DISHONORABLE
Gentlemen

THE BENNET GANG DUOLOGY

VOLUME ONE

A PRIDE & PREJUDICE VARIATION

SUMMER HANFORD

To Laura;
Enjoy!
Summer
Hanford

COPYRIGHT

This is a work of fiction. Names, characters, businesses, places, events, locales, and incidents are used in a fictitious manner and researched for historical accuracy insofar as this author was able. Fictitious names, characters, businesses, places, events, locales, and incidents are products of the original work *Pride & Prejudice* or of this author's imagination. Any resemblance to reality is coincidental.

Amazon Edition
ISBN: 9798315076674

The Bennet Gang Volume One: Dishonorable Gentlemen

Copyright © 2025 by Summer Hanford
Cover Copyright © 2025 by Summer Hanford
Map Copyright © 2025 by Summer Hanford

Cover by J. M. Girard
Map Art by Marcela Hanford

No AI was used in the creation of this novel or its components.

Please do not reproduce or distribute this work without express permission from the author: summer@summerhanford.com

www.summerhanford.com

Thank you!

ACKNOWLEDGEMENTS

With special thanks to Doris, Linda, and all of my amazing beta readers.

Dear Reader,

After enjoying this story, you'll find information about signing up for my mailing list, where you will have the opportunity for prizes, information about new releases and in person events, and more. I hope you'll sign up and join us by visiting:

www.summerhanford.com/pride-and-prejudice-variations

Variations by Summer Hanford

Once Upon a Time in Pemberley*
Mr. Darcy's Matchmaker*
Mr. Darcy's Bookshop*
The Adventures of Anne de Bourgh of Rosings, v.I*
The Adventures of Anne de Bourgh of Rosings, v.II*

By Summer Hanford & Renata McMann

To Catch a Poisoner*
Charitable Endeavors
Pride & Prejudice and Planets*
To Fall for Mr. Darcy*
Mr. Collins' Will
More Than He Seems
After Anne
Their Secret Love
A Duel in Meryton*
Love, Letters and Lies
The Long Road to Longbourn*
Hypothetically Married*
The Forgiving Season
The Widow Elizabeth
Foiled Elopement
Believing in Darcy
Her Final Wish
Miss Bingley's Christmas
Epiphany with Tea
Courting Elizabeth
The Fire at Netherfield Park
From Ashes to Heiresses*
Entanglements of Honor
Lady Catherine Regrets
A Death at Rosings
Mary Younge

Poor Mr. Darcy
Mr. Collins' Deception
The Scandalous Stepmother
Caroline and the Footman
Elizabeth's Plight (The Wickham Coin Book II)
Georgiana's Folly (The Wickham Coin Book I)
The Second Mrs. Darcy

Pride & Prejudice Variation Collections:

A Dollop of Pride and a Dash of Prejudice:
Includes from above: Their Secret Love, Miss Bingley's Christmas, Epiphany with Tea and From Ashes to Heiresses.

Pride and Prejudice Villains Revisited – Redeemed – Reimagined A Collection of Six Short Stories.
Includes from above: Lady Catherine Regrets, Mary Younge, Mr. Collins' Deception and Caroline and the Footman, along with two the additional flash fiction pieces, Mrs. Bennet's Triumph and Wickham's Journal.

Georgiana's Folly & Elizabeth's Plight: Wickham Coin Series, v. I & II
Includes from above: Elizabeth's Plight and Georgiana's Folly.

Historical Romance by Summer Hanford

His Yuletide Kiss

The Duke's Bequest Series:
Sleigh Bells & Slander
Wildflowers & Wiles
Heartache & Holly
Meadows & Mischief
Grace's Story

Crown & Dagger Historical Fiction:
Kestrel
Red Fox
Forest Hart

Epic Fantasy by Summer Hanford

Rise of the Summer God Series:
Daughters of Awen
The Battle of Greypass
Wyvern's Call
Shroud of Fate
Shards of Deceit
A Destiny of Truth

Trial by Moonlight

Thrice Born Series:
Gift of the Aluien
Hawks of Sorga
Throne of Wheylia
Plains of Tybrunn
Shores of K'Orge
Thrice Born Chronicles

*available as an audio book

DISHONORABLE
Gentlemen

CHAPTER ONE

The Heist

Seated across from Darcy, his friend Charles Bingley tugged back the curtain again as his carriage trundled down a narrow lane in Hertfordshire. Trying to ignore Bingley's fidgeting, Darcy angled the book he held in an attempt to catch the fading light of the lowering sun. Bingley peered out for a moment, then yanked the curtain closed once more, fortunately not interfering with Darcy's light on the other side of the carriage.

Bingley pulled out his watch and flipped it open, then pushed aside the curtain so he had enough light to read the time. "Mr. Morris and I agreed on five. He's surely gone by now. At this rate, we will be lucky if we have enough daylight to inspect the exterior of the house, and I doubt anyone will be available to give us entry." Bingley snapped his watch closed, shoved it away, and then tugged the curtain across the window.

"We will seek rooms at the nearest inn and view the estate come morning," Darcy said, not looking up from his book. "Mr. Morris will make no protest. It is his purpose as agent for the estate to accommodate us. You worry for nothing."

Bingley peered out the window again. "I cannot believe all those sheep were blocking the London road. You would think between the dogs and the farmer, they would have been able to move them quickly, rather than send us back to the previous fork. It cannot please them to have traffic diverted from their village. What is it called? Meryton?"

"So you informed me when we set out," Darcy said by way of agreement. "And let us hope it boasts an inn. I would rather stay than repeat the journey from London tomorrow."

"Meryton is in possession of an inn, according to Mr. Morris. I had thought we would have a look about, perhaps dine at the inn, and head back, the horses nicely rested."

"We can as easily dine and remain, if they have room." Which seemed likely to Darcy in this backwater. "We will send a rider for our cases. One of my carriages can bring them, along with our valets. Better to see this estate you want to let first thing in the morning with fresh eyes."

Bingley groaned. "You and mornings. It's unnatural to be out of bed before ten, Darcy. Unhealthy, even. I am certain the cold morning air is how one catches a chill."

"Have you ever known me to catch a chill?" Darcy permitted scorn to touch his voice.

"Well, no. Not now as you mention it." Bingley tugged at his cuffs. "Yes. Very well. We will inspect Netherfield Park in the morning. Not an auspicious name, that. If I purchase the place, I will have to see about getting it changed. I mean, 'nether field?' It sounds rather desolate. Like what you would call the very last place you wished to farm. Or somewhere to which one might consign ill-behaved sheep. Such as those that blocked the road from London."

"We were changing direction," Darcy reminded him, turning a page in his book. Bingley's mind had a tendency to wander, and Darcy wished to reach whatever paltry accommodations Meryton offered sooner rather than later if they were to send a man back to London.

"Right. Changing direction to seek the inn." Bingley raised a hand, poised to knock on the ceiling to alert the driver to their need for him. "I'll direct my man to take us to the village rather than the estate, assuming he took note of the way, and—"

The carriage clattered to a halt.

"You should speak to your driver about his technique," Darcy groused, finally looking up from his book.

"I did not yet signal a stop." Bingley tugged the curtain open once more. To the sight of a pistol barrel.

"What have we here?" a low-pitched voice grated out in a thick French accent. "As wealthy looking a couple of gents as I ever did see." The pistol waggled at Bingley. "Let's have your purse then, monsieur."

Bingley gaped at the pistol, held firmly by a hand encased in a black leather glove, attached to an arm with an equally dark shirtsleeve. Above that, sharp eyes regarded them from behind a mask that covered the upper half of a somewhat grimy face.

"Do not be absurd," Darcy snapped on behalf of his friend. "What is the meaning of this?"

"This, your lordship, is what we outside London call highway robbery," the man said.

A rather young man, Darcy guessed by the fellow's slight build and what, by his estimation, was an artificially deepened voice. "I do not get robbed," Darcy stated. "Be off with you and we will not press charges." There was a vast deal of difference between robbing a man and shooting him, and Darcy suspected the youth would not actually attempt the latter.

The man chuckled. "You are a funny one, no?" Raising his voice he called, "Enaj, these fellows need some extra persuading."

Enaj? Darcy found the name odd. Foreign, by the sound of it. French, like the man pointing a pistol at him? More likely émigrés from one of the colonies.

"Here now, your masters do not want to behave," another roughened, French-accented voice said somewhere without. "Down from your perch with you. That is right. Up there by the horses. Hold their reins tight. I would not want to see you trampled, mon homme. Remember, I have an eye on you."

A moment later a second pistol appeared, this time on the other side of the carriage but likewise held by a black leather glove. "Now, what have we here?" Enaj asked.

The face that appeared in the window, the upper half masked in black, had a narrow chin and a scraggly mustache, emphasizing Darcy's impression of youth. Young men with not enough to occupy them, up to no good. Once he discovered who they were, he would see them placed in the regulars, if they were citizens of England. If they survived the experience, they would be the better for it.

And if they were not meant to be in the British Isles, Darcy would see them removed back to France, or to whatever colony they'd come from.

"This exalted fellow says he does not get robbed," the first bandit said, still peering in the other window. "You will have to persuade him."

"Must I?" Enaj asked with a sigh. "You know I do not find it so amusing as you."

"You would rather I attempt to make our point? I am a fair shot, but nowhere near so good as you. You jeopardize monsieur's pretty face with your reluctance."

"I say," Bingley cried. "What do you mean about Darcy's face?"

Darcy cast him a quelling look. If the young men recognized his family name, they might decide to add kidnapping to their dubious list of achievements. His estate could muster quite the ransom.

The first bandit gestured with his pistol, causing Bingley to flinch. "Enaj here is going to shoot a hole in your friend's hat, monsieur."

"And what, precisely, will that prove?" Darcy asked coldly.

"Oy," Enaj called, stepping back from the window, out of Darcy's reach, and turning to face the front of the carriage. "I said stay with the horses, by which I meant stay with the horses."

"It will prove," the first bandit said, ignoring Enaj's activity on the other side of their conveyance, "That these here pistols are loaded and that we know what we are doing with them."

Enaj turned back to Darcy. "Take off your hat, monsieur, and hold it out before you."

"I most certainly will not," Darcy said with considerable affront.

The first bandit stepped out of sight but could be heard calling, "Hold onto those horses tight, mon homme. The shot might startle them."

"I urge you, monsieur, to remove your hat," Enaj repeated.

"Absolutely not," Darcy said stiffly. Whoever these youths were, they were going too far.

"Very well," Enaj said. "It should not matter. I rarely miss."

Enaj backed up, watching Darcy down the barrel of his pistol, and backed up some more. Finally, he stood quite some distance away, engaging Darcy's nerves despite every effort to maintain a proper level of uncaring reserve. Why was the lad making the shot so difficult? Or did he simply play on Darcy's resolve, hoping that if he drew back far enough, Darcy would relent out of fear that no one could make the shot? It was, after all, at an angle and through a carriage window, into the darkened interior, with the sun dropping low, casting long shado—

A loud report sounded.

Bingley yelped. The horses reared, jolting the carriage. Their driver cursed. Smoke curled between the carriage and Enaj, who waved a gloved hand to clear it away, then stuck the spent pistol through his belt. He pulled free a second one.

"The devil take it, Darcy, he shot a hole right through your hat," Bingley cried.

Darcy removed the article. Indeed, a hole went in one side and out the other. A glance showed a ball embedded in the wall inside Bingley's carriage, beside the opposite window.

"Here," Bingley cried. He reached into his coat and pulled out a tightly folded packet of banknotes, then thrust his hand out the window.

The first bandit instantly reappeared, taking the money. "Merci," he said with a bow, then straightened to regard Darcy with a smug, aggravating grin.

Peripherally, Darcy was aware of Enaj moving nearer again, but he kept his focus on the first bandit, by far the more aggravating of the two. "Your companion shooting my hat in no way means that either of you have any intention of shooting me," Darcy said stiffly, dropping his hat to the seat beside him. "And you owe me a hat."

"It does not mean we will, no," the first bandit agreed. "But I am starting to *want* to shoot you, monsieur."

"Azile," Enaj said sharply.

The worry in Enaj's voice, far more than the threat issued by this Azile, spurred Darcy to reach into his coat. He drew out his wallet, but did not hand it over. "Know that I do this under protest and with the firm belief you have no intention of actually harming us."

"No no," Enaj said, once more turning his pistol in the direction of the horses, where their driver must still be. "You remain there and mind your charges."

"Give them the money," Bingley said in a low voice. "That Enaj fellow still has a shot left, and the other one has two. Even if they do not want to shoot us, the longer we drag this out, the greater chance of some ill befalling us or my driver."

"Very well," Darcy said stiffly. He weighed the wallet in his hand. If he could get the one called Azile to bend down, Darcy could shove open the carriage door, hopefully slamming it into the bandit's head, then jump out and subdue him.

Darcy tossed his wallet out the window.

Azile snatched it from the air, presumably with his off hand as his right held the pistol. He cast Darcy a quick grin, almost as if he guessed the plan Darcy had so rapidly concocted. "Merci, good sirs. It has been a rare pleasure." Azile moved backward as he spoke, then raised his voice to call, "Enaj. Go."

Both youths backed away into the trees that lined the road, one to each side. Darcy slid across his seat, looking out in time to see Azile disappear among the broad trunks. Bingley, watching in the direction Enaj had gone, let out a sudden, loud breath.

"Well, that settles it," Bingley exclaimed. "I am not meant to take this Netherfield property. 'Nether' indeed, I say. First a herd of overly obstinate sheep block our way. Then we are set upon by bandits. And they ruined your hat."

Darcy frowned down at the beleaguered object before addressing Bingley. "Has it not occurred to you that the blockade of sheep milling about on the London road was by design? To send us here to this narrow, forested lane?"

"Sirs." The face of Bingley's driver filled the window. "Sirs, are you well? The dastards are gone, off into the woods. Did that shot catch either of you? Any harm done?"

"Only to Darcy's hat," Bingley said in obvious relief. He scrubbed a hand over his face, knocking his own hat askew. "I say, I've never been robbed before."

"Nor have I," Darcy admitted. "I did not appreciate the experience. What manner of backwater is this?"

"Sirs, will we be heading back to London, then?" the driver asked. "I'll be needing to light the lanterns soon."

"Did you mark the location of that village, Meryton?" Bingley asked. He looked at Darcy. "I don't know about you, but I could use a pint. Robbed. Of all things."

"If we go to the village, we will need to remain until funds arrive," Darcy replied in a tone of protest. "Need I remind you that 'robbed' means we were relieved of our wallets?"

"I am certain a simple promise of payment will suffice," Bingley said with a shrug.

"Perhaps in London it would and certainly in Derbyshire, but these people do not know us. We would put them in the unenviable position of insulting us with their refusal or putting their faith in two gentlemen completely foreign to them, one with two holes in his hat."

Bingley stared at him, his expression mutinous, but Darcy had strong opinions on the subject of gentlemen availing themselves of items and services for which they did not pay. Or of those posing as gentlemen doing so. The village nearest his estate of Pemberley had suffered greatly from the habit. To be certain, it had been one man in particular who had abused the shopkeepers' goodwill, one Mr. George Wickham and him not even a gentleman, but Darcy still abhorred the imposition.

While putting right Wickham's debts, Darcy had seen the harm done to livelihoods by the practice. After all, the merchant's funds were already spent and gone, simply to have the item available in their shop. If they received no payment at the time of purchase, they had no goods nor, in many cases, the ability to purchase more until paid. Even an honest gentleman did not always meet his debts expediently enough to avoid causing undue hardship.

"Either we dine in Meryton and remain the night, thus giving fresh funds the opportunity to catch up with us, or we return to London," Darcy stated. "I leave the decision up to you."

Bingley cast him a sour look. "Yes, but you give me only two options, neither of which appeal to me." He thought for a moment, the struggle to be amenable clear on his face, then shrugged. "To Meryton it is. I am done riding about in this carriage for the day."

"The village, then, sir?" the driver asked.

"The village," Bingley said firmly. "To whatever they have for an inn."

The driver nodded and returned to his perch. Soon, the carriage was moving again.

"Tomorrow, we should make an effort to report this incident to whomever passes for authority here," Darcy said. There would, he assumed, be a local magistrate.

"Most assuredly," Bingley agreed, his ill humor already passed. "Will you permit me to purchase you a new hat?"

"You did not shoot a hole in this one." In truth, Darcy wondered if his valet couldn't repair the article, and then see it donated. Darcy did not wear mended hats. "Azile and Enaj are who owe me a hat, not you."

Bingley shrugged. "If you change your mind, let me know."

It was well dark by the time they reached Meryton, but people still strolled the streets. The local assembly hall was open, and quite a few shops. It seemed, in truth, a lively sort of place. The coachman brought them to the inn, and Darcy donned his hat as he stepped free of Bingley's conveyance. He could not very well go about bareheaded, after all, holes or not.

Before they could go in, an overwide carriage rolled up the street, pulled by six white horses. The carriage itself was cream, a color which might have been attractive if the white-gray of the horses didn't make it appear dingy, at least by lantern light. The conveyance also boasted a plethora of carved cartouches, medallions, and other embellishments, all gilded. Even the driver wore cream and gold. Overall, the effect was ostentatious to the point of being vulgar. Darcy shook his head, unable not to stare at the monstrosity as it trundled by.

They entered the inn to find a counter before them, a noisy public room and a hallway to the left, and a staircase to the right. Striding up to the counter, Bingley rang the bell.

A moment later, a man came out of the public room, wiping his hands on his apron. He took up a stance behind the desk and asked, "May I be of assistance, sirs?"

"Do you have an adequate private dining room?" Darcy asked.

"We have three, sir," the man said with sufficient deference. "None are occupied this evening."

"We will dine in the finest of the three," Darcy informed him.

"Certainly, Mr....?"

"Darcy, of Derbyshire, and my companion is Mr. Bingley. We also require two rooms for us and two more for our valets, who will arrive quite late, as well as one for our driver. Again, the finest you have for such purposes. Lastly, we wish to hire a man to ride into Town with a missive. Immediately."

"Certainly, Mr. Darcy. Will you require paper and ink to be brought to your dining room?"

Darcy gave the man credit for his observation that they carried nothing with them. "Indeed, that would be most welcome."

"If you will give me a moment, Mr. Darcy, Mr. Bingley, I will have your dining room made ready for you."

"Very well," Darcy replied.

"Your quarters will be made up while you dine, and I will have a rider ready to make all haste to London. You may give your missive to any member of my staff once it is ready. They will know what to do." The man, Darcy assumed him to be the proprietor, gestured to the noisy space to their left. "You may wait in the public room if you like."

"That sounds just the thing," Bingley said before Darcy could refuse.

With a nod, the proprietor hurried away down the hall.

Bingley pivoted and went in the direction of the public room, his movements quick and decisive enough that Darcy had the keen suspicion his friend knew he did not wish to enter. Darcy followed more slowly to find that Bingley had already claimed a table, doffed his hat, and caught the attention of a serving girl. He waved Darcy over, saying, "Two pints of your finest," to the girl, then began tugging off his gloves.

The serving girl turned in the direction of Bingley's wave and spotted Darcy. Her eyebrows went up and she blurted, "Sir, there's a hole in your hat."

"I am aware," Darcy said stiffly, removing the abused article.

"We were set upon by bandits on the roadway," Bingley said with a shudder. "Quite the experience, I can tell you. They shot my friend's hat."

"Oh dear." The girl's tone was aggrieved but bright interest lit her eyes. "Was it, then, the Boney Bandits?"

"How should we know?" Darcy said sourly as he sat. "They did not offer their card."

That earned a nervous giggle from the girl.

"They were called Enaj and Azile," Bingley told her. "Why Boney

Bandits? Because they're so scrawny?"

She shook her head. "No. On account of them being Frenchmen."

Twin lines of confusion appeared on Bingley's brow.

"Like Napolean Bonaparte…Boney?" the serving girl clarified, her expression clearly revealing what she thought of Bingley's intellect, though Darcy didn't find the connection obvious either. Raising her voice, she cried to the room at large, "The Boney Bandits had at these two gentlemen."

That set up a clamor. A rather cheerful sounding one, to Darcy's ear. His mood grew more sour. "Are they pleased we were robbed?"

"Oh no," the girl said solemnly. "They're something of local legends, though, the Boney Bandits. Half the ladies in Meryton are in love with them. Every time the magistrate has new wanted posters put up, they get nicked."

"Stolen?" Bingley repeated blankly.

"Aye," the girl replied, that twinkle back in her eyes. "To go up on ladies' bedchamber walls, or be tacked up on the insides of wardrobe doors, if they be discreet ones. You'll be quite the sought after guests, I must warn you. Everyone will want to hear the tale. I'll be back with your ale."

As she walked away Bingley shook his head. "This village seems a bit mad, I must admit."

"I could not agree more," Darcy replied. "But we are here and will make the best of the evening that we can." And tomorrow, they would report the incident to the magistrate, although Darcy already had the suspicion that would prove useless, and then depart, never to visit this forsaken backwater again.

CHAPTER TWO

Jane's Remorse

At the base of Oakham Mount, Elizabeth dismounted and led her horse around several boulders. No matter how many times they passed this way, Tuck still refused to navigate the narrow path on his own, so thoroughly did the boulders appear fused as one. Reaching the tallest, which stood nearly touching the base of the mount, Elizabeth swept aside a screen of vines and led Tuck through. She picked up the single shielded lantern left at the mouth of the tunnel, unsurprised that Jane had already returned. The vines once again a wall behind her, Elizabeth unshielded the light and led Tuck down the tunnel.

They came out into a large cavern that hollowed out the hillside. Around them were arrayed familiar racks of weapons, some elegant and sharpened, and others dulled for practice, as well as hooks adorned with padded coats, vests, and other vestments to be worn while training. Leaving Tuck in the middle of the domed chamber, Elizabeth went first to the cabinet that the rack of padded armor hid, unloading and cleaning her pistols before secreting them away alongside their other firearms. She crossed to another rack to stow her rapier and various daggers, then returned to a slightly impatient Tuck.

Taking back up his reins, Elizabeth led her horse through a hidden door at the back of her late stepfather's stable, the structure being built half into the line of hills that ranged from her former home of Longbourn, past their estate just outside the village of Meryton, and onward to Netherfield Park. Jane was in the center of the stable brushing down her horse, Robin, and Elizabeth led Tuck over. Robin nickered softly in greeting and Jane spared Elizabeth and Tuck a smile.

Grabbing up a cloth, Elizabeth quickly wiped the chalk dust from Tuck's nose, smeared there so that any who saw him would recall a white blaze and so, even if they had occasion to enter the stable, would never associate her bay with Azile's mount. Then Elizabeth left him to duck into the tack room and change, bundling away her highwayman's garb and their loot into more of their stepfather's secret compartments. The hill side of the stable, appearing to be a wall of stacked stone, was riddled with concealed cubbies. Having served as a spy for the Crown for many years, Papa Arthur had a deep love for secret passageways, hidey-holes, and hidden talents. With his passion for intrigue and secrets, Elizabeth sometimes wondered if they had found all the passageways and compartments he'd hidden in their home. With Papa Arthur gone these seven years past, they might never know.

"Your face," Jane warned when Elizabeth came back out.

"Worry not. I realize I appear as if I have been eating mud cakes." Elizabeth took up the cloth she'd used to dust the chalk from Tuck's face and applied it, along with a bit of water, to her own. When she was done, she turned to Jane. "How is this?"

Before Jane could answer, the stable door cracked open. Elizabeth tamped down a shock of worry even as she saw it was only their sister Mary, which was as it should be. They'd long ago talked Mama into only hiring a temporary man for the stable, not a difficult task given her dislike of horses. Mr. Clarke came over from one of the tenant farms each morning and, more briefly, evening, to care for their mounts, and could be paid extra for the use of himself and his team when they required a coachman, but he didn't stay on. That way Elizabeth, Jane, and Mary knew precisely when their domain would be invaded.

Mary came to Tuck's side and began unbuckling his tack while Jane continued to brush Robin. She liked to make his coat shine. Over Tuck's back, Mary asked, "Was it a profitable outing?"

Elizabeth grinned, taking the heavy saddle from her sister and turning to drape it over the rail of Tuck's stall. "Very profitable. Either we robbed two men of their life's savings, or we picked an exceptionally good carriage to hold up."

"Oh." Jane's face pinched with worry, the brush in her hand stilling. "You do not believe we took their life's savings, do you?"

Elizabeth shook her head. "Most certainly not. Did you see the arrogance of the one whose hat you shot? Such condescension can only come from excessive wealth."

"I hope you are correct." Jane resumed brushing. "If I discovered we took all someone has, I would insist we return it."

"Not the church's portion," Mary said crisply. "I intend for the vicar to receive a large donation on Sunday and, Elizabeth, you know better than to stop and count money. You are to return directly here after a robbery. We agreed on that."

"I did not stop and count the money. Their purses are so fat, though, that I know they must contain a considerable sum. You will not even be able to give the church its portion all at once. It will not fit in the box."

"It cannot be that much," Mary said and traded a brush for Tuck's bridle. "I will count it later and make up a bundle for the church and the ones for us to distribute."

Jane smiled at that, for she loved the days when the three of them would sneak about Meryton, Longbourn, and the surrounding countryside and leave small parcels of money for the needy to find. Tucked into the pocket of an apron left out to dry on the line, or slipped under a pie cooling in a window. Or, Elizabeth's personal favorite, wrapped in paper and left under a brooding hen.

"I see the new paste I developed worked well," Mary said to Jane. "Unless, that is, your mustache fell off?"

"It remained firmly in place, and yet this new concoction did not adhere so firmly that I needed to scrub off half my skin to remove it."

They had, about a year ago, had an alarming incident where one of Mary's attempts at glue had worked so well that they'd encountered a great deal of difficulty removing Enaj's mustache from Jane. Then, by the time they got it off, she had an incriminating pink line across her upper lip, the skin quite irritated. Fortunately, they had managed to bundle her into the house and apply a soothing ointment without anyone seeing her. By the following day, she'd appeared nearly normal. At least normal enough that a bit of powder could hide the mark until it completely healed.

"Maybe Azile should grow a mustache," Elizabeth mused.

"And leave ladies all over Meryton scrambling to pencil mustaches onto the posters they hide in their chambers?" Jane asked with a laugh. Then her expression became solemn and she turned to set Robin's brush down.

Elizabeth grimaced, knowing what was coming next. Jane was always filled with remorse after they robbed someone.

"Do you... Are you both still certain that what we are doing is right?" Jane asked. "When Papa Arthur taught us to fight and ride and shoot, it was to keep us active and so we might defend ourselves. I do not believe this sort of behavior is what he had in mind."

"I believe this is precisely what he had in mind," Elizabeth said firmly, as she always did when Jane got this way.

Their mother's second husband, retired General Arthur Oakwood, had adored teaching them such fine arts as swordsmanship and pugilism. He often said he wouldn't always be here to care for his Bennet Gang, as he liked to call the five of them, but that he would teach them to care for themselves. He hadn't been able to interest Kitty in learning anything, even the French he'd taught Jane, Elizabeth and Mary, and begun to teach Lydia, Thomas, and Matthew. Nor had Papa Arthur had time to teach Elizabeth's youngest three siblings anything more, or to buy Lydia a horse, having died when she was but eight. Still, he'd instructed Jane, Elizabeth, and Mary well. More than that, after he left them, they kept up their training in secret. Especially Elizabeth and Jane, who showed more aptitude for all things martial than Mary.

"And the two gentlemen we robbed this evening were entirely unknown to me," Jane continued, ignoring Elizabeth's words. "They are not part of the troubles hereabouts. We had no right to take their money."

Elizabeth snorted. "They are wealthy gentlemen. I am certain they are part of someone's troubles."

"We do not know that," Jane said firmly. "Not all gentlemen are like those in this area. They simply cannot be. Papa was not," she added, to stave off Elizabeth's rebuttal.

"So you say." Mary gave a little sigh where she stood on the other side of Tuck from Elizabeth, brushing him as he munched on hay. "I hardly remember Papa Thomas."

Their father, Thomas Bennet, had died before Lydia was even born, plunging them into mourning. When she'd arrived a girl, their hideous relations, Mr. Collins Sr. and his sons, had inherited their home, Longbourn, which was entailed away from female offspring. The Collins had moved in with alacrity, unceremoniously kicking out the grieving new mother and her five daughters. If not for their relations on their mother's side, Elizabeth had no notion what would have become of them in the year before their mother met General Arthur Oakwood. The Phillips kindly putting a roof over them, and Mr. Gardiner giving some of his then meager funds to help feed them, were all that had saved them after Mr. Collins Sr. took possession of Longbourn.

A sycophantic, conniving man, Mr. Collins Sr. had rapidly risen in the eyes of the local populace. In little time, he'd been named as the local magistrate, a position his son now held. Until his death, Mr. Collins Sr. had worked diligently at squeezing every penny from his tenants, and had convinced the other men of the region to do likewise. He'd lobbied for, and seen, many local statutes changed, and local taxes raised, and one of his associates placed in the role of tax collector. Not that the money went to anything but lining the pockets of the greedy and overprivileged. Now, it was nearly impossible for good, honest people to survive in and around Meryton, but likewise few had the means to leave.

And Elizabeth simply would not stand for it.

Nor, sadly, could she do anything to change it. As women, she, Jane, and Mary had little say in their local governance. Even their mother, a longstanding matron of the community, wielded no power when it came to laws, fines, and taxes.

"This is the part where you tell me that Papa Thomas was a good man who loved us, cared for us, and would be every bit as proud of what we are doing as Papa Arthur would be," Mary urged, drawing Elizabeth from her churning thoughts.

"Mr. Bennet was a good man," Jane said quietly.

"But he would be more amused than proud," Elizabeth added with a sad smile. Even though she'd been only five when their father died, she clearly remembered his wry humor.

"Jane. Elizabeth. Mary," their sister Lydia's voice called from outside the stable. "Are you in there?"

Elizabeth cast a quick look around, but nothing that would indicate their true purpose in the stable met her searching gaze. Calmly setting down her brush, Jane led Robin to his stall. Mary resumed grooming Tuck, and Elizabeth went to the wall by the stable door, where their gardening implements were hung. She snatched down a trowel and a small rake.

Lydia pushed the stable door open. Her gaze settled on Elizabeth, who immediately set to returning the trowel and rake to their places, as if stowing gardening tools had been her occupation for some time.

"There you are." Lydia smiled, coming farther into the stable.

To Elizabeth's dismay, Kitty followed.

Her nose scrunching, Kitty yanked out a handkerchief to press to her face. "How can you stand the smell in here?"

"Smell?" Jane asked mildly, turning from securing Robin.

"It smells like hay and horses," Elizabeth added.

"Precisely." Kitty gave a condescending sniff, then started sneezing. "Ugh. I will go tell Mama we found them." Pivoting, she left.

Lydia looked at the three of them eagerly. "When you weren't in your garden, I said to look here. I thought you'd be finishing up." She smiled at Elizabeth before turning to Mary. "But why are you brushing Tuck and not Mare Marian?"

"We already brushed Mary's mare," Elizabeth said easily. Not a complete lie, as they had brushed Mary's white mare many times in the past.

"And I think Tuck is done now, as well." Mary set her brush aside and led Tuck away.

"I have an apple for Mare Marian." Lydia pulled a rather small, pathetic apple from her skirt pocket. "Can I give it to her?"

From where she was stabling Tuck, Mary nodded, casting her horse a fond smile.

Lydia skipped across the stable and held out the apple to the eager mare. "You know, I could help brush her."

"I do not require help," Mary said instantly.

Lydia sighed and patted the mare's nose as she ate the apple.

Elizabeth wished their youngest sister could help them, but Lydia was too flighty to be trusted with their secret. Still, she clearly pined for friendship, and Elizabeth felt sorrow at excluding her. Lydia did not even have a horse, for their mother wouldn't buy her one or pay for her to learn to ride. Papa Arthur had been the impetus behind such things. He would surely have bought Lydia a mount for her tenth birthday, as he had for Elizabeth, Jane, and Mary, though Kitty had refused the gift of one.

Papa Arthur had been certain he could wear her down and start training her in riding and other, more martial pursuits, as he had the three of them, but he hadn't lived long enough to try. It was shortly after Kitty's tenth birthday that the *incident* had taken place. Papa Arthur had been robbed not only of convincing Kitty to learn to ride and of one day buying Lydia a mount, but of watching the two sons the now Mrs. Oakwood had given him grow up.

"Why have you come looking for us?" Jane asked, joining Lydia in lavishing attention on Mare Marian, who did not get ridden very often as Mary preferred to be in charge of the ledger, distribution, and false mustache making side of their venture. Not to go gallivanting about, as she called what Elizabeth and Jane did.

"Mama has a note from Mr. Lucas at the shop," Lydia said. "He has more of her favorite bonbons in. She wants to speak with you about going into the village tomorrow."

Elizabeth exchanged a look with Mary, wondering if her sister could have any bundles ready for distribution by the time they went on their mother's upcoming bonbons mission. Mary returned the slightest nod.

"We had best go in, then," Jane said. "Mama will not be satisfied until she has repeated the story."

Elizabeth grimaced but nodded, knowing Jane was correct.

To the tune of Lydia prattling on about the bonbons story their mother would undoubtedly tell, they finished with the horses and closed up the stable, then all set out for the house.

"We looked for you in your garden first," Lydia said as they walked up the path. "It is looking lovely. I could help in there, you know. I want to learn to arrange flowers."

"There will be no new flowers until spring," Mary said.

"I could cut ivy and maybe dry flowers."

"We are cultivating the ivy."

Elizabeth squelched down guilt at how Lydia's face fell. She truly felt sorry for her youngest sister. Spurned by their mother for being born female, Lydia lived in Kitty's shadow. Mama doted on Kitty, unquestionably her favorite. It worked well for Elizabeth, Jane, and Mary, who'd nurtured a reputation for spending hours in the walled garden Papa Arthur had built on the estate. A garden that had one gate facing the house and a second facing the stable.

But Lydia had no one. Kitty looked down on her. Their mama disdained her. For their part, though they were sympathetic, Elizabeth, Jane, and Mary couldn't have Lydia around. Not if they wanted time to practice their unladylike arts of combat, and to be able to sneak away and back at will.

Not that they snuck away often. Much of the time, aside from when they practiced, they truly were working in the garden or riding for pleasure. They'd long ago agreed not to rob people too often. They didn't need to stir Mr. Collins into taking serious steps to capture them.

Not that he would ever find them out, but he could make their work more difficult.

When they reached the house, they went to wash up, knowing their mother felt the same way about the smell of horses as Kitty, for where else had Kitty learned such airs? Lydia followed Elizabeth to her room, chatting away as she washed in a basin and fixed her hair. By the time she and her youngest sister entered Mrs. Oakwood's favorite drawing room, Elizabeth had already endured several more reiterations of Lydia's thoughts on the bonbons story, as well as her younger sister's conviction that their young brothers, Thomas and Matthew, were also tired of hearing it.

They entered to the sight of Jane standing before their mother's favorite sofa, nodding along, with Mary, Kitty, Thomas, and Matthew seated about the room. Elizabeth despised how Jane always stood before their mama like an errant schoolgirl, enduring Mrs. Oakwood's rants. Not because their mother was in any way cruel to Jane, but because Jane's subservience reminded Elizabeth that her older sister still felt responsible for their stepfather's death.

"...know that Mr. Lucas, bless the man, gets them in especially for me," Mrs. Oakwood was saying. "He always has. As well he should, as it is a wonder I can eat confections at all." She heaved a great sigh.

Elizabeth settled onto the sofa behind Jane, the cushions stiff and the feet carved into lions' paws grasping rounded ornaments. Lydia dropped down beside her.

"Why is it a wonder, Mama?" Kitty asked dutifully where she sat beside their mother, the question issued as much to please Mrs. Oakwood as to torment the rest of them, Elizabeth imagined.

Where their brothers sat together at a small table, cards before them, Thomas scrunched his nose.

Knowing Mrs. Oakwood couldn't see them with Jane standing before her, Elizabeth and Lydia mouthed along with their mother's words as she answered Kitty with, "It was a lovely winter's day, sunny and bright. Oh, but for the sunshine to bring such sorrow on that fateful day."

She paused for a fluttering of her handkerchief, mimicked by Kitty where she shared their mother's sofa.

"I told your father, girls, my poor sweet Thomas, after whom you are named, Thomas, that I was with child and certain, so certain, that this time I would bear a boy."

She paused again. Fortunately, Jane still stood before Elizabeth and Lydia, preventing their mother's usual accusatory glare from landing. Even so, where she sat beside Elizabeth, Lydia dropped her gaze to study her hands, amusement leaving her face.

"My dear sweet Thomas was filled with such elation, he ordered his mount saddled and rode with all haste for Meryton, to purchase for me my favorite confections. And that was the last I ever saw of him."

The sob Mrs. Oakwood issued then had lost all ability to evoke sorrow in Elizabeth, the performance being too oft repeated. She nudged Lydia with her elbow, giving her youngest sister a little smile when Lydia darted a look at her.

"After they found him, his neck broken and his horse run off, I could not eat sweets again," Mrs. Oakwood wailed. "Not for the remainder of my pregnancy. Not for my year of mourning."

'But then,' Elizabeth mouthed along with her mother.

"But then, General Arthur Oakwood rode into Meryton, and my Kitty, whom you were meant to be watching, Elizabeth." Mrs. Oakwood leaned to the side to cast a scowl around Jane, at Elizabeth. "My Kitty ran into the roadway and General Oakwood, darling man that he was, was thrown as he avoided trampling her, and I nearly lost another great man to horses."

"But you did not, Mama," Kitty put in eagerly.

"I did not. Instead, I assisted General Oakwood into the Phillips' parlor and set to nursing him back to health, and once he was well, he did not continue on his journey north, but instead asked for my hand and here he remained, and purchased this land and built this lovely estate, and lived as my dear husband until his d-death." Their mother burst into loud sobs.

"And the bonbons," Kitty urged, as unmoved by their mother's dramatic weeping as Elizabeth.

"Yes, the bonbons." Mrs. Oakwood sniffed loudly. "When he was well enough to walk again, General Oakwood daily fetched me bonbons from Mr. Lucas's shop. He taught me to love sweets again, the sweet, sweet man."

Jane nodded. "Yes, Mama, but how many do you mean for me to purchase and is there anything else you want from the shops tomorrow?"

Elizabeth couldn't see their mother, who'd left off leaning sideways to glare at her, only Jane's back, but she didn't mind. Her attention wandered as plans were made for the excursion into Meryton, as if they did not walk there several times a week, Mama and Kitty discussing who would go and how much would be spent, and on what. Elizabeth didn't attend to them. While Mrs. Oakwood's theatrics didn't touch her, for some reason Elizabeth still felt more sorrow than usual at her mother's oft-repeated tale.

She couldn't help but wonder what their life would be like if Papa Arthur hadn't dueled, and slain, Mr. Collins Sr., and subsequently died of the wound he'd sustained in the bout. If not for that fatal shot, he could be with them still, buying their mother bonbons and living in the lovely home he'd caused to be built, tending the walled garden with them and teaching Lydia to fence, shoot, speak French, and ride.

Or if Mr. Bennet had not died. If he had fathered Thomas and Matthew, and they'd been permitted to remain in Longbourn. Why, then she would not even know how to fight, or to speak French nearly like a native, or shoot a pistol. Then, she would be like any other young lady, and would meet a man like the one they'd held up today, Mr. Darcy his companion had called him, and marry him rather than rob him.

Smiling, Elizabeth shook her head, unable to imagine such a life. She loved to fence and to ride, and even though he was undeniably handsome, she would never marry a snobbish gentleman like Mr. Darcy. A gentleman, she recalled with a grin, who now had some well-deserved holes in his hat

CHAPTER THREE

Fate Intervenes

Darcy woke with the sun, for there had been little to occupy him in Meryton the previous evening and they'd made an early night of it. Bingley had attempted to orchestrate a jaunt to the local assembly hall, but Darcy had flatly refused. He'd reminded his companion that he did not prefer to dance with ladies outside his acquaintance, effectively putting an end to the evening. Even the arrival of his cases with his valet, Partick, had little disturbed Darcy's rest. He woke refreshed and ready to depart Meryton at Bingley's earliest convenience. Not that they would travel together, as his and Bingley's men and luggage had arrived with Darcy's carriage.

Once he was dressed, Darcy was pleased to discover that Patrick had toast and coffee on hand. A man could starve to death waiting for Charles Bingley to wake, for he seldom breakfasted before eleven. Patrick knew Darcy preferred a light meal to tide him over until then.

But Darcy was in no mood to lounge about. Though clean and well cared for, the inn in Meryton had nothing in the way of suites, where there might be an adjacent parlor for his use. Each chamber held only a bed, a small table with one chair, a wardrobe, and a single window. While he might have read in a parlor, Darcy was not one to hang about a bedchamber all morning.

Out the lone window, he could see that while the rising sun had reached him, its warming rays readily evoked fog from the cool earth. Soon, the village would be shrouded and the inn room would feel more like a cave than a sanctuary. All the more reason not to linger.

What he needed after yesterday's aggravating events was a ride. As they were departing shortly, he hadn't asked for his riding mount to be brought, but surely the inn boasted something more adequate than a saddleless carriage horse? Perhaps Darcy would take in the vista of this Netherfield Park, to better assure Bingley that he'd made the correct decision in no longer wishing to see the place.

A short time later, Darcy had secured an acceptable enough mount and directions not to Netherfield Park, but rather to a hillock overlooking the estate. The idea of surveying the place from a distance appealed to him even though the rising autumnal morning mist, which had bloomed into a dense miasma, made him question how much of a view the hillside would offer.

He set out regardless, waving off Patrick's offer to accompany him. The inn had only the one spare mount, and Patrick had arrived from London in the small hours. He likely needed rest as much as Darcy did a ride, and Darcy doubted the two intrepid highwaymen would be about so early. Like as not, they'd imbibed themselves into a stupor celebrating the not-insignificant funds they'd robbed from him and Bingley.

Darcy set out through the swirling mist, the September air chill and clinging. The innkeeper's directions proved sound, and soon enough he found the narrow trail leading from the main roadway and upward into the fog. Seeking higher ground, Darcy urged his borrowed mount up the path, thick tendrils of mist clinging to them.

As he'd feared, though the morning fog grew more ethereal at the top of the hill, the dense miasma he'd ridden through in the village filled the lower ground before him. He could see naught of Netherfield Park save a veritable graveyard of squat stones… chimneys poking up from the mist.

He imagined the sun would burn away the obscuring shroud soon enough, but the view and the chill recalled to him that the private dining room they'd employed the evening before held a fireplace. Perhaps a bit more coffee and as close as he could find to this morning's paper would be a better use of his time. Deciding his attempt to survey Netherfield Park to be fruitless, Darcy turned his mount.

A lovely silhouette drifted through the mist before him, her profile elegance itself. Darcy blinked, certain she was a figment conjured from his imagination, but the woman did not vanish. Moving away from him, she walked across the hillside at an angle that took her ever deeper into the morning fog. He did not believe she took note of him, though he couldn't be certain for the swirling mist obscured the details of her face.

Dismounting, because the fog atop the hill was thick enough that he did not lightly leave the trail, Darcy led his horse after her. He could not say why, as he wouldn't presume to approach an unknown lady in the mists atop a hill. He only knew that he did not want to lose sight of her.

He followed her along the hilltop, catching glimpses of dark curls and a pale blue gown. She strode quickly, though he did not think with purpose or haste. Perhaps simply for the joy of walking.

And then she vanished.

Darcy rushed forward. His foot slipped and he lurched back, happy for his grip on the horse's reins. A sharp drop lurked before him. The woman was nowhere to be seen.

Looking about in the mist, he couldn't spot where she'd gone. Fear caught his breath, though logic told him that if she'd fallen, she would have cried out.

He stood scanning the mist, but she did not reappear and the fog-shrouded hilltop seemed devoid of sound. Imperceptibly, the sun rose higher and the haze about him thinned. Darcy narrowed his gaze, peering over the edge, unwilling to depart without knowing her fate. Little by little, the mist cleared, ephemeral tendrils slipping away over the edge of the cliff to form final, fleeting pools in the dells below.

Finally, his seeking gaze found a narrow cleft cutting through the bluff on which he stood. She must have descended via that path.

But the horse could not follow, and she would be far from them by now with her sure, rapid strides. Besides which, he was behaving like a madman, following a dimly seen woman through the mist. That was how tragic fairy tales began, and Darcy was not one for fairy tales.

Retracing his steps, he returned to the head of the path and a view of a solid, pleasant enough manor house set in lovely, well-manicured grounds. The lingering tendrils of fog cast Netherfield Park in an enigmatic, bewitching light, and Darcy wondered if the woman had come from there. No one was in residence, but Bingley had mentioned that staff came by almost daily to tend to the place and could be easily retained if he leased it. The apparition Darcy had seen, the unearthly, lovely vision in the mist, could have been a maid.

Somehow, he could not believe she was.

Shaking his head, he retook his saddle and rode back to the inn to find that paper and coffee.

Bingley didn't keep him waiting as long as he expected, arriving in the private room at the early-for-him hour of half ten. As he entered, Darcy looked up from a paper he hadn't truly been reading, his mind on the woman he'd glimpsed in the mist, and offered a greeting.

Bingley dropped into a chair, gesturing for coffee. "I have it from the innkeeper that the magistrate, a Mr. Collins of Longbourn, is generally in his office around noon, so we've only to make a leisurely breakfast of it and we're certain to find him. Then we can pop over and let Mr. Morris know that I'm no longer interested in the estate."

Darcy would prefer to speak with Mr. Morris first, for he didn't know how much more leisurely his breakfast could be, but as he had no pressing business back in Town, he nodded. "I rode out earlier to take in Netherfield Park. It is auspicious enough in appearance." Though nothing compared to Darcy's estate of Pemberley, in Derbyshire. But then, little compared to the Darcy lands.

"Is it?" Bingley brightened for a moment, then shook his head. "No. I will not take the place. Being set upon was a sign."

"Undoubtedly," Darcy agreed and returned to not actually reading his paper, the activity not hampered by Bingley's chatter as he ate.

Not two hours later, the noon hour found them before the inn, eyeing an imposing stone structure across the street.

"That building houses the magistrate's office, according to the innkeeper," Bingley said.

As they stepped into the roadway, the same ridiculously grandiose carriage Darcy had noted the evening before rolled to a halt across from them, obscuring their view of the entrance to the magistrate's office. After a moment, it pulled away, leaving behind the sight of the door swinging closed. Darcy's eyebrows shot up. Did the carriage belong to this Mr. Collins? That did not bode well for the man's sensibility. Regardless, they crossed the street and went in.

The outer office, which held a young man at a desk that was set so as to bar their way forward, proved as offensively ostentatious as the carriage. With mounting distaste, Darcy took in the blood red carpet, elaborate, gilded molding, and a fresco of rotund cherubs and half-clad women dominating the ceiling. About the walls, their large, ornately carved and golden frames nearly keeping the eye from the artwork within, large oil paintings of a similar theme cluttered the walls.

"I say, you do not see that every day," Bingley muttered under his breath, dropping his gaze from the bright colors of the mural above.

"Fortunately," Darcy replied, then strode forward to the desk.

The man there, who Darcy guessed to be about Bingley's age of two and twenty, did not look up. Merely kept going over some sort of ledger, peering intently at rows of numbers through wire-rimmed spectacles.

Darcy pulled a card from his coat pocket and slapped the expensive rectangle of vellum down on the desktop.

With a start, the clerk glanced up. He shoved a clean page into the ledger and closed it as Bingley joined Darcy before the desk. Taking up Darcy's card and squinting at it through his lenses, the clerk asked, "How may I be of assistance, Mr. Dacy?"

His eyes going a bit wide, Bingley rushed to say, "It's *Darcy*. Mr. Fitzwilliam Darcy of Pemberley. And I am Charles Bingley." He handed over his card as well.

The clerk nodded vigorously. "And how may I assist you, Mr. Darcy? Mr. Bingley?"

"We are here to speak with the magistrate." Darcy permitted a certain condescending coldness into his voice.

"May I inquire about what?" the clerk asked.

Darcy pressed his mouth closed, unaccustomed to being questioned with such impunity. That he wished to speak with this Mr. Collins should be enough.

Bingley glanced from Darcy to the clerk and back, then replied, "To, ah, report a crime."

"I will see if Mr. Collins has space in his schedule." Taking their cards, the clerk stood. He nodded to them gravely, then disappeared through the door at the back of the room.

"I have ever-diminishing hope that speaking with the magistrate here will be worth our time," Darcy stated quietly.

Bingley looked about the room. "I concur." His countenance brightened. "Still. No harm in it, and then we can be on our way with a clear conscience of having done our civic duty."

At the back of the room, the eyes of a particularly large, lush, and underdressed woman lounging against a backdrop of brightly painted lawn swung aside. Darcy blinked, startled, as the painted woman's eyes were replaced by a pair of watery blue ones peering out from behind the wall. He drew his eyebrows together, uncertain if he was seeing what he thought he was. The blue eyes jerked back and the painted ones swung into place.

Was this Mr. Collins fellow spying on them?

A moment later the door opened and the clerk stepped out. "Mr. Collins will see you now."

Bemused, Darcy started forward, Bingley beside him.

If the outer room was ostentatious to the point of distaste, Mr. Collins' office took the theme into the ridiculous. All about the walls, white carved marble women stood at regular intervals, the tall vases on their heads giving the appearance of holding up the ceiling. That, fortunately, was merely blue and cloud-filled, though the color was somehow unsettling. The artist, Darcy felt, had employed too much of a green tinge, rendering the cloud-dotted sky somehow sickly.

Behind a desk that would require six stout men to move it, blood-red, gold-embroidered curtains masked a window that undoubtedly faced an alleyway. Around the room, more scantily clad statues hoisted candelabras, a dozen candles burning in each. The thick rug underfoot, some sort of royal purple gone puce, clashed with everything, and every open bit of wall was either hung with more red and gold curtains, or covered with gilt-framed oils.

"Greetings, gentlemen," the tall, stout man behind the desk said, rising from an uncomfortable looking blue velvet and silver painted chair. "My assistant claims you would like a word with me, which, to be certain, I am happy to grant such exalted gentlemen as yourselves, no matter your standing. As my father, Mr. Collins Sr., the late Mayor of Meryton, always quoted, charity begins at home."

Somehow speaking with them was an act of charity even though they were exalted, which they seemed to be even though Mr. Collins had no notion who they were? Darcy fought off the urge to shake his head in confusion.

"Ah, yes, well, Charles Bingley at your service," Bingley said, moving forward to stand before the monstrous desk. There being nowhere for them to sit, he bowed and continued, "We merely wished to report that we were set upon by a pair of French bandits yesterday evening."

Darcy joined Bingley before the desk as Mr. Collins dropped back into his chair with a grimace. Closer inspection revealed that the man before them, perhaps nearing thirty, had the embellished accoutrements of his office tailored in a manner that hearkened to the Prince Regent's garb. Mr. Collins' attempt at hiding his over-indulged physique was about as successful as Prinny's.

"Those damn Boney Bandits," Mr. Collins growled. "Every time I think I've scared them off, they pop up again to accost innocent travelers, if such fine gentlemen as yourselves can ever be called innocent in all things, as surely you are, though we all know none of us are." Here, he supplied a wink. "Those merely passing through Meryton to…" He trailed off with a questioning look.

Darcy stared down at the man before him in mild disgust.

All affability, Bingley supplied, "We were on our way to view this Netherfield Park place. I was thinking of leasing it, you see."

"Ah, yes, such an eyesore, empty as it is. A real tragedy that the owner remains in London, though certainly one can see the superiority of London, dismal though it may be. Lovely estate, Netherfield Park. My father always said that if we weren't burdened with Longbourn, we would have taken

Netherfield Park, if only to save it from becoming what it has become. Terrible shame."

"Ah, yes, well, a man needs an estate to be taken seriously and to pass along to his offspring, as it were," Bingley replied, though Darcy didn't feel his friend had understood Mr. Collins' rambling any more than he had. "So I, that is we, set out to take a look, but it simply won't do, so we will be off once we supply the details of the robbery."

"Pass on to your offspring?" Mr. Collins repeated sharply.

"Well, yes, once I have some." Bingley smiled easily. "Need a Mrs. Bingley first, I'd say."

"You planned to purchase Netherfield Park, not lease it?" Mr. Collins pressed, his eyes narrow. "It is my understanding that the property is for lease only, not for sale."

Bingley looked to Darcy, who shrugged his ignorance both of the exact nature of the availability of Netherfield Park and of the source of Mr. Collins' clear agitation.

Turning back to the magistrate, Bingley said, "Mr. Morris gave me to understand that if I was pleased with the place, I might make an offer."

"Which is not the point of us seeking a word with you, sir," Darcy said firmly. Bingley's affairs were no business of this Mr. Collins, be he magistrate hereabouts or not. "We simply wish to report a robbery."

"Right. Yes. Robbery." Mr. Collins stood, making a shooing gesture. "Report the details to my clerk and I will raise the bounty again, though I doubt it will help. Hated as those Boney Bandits are, the citizens hereabouts love them too dearly to turn them in. My father, Mr. Collins Sr., always said, it takes fools to know fools, and trust me, I know the people hereabouts well enough to understand them. I am afraid I must be off to drop in on Mr. Morris. We have a meeting. Yes, a meeting. Scheduled for now. Cannot be late." Throwing his arms out wide, Mr. Collins came around the desk, ushering them before him as one would corral chickens.

Thoroughly affronted, Darcy pivoted and strode from the room. He would have continued from the building, but Bingley turned aside at the clerk's desk. Mr. Collins locked the door to his office, then passed them without a glance. A pinched, angry look on his face, he left.

"He seems rather distraught," Bingley observed, his brow creased with confusion.

"Oh dear." The clerk looked after his employer with worried eyes. "Whatever did you tell him?"

"We attempted to tell him about being robbed yesterday evening," Darcy stated.

"Ah, yes, the Boney Bandits. The whole village is speaking of it." The clerk shook his head. "That will not be what upset him. He will simply raise the reward again."

"Can nothing be done about them?" Bingley asked with clear curiosity. "A trap laid or whatnot?"

The clerk, who'd been looking after Mr. Collins, turned to Bingley with a shake of his head. "They do not strike often, and never in the same location twice. We would not know where and when to set one." Opening his desk drawer, he pulled out a bundle of papers. Sifting through neat rows of numbers, dates, and figures, he pulled free a graph, then slid it across the desk. "The only predictor I have found is the size of their haul. Insofar as I can tell, the more they get off their, well, victims, the longer until they strike again."

Darcy studied the neat chart, impressed by both the clerk's draftsmanship and the bandits' restraint. The so-called Boney Bandits were economical, were they? How odd for highwaymen. "Does not the fact that they are French make them easy to track down?"

The young man shook his head again. "I am afraid not. For one, they are favorites hereabouts. For another, I honestly do not believe anyone knows who they are. Either their English is very good and used at all other times, or their French is a ruse. I cannot say which."

Darcy found both difficult to believe. He felt certain that if he saw the two young men again, unmasked, he would know them. Especially that aggravating Azile with his obvious amusement over robbing them.

"Yes, well." Bingley shrugged. "It sounds as if it will do little good, but Mr. Collins asked us to supply you with the details of the event, Mr...." Bingley trailed off, waiting.

"Mr. Collins," the young man said. Seeing their frowns, he elaborated, "Mr. Robert Collins. The magistrate is Mr. William Collins. I am his brother. His father—" Robert Collins broke off, flushing. "That is, our father married my mother before I was born, it being a second marriage for both."

Darcy took in the odd phrasing and the young man's scarlet face and decided that his mother hadn't married Mr. Collins very long before he was born, which explained the complete lack of resemblance. But even if, as Darcy suspected, no blood bonded the two men, the esteem the careful charts and graph had garnered in Darcy crumbled under the revelation of their connection.

"And you need not trouble yourselves," Robert Collins continued. "I already noted the details of the event. As I said, the whole village is speaking of it."

"Did they report that the devils shot Darcy's hat?" Bingley's voice radiated indignation.

"Ah, yes." Robert Collins had the decency to give an apologetic grimace. "That detail has been oft repeated." He cleared his throat, his gaze dropping to his chart. "It would be helpful to know how much they took off you, however, if you do not consider it an imposition? That will allow me to narrow down the timing of their next appearance."

Darcy found everything about their trip to Hertfordshire to be an imposition, but he supplied the sum, as did Bingley, the combined amount causing Robert Collins to go a bit slack-jawed.

"Ah, on behalf of Meryton, let me tender our sincerest apologies, Mr. Darcy. Mr. Bingley." Robert Collins flipped open the ledger he'd been studying when they arrived. "I can look through the budget. There must be something here that can be diverted to replacing your hat, Mr. Darcy. It seems the least our community can do for you."

"That will not be necessary," Darcy said firmly. He wanted neither this village's funds, nor anything more to do with Meryton. Turning to Bingley he continued, "Is your sense of civic duty satisfied?"

"I suspect it must be," Bingley replied.

"Then all we require are directions to a Mr. Morris." Darcy hoped the man was near and would be in, and finished with his meeting with Mr. William Collins. It was high time they departed Meryton.

"Yes, certainly. Three doors down on the right. His office is beside Mr. Phillips." Robert Collins reached for a sheet of paper. "I can write down the address for you."

"That will likewise not be necessary." Darcy imagined they were capable of counting to three.

Bingley offered Robert Collins a dip of his head. "Thank you for your time."

The young man stood to bow. "Thank you for yours, sirs."

Darcy nodded as well, then followed as Bingley led the way back across a room Darcy hoped never to set foot in again.

As Bingley reached the door, Robert Collins blurted, "But what did you say that has my brother so agitated?"

Bingley looked over his shoulder. "That I had thought to purchase Netherfield Park," he said to Robert Collins. Adding a confused shrug for Darcy, Bingley stepped out into the street.

A feminine cry sounded. Bingley lurched to the side as the door swung closed behind him. In a shock of worry, Darcy hurried through the door after his friend.

CHAPTER FOUR

Sneaking

Elizabeth whirled at her sister's cry of alarm. A man had Jane by the shoulders. Elizabeth's hand went to her hip, only to find no sword or pistol waiting there. She started to drop down, to pull free the small knife hidden in her boot.

The man released Jane, stepping back, and Elizabeth straightened as a second man emerged from the door to the magistrate's office. Mr. Darcy, Elizabeth thought, realizing she recognized both gentlemen. Their visages evidencing various states of surprise, Mary, Lydia, and Thomas clustered on the other side of Jane and the two men.

"I beg your pardon, miss," the gentleman who'd run into Jane blurted. "I did not see you. A thousand apologies. Are you harmed?"

Jane had a hand to her chest, her cheeks flushed and her breath rapid. "Oh, no, my apologies, sir. I did not realize you were exiting the building. I would have moved from your path."

He shook his head. "It is I who blundered into you, looking over my shoulder while walking. What a fool I am, to endanger you in such a way." He bowed. "I beg your forgiveness."

"You do not need to, sir. I am certain we were both in the wrong."

Shaking his head again, the man opened his mouth to speak.

"Jane, you were merely walking along a street we have walked many times," Elizabeth cut in, aware that her sister would simply apologize again as, apparently, would this man they'd robbed.

"Yes, which is why I was not being attentive enough," Jane replied firmly.

Did Jane realize these were the men from yesterday? Was guilt the source of her adamant refusal to accept an apology for being nearly trampled? Elizabeth's gaze darted to Mr. Darcy's hat. She noted where someone, she suspected a skilled valet, had made a valiant attempt to minimize the holes.

Mr. Darcy's mouth flattened as he regarded Elizabeth from beneath the beleaguered article. She cocked an eyebrow, daring him to recognize her. It was rather a shame he scowled so, for the expression spoiled a countenance every bit as handsome as she recalled.

"I am adamantly at fault," Mr. Darcy's companion said firmly. "I will do all in my power to make amends."

Standing as tall as his thirteen years allowed, Thomas said, "My sister appears unharmed and has accepted your apology, sir. I am certain that will do."

Mr. Darcy's companion turned to him, then bowed again. "Charles Bingley at your service, sir."

Shoulders thrust back, Thomas bowed in return. "Thomas Oakwood." He gestured to Jane. "This is my sister, Miss Jane Bennet, who you mistakenly accosted, and these are three of our other sisters, Miss Elizabeth Bennet, Miss Mary Bennet, and my sister Lydia."

Mr. Bingley issued yet another bow and gestured to Mr. Darcy. "Mr. Oakwood, Miss Bennets, it is a pleasure to meet you. May I present my companion, Mr. Fitzwilliam Darcy?"

Mr. Darcy bowed to them as well, the gesture somehow grudging for all its fluidity.

Elizabeth curtsied, coming up to find that Mr. Darcy still studied her intently. She met his gaze with a fresh look of inquiry, regretting her earlier surety. After all, it wouldn't do for him to actually recognize her as Azile.

"Are you recently arrived in Meryton?" Lydia asked brightly, ignoring the fact that Thomas had introduced her as a child might be introduced, not as a young lady out and ready to speak with impunity in the presence of two newly encountered gentlemen.

"We are merely passing through," Mr. Darcy replied, the look he turned on Elizabeth's little sister offended and aloof.

"Oh? On your way north or south?" Elizabeth asked innocently, pleased all over again to have taken Mr. Darcy's money. In view of his hauteur, she'd been right in her initial assessment that he must be an annoyance to someone.

"Well, in actuality, we are here so I might tour an estate," Mr. Bingley replied to Elizabeth's inquiry, though his attention was fixed on Jane. "I'm thinking of leasing the place. Perhaps even of purchasing it. A man needs an estate, you see."

"Certainly," Jane murmured, looking down, her cheeks pink.

"You are thinking of leasing Netherfield Park?" Mr. Darcy asked sharply, turning to his friend.

Mr. Bingley nodded, all the while smiling at Jane. "Yes. I mean to speak with Mr. Morris about doing so momentarily."

Elation and hope sped through Elizabeth. Their horrible cousin, Mr. Collins, was magistrate by appointment, having been put up for the position by Mr. Parkland, who owned Netherfield Park. Not one to trouble himself with his country seat, Mr. Parkland left the estate to the staff, and his duties in Meryton first to Mr. Collins Sr. and now to his son.

Jane smiled at Mr. Bingley, and for once Elizabeth agreed with her sister's quick joy as Jane said, "Oh, but that would be wonderful. Netherfield Park has stood empty for far too long."

Mr. Bingley leaned forward, his entire being eager. "Then you approve of the notion, Miss Bennet?"

"I thought we agreed that being accosted on the roadway was a sign," Mr. Darcy said flatly.

Mary's eyes went wide. She turned a questioning look on Elizabeth.

Mr. Bingley glanced at Mr. Darcy with a frown and Elizabeth wished anew for a weapon. She'd march Mr. Darcy off down the street where he couldn't dampen Mr. Bingley's enthusiasm.

"Are you the two gentlemen who got to meet the Boney Bandits yesterday?" Lydia cried. "I am so envious. What were they like? Is Enaj as handsome as they say, just like his reward posters?" She let out a sigh. "I have nearly all of them."

Jane went pinker still.

Mr. Darcy turned a horrified look on Lydia.

Mr. Bingley frowned, though more in confusion than dismay. "You want to meet a pair of highwaymen, Miss Lydia?"

"Well, they're ever so handsome in their posters." Lydia clasped her hands before her. "Everyone wants to meet them. Even our sister Kitty, who is too good for most gentlemen."

Mr. Bingley blinked in confusion. "But, they are bandits. Robbers of the innocent. Dangerous men."

"They have never been known to harm a soul," Mary said firmly, speaking for the first time. "And it is rumored that they give most of what they acquire away."

"Give it away?" Mr. Darcy exclaimed.

Elizabeth imagined that Mr. Darcy sounded more offended than ever. Did he believe that highwaymen must be greedy? Directing her words at him, she said, "So rumor has it. It is what passes for charity hereabouts." As it must, with the local landholders all either absent, Mr. Collins, or under Mr. Collins' sway. Their estate, built by Papa Arthur, was generous with their tenants, but Elizabeth, Jane, and Mary could never convince their mother to further spread her wealth, especially to the beleaguered of Longbourn. Fanny Oakwood, formerly Bennet, somehow contrived to hold her ousting from her previous home as partly the tenants' fault, as if they had any say in the entail.

Mr. Darcy's brows drew into a rather dire vee and he said flatly, "I see." Elizabeth doubted he did.

He turned fully to Mr. Bingley. "We should be on our way."

"Yes, to speak to Mr. Morris about touring Netherfield Park." Mr. Bingley put forth the words with a hereto unseen firmness.

The two men locked gazes.

"I do hope you will like Netherfield Park, Mr. Bingley," Jane said softly into the tense silence. "It would be a boon to the whole neighborhood to have you among us."

Breaking his tableau with Mr. Darcy, Mr. Bingley smiled at her. "I am certain the estate will suit me well, Miss Bennet." He bowed. "Mr. Oakwood, Miss Elizabeth, Miss Mary, Miss Lydia. A pleasure to meet you all." He bowed yet again, then raised shining eyes to regard Jane. "Miss Bennet."

Elizabeth curtsied along with her sisters, Thomas bowing. Mr. Darcy gave a scant mimicry of that obeisance and the two gentlemen departed, going in the direction of the Phillips' residence.

As soon as they were gone, Mary whirled to Elizabeth. "Were they—"

"The gentlemen who were robbed yesterday?" Elizabeth cut in. "You would have to ask Lydia. She seems to have heard the morning gossip. I was out walking this morning, not chatting with the maids."

"They are," Lydia said, enthusiastic at being included. "Their carriage was diverted from the main road by Mr. Pierson's sheep, which somehow got out, and they were robbed and one had his hat shot through by Enaj." She issued another dreamy sigh. "They're so lucky. I would give all my favorite ribbons to meet Enaj."

Her cheeks still pink, Jane turned away to resume their walk to Mr. Lucas's shop.

They entered the shop to the cheerful jingle of the bell and the sight of Charlotte Lucas looking over from where she dusted shelves of sundries. With a cheerful smile, she made her way to the counter, hanging the duster on a peg when she reached the front of the shop.

Lydia and Thomas immediately disappeared deeper into the shelves, though in opposite directions. Lydia to peruse ribbons she hadn't the pin money to buy, but which she might prevail on her older sisters to purchase for her out of pity, for their mother gave Lydia the least. Thomas undoubtedly sought the shop's small collection of lead soldiers, for which he was eternally saving. Elizabeth believed he had nearly enough for a cavalryman.

Mary wandered off as well, unobtrusively studying a set of silver teaspoons locked in a glass-fronted case while Elizabeth made her way to the counter with Jane.

Behind the counter now and wiping her hands on her apron, Charlotte greeted Elizabeth and Jane with, "You must be here for your mother's bonbons."

"You know us well," Jane replied.

"Or at least, you know what will happen when your father sends a note around, informing our mother of the availability of sweets," Elizabeth added.

Charlotte chuckled. "Well, yes, Papa knows what he's about."

Indeed he did. Mr. Lucas ran a respectable shop that contained most non-specialty items a person could want. Various preserved or less perishable foodstuffs. Assorted dishes. Some bolts of cloth. Whatever he thought the people of Meryton might require.

Not that Mr. Lucas was in his shop much, taking his role as Mayor of Meryton very seriously. A role he defined by being constantly out and about, speaking with any and everyone. Nor was Mrs. Lucas usually in evidence, for she did fine needlework for the ladies of the village who could afford it, and was usually in the family's rooms above.

Out of the corner of her eye, Elizabeth watched as Mary inched nearer to the small doorway beside the counter. The one leading into the stockroom.

"I will go get them from the back. I haven't had time to wrap them up yet," Charlotte was saying to Elizabeth and Jane. "I did not realize you would be by so early, but I should have. You two are always early risers."

"Perhaps unfortunately so," Elizabeth said before Charlotte could turn to where Mary was about to step through the doorway. "You will never guess what happened to Jane on our way to you. She was nearly trampled by a wealthy gentleman."

"Trampled?" Charlotte said with surprise. "But who would trample you, Miss Bennet?"

"It was an accident," Jane said softly, shooting Elizabeth an annoyed look.

But Elizabeth wasn't done. She needed to give Mary time for her work, so she continued with an exaggerated, overly dramatic recounting of the incident with Mr. Bingley and his haughty companion. She could tell Jane was unimpressed with the tale, but the telling seemed the easiest way to keep

Charlotte from catching Mary in the act of hiding funds.

Finally, seeing Mary slip back into the front of the shop and drift away down an aisle, Elizabeth concluded with, "And from the way he looked at Jane, I believe this Mr. Bingley will let Netherfield Park simply to be near her."

"His looks were nothing but polite regard," Jane said softly, her cheeks red.

"Well, this is fine news." Charlotte glanced about, then lowered her voice even though they were the only ones in the shop. "If this Mr. Bingley would buy Netherfield Park, and if he is as enamored with you, Miss Bennet, as you claim, you could convince him to oust Mr. Collins as magistrate."

"Do not imagine it was not my first thought," Elizabeth replied by way of agreement. And once Mr. Collins was no longer magistrate, Mr. Robinson would no longer be tax collector. He and Mr. Collins' other cronies would lose their hold over the local populace.

"Truly, you are putting the cart ahead of the horse," Jane said. "We merely exchanged greetings."

"After which he said he would let Netherfield," Elizabeth could not help but point out.

Jane frowned at her. "He came here for that purpose."

"But it seemed clear that his companion, that Mr. Darcy, meant to dissuade him."

"If anything was dissuading him, it was likely being robbed yesterday," Jane cast back.

"Your Mr. Bingley is one of the gentlemen who the Boney Bandits got yesterday?" Charlotte asked, startled.

Her footfalls announcing her before her voice, Lydia said, "He is."

Their youngest sister joined them at the counter, her expression eager and two pink ribbons in hand. Lydia launched into a rendition of the tale of the gentlemen being separated from their funds by Azile and Enaj, picked up that morning from some of the maids. Elizabeth listened with amusement and Jane with mortification, while Charlotte tried several times to assure Lydia that she'd already heard the news, simply not the names of the gentlemen involved. But Lydia would not be interrupted.

Finally, Lydia finished her story and turned to Jane, holding up the ribbons. "Is there enough money, do you think, for me to have these? They aren't much." She looked down. "I can pay you back the next time Mama gives me pin money."

"I will buy them for you as a present," Jane said immediately.

Lydia's chin came up to reveal a bright smile. "Thank you. You're the best sister."

Elizabeth raised her gaze ceilingward, but she felt more amusement than annoyance.

Charlotte glanced over her shoulder at a large clock. "Let me wrap everything up for you. My father will return soon."

They exchanged commiserative looks at that, for none of them wanted to hear the tale of how Mr. Lucas would surely have won the favor of the King if Mr. Collins Sr. hadn't stolen his opportunity to deliver a speech. The Collins being their relations, something Elizabeth preferred not to own up to whenever possible, the sight of them always seemed to draw out the sad tale, which Mr. Lucas would conclude by listing all the advantages the King's favor would have given him. He was certain he would be a shopkeeper no more, but instead have an estate, and the funds for him and Mrs. Lucas to attempt the begetting of more offspring than Charlotte.

But instead, Mr. Collins Sr. had preempted Mr. Lucas's opportunity to address the Crown. He'd received no such rewards as Mr. Lucas dreamed of, but Elizabeth didn't know if that was because the dream was false, or because Mr. Collins Sr. had been incapable of winning the King's favor.

Charlotte went into the back room and returned with the bonbons, then unfurled a length of thin brown paper. As she worked, she said, "Do you imagine this Mr. Bingley will take possession of Netherfield Park in time for the next assembly? It's a shame he missed the one last night."

"Was it a fine affair?" Elizabeth asked.

"Elegant enough. It would have been more enjoyable with you there." Charlotte wrinkled her nose. "Although, there were not enough gentlemen as it was."

"Kitty did not wish to attend," Lydia said, not looking up from carefully coiling her pink ribbons. "And Mama said there was no reason for her to go to the trouble to chaperone Jane, Elizabeth, and Mary because she despairs of them ever marrying."

Charlotte handed over the wrapped bonbons. "Well, perhaps if this Mr. Bingley attends the next event, Miss Kitty will wish to as well."

Out of the corner of her eye, Elizabeth took in Jane's frown.

"And I will attend, if Mr. Bingley attends," Thomas said, coming up to the counter with a lead infantryman in hand. "I would like to purchase this, please, Miss Lucas."

"I thought you were saving for the cavalryman," Lydia protested.

Thomas shrugged. "This way, my army grows now."

"Why will you attend if Mr. Bingley attends?" Elizabeth asked their brother.

Thomas stood tall. "I am the man of the house, am I not? If Mr. Bingley is going to court our Jane, I must supervise."

Lydia shoved her ribbons into the pocket of her gown. "Why does Tommy get to attend assemblies if I'm still too young? I'm two years older than he is."

"Because you are a young lady and not yet out," Mary said crisply, startling Elizabeth.

She looked over her shoulder in mild annoyance. She always forgot how softly Mary could tread.

"We do not know that Mr. Bingley will court me," Jane murmured.

"Well, he won't court Kitty, no matter how many times Mama and her say she's the prettiest," Lydia muttered.

"May I purchase this sheet music?" Mary asked Charlotte.

"Certainly."

They settled up with Charlotte and started back home. Mary, Lydia, and Thomas were all in fine spirits, pleased with their purchases. Or, in Lydia's case, gifts. Jane, to Elizabeth's eye, seemed distracted and thoughtful, and Elizabeth wondered if her sister had taken to Mr. Bingley as much as he'd appeared to take to her. Jane's feelings were often difficult to guess, an advantage for Enaj, but an annoyance for Elizabeth when she wanted to understand her sister.

The walk back wasn't overly long and Lydia and Thomas raced ahead, both eager to add to their collections. Leaving Jane's side, for her sister seemed disinclined to converse, Elizabeth lengthened her stride to walk with Mary.

In a low voice, Elizabeth asked, "Did you find a good place to leave the Lucases' portion?"

While the Lucases did well enough, they could still use a bit extra to assist with the steep taxes Mr. Collins and his cronies had added to the books, some of which seemed designed to put Mr. Lucas out of business. An imposition likely put in place because he was elected mayor time and time again, a position Mr. Collins wished to add to his already held post of magistrate.

"Yes," Mary replied in an equally soft voice, though the road was empty of all but their siblings. "I put the funds in the shop's ledger."

Worry filled Elizabeth. "Will Charlotte not find the sum today, then?" They had to be careful that no one ever suspected they left the caches of money credited to Enaj and Azile.

Mary shook her head. "She keeps a daily ledger at the counter, but in back, she has a weekly one into which she enters those sums. She will not find the funds until the end of the week, by which time nearly every person in Meryton is likely to have set foot in the Lucases' shop."

Elizabeth cast Mary a quick smile. "I should have known better than to doubt you."

"Yes. You should have." Her visage holding less censure than her tone, Mary continued. "Now, let us go listen to Lydia tell Mama of Mr. Bingley trampling Jane, and that Netherfield Park may be let at last. It should be entertaining."

"That is one word for it." Elizabeth wondered if she should plug her ears with cotton.

She also wondered if Mr. Bingley truly would let Netherfield Park. Mr. Darcy obviously opposed the idea, and his very presence spoke to Mr. Bingley's regard for his opinion. Had Elizabeth and her sisters truly ruined the first step in finding Netherfield Park a new master and seeing Mr. Collins replaced as magistrate? Elizabeth hated to think that after all of Azile and Enaj's hard work, they could be responsible for spoiling such an opportunity. If Mr. Bingley didn't at least let Netherfield Park, Elizabeth would never forgive herself. Or that haughty Mr. Darcy.

CHAPTER FIVE

Speculation

Several weeks after his first glimpse of Netherfield Park, Darcy sat on what he was forced to admit was an elegant and comfortable sofa, in one of the manor house's well-appointed drawing rooms, in the company of Bingley and three of his relations. Against Darcy's advice and wishes, Bingley had indeed let the place. Now, he wished them to attend some sort of local assembly. On his previous visit to Meryton, Darcy had caught a glimpse of the sort of company they could expect. He was not enthusiastic about the idea of mingling with such rabble.

In truth, he wasn't enthusiastic about having returned to the region at all. Despite Robert Collins' graph, Darcy did not feel safe in an area where a team of French bandits were on the loose. Bandits apparently sheltered by the populace out of some misguided sense of gratitude. If this Azile and Enaj learned of Darcy's vast estate and wealth, they would surely target him for further abuse.

Which was why Darcy had written to his cousin, Colonel Richard Fitzwilliam, about using his connections to have a militia troop sent to the region. The presence of a unit of redcoats would see the so-called Boney Bandits scuttle off into their lair to hide. Fortunately, Richard had replied that such a unit would be dispatched. Darcy only hoped they would arrive soon.

But whenever they arrived, it would not be before the assembly Bingley wished to attend that evening. Not that bandits were what Darcy feared from the event. Rather, he dreaded the uncouth denizens of this staunchly rural corner of Hertfordshire.

Except that there was one particular member of the local community he wouldn't mind encountering, but he had no means by which to ascertain if she would be present.

"…will be a fine occasion," Bingley was saying where he stood with his back to the grand, swan-themed fireplace that dominated one end of the room. Despite Darcy's reluctance, Bingley's words were not aimed at him. Rather, Bingley addressed his younger sister, Miss Caroline Bingley.

"There can be no such thing as a fine occasion in such a rusticated corner of England," Miss Bingley replied from the settee across from Darcy. "I cannot see why you brought us here. I took the carriage through that Meryton place today. It has but one street of shops. One, and that is dirt. Not a cobblestone in sight. Really, Charles, I do not know what you were thinking, taking on this place."

"Caroline is correct," Mrs. Hurst, older sister to the two, added. "There is no society here worth knowing. Do you not agree, Mr. Hurst?"

"What?" Mr. Hurst looked up from his paper, peering over at the chair in which his wife sat.

"Do you not agree that there is no society here worth knowing," Mrs. Hurst repeated loudly.

"Quite right," Mr. Hurst mumbled and returned to reading.

Darcy wished he'd thought to bring a paper into the room so that he, too, would have an excuse not to attend to the siblings' debate.

"Nonsense," Bingley declared. "There are at least two families very worth knowing, and I'm certain the remainder of the populace is pleasant company. Why, I was down at the public house the day after I arrived, and the Mayor of Meryton himself sat down to chat with me. Mr. William Lucas. Couldn't be friendlier or more welcoming. The whole village is."

"Two families?" Miss Bingley repeated with clear skepticism. "Pray elaborate."

"Yes, do." Mrs. Hurst's tone of disbelief mimicked her sister's.

"Well, for a start, there are the Collinses of Longbourn."

Darcy struggled to contain an unbecoming bark of laughter at that.

As if sensing his disagreement on the Collinses suitability, Bingley cast him a quelling look before continuing, "Two brothers, both unmarried, and the elder serves as the local magistrate, and is in possession of a fine country estate."

Miss Bingley sniffed. "It cannot be that fine of an estate if I have never heard of it. In London, I associate with everyone worth knowing."

Darcy doubted that was true, the Bingleys' wealth having come from a background in trade from which they were the first generation removed. He could believe, however, that Miss Bingley took the time to know of everyone in London worth knowing.

Ignoring his sister, Bingley barreled on with, "And there are the Oakwoods and Bennets of Dovemark. It's a new estate, but I rode past and it is elegantly done."

"Really, Charles, they sound even less bearable than these Collinses," Mrs. Hurst huffed.

"Oakwood?" Miss Bingley repeated thoughtfully, an avaricious glint in her narrowed eyes. "Mr. Darcy, do you know of any Oakwoods? I have a vague memory of a member of the peerage with that surname. An earl, I believe, in Nottinghamshire."

"I am not familiar with the family name Oakwood," Darcy replied, for he was not. But then, he did not memorize lists of the peerage, their family names, and their connections, as Miss Bingley did.

She leaned forward on her settee. "Will you ask your aunt in Kent, or your uncle, the Earl of Matlock? Surely, if there are Oakwood's among the peerage, they will know the details."

Darcy would do no such thing, not being prone to idle gossip or wishing to be a party to Miss Bingley's ambitions. "When next I write to each, I will ascertain if there is a place in my letter for that query." Which there would not be.

"And when will you write to them?" Miss Bingley asked eagerly.

"I have recently corresponded with both my aunt and my uncle. I cannot say when I will do so again."

Miss Bingley sat back with a frown. "Perhaps I will write to Miss Grantley. Living in London, she will be free to ask about." Miss Bingley glanced left and right, as if more people may have appeared in the drawing room. "Here, there is no one of whom to make inquiries."

"You could inquire of Mrs. Oakwood, or of her son, Mr. Thomas Oakwood," Darcy felt obliged to point out.

That glint returned to Miss Bingley's eyes. "Is Mr. Oakwood attached? Will he be at this assembly, do you believe?"

"I have every reason to believe the gentleman is not spoken for," Darcy replied in all honesty. Taking in the bright interest in Miss Bingley's eyes, he felt a twinge of guilt for raising her hopes and opened his mouth to reveal Mr. Oakwood's youth.

"He is very likely to be at the assembly," Bingley cut in before Darcy could speak. "Mr. Lucas has it from his daughter, who is friends with the Miss Bennets, that they are inclined to attend. As Mr. Oakwood is their brother, it follows that he may as well."

Raising an eyebrow, Darcy cast Bingley a look of mild reprimand. He must be desperate to join in the local festivities indeed, for Miss Bingley would not take kindly to being misled.

"How is it that a Mr. Oakwood is brother to these Miss Bennets?" Mrs. Hurst asked.

Bingley turned to her. "I had occasion to make inquiries of both Mr. Lucas and Mr. Morris. The Miss Bennets are the daughters of a Mr. Bennet, who was master of Longbourn. Upon his death, the estate passed to Mr. Collins Sr., now deceased." Bingley paused, frowned, then shrugged. "How Mr. Collins Sr. passed appears to be some sort of local secret, but regardless, the widowed Mrs. Bennet remarried to a General Arthur Oakwood, and by him has two sons."

Miss Bingley, who had listened with an ever-growing frown, snapped, "If that is the case, either these Miss Bennets are on the shelf or Mr. Oakwood is still in strings."

A ruddy glow overtook Bingley's face. Darcy felt no sympathy. Bingley had to know his attempt to mislead his sister would be found out.

"He's not so young as all of that," Bingley muttered.

"I would place him at no more than fourteen, but he could be as young as eleven," Darcy stated for clarity's sake.

Miss Bingley glared at her brother.

"Still," Mrs. Hurst said into the charged silence. "If these Bennets are relations of Mr. Oakwood, and he is related to an earl, they might be worth cultivating, even if they are on the shelf."

"They are not on the shelf," Bingley said firmly. "They are lovely young women. At least, the four we met were."

"Four?" Miss Bingley and Mrs. Hurst chorused.

Exchanging a worried look with her younger sister, Mrs. Hurst asked, "How many of them are there?"

"Ah, I have the impression there are five," Bingley replied.

"Mrs. Oakwood certainly is a prolific sort of woman," Mrs. Hurst, who had been married for several years already with no offspring, said in a tight, hard-edged voice.

"Five, and all misses still?" Miss Bingley looked from her brother to Darcy and back. "You said, 'we met.' Does that include you, Mr. Darcy?"

"It does," he replied shortly. He was growing increasingly dissatisfied with the conversation. Such mercenary machinations were best kept to family, which he was not. Perhaps he would ride before tea.

Still looking at him, Miss Bingley asked, "Were they hideous, then? Five daughters, and none spoken for. They must be repulsive in some way."

Darcy frowned. He should have made his excuses the moment the notion of riding came to him. "The elder two are comely, and the third reasonable."

"And the fourth?" Miss Bingley pressed.

Darcy shrugged. "I cannot say. She is too young to have revealed her potential." About the age of his sixteen-year-old sister Georgiana, he would hazard.

"And we did not meet the final sister," Bingley interjected. "And if you are so interested in them, it behooves us to attend the assembly on the chance they will. You can assess them for yourself."

"Yes. Perhaps we should attend," Miss Bingley turned to her sister. "Louisa?"

"Oh, very well. I daresay it cannot do us too much harm to take in the locals." Raising her voice she asked, "What do you think, Mr. Hurst?"

He looked up from his now drooping paper, blinking rapidly. "Yes?"

"We will attend an assembly later," Mrs. Hurst stated loudly.

"Right. Assembly. Fine activity." Mr. Hurst dropped his chin back to his chest.

"Mr. Darcy?" Miss Bingley asked, transforming her visage into beseeching sweetness that would be far more effective were he not familiar with her shrewish side. "Do say you will join us."

"Before you reply, Darcy," Bingley cut in. "Let me remind you that if my sisters and the Miss Bennets are in attendance, you will have a bevy of partners with whom you are acquainted."

Did Darcy imagine the smug edge to Bingley's words? Regardless, he would not be so ill-mannered as to refuse to accompany his host and the remainder of the household.

And if the Bennets and Oakwoods did attend, Miss Elizabeth would be there.

Darcy tamped down that thought and replied, "I imagine it will be endurable."

"Wonderful." Bingley rubbed his palms together in something akin to glee. "We will have a jolly good time, I assure you."

Darcy doubted that but kept his peace as he stood. "I plan to ride before tea."

"Care for company?" Bingley asked.

"That is up to you." With that, Darcy bowed and retreated from the room, pleased to suppose that Bingley knew him well enough to take his noncommittal reply as a refusal.

His supposition proved correct, for when Darcy made his way to the stable a short time later, he found only his mount saddled and waiting. Relieved, for he wished solitude before being forced to endure the press of an assembly, Darcy waved off a groom's offer of attendance and set out. Soon enough, he and his horse looked off the bluff from which Darcy had first glimpsed Netherfield Park through the fog.

No mist obscured the estate today and he had to admit that it was a well-situated, impressive sort of place. Not as lovely or elegant as Pemberley's manor house, but then, what was? Still, the grounds were well tended and the manor house cared for, if boxy and austere. Darcy would have recommended Bingley let the place if not for the Boney Bandits.

That thought made him look about, wondering if he should have accepted the attendance of the groom after all.

But how could he be unsafe in this place, within sight of the manor house, where a woman had the courage to walk alone? He simply could not conceive that bandits frequented this hilltop. He would, and realized that in a way he had, stake his life on the idea that neither Azile nor Enaj had ever set foot here.

All of which brought him to his true reason for accepting Bingley's invitation to Netherfield Park. The woman in the mist.

Yes, he'd but glimpsed her mist-shrouded profile, but obscured as her features had been, he'd been assailed by the instant sense that he knew her. Not so much that he'd seen her before, but a recognition of her essence such as he'd never experienced. That was why he'd followed her to a clifftop in the morning fog, and why he resided as Bingley's guest now.

Darcy didn't know if Miss Elizabeth Bennet was the woman he'd seen. He could not even name the mist-hidden woman's hair color except to label it as not-blonde. He did think her to have been about Miss Elizabeth's height, but he'd been ahorse when he'd sighted her, and she'd been a fair distance away.

Still, Darcy had again felt that spark upon meeting Miss Elizabeth. That inexplicable jolt of recognition.

Was Miss Elizabeth his mist-woman, or had he suffered some ailment that day in Meryton? Some affliction that caused him to…to what? Imagine being strangely beguiled by unknown females? What ailment could do that?

Even if such a disorder existed, why the woman in the mist and Miss Elizabeth? Why not Miss Bennet, objectively the prettiest of the misses he'd met? Or Miss Mary, who was comely enough. Insofar as Darcy had seen, her only flaws were a tendency for dowdiness in garb and style, and standing with her lovelier sisters. Hardly extreme enough faults to stave off a mysterious affliction.

Darcy shook his head, aware that the same thoughts had run around and around in his mind for days. He urged his horse back from the cliff's edge, then turned him. Almost against his will, Darcy directed the beast along the crest of the hill, away from Netherfield Park. As near as he could guess to the path his mist-woman had taken.

More quickly than he'd expected, he found the cleft he'd noted on his previous visit. Dismounting, he inspected the descent to find it steep indeed. He could manage it, but could a gently bred lady?

Not that Miss Elizabeth seemed in all ways gently bred. He couldn't pinpoint any precise behavior in their brief meeting to suggest as much, but Darcy sensed a firm will beneath her fair façade. She'd also been quick and, he suspected from the amusement that had bordered on mocking he'd seen glinting in her eyes, judgmental. Were those traits he thought his mystery woman possessed?

He shook his head. He'd been a fool to accept Bingley's invitation. Like as not, the woman on the hillock had been a figment of his imagination. Something stirred loose by the fog and the drama of the afternoon before. What did he truly believe he would accomplish in Hertfordshire except to be a target for insipid misses and intrepid highwaymen?

Remounting, he turned his horse back in the direction of the manor house. Foolish or not, he was here now, and he was obliged to ready for tea and, later, to attend an assembly. He was not particularly looking forward to either.

CHAPTER SIX

The Netherfield Contingent

Elizabeth stood on the far side of the assembly hall with Jane and their friend Charlotte Lucas, studying their neighbors with interest. While her mother and Kitty generally decried public assemblies as not having anyone worthy of Kitty and the dowry Mama had bestowed upon her, Elizabeth took delight in them. She enjoyed the liveliness and being among people, and especially the opportunity to socialize with Charlotte. Mama did not approve of the daughter of a shopkeeper calling on them, and Elizabeth couldn't call on Charlotte, who was generally working in the shop and hadn't the space or staff to accept afternoon calls. Thus, opportunities to be in the company of her friend were few.

But in that moment, while Jane and Charlotte peered eagerly at the hall's entrance awaiting the arrival of the Netherfield Park contingent, the reason Mama had permitted them to attend, Elizabeth watched Mary. She, Jane, and Mary had been all over Meryton and the surrounding communities for days, hiding caches of funds where they could be discovered by a needy populace. Mary kept diligent records of their donations, and Elizabeth knew she hoped to complete the distribution of Mr. Darcy's and Mr. Bingley's stolen wealth that evening.

In a frumpy gown, her hair pulled back severely, Mary glided through the throng. On occasion, Elizabeth had seen her younger sister feign tripping in order to blunder into someone so she might place funds on their person, but that had not been necessary yet tonight. Unremarked upon by most and possessed of nimble fingers, Mary could generally slip a sum into a coat or even a reticule without anyone the wiser. Elizabeth liked to tease her that when Jane married and Azile and Enaj retired, Mary would turn to pickpocketing to secure 'charity' from the wealthy.

She watched Mary slip around a circle of chatting gentlemen and wondered if she'd augmented any of their wallets. Even though she knew what her sister was about, Elizabeth couldn't catch her in the act. Papa

Arthur had called her a gifted pickpocket. Not something on the usual list of accomplishments for a young lady.

But then, neither were riding astride, fencing, pugilism, or marksmanship.

Nearer to the entrance, Mama, Kitty, and Thomas waited, a noticeable gulf around them. Thomas, being but thirteen, did not truly fit in at an assembly. At least, not in his role as head of the household, rather than off somewhere playing with other lads. Normally, Mama would have left him home with Lydia and Matthew, but she wanted him to introduce her to Mr. Bingley.

Aside from that wish, Elizabeth knew her mother and Kitty preferred to remain aloof. As Dovemark exceeded all but Longbourn and Netherfield Park in size, Mama didn't consider their neighbors worthy of her favorite daughter. Especially once Mama had bestowed upon Kitty the whole of the five thousand pounds that had been her dowry. Mrs. Oakwood often said that her dowry had made her worthy of a gentleman and therefore, as Kitty was already a gentleman's daughter, the same dowry should secure her a peer.

A collective gasp sounded, cutting into Elizabeth's musings. She turned her attention from her relations to the entrance, eager to see who Mr. Bingley had brought to their assembly with him. Rumor had flown about, describing all sorts of gentlemen and ladies as being in attendance at Netherfield Park.

Her excitement went as flat as a ruined soufflé. There, paused in the doorway to preen under the many eyes turned his way, stood Mr. Collins. Somehow, he managed to appear both imposing and ridiculous all at once. The first due to his height and bulk, the second accomplished by his red, square cut coat. A garment which boasted so much gold embroidery that Elizabeth assumed the weight of it to be behind the sheen of sweat coating Mr. Collins' loathsome face.

"What is he doing here?" Charlotte muttered.

Looking past her, Elizabeth took in Jane's white face.

Skirting his brother, Robert Collins disappeared into the gathered throng, mostly ignored. While some in Meryton disliked their cousin Robert simply for being a Collins of Longbourn, most accepted him as the complete opposite of his older brother. In fact, rumor whispered about the village said that Robert Collins was no Collins at all, having been born a mere five months after Mr. Collins Sr. married his mother, a wealthy widow who had died not long after his birth.

Elizabeth might even concede to Robert Collins being a pleasant individual, did she not loathe all Collinses. His true progeny or not, she couldn't forgive Cousin Robert for being raised by the man who had cast them from their home, who'd robbed so many of their hard-earned funds, and who, worst of all, had shot Papa Arthur.

From where he still stood in the entrance, Mr. Collins' gaze settled on Jane. His eyes narrowed, avarice flashing within.

"I...perhaps I should depart," Jane murmured.

"He never attends assemblies." Charlotte twined her hands together before her. "What do you believe he would say if I approached him and reminded him of the outstanding sum he owes my father's shop?"

"I imagine he would form any number of repugnant expressions with those too-thin lips and simply walk away," Elizabeth replied, most of her attention devoted to Jane and the worry on her face. "He would not dare to ask you to dance."

Jane swallowed, nodding.

Charlotte looked back and forth between them, her brow creased, and whispered, "Surely, your father proved that Mr. Collins has no right to approach you."

"Papa Arthur has been gone for nearly seven years," Elizabeth replied just as quietly, as Mr. Collins started across the room in their direction. "Mr. Collins may require a fresh lesson in chivalry."

Charlotte shook her head, her gaze going to Thomas. "You cannot expect Mr. Oakwood to duel him."

Elizabeth would much rather do so herself. Azile would teach their foul cousin a stern lesson. Or, if the lout preferred pistols, Enaj could have the honor.

"I should leave before he can speak with me," Jane said anxiously.

"No." Elizabeth would not have her sister run away, nor miss an opportunity to dance with Mr. Bingley. "Charlotte and I, between us, can keep him from you. Let us take a turn about the room."

Even as she spoke, unwitting aid came in the form of their mother and Kitty. Mrs. Oakwood, who forgave Mr. Collins the sins of his father and refused to believe he had any of his own, thrust Kitty into his path. Their mother made no secret of her hope that her favorite daughter would reclaim Longbourn for them as Mr. Collins' wife. His face pinched with dislike, Thomas joined them.

Mr. Collins eyed the curtsying women with a frown, his mouth opening and closing in a quick reply. His attention snapped back to Jane, but Mrs. Oakwood was speaking. While Elizabeth could not hear her mother's words from across the room, she felt confident that Mr. Collins would be occupied for some time. When Mama wanted to talk, little could halt her.

Elizabeth took Jane's arm and turned her away. In silent support, Charlotte came around them to walk on Elizabeth's other side, both of them between Mr. Collins and his prey, though only Charlotte was as tall as Jane. As they walked, Elizabeth kept her attention half on their horrible cousin, sneaking peeks around Charlotte. The moment Mr. Collins turned fully to her mother and Kitty, Elizabeth yanked Jane into an alcove. Charlotte followed.

Releasing Jane, Elizabeth peeked out. "He is looking about now, but Mama is still talking. I do not believe he saw where we went."

"We cannot hide here all evening." Jane rubbed at her brow. "If I depart, at least you and Charlotte may still enjoy yourselves."

Elizabeth shook her head. "As soon as he stops searching, we will move nearer to the entrance. We will be behind him then. People rarely turn fully around." At least, that was what Papa Arthur had taught them, and what Elizabeth's experience showed to be true.

Charlotte chuckled. "Were you a man, you could be a general like your papa, Miss Elizabeth."

A shock of worry raced through Elizabeth. She knew better than to appear so calculating before anyone but Jane and Mary. She smiled easily, though. "I simply want Jane to have every opportunity of dancing with Mr. Bingley. She is going to charm him, and then he will purchase Netherfield Park and put someone other than Mr. Collins up for magistrate."

Charlotte sighed. "Oh, if only that were true. It would be wonderful."

"It will be," Elizabeth said stoutly, and turned to peek at Mr. Collins again.

"You cannot know that," Jane murmured.

"I can and I do," Elizabeth cast back.

"Miss Elizabeth very well may be correct," Charlotte put in. "After Mr. Bingley met with Mr. Morris, Mr. Morris told my father that Mr. Bingley asked after you quite extensively, Miss Bennet. And later, when he met Papa, he asked about you all over again. The whole village is speaking of how he's only let Netherfield Park because he ran into you on the street. Quite literally."

"Oh dear." Jane cast Elizabeth a worried, warning look. "That is a great deal of gossip."

"But all of it good," Charlotte said staunchly. "No one ever has a bad word to say about you."

Elizabeth answered her sister's worry with the barest nod. She felt it as well. The weight of knowing they were the subject of too much attention. Still, she kept her voice light as she said, "The only reason for you not to wed Mr. Bingley would be if you decide he does not suit you, but do not believe for a moment that I missed the way you looked at him when you met."

The blush of Jane's cheeks darkened in the dim light of the alcove. "You do realize that he must also believe that I suit him? He may not, you know, despite Mr. Morris starting rumors he ought not start."

With a shrug for what couldn't be undone, Elizabeth reached for Jane's hand. "Come. Kitty and Mama have our cousin well occupied. Now is our chance."

They slipped from the alcove and around the edge of the room, quickly gaining a space beside the opening into the hall's modest foyer. Mr. Collins had begun scanning again, but as Elizabeth predicted, he did not turn around. He bowed to their mother and Kitty, ignored Thomas's presence, and moved deeper into the room, searching. Some of his lackeys, Mr. Robinson and Mr. Goulding among them, moved through the crowd, angling to intercept him.

Elizabeth cast her gaze over the assembled men and women. Several had begun to line up for a set, but she saw no sign of Mr. Bingley having arrived during the brief moments they were hidden. She did, however, catch sight of Mary's severe coif. Not moving through the crowd as usual, she stood speaking to . . . Robert Collins.

Elizabeth frowned. In saving Jane had she neglected Mary? She would not want to doom her sister to a set with a Collins.

But as Elizabeth watched, he bowed, and Mary curtsied, and they moved apart. Elizabeth let out her breath. Whatever Cousin Robert had wanted, Mary had obviously dealt with, employing her usual efficiency.

A clatter of footfalls and the well-shaped vowels of cultured voices bubbled from the foyer. Elizabeth nudged Jane, who turned, her expression eager, and stepped forward into the open doorway.

To almost collide with an equally keen Mr. Bingley.

He took a half step back, blinked at Jane, and broke into a grin. "Miss Bennet. I'd hoped to find you in attendance."

Jane smiled back. "And I you, though perhaps we should endeavor not to keep meeting with such abruptness."

A tall young woman, along with a slightly older one and an undistinguished gentleman, all spilled in around Mr. Bingley. To Elizabeth's surprise, the emotion elicited by his presence rather than his expression, Mr. Darcy appeared behind Mr. Bingley, glowering. Much as his ill-humor amused her, it also contradicted her earlier impression of the gentleman. His sternness did not, in fact, infringe upon his comeliness as she'd first decided. Still, she would prefer to see him smile.

"Miss Bennet, Miss Elizabeth, may I present my sisters, Mrs. Hurst and Miss Bingley, and my brother by marriage, Mr. Hurst." Mr. Bingley looked about with a slight frown of confusion. "Darcy should be here somewhere as well."

"I am," Mr. Darcy said flatly, making no move to come around Mr. Bingley to join them.

Mr. Bingley's frown vanished. "Right, and you already know Mr. Darcy. Louisa, Caroline, Hurst, this is Miss Bennet, and Miss Elizabeth, and…" He trailed off with a questioning look at Charlotte. "Your fifth sister?"

Elizabeth would not mind if that were true, but as it was not, she replied, "Our friend, Charlotte Lucas. Her father is Meryton's mayor and owns the village's largest shop. Surely, you have taken note of Lucas's Sundries, right in the center of the main street?"

"Certainly. A pleasure to make your acquaintance, Miss Lucas," Mr. Bingley said enthusiastically. "I have met your father. Fine fellow."

Beside her brother, Miss Bingley exchanged a grimace with Mrs. Hurst.

Charlotte curtsied at least as well as any gentleman's daughter and said, "Thank you, Mr. Bingley. It is a pleasure to make your acquaintance as well."

"Our other sister is here, however. With our mother and Thomas. I am certain they will be delighted to meet you." Elizabeth turned to point them out and caught sight of Mr. Collins pushing his way through the throng in their direction. Swiveling back to Mr. Bingley, she said, "But a set is starting. Better you should dance first and endure introductions later. They can be so time consuming, do you not agree?"

Mr. Bingley and his companions stared at her, obviously uncertain how to reply. Miss Bingley's eyebrows appeared ready to climb up to join the towering ostrich feathers that topped her head, and Mr. Darcy's expression spoke of someone who had bitten into an apple to find half a worm.

Jane blushed and hissed, "Elizabeth."

Charlotte, however, looked past her and sighted their nemesis. She gave Elizabeth a meaningful stare, then curtsied. "I am pleased to meet you all, but if you will excuse me?" The gentlemen offered quick bows as, squaring her shoulders, Charlotte marched off to intercept Mr. Collins.

Elizabeth would assure Charlotte later that she was the very best of friends, but knew she could not delay Mr. Collins for overlong. He was not above a certain amount of rudeness, especially to someone of Charlotte's standing.

"My apologies, Mr. Bingley," Jane said sweetly. "I do not know what possessed my sister to be so forward."

"I was overcome by my desire to see you happy." Elizabeth caught Mr. Bingley's gaze, no easy feat for he'd fixed his attention on Jane. "Jane does so love to dance, and a set is starting this very moment."

"Elizabeth," Jane protested again.

Beyond her, Elizabeth took in their mother, Kitty, and Thomas drawing nearer through the crowd, a fresh obstacle in her quest to see Jane and Mr. Bingley manage a set. Elizabeth could think of no way to delay them but to intercept them, but if she left Jane's side, would her sister coax an invitation from Mr. Bingley? The musicians strummed the opening chords.

Mr. Bingley recovered from his initial shock to bow to Jane. "It seems, Miss Bennet, that your sister will not be satisfied until you do me the honor of partnering me for this set, if you will?"

Her cheeks aflame, Jane nodded and placed her hand in the one he proffered. Mr. Bingley tucked her hand on his arm and immediately drew her away in the direction of the about-to-begin dance.

Relief washed through Elizabeth. Turning, she followed the progress of the two through the crowd. Their goal the end of the line of dancers, their path took them near enough to Charlotte and Mr. Collins to make Elizabeth hold her breath. Sighting Jane, he turned, but Charlotte sidestepped, remaining between them.

"I believe I require punch," a pinched voice said. "Mr. Hurst, escort me."

Mr. Hurst offered his wife his arm. The two moved away without another word.

"Country manners certainly do differ from London ones, do you not agree, Mr. Darcy?" Miss Bingley flipped open a feather fan as she spoke, then studied Elizabeth over it.

Mr. Darcy scrutinized her as well, his coolness offset by the perplexed line of his brow. "Not all country manners. I find the manners in Derbyshire dissimilar to those displayed here in Hertfordshire."

"Oh, certainly, one would not see anything uncouth in Pemberley. Not with you and dear Georgiana as guides."

"It is my sorrow to have represented all of Hertfordshire so poorly," Elizabeth cast back with no trace of sadness or apology in her voice. She would offend the Prince Regent himself to keep Mr. Collins away from Jane.

Miss Bingley's gaze slid from Elizabeth to take in Mr. Collins, who now stood alone, glaring at the dancers with sullen hostility. "It does, however, occur to me that your eagerness may be born of sisterly affection, Miss Elizabeth."

Mr. Darcy cast Miss Bingley a surprised look before following her gaze to Mr. Collins. Immediately turning away, as if the sight of Elizabeth's cousin disgusted him as much as it did her, Mr. Darcy refocused on Elizabeth. "Sisterly affection is laudable."

They would condescend to be understanding, would they? Amused, Elizabeth replied, "Indeed. Being one of five sisters, I hold sisterly affection as quite sacred."

"As do I." Miss Bingley lowered her fan. "And I imagine you must often fend off the attentions of unsuitable gentlemen who simply want a connection to the Oakwood line."

Though she did not wish to spoil the growing accord between them, Elizabeth could not affirm that. "I am afraid I know little of the Oakwood line. Or, indeed, if there is one outside of my brothers Thomas and Matthew."

"You have no relations in, perhaps, Nottinghamshire?" Miss Bingley asked with ill-concealed intentness.

Elizabeth had devoted little time to considering what other relations Papa Arthur might have, and so answered slowly, "My stepfather did not speak of his family often." Now that she gave the matter consideration, it seemed odd. But then, Papa Arthur had been so involved with them. So present. Buying Mama bonbons. Overseeing every detail of the construction of their home. Teaching her, Jane, and Mary to ride and the gentlemanly arts of war. As well as French and skills that Elizabeth suspected could only fall under the category of spy craft. "He was more likely to speak of his time serving the Crown, though there was much he could not tell us of that."

Much of the interest in Miss Bingley's face drained away. Her fan came back up, fluttering.

"Why could a general not speak of his service to the Crown?" Mr. Darcy asked.

Elizabeth took in his glower with the growing suspicion that Mr. Darcy always appeared slightly offended. "He never said as much, but I always suspected that his service to the King fell under the category of clandestine. I do know he spent considerable time in—" She broke off, full of chagrin. In a bid to impress the two, she'd nearly spoken about France.

She, Jane, and Mary never brought up their stepfather's time in France. Not with those outside their family, who might make the connection between them and the Boney Bandits, nor those inside the family. Their mother and younger siblings were unlikely to recall Papa Arthur's French lessons if not reminded.

"Time in?" Mr. Darcy repeated, his frown all for her now.

"In the regulars." Elizabeth worked not to hurry her words, a sure sign of guilt. "I imagine it is considered improper to speak of such things to us girls."

"Certainly." Miss Bingley gave a delicate shudder. "War is no subject for ladies."

"Where did your stepfather serve?" Mr. Darcy asked.

Elizabeth turned an innocent look on him. "I believe we only now established that Miss Bingley and I are not meant to converse about such matters, Mr. Darcy."

Miss Bingley flicked her fan at Mr. Darcy. "You must excuse Mr. Darcy for being a man. They are obsessed with all things martial, and one of his cousins serves, so he has an even more vested interest in such matters."

"I will if you insist." Elizabeth couldn't quite contain a smile as, with as much sincerity as she could muster, she said, "Mr. Darcy, I forgive you for being a man."

His eyes narrowed.

"Elizabeth, whatever do you mean by keeping this lovely lady and gentleman trapped here in the doorway?" her mother's voice cried.

Elizabeth turned to find that Mrs. Oakwood, Kitty, and Thomas approached. Unable to resist tormenting her mother, Elizabeth replied, "You are correct, Mama. I'm certain Miss Bingley and Mr. Darcy would like to leave this inauspicious location and explore the hall."

Mrs. Oakwood huffed as she halted before them. "Nonsense. I forbid anyone from moving until I have been introduced to these fine people."

"But if you do not know them, how do you know they are fine?" Elizabeth asked.

Thomas giggled. Kitty, her expression offended on their mother's behalf, jutted out an elbow, catching Thomas in the shoulder. He rubbed his coat sleeve, glaring at her.

"Really, Elizabeth. Sometimes I believe there is no hope for you."

"Yes, Mama," she agreed, quelling any other reply in view of how frantically Miss Bingley's fan had begun to flutter.

Thomas stepped forward to bow, then cleared his throat. "Mr. Darcy, may I present my mother, Mrs. Oakwood, and my sister, Miss Catherine."

Elizabeth's mother and sister curtsied.

Mr. Darcy bowed in return. "Mr. Oakwood, it is pleasant to see you again. Mrs. Oakwood, a pleasure. Miss Catherine, there are many Catherines in the annals of my family. A formidable name."

Mr. Darcy started to turn to Miss Bingley but Mrs. Oakwood preempted him with, "We call our Catherine 'Kitty.' Kitty is such a fine, lively name, do you not think? It speaks of a young woman who is vital and joyous, rather than someone sour or ancient. You can always tell when a Catherine has been labeled a—"

"Mama," Elizabeth cut in, her tone begging for silence on the matter. Somehow, she could not picture anyone using the nickname Kitty in Mr. Darcy's family.

"What?" Mrs. Oakwood blinked at her. "I am certain all the Catherines in Mr. Darcy's line are Kittys." She turned a preening smile on Mr. Darcy. "Aren't they?"

"No."

Mrs. Oakwood's jaw hinged open.

Behind her fan, Miss Bingley coughed, the sound suspiciously like suppressed mirth.

Mr. Darcy gestured to her. "May I introduce Miss Bingley?"

Miss Bingley offered an elegant curtsy, though her face spoke of how little she felt the recipients of the gesture warranted the courtesy.

Mrs. Oakwood turned to Thomas. "Thomas, properly greet the lady."

Thomas huffed a sigh, then reached out and caught Miss Bingley's hand. "Miss Bingley, it is an honor to welcome a lady so lovely as yourself to Meryton." He bowed over her gloved fingers.

Her fan drooping, Miss Bingley looked down at him in mild horror. "Yes. Well. Thank you." She retrieved her hand and turned to Elizabeth's mother. "Mrs. Oakwood, you are not a moment too late. I was asking Miss Elizabeth about your late husband's relations but she has proved a paltry source of information on the subject."

Elizabeth's mother waved that off. "As will I, to be certain. My Arthur did not care to speak of his family, and I am not one to press, mark my word. I'm very skilled at seeing when a person wishes to speak, and when they do not, and my Arthur did not care to converse about his relations, no matter how many times I asked nor for how many years I pressed him. He said they weren't worth knowing."

"Ah, I see." Apparently not one to be easily defeated, Miss Bingley continued, "But certainly you know where they are to be found. After all, you must have notified them when he passed."

"I certainly did not. I left that to Mr. Phillips, didn't I?" Mrs. Oakwood yanked a handkerchief from her lace-draped sleeve. "Oh, my poor Arthur."

"I beg your pardon," Miss Bingley said with sudden contrition. "I did not realize his passing was recent."

"It was seven years ago," Elizabeth said blandly.

"And we are all still terribly sad about it," Kitty snapped, glaring at Elizabeth before pulling out a handkerchief of her own and adding her sniffles to their mother's.

"I am going to have some punch," Thomas said firmly. "Miss Bingley, would you care to accompany me?"

Her expression bemused, she nodded, though she pretended not to see the arm he offered. Shrugging, Thomas dropped his arm and set out, Miss Bingley by his side.

"Punch will suit me as well, if you will excuse me," Mr. Darcy said.

Mama lowered her handkerchief. "If you are going, Mr. Darcy, and as you are not yet dancing, I am certain my Kitty would care for punch, and when you return with it, we will discuss what we may do about your lack of a partner."

Mr. Darcy's face pinched.

"Let me show you to the refreshments," Elizabeth offered quickly.

His nod seemed reluctant but he gave it. They set out after Thomas and Miss Bingley.

Halfway to the punch table, Elizabeth lightly touched Mr. Darcy's arm to gain his attention, then drew him aside. She halted by a row of unoccupied chairs set against the wall and he regarded her leerily, appearing quite perplexed.

He did have a knack for being rather stern, the effect enhanced by his strong jaw, broad shoulders, and height. Elizabeth wondered if he always held his face the way he did now, with lines of thought creasing his brow. She had the strangest compulsion to smooth them. "I would like to apologize for the behavior of my family, and of myself," she said, wondering if those lines would ease. "Miss Bingley was correct that my desire to see Jane dance with Mr. Bingley stemmed in great measure from my desire to ensure she was not asked by another. I assure you that while I am not bashful, I am not usually so very forward either."

"No, I cannot picture you as bashful," he said slowly. "Nor, based on our brief acquaintance, did I imagine you to be ill-mannered."

"I truly do apologize."

"May I assume the gentleman who evoked such extreme necessity is Mr. Collins?"

Elizabeth studied Mr. Darcy's face, trying to deduce why he asked. He'd shown marked disgust when he sighted her cousin earlier, but had that disgust been a ruse? Being new to the region and with him and Mr. Bingley seeming so upright, she couldn't quite believe the two were in league with Mr. Collins. Yet, so many of the gentlemen of her acquaintance bowed to the man, some out of fear, like her Uncle Phillips, but others out of avarice for the funds his corruption brought them. It would not shock her to add two more to the list.

A sick, sinking feeling swirled in her gut, for she, Mary, and Jane already held such hopes for Mr. Bingley. Elizabeth tamped her worry down. She had no reason to suspect Mr. Darcy of holding any regard for her horrible cousin.

Except that he and Mr. Bingley had been in Mr. Collins' office that day they'd stepped out onto the street, and then Mr. Bingley had let Netherfield Park. Elizabeth had assumed because he was smitten with her sister, but what sort of reason was that for a gentleman to take on a new residence? Based on her experience, gentlemen were self-serving and avaricious. Could she truly hope that Mr. Bingley and Mr. Darcy were any different?

CHAPTER SEVEN

Keep Away

The silence that met his question growing awkward, Darcy added, "I do not wish to give offense. I have met the gentleman only once, when Mr. Bingley and I reported the incident we endured upon our first visit here, so my judgment of him is admittedly hasty." Why did Miss Elizabeth scrutinize him with such angry suspicion?

"And, in your hastily formed opinion, what think you of our local magistrate?" she asked, the words sharp.

Darcy cleared his throat. He did not know what answer she sought, but he would not lie. "My assessment of the man is not favorable."

Much of the tension eased from her graceful frame. "I am afraid I cannot say that he improves upon further acquaintance."

"A sentiment with which I assume Miss Bennet agrees?" Darcy ventured, seeking a return to the earnest, beseeching young woman of moments before, not this sharp, suspicious creature.

A hard, cold glint shadowed Miss Elizabeth's eyes. "Very much so."

He sought about for a lighter topic. He knew so little about this woman he suspected to be his vision in the mist, but he longed to learn more. Did she enjoy reading? Drawing? Dancing? Should he ask? Usually, when in the company of unmarried misses, Darcy need not bear the burden of conversation. He'd done nothing to cultivate the knack.

Before he could attempt a verbal foray, Miss Elizabeth drew in a slow breath, then said, "By way of apology for my earlier behavior, please allow me to bring Kitty her punch. If you return with it, my mother will use any good manners you possess to see you dance with her." Miss Elizabeth blinked once, appearing slightly startled, then hastily added, "That is, unless you want to dance with Kitty?"

Darcy studied Miss Elizabeth's face, taking in how much younger she appeared in her moment of uncertainty. No, he did not want to dance with Miss Kitty. "I would much rather dance with you."

Darcy did not know from whence the words sprang. He should have conversed with her for longer before tendering such an offer. She could be a wholly unengaging companion. Someone it would be a trial to stand up with, even were she his mist-woman.

Which he felt more and more that she must be. Her elegance, her dark curls, her height, all pointed to her being the lady he'd glimpsed the morning he'd first set eyes on Netherfield Park through the fog. As did his certainty, when he'd met her on the street before Mr. Collins' office, that it was not their first encounter.

As he watched her, it occurred to him that she had not accepted his offer to dance. In fact, her attention had moved past him. He followed her gaze to where Bingley and Miss Bennet had begun the second dance of their set. She hardly seemed aware that Darcy stood with her, or of the offer he'd tendered.

"Is silence to be my reply?" he blurted, chagrined. Women planned their evenings around securing a set with him, though he bestowed the honor on few.

Miss Elizabeth returned her attention to him with a raised eyebrow. "Did you ask me a question to which I was meant to reply?"

"I asked if you would do me the honor of a set."

"No. You stated that you would rather dance with me than with my younger sister." She pressed her full lips together, her eyes bright.

Was she attempting not to smile at him? Not to...mock him? Darcy stared down at her, seeking words to express an emotion he could only label as aggravation.

"Am I to understand that in the usual course of things, any hint that you might dance with a lady is seized upon, Mr. Darcy?" Miss Elizabeth asked. The humor she would not permit her lips to express danced in her eyes. "Was I meant to leap at your not-quite invitation?"

Was she always so contrary? So vexing? He should walk away. That would show her...what, exactly? That her words had struck a blow?

Her expression gentled. "It seems to me that if you desire something a worthy amount, asking for it is a small concession."

She had a fair point. Darcy cleared his throat. "Miss Elizabeth, may I have the next set?"

Rather than answer, she looked past him again, then murmured, "I am uncertain."

Shock raced through him, followed hard by displeasure. Why make such a point of him asking if she had no answer?

Miss Elizabeth nodded in the direction of the dancers. "I require assistance in keeping Jane away from Mr. Collins, whom she loathes even more than I do. Will you agree to render that assistance and, if possible, to engage others of your party in the effort? If so, I would be pleased to dance with you. If not, I am far too busy to indulge in what I imagine would be a delightful set as your partner."

The woman was mad. He should have known. If she was his vision, she had walked about alone in some of the densest fog he'd ever seen, and then all but climbed down a cliff face. None of that was normal behavior for a gently bred lady.

"I am afraid I must insist on an answer, Mr. Darcy. Time is running short."

Her words added to his annoyance, but rather than reply, he followed her gaze again to see Bingley leading Miss Bennet through their second dance. Both smiled, Bingley in a silly way and Miss Bennet with simple cheer. On the other side of the rows of dancers, Mr. Collins watched, arms folded across his chest, glowering and blatantly avaricious.

A surge of chivalry reared up in Darcy. He had no designs on Miss Bennet. No obligation to her. Yet, to see such an obviously sweet creature hounded by such an odious fellow as Mr. Collins, it wasn't to be borne. "You have my assistance, and that of anyone else in my party I can bring to aid us."

Miss Elizabeth's answering smile was like the first rays of sunlight streaming down between fragmenting storm clouds after a rain. She quickly schooled the expression into a more demure shadow of its former glory, but happiness still glowed in her expressive eyes. "Thank you."

As one, they set out to reach the dancers. Darcy caught Bingley's eye, and Miss Elizabeth likely did the same with her sister, and when the set ended, the two came to join them. Fighting his way through the dispersing throng, Mr. Collins cut across the center of the hall.

Darcy bowed. "Miss Bennet, may I have the pleasure of this set?"

She blinked, surprised.

"I was escorting Miss Bennet to the punch table," Bingley said a touch sharply.

"He was," Miss Bennet agreed.

"Jane, you truly should go with Mr. Darcy. I will see Mr. Bingley to the punch." Miss Elizabeth lowered her voice to add, "And an explanation."

Over Bingley's shoulder, Darcy saw Collins drawing near and reiterated, "Please, Miss Bennet? It would be my honor."

She looked to her sister.

Miss Elizabeth nodded earnestly.

Miss Bennet dipped a curtsy to Darcy. "Thank you, sir."

Offering his arm, he whisked her away, aware of the ire radiating off Bingley as he did so.

Darcy took her to the far side of the hall, forcing the square of dancers forming up nearest the musicians to break apart to accommodate them, thus reordering everyone going down the line. Miss Bennet blushed prettily and apologized profusely. Darcy cared not if he aggravated a handful of locals while completing the mission he'd undertaken. Past the assembling dancers, he watched Miss Elizabeth speaking rapidly to Bingley, whose anger melted into confusion, then reformed into determination. Mr. Collins reached the end of the room where Darcy and Miss Bennet stood, but before he could approach them, the musicians launched into a lively quadrille.

Proficient as he was, Darcy was able to devote most of his attention to the room at large as he executed the steps. He sighted Bingley and Miss Elizabeth speaking to the Hursts, then to Miss Bingley and Thomas Oakwood. At some point, Charlotte Lucas joined them, and Miss Mary. When next the dance brought Darcy around, the group had separated.

"Thank you," Miss Bennet whispered as they met in the center of their square, having obviously come to understand his and Miss Elizabeth's insistence.

Darcy nodded, trying to keep track of their co-conspirators among the crowd. It was not until halfway through the set that he noticed Miss Kitty partnering Robert Collins not far away. A few turns later, Miss Bingley and Mrs. Hurst had converged on Mr. Collins.

Mr. Hurst danced with Miss Bennet next, and then a gentleman Darcy didn't know partnered her for a set. As the night wore on, more and more of those gathered in the hall joined in the scheme. It seemed Miss Bennet was well liked, and Mr. Collins far less so, though Darcy suspected that some of the gentlemen who aided their endeavor simply wished to dance with such a lovely partner.

It was not until the assembly was winding down, all three of the gentlemen in Darcy's party having partnered Miss Bennet for not one, but two sets, and also having endured several dismal conversations with Mr. Collins, that Darcy finally partnered Miss Elizabeth. He could tell by her cheerfulness that she was well-pleased with the success of their efforts and a warm feeling of accomplishment suffused him, adding to the ambiance of the low-burning candles.

Their first dance was lively, giving little time for conversation, but the second slow. An older style, with stately steps to permit the dancers to recover from their exertions, and to wind down the evening. Candlelight glittered in the smattering of crystals in Miss Elizabeth's hair, and in her dark eyes, and Darcy suspected he had never before fitted so well with a partner.

She must be his vision from the mist.

"Thank you for your assistance this evening, Mr. Darcy," Miss Elizabeth murmured. "I imagine this assembly was not akin to your typical outing."

The steps drew them apart, giving him ample time to consider his reply. When next Miss Elizabeth came to his side, Darcy said, "Indeed, this evening was an aberration for me, but not a terrible one. In truth, I could be prevailed upon to admit enjoyment." Certainly, having a mission other than avoiding marriage-minded misses and their mamas was a pleasant change.

Executing a slow turn, Darcy caught sight of Mr. Collins standing off to one side, tapping his foot out of time and scowling at the dancers. "Has Mr. Collins been pressing his suit for long?"

Miss Elizabeth's expression pinched.

The music drew him away from her again.

When they met once more, she said, "Some years ago, he pursued her sharply and was…rebuffed. Since then, he has left her, all of us, blissfully alone. Until this evening."

Frowning, Darcy asked, "What changed?"

Miss Elizabeth assessed him from the corner of her eye as they moved through the steps of the dance. Once they were facing one another again, she said, "I believe his renewed attentions are the result of a rumor running through the village."

"Dare I ask the content?"

She shrugged. "It seems the whole of Meryton has already decided that Mr. Bingley will offer for my sister."

Coldness washed through Darcy. Had the entire evening been some elaborate ruse to trap Bingley? "A rumor begun by whom?"

Miss Elizabeth raised her eyebrows, likely at his clipped tone. "By what I am to understand were numerous unsubtle inquiries made of Mr. Morris and then of Mayor Lucas," she cast back, her words nearly as hard-edged as Darcy's had been, then added with emphasis, "By Mr. Bingley."

Darcy grimaced, having no delusion that Miss Elizabeth's quick mind hadn't followed his angry and suspicious thoughts. Meeting her gaze, he dipped his head in mute apology as the steps drew them apart again.

Coming to a halt across from her, he realized the set was over. He'd squandered his final moments of the dance offending her. Along with the other gentlemen, he bowed. Across from them, the ladies curtsied, Miss

Elizabeth's obeisance the most graceful by far.

She possessed the agility of a dancer. That sureness and strength of form. He wondered how she came by it. Gently bred ladies were often elegant, but not accustomed to a life that held any rigor.

He stepped forward, offering his arm to escort her to where her family was gathering, and asked, "Do you ride?"

Though the tension his unsubtle accusation had evoked still showed in her features, she placed her hand on his arm. "I am not known as a great rider. I do walk daily. I enjoy the exertion."

Seizing on the opportunity she provided, he asked, "Have you taken in the view of Netherfield Park from the nearby hilltops? It is worth seeing."

She slanted a look at him. "It is a view with which I am familiar."

Feeling strangely daring, Darcy said, "Although, I have noted that on occasion, a fog rolls in to obscure the sight, especially quite early in the morning."

Miss Elizabeth nodded, her lovely profile revealing little of her thoughts.

Was it the same profile he'd glimpsed through the mist?

They reached her relations, gathered together with his party. Near the broad doorway leading into the foyer, Charlotte Lucas looked back to offer Miss Elizabeth a wave, which she returned with a smile. Miss Lucas walked with an older man and woman, presumably Mr. and Mrs. Lucas, all of them well-dressed. If Darcy did not know they were shopkeepers, he might have guessed Mr. Lucas to be a country squire.

"…will certainly have to call on us at your earliest convenience, Mr. Bingley," Mrs. Oakwood was saying when Darcy and Elizabeth reached the group, a sullen Miss Kitty at her side. Casting a triumphant look at Miss Bennet, who appeared to study the toes of her slippers, Mrs. Oakwood continued, "Not that anything could keep you away, I suspect. Nor you, Mr. Darcy. Not when you are both so obviously fond of my Jane."

Pink colored Miss Bennet's downturned cheeks. At her side, Miss Mary cast her a pleased smile. Fresh suspicion bloomed in Darcy.

"Ah, yes, well," Bingley fumbled, his own face ruddy.

"We will be delighted to call," Miss Bingley stated for him. "Will we not, Louisa?"

"Yes." Mrs. Hurst's voice was far more neutral than at the start of the evening. "Delighted."

Mr. Hurst, who stood beside young Master Thomas, nodded along with his wife's words.

Had they, too, enjoyed the diversion of not permitting Mr. Collins to dance with Miss Bennet? Darcy had witnessed all three assisting in the effort, but had assumed that Mrs. Hurst and Miss Bingley would have soured on the idea after each made the ultimate sacrifice…a set with Mr. Collins.

"And I will be calling as well," a voice said loudly from behind Darcy.

He turned, drawing Miss Elizabeth around with him as her hand still rested on his arm. Mr. Collins barreled down on them, his expression smug.

A tremble went through Miss Elizabeth. Darcy looked down at her in alarm, wondering what frightened her so.

Anger flashed in her eyes.

She did not shake with fear, he realized, but rage. A glance showed that Miss Bennet had looked up from her contemplation of the floor, all color leaving her cheeks. Her clear blue eyes held a loathing that seemed entirely foreign on such a sweet visage.

"Certainly you will call as well, Mr. Collins." Mrs. Oakwood beamed at him, showing no sign that she noted the dislike on every face.

Nearly every face, Darcy realized. Miss Kitty stepped forward, batting her lashes. "You will call on me, will you not, Cousin William?"

Mr. Collins bowed. "I will call on all of my fair cousins, for we have for too long been estranged."

"For good reason, sir," Miss Elizabeth snapped.

As one, Mrs. Oakwood and Miss Kitty cast her quelling frowns.

Mr. Collins turned a smug, condescending look on her. "Yes, with very good reason, and I will admit that it has been a struggle, one understandably too momentous for the gentle minds and hearts of females to undertake, but I have forgiven you all for the loss of my dear, beloved father. So you see, you are bound to extend me the same courtesy. After all, 'forgive, and you will be forgiven.'"

A fresh tremble of anger went through Miss Elizabeth.

Darcy looked from face to face. What did Mr. Collins mean, he'd forgiven them the loss of his father?

"It is decided, then," Mrs. Oakwood said brightly. "Everyone will call."

"I will look forward to receiving you, Cousin William," Miss Kitty simpered at him.

Miss Elizabeth released Darcy's arm. Her features set and her smile strained, she curtsied. "Mr. Darcy, Mr. Bingley, Mr. and Mrs. Hurst, Miss Bingley, it has been a distinct pleasure to be in your company this evening. If you will excuse me, I require fresher air."

"I have already called for the carriage, Elizabeth," Mrs. Oakwood exclaimed. "If you will simply wait a moment, I am certain a boy will be in to announce its return."

Miss Elizabeth shook her head. "It is not far. I will walk." She looked to Miss Bennet and Miss Mary.

"I will join you," Miss Mary said quickly.

"As will I." Miss Bennet dipped a curtsy. Her gaze found Bingley as she straightened. She offered a quick smile, no less strained than her sister's, and whirled away.

Miss Mary offered a quick farewell as well, and the three departed. Master Thomas started to bow, as if he might take his leave and follow, but his mother's glare halted the motion.

Mrs. Oakwood huffed, turning back to Darcy's companions. "You will accept my apologies for Elizabeth. She has always been wayward. She suffers for not having a strong male presence in her life."

"Think nothing of it," Miss Bingley replied with raised eyebrows.

"It would do you credit to take her in hand, Mrs. Oakwood," Mr. Collins said, his smile condescending. "No man wants such an impertinent miss in his household and once your eldest is married, I am certain her husband will put Miss Elizabeth right. It is the duty of a mother to see to these things, do you not agree?"

"Oh yes. Certainly, Mr. Collins," Mrs. Oakwood rushed to say.

"My husband will have every sway over my unwedded sisters," Miss Kitty added.

Darcy eyed the three with mounting disdain, a feeling he saw repeated on the faces of Miss Bingley, Mrs. Hurst, and even Mr. Hurst.

For his part, Bingley merely gazed longingly in the direction Miss Bennet had gone, not appearing to have heard anything said after her departure. Darcy reflected that if a conspiracy were afoot to unite the two, it was hardly needed. Bingley appeared quite smitten.

A footman strode in, scanned the dwindling occupants of the room, and approached Bingley. "Your carriage is without, sir."

Bingley tore his gaze from the doorway. "Yes. Right. Well, a pleasant night all. Splendid event."

Making his bow along with the others, Darcy then trailed them out and into Bingley's conveyance, fortunately large enough to easily hold six, and them only five. Once they were inside and on their way, Bingley craning his neck out the window in an obvious attempt to catch another glimpse of Miss Bennet, Miss Bingley looked about at them all. The flickering light cast by the lanterns they passed mingled with the steadier glow of those mounted on their carriage to dance across her even features, illuminating her bland expression.

"That was an interesting evening," she stated.

"Very." Mrs. Hurst turned to her. "Do you imagine they truly are well connected? Often, such eccentricity stems from being wealthy and connected."

"True." Miss Bingley's face pinched in thought. "After all, if such eccentricity were paired with a lack of wealth and connections, they would simply be mad."

"What was that business about Collins' dead father?" Mr. Hurst put in.

Silence met that, until Bingley turned back from the window to say, "No idea. I can tell you that there is quite a bit of dislike between Miss Bennet and the man, though. She said she would depart with alacrity rather than stand up with him, or even speak with him."

"Miss Elizabeth said that he courted Miss Bennet once, years ago, but has ignored her since, until now," Darcy found himself saying. He did not care to gossip, but the situation was too odd to ignore.

"Did she?" Bingley frowned. "Why start up again now?"

Miss Bingley raised her eyes heavenward, the whites glinting in the passing lantern light. "Obviously, he was biding his time, Charles. You have spurred him into a fresh suit."

"I have?"

In the dim light, Darcy couldn't tell if Bingley's color heightened, but he tugged at his cravat nervously.

"Yes, you have," Mrs. Hurst snapped. "And you had best guard your behavior better until we learn if they are connected or simply a bevy of madwomen, or you will be in too deep to extract yourself."

Silence again filled the carriage.

"They seem intelligent," Miss Bingley said quietly after a time. "Certainly, they appear modish and attractive, although Miss Kitty's gown was adorned with enough bows to supply the local milliners for a year."

"And I have never before beheld so many ruffles as Mrs. Oakwood had on her cap," Mrs. Hurst declared, her tone far less charitable. "And Miss Mary is quite severe in her tastes. She looked practically dowdy."

"I heard from a Miss Long that Miss Mary is the most accomplished of the five," Miss Bingley replied in a less aggrieved tone. "Perhaps she simply wishes to appear studious. Apparently, she plays pianoforte and speaks French."

"Well, that is something, at least," Mrs. Hurst allowed. "But Charles, do say you will guard your behavior with greater care until we learn more about them."

Bingley shrugged, looking back out the window into the night.

On the other side of the seat they shared, Darcy mimicked him. Across from them, Mrs. Hurst and Miss Bingley delved into even greater speculation, Mr. Hurst silent between them. Darcy did not attend as they left Meryton behind for the deeper darkness of the countryside. He kept his gaze on the stars and his thoughts on Miss Elizabeth as Bingley's driver took them back to Netherfield Park.

CHAPTER EIGHT

Complications

By flickering lantern light in the cavern hidden behind the stable, Elizabeth parried Jane's thrust, pressing her sister back. Dropping low, Elizabeth pivoted. She brought up her blunted practice blade and swung, intent on knocking aside the knife she knew sped in her direction.

The dulled knife Mary had launched at her bounced off Elizabeth's padded jerkin, then clattered to the floor.

Mary's mouth fell open in shock. "You missed. I mean, I hit you."

Elizabeth looked down at the knife where it lay on the smoothed stone. She straightened, frowning.

"Are you unwell, Elizabeth?" Jane asked, coming around her to peer at her face. "Perhaps we should not be practicing on so little sleep? We did remain at the assembly rather late."

"I took plenty of rest." Elizabeth winced at the note of annoyance in her voice, also unusual.

Jane regarded her with worried eyes. "But you never miss. Mary has not hit you in years."

Elizabeth drew her shoulders back, resting the blunted tip of her practice blade on the stone at her feet, her hands folded on the pommel. "I am perfectly well."

"You are distracted," Mary said. "You are daydreaming about someone wealthy and handsome, no doubt."

Elizabeth kept her face bland but Mr. Darcy's handsome visage, determined as he strode forward to intercept Mr. Collins in conversation, filled her mind. Once he'd committed to Elizabeth's scheme of keeping her sister away from Mr. Collins, Mr. Darcy had undertaken the task with a dedication and intensity that impressed her, and had laid to rest any worry that he and Mr. Bingley were in collusion with the master of Longbourn.

He'd also seemed, at times, to actually enjoy himself. Once or twice, Elizabeth had glimpsed mischief in his eyes, the expression delightful there.

In their brief acquaintance, he generally seemed guarded and stiff. Was there anyone in his life who made certain he engaged in fun now and again?

"You were thinking about Mr. Bingley?" Jane asked slowly, agony in her voice.

Elizabeth shook her head. "I was certainly not thinking about Mr. Bingley."

Red suffused Jane's cheeks. "Oh. Well, that is good." She crossed to the rack where they stored their practice swords.

Mary came forward to collect the knife she'd thrown, saying, "I did not mean Mr. Bingley."

In the act of returning her blade to its place, Jane looked over her shoulder. "Who, then?"

Mary eyed Elizabeth. "Mr. Darcy."

Heat raced up Elizabeth's neck, for Mary was correct. As much as she'd meant to concentrate on their sparring, memories of Mr. Darcy at the assembly continually encroached.

"Were you thinking about Mr. Darcy?" Jane asked, turning from the sword rack.

Elizabeth shrugged, trying to make the motion casual. "I was, but not in the way Mary is suggesting."

Mary snorted. "How many ways are there to think about a tall, handsome, wealthy gentleman?"

Elizabeth presumed there were a great many. She tried not to get lost in imagining them.

Taking up a cloth to wipe her hands, Jane said, "Oh, come now, do tell. I have already bored you nearly insensible by recounting my every interaction with Mr. Bingley."

Elizabeth shook her head. "You could never bore anyone, but I was not thinking about Mr. Darcy like that." At least, she'd been trying not to. "It is something he said as he was escorting me back to you all after the final set." Her cheeks grew hot. "I do not know what to make of it."

"Well, tell us and we will help you decide," Mary ordered. She replaced Jane by the sword rack, lining up her practice daggers in their space below the longer blades.

"We are done sparring?" Elizabeth asked. "I will concentrate. On my honor."

"Jane put up her sword," Mary replied. "I assumed we were done. And do not think you can change the subject so easily."

Ignoring Mary, Elizabeth cast a questioning look at Jane. "Are we done practicing for the day?"

"I thought I would do some mending." Jane started on the laces of her padded jerkin.

Elizabeth was in no way fooled by her sister's casual reply. "You want to be in the house. You hope Mr. Bingley will call."

Jane looked down. "Perhaps."

"A deduction that in no way tells us what Mr. Darcy said to you, Elizabeth," Mary put in, starting to remove her padding as well.

Elizabeth knew her sister wouldn't relent. Once Mary focused on something, she was tenacious. Trying not to let the annoyance she felt into her voice, Elizabeth told them, "He truly did not say much. We were speaking of walking and he asked if I have taken in the view of Netherfield Park from the hills, early in the morning."

"That seems harmless enough." Jane sounded relieved.

"I would think so, and his voice held no inappropriate undertones, but his eyes…" Elizabeth trailed off. His eyes, though glimpsed only out of the corner of hers, had practically blazed with interest.

"His eyes what?" Mary asked.

Searching for the right words, Elizabeth said, "I cannot quite describe it, but I formed the impression that he wants to encounter me there. On the hillock overlooking Netherfield Park, early in the morning."

"Surely not," Jane protested, hanging up her jerkin.

Mary frowned, considering. "To what end?"

Elizabeth shook her head. "That is the question that has me so preoccupied."

"Do you think he sought a…a rendezvous?" Mary ventured.

"He could not have." Jane sounded quite insulted on Elizabeth's behalf. "He is Mr. Bingley's friend and a perfectly upright gentleman."

Or perhaps her sister was offended on Mr. Bingley's behalf, Elizabeth mused, and said, "He could not have been suggesting a rendezvous because he offered no date." Giving up on more practice, she crossed to stow her blade with the others, then started unlacing her jerkin.

"But he did offer a time," Mary said thoughtfully, hanging her jerkin beside Jane's. "Perhaps you were meant to add a date? Maybe that was to be the next step in the conversation. What did he say next?"

"That sometimes fog obscures the view."

"That does not sound like an invitation to a rendezvous," Jane said firmly.

"Unless he means for Elizabeth to meet him up there the next time we have a foggy morning."

Jane cast Mary an annoyed look before asking Elizabeth, "Have you been going up there?"

Elizabeth hung up her padding and reached for a cloth to wipe her hands. "Not of late. Not since Mr. Bingley took up residence." But it had been foggy the last time Elizabeth walked along that stretch of hilltop. Densely so. Later that same day, they had met Mr. Darcy and Mr. Bingley for what the two believed was the first time. Which made Mr. Darcy's choice of conversation all the more curious.

"Perhaps Jane is correct about the need for mending," Mary mused. "If the Bingleys, Hursts, and Mr. Darcy do call, you can see if he brings up walking and fog again."

"I cannot imagine he will." Somehow, despite his odd statements about the view of Netherfield Park, Elizabeth couldn't picture Mr. Darcy as a rake. He seemed far too serious for dalliances. "Likely he meant nothing by his words."

And even if he were a rake, her lack of response to his sallies about the hilltop would ensure he took such attention elsewhere. Which suited her. Elizabeth wouldn't be the one to break up the Boney Bandits. They all knew Jane would fall in love and do that.

And if she could fall in love with Mr. Bingley, as she seemed inclined to do, and Mr. Bingley could be persuaded to purchase Netherfield Park and see that a more just man was put up for magistrate, there would be no more need for the Boney Bandits. Elizabeth and her sisters could become just like all the other marriage-minded misses.

"Mending, then?" Mary asked, looking back and forth between them.

Elizabeth folded the rag she held. "I do have a tear in the hem of my cloak."

Smiling happily, Jane went to the door to the stable. She slid aside a small panel and peered out.

They always checked to ensure that no one had come in while they were in the cavern. It pleased Elizabeth that her sister hadn't forgotten caution in her excitement over the possibility that Mr. Bingley might call.

Jane opened the heavy door and stepped through, Mary following her.

Elizabeth caught up the lantern, the only source of light as they hadn't troubled to light the many candles that filled sconces set about the large space. She turned in a slow circle, taking in the rough walls of the cavern, discovered by Papa Arthur before he purchased the land on which to build their home. They'd spent so many happy hours here, first learning from Papa Arthur and then sparring together. Was all that truly about to end simply because a man had smiled at her older sister?

Elizabeth sighed. She did not want to be like every other marriage-minded miss. She wanted to be a part of Papa Arthur's Bennet Gang, even if the Boney Bandits must lose Jane.

"Elizabeth, are you coming?" Jane called back. "We need time to make ready before they call."

Elizabeth lowered the lantern. No, not because a man had smiled at Jane, for many had over the years. Because the right man had. Mr. Charles Bingley.

Suppressing her sorrow in view of Jane's happiness, Elizabeth slipped through the secret door, following her sisters.

After extinguishing the lantern and returning it to a shelf set just inside the door, they closed it, rendering the passageway invisible in the stacked stone wall. They helped each other check that their gowns and coifs were in order, then exited the stable to find Lydia coming out of the walled garden. Sighting them, she brightened and hurried up the path. "There you are. I was worried you'd gone riding. Jane, Mama says you must come in and ready for callers." Lydia looked from their eldest sister to Elizabeth and Mary. "She didn't say anything about you two."

Elizabeth exchanged a wry look with Mary. No, Mama wouldn't care where they were. Only that Kitty and Jane were available, and the latter was a new concern. Before Mr. Bingley's marked attention the evening before, Mama wouldn't have shown interest in where Jane was, either.

Not seeming to note their amusement, Lydia prattled on to Jane, saying, "Mama is certain Mr. Bingley and Mr. Darcy and Mr. Collins will call, and she says she does not care which of them you marry so long as you marry one and Kitty the other, and Kitty said she wants to marry Mr. Collins and have Longbourn, but Mama said she should want to marry that Mr. Darcy, because he is worth ten thousand a year, even if he did not dance with her. Mama said she was certain you, Jane, had squandered any opportunity of happiness after ruining your chance with Mr. Collins all those years ago, but that now you might make up for your bad behavior by securing a wealthy gentleman."

Jane halted, drawing the rest of them up short.

Taking in her sister's white face, Elizabeth asked, "Jane? Are you unwell?"

"You do not truly believe that Mr. Collins will call?" Jane said quietly.

Lydia scrunched up her nose. "I know his papa killed Papa Arthur, and Papa Arthur killed him, but it was so long ago. And Mama says Mr. Collins had nothing to do with it. She says we must forgive him because there are five of us and we all need to marry."

"He had everything to do with it."

Jane spoke with such low ferocity that Lydia, her eyes going wide, stepped back from their older sister. Lydia swallowed. "H-he did?"

"If he calls before Mr. Bingley, you can say you have a sore head and leave," Elizabeth said quietly. "You cannot forgo the opportunity to see Mr. Bingley simply because of our horrible cousin may also call."

"And if Mr. Bingley arrives first, we can suggest a walk," Mary added.

Jane shook her head. "Mama will not allow it. Not knowing there might be more callers."

"I can help." Lydia looked eagerly from one to the other of them. "I can keep talking about a walk no matter what Mama says. I can wear her down."

Jane cast her a grateful look but said, "She will likely send you and Matthew to your schoolroom. Maybe even Thomas."

Lydia stamped a foot against the stone of the walk. "I wish I were older. I want to help."

"You will be sixteen soon," Elizabeth said soothingly. "Mama let Kitty be out when she was sixteen."

"She made the rest of us wait until we were eighteen," Mary said.

Elizabeth cast her a quelling look.

Jane sighed. "None of that will be decided by lingering here." Squaring her shoulders, she resumed walking, though with a hint of a gallows' march to her steps.

Elizabeth exchanged a worried look with Mary, then they all followed.

They entered through the kitchen and went up to their rooms via the maids' stairs, avoiding the front of the house where they might encounter callers. None of them spoke as they slipped into their rooms to change.

Elizabeth had hardly closed her door when a soft knock sounded.

"It's only me," Lydia's voice said.

"Come in," Elizabeth called back.

Lydia entered, then closed the door firmly behind her before meeting Elizabeth's inquiring gaze. Lydia raised her chin, her expression mulish but her voice soft as she said, "I want to know what happened. I want to know why you and Jane and Mary hate Mr. Collins so much."

Elizabeth studied her younger sister, taking in Lydia's childish gown, which looked a touch absurd on her less-than-childish figure. Having grown a great deal in the past year or so, Lydia now towered over Thomas and Matthew, and Elizabeth as well.

"You just said I'm nearly old enough to be out." Lydia stamped a foot in the thick carpet that warmed Elizabeth's floor. "I need to know. I have to learn about dealing with gentlemen."

"You have to learn to stop stamping your foot like a child about to throw a tantrum," Elizabeth cast back.

Scarlet suffused Lydia's face. She sucked in a deep breath, smoothing her palms along the sides of her skirt. "I am sorry. I will endeavor not to stamp my foot, but you truly must tell me."

Lydia was right, Elizabeth decided. Even though it was more Jane's story than hers, Lydia should know. She would need to deal with gentlemen, and Mama treated her more as a maid than a daughter, so she would receive no advice there. Not that Elizabeth ever had, either. Mrs. Oakwood's advice was reserved for Kitty, the daughter who had brought Papa Arthur into their lives by running into the street. "If you help me ready so I need not call a maid, I will tell you." She grimaced at her words, feeling a flash of guilt at asking Lydia to play the maid after her uncharitable thought about their mother moments ago.

Lydia nodded eagerly. "I will. Only please tell me."

Elizabeth turned and lifted her hair out of the way so Lydia might get at the row of buttons down her back. Taking a moment to gather her thoughts as Lydia started on the buttons, Elizabeth said, "In truth, there is not very much to tell." Yet, what there was, was difficult. Elizabeth swallowed. "One day when Jane was—" She broke off, having not considered Jane's age at the time in light of Lydia's age now. "When Jane was your age, in fact, she was out walking and Mr. Collins came upon her. He…" How to phrase such a thing? "He had been showing Jane marked attention of late and, finding her alone, he attempted to take certain liberties."

Lydia gasped, her hands stilling in their work on the buttons. "But only tried?"

Elizabeth nodded. "Fortunately, Jane managed to strike him right on the nose, and that drove him off." In truth, having been training with Papa Arthur for over five years at that point, Jane's punch had nothing to do with luck and had broken Mr. Collins' nose.

"Jane must have been very upset." Lydia resumed her work on the buttons.

"She was very upset, yes. She came straight home to tell me and Papa Arthur." Who'd become so coldly enraged that Elizabeth still shivered, recalling his face. "It may have ended there but, unfortunately, Mr. Collins had a broken nose and developed two blackened eyes as well." Even though it had caused so much trouble, Elizabeth still savored the memory of her cousin's damaged face. "He could have done the decent thing and hidden away until he healed, or concocted a story, but instead he started telling anyone who asked that Jane had permitted him liberties. He claimed that, once he was lulled into believing in her affection, she struck him by surprise." That was the best Elizabeth could do in describing to her young sister the revolting tale Mr. Collins had truly spread.

"Oh dear." Lydia helped Elizabeth from her gown, and they both moved to the wardrobe.

Elizabeth reached for the nearest tea-appropriate garment.

Lydia batted her hand away. "The yellow makes you look sallow. You should never wear it. You'll look much prettier in the blue." She pulled the gown free.

Bemused, Elizabeth shrugged. She had little care how she looked. It was Jane who must win Mr. Bingley.

They got Elizabeth into the gown and Lydia began on the new set of buttons before asking, "Then what happened?"

"Mr. Collins and his father called, saying that Jane and our cousin must marry, her being compromised." Elizabeth could still recall being younger than Lydia was now, huddled with their ears to Papa Arthur's study door, listening to the men argue. "Papa Arthur said there had been no compromise and Jane would never marry our cousin. They argued, and Papa Arthur challenged Mr. Collins, so he might prove Jane's innocence."

Behind Elizabeth, Lydia sighed. "That is so brave. I hope a man will fight a duel for me someday." She buttoned another button. "But I thought Papa Arthur dueled Mr. Collins' father, not Mr. Collins."

"He did. Mr. Collins' father championed him. He said that at eighteen, Mr. Collins was too young to duel."

"Eighteen is not too young to duel."

Elizabeth shrugged. "I agree, but our cousin is a coward."

"Sit down and I will fix your hair," Lydia ordered.

Complying, Elizabeth continued, "So they dueled, and I think you know the rest."

In the mirror before Elizabeth, Lydia nodded. "Papa Arthur and Mr. Collins Sr. dueled, and Papa Arthur shot Mr. Collins Sr. dead, but he was shot too. He died a week later."

Elizabeth squeezed her eyes closed, but that in no way blotted out the memories. Their stepfather, unconscious from the shot to his head and slowly leaving them. Their mother's wails as she begged him to wake up.

"It was a terrible week."

"I know," Lydia said softly. "I was only eight, but I remember. We could hear Mama crying in the nursery. Nanny Hill tried to keep us at our lessons, but Mama kept crying and crying. Did you see the duel?"

Elizabeth met her sister's gaze in the mirror, surprised. "Ladies do not attend duels, and I was only thirteen."

"Yes, but you are always sneaking about." Lydia reached for a hairpin. "And you don't do as you're told."

Elizabeth shook her head.

"Hold still."

Stilling, Elizabeth clarified, "I did not see the duel. I am not certain if Mr. Collins even went, or Cousin Robert. I know that Papa Arthur was there, with Uncle Phillips as his second, and Mr. Collins Sr. and his second. Mr. Jones was there as well. Or he was nearby, at least, because he came back in the carriage with Papa Arthur."

Lydia coiled Elizabeth's hair and stuck in a pin. "How can Mama say that it wasn't Mr. Collins' fault? He accosted Jane and then spread a horrible rumor about her."

"Mama did hate him at first." Elizabeth remembered the ranting, the cursing of all things Collins. "But, as you said, it has been nearly eight years. She still hates the elder Mr. Collins. Mama would never stop hating the man who shot Papa Arthur. But she wants one of us in Longbourn. She wants us all married well. I think she simply eased some of the memories from her mind. Let them go, so they will not interfere with the plans she has now."

Lydia put in another pin. "Well, I agree with you and Jane and Mary. I hate Mr. Collins. He is horrible." She pursed her lips for a moment. "Is that why Jane never walks alone?"

Elizabeth blinked, startled by the question. Slowly, she said, "She does not, does she?" How could Elizabeth not have noticed?

"You walk alone lots, and Mary does sometimes, but Jane never does." Lydia tipped her head to the side, thinking. "I am not allowed to yet, and Kitty doesn't walk unless someone is escorting her, but that is because she doesn't like walking. She likes sitting with Mama."

"Hm." Elizabeth would have to take more note of that. She would also bear in mind how observant Lydia was, for she hadn't realized.

"Since I hate Mr. Collins, I will make certain Jane is not made to endure him."

Elizabeth couldn't help but smile at her youngest sister's bravado. "That is very kind of you, but you know Mama will not permit you to receive callers with us."

"I can still help. I'll get Thomas and Matthew to help, too."

Elizabeth raised an eyebrow. "Will Nanny Hill not have something to say about that?" Their long-time nanny and mother-in-law to their housekeeper, Mrs. Hill, Elizabeth recalled Nanny Hill as always having activities to occupy them when she was in the schoolroom.

"Nanny Hill will be asleep, like usual. She takes a nap every afternoon." Lydia gave Elizabeth's hair a final pat. "There. You look lovely."

Drawing her thoughts from her worries, Elizabeth focused on her reflection.

Lydia had done her hair more elaborately than Elizabeth would have troubled a maid to do. In a different, more forgiving style than Elizabeth usually wore, as well. Turning her head to the left, then the right, she concluded that she did, indeed, look lovely.

She met Lydia's gaze in the mirror. "Thank you."

Lydia smiled happily. "Mr. Darcy won't be able to take his eyes off you."

Elizabeth fought against the heat that threatened her cheeks. "You should not know anything about that, and neither do I." Her youngest sister was such a terrible gossip.

In the mirror, Lydia merely smiled.

CHAPTER NINE

Earlier That Morning...

Darcy had risen long before Bingley and his relations, a gnawing worry over his final conversation with Miss Elizabeth at the assembly ruining any chance of more sleep. How had she interpreted his words regarding fog and the view? He'd issued them in the hope that she might reply with something similar to, 'Yes. The fog was very dense when I walked there the morning we met you and Mr. Bingley.' Instead, she'd regarded him askance. At first, he could think of no reason for his question to elicit such suspicion, but upon reflection, he realized that taken in the right light, his words could be construed as an assignation.

If he did not take more care, he was the one who would end up trapped, not Bingley.

Darcy worried about what Miss Elizabeth might think of his parting remarks as his valet fussed over his cravat, and continued to do so as the man helped him into his coat. Nor did the trajectory of his thoughts change as he strode to the stable, where he'd requested his mount be waiting. Not until he was astride and urging his mount down the path away from the manor house did another thought intrude.

What if Miss Elizabeth had taken his words as an attempt to rendezvous, and awaited him atop the hillock even now?

Were that the case, he'd be a fool to go there.

Yet, somehow, that was the direction his mount took. Soon enough, the beast's shod hooves clattered on the steep trail that wended up into the low line of hills ending near Netherfield Park, and Darcy's breath quickened. Not at the effort of the climb, for his horse did the work, but in expectation.

Although, to be certain, were Miss Elizabeth atop the hillock admiring the view, that would mark her as simply another husband-hunting miss intent on claiming the Darcy name and fortune. Were she there, he would not deign to have aught to do with her, reverting to cold politeness in public and never permitting her a word otherwise. Were she there...

He claimed the summit with expectation tight in his throat.

No woman, mysterious or otherwise, awaited him atop the hill. Only a view of Bingley's leased manor house. Darcy looked about, his gaze probing. A sparrow alighted on a scrubby, leafless bush, ignoring him as it cleaned its beak on a nearby branch. Nothing else moved except by the will of the light breeze.

Disappointed, Darcy returned to a breakfast he didn't much attend to, where he proceeded to pretend interest in a day-old paper and murmur noncommittal responses. His thoughts swirled with visions of Miss Elizabeth Bennet and the woman in the mist.

Were they one and the same? If so, Miss Elizabeth hadn't thought to take in the view this morning. But then, no fog shrouded the land. Perhaps she only walked the peaks enveloped in a screen of mist? Or, even though he did not intend to meet her atop the hill, had he somehow implied that she should wait for a foggy day?

Darcy mulled over that prospect for the remainder of the morning, and through luncheon. He managed to tamp down musings about Miss Elizabeth for a time after that light meal, as he and Bingley rode about the estate taking stock. But when they returned to change for making calls, Miss Elizabeth Bennet claimed Darcy's thoughts once more.

His mind remained fixed on the notion that Miss Elizabeth may have misconstrued his words even as Bingley's carriage rolled to a halt before a tall, modern dwelling about half the size of Netherfield Park. Dovemark, residence of the Bennets and Oakwoods.

"A pretty sort of place," Miss Bingley allowed. With a slight frown she added, "French inspired, one might think."

Bingley cast her a quick look. "Doesn't appear one bit French to me." He gestured. "Not all cluttered and ornate, is it?"

Miss Bingley turned a condescending look on her brother. "I am speaking of the architecture on the Mediterranean coast." She smiled at Darcy. "Mr. Darcy's library at Pemberley has a lovely travel journal with quite intricate renderings. Dovemark reminds me of those. Do you not agree, Mr. Darcy?"

Darcy could only nod, for the clean, simple lines and soaring height of the structure, coupled with numerous tall windows, did speak of the drawings to which Miss Bingley referred.

"I will allow that it sits well against that line of hills." Mrs. Hurst swiveled to ask her husband, "Do you not agree, Mr. Hurst?"

Mr. Hurst leaned forward to peer out the carriage window past his wife, where a footman could be seen coming down the steps of the house. "Hills.

Yes. Quite nice. Tallest bit that, behind the house, is it not? Steep, even. Same line of hills as dominates the northern view from Netherfield, Bingley?"

His attention on the house, Bingley shrugged. "Seems likely. Imposing sort of place, this Dovemark. I approve."

The footman opened the door. With a bow, he offered Mrs. Hurst his hand.

As her sister descended, Miss Bingley, who sat across from Darcy, added, "Though it is easy to see that Dovemark is nothing compared to Pemberley."

Darcy offered no denial as they disembarked one by one. Nowhere compared to Pemberley.

They entered to find the elegance promised by the exterior borne out in an entrance hall done in warm cream, sage, and soft brown wood. Unfortunately, the beauty of the space was almost completely obscured by numerous small, and rather poor, watercolors. Ensconced in ornate golden frames, they covered the entrance hall walls, drifted down the corridor, and climbed up the staircase. Darcy would hazard to guess that over a hundred of the less than lovely renditions met his gaze, which he sought to place on anything else.

After turning over their cards and outerwear, and a brief wait as the butler disappeared and returned, they were escorted deeper into the house. Darcy thought that, perhaps, the paintings threading down the hallway were newer. They seemed to show a very small increase in skill. Regardless, they were not something he would display with such prominence or in such quantity, even if someone as dear as his younger sister had painted them. Fortunately, the watercolors tapered off as they walked, permitting the home's elegance to once more shine.

They followed the clomping butler, his tread pronounced enough that Darcy wondered if the man sought to convey a level of disapproval. As they passed open doorways, Darcy took in drawing rooms that faced the light at opposing times of the day, a well-appointed library that held no candle to Pemberley's, what appeared to be a study, two maids within dusting, and a large dining room. He began to suspect that the narrow façade of Dovemark belied the home's size.

A moment later, Darcy and his companions still following the heavy tread of the butler, a voice threaded up the hall. Mrs. Oakwood's, were Darcy not mistaken. He made no effort to listen, but soon enough her high, somewhat grating voice coalesced into discernable words.

"...pleased to see Mr. Bingley and Mr. Darcy dancing with you, Jane," the matriarch was saying. "And the way Mr. Bingley in particular gazed on you, he's certain to offer for you, just as my sister Phillips said after speaking with Mrs. Lucas and Mrs. Morris. I never thought you would come to anything after you ruined your chance with Mr. Collins, but—"

"Mama," Miss Elizabeth's voice cut in.

Miss Bingley and her sister exchanged looks that held a mixture of amusement and condemnation.

"But that, to be certain, matters not at all, as my dear Kitty will reclaim Longbourn for us," Mrs. Oakwood continued, ignoring Miss Elizabeth's interruption. "It is Kitty, after all, who is meant to marry well. Ever since she brought Mr. Oakwood to us, I've known she was destined for wonderful things. I assumed for Mr. Collins, but that was before that Mr. D—"

"Mama," Miss Elizabeth repeated, louder. "Footfalls."

"Do not interrupt me when I am speaking," Mrs. Oakwood said sharply. "You, Elizabeth, are too impertinent to attract the notice of any man, leastwise not in a welcome way, and so must contain yourself so as not to spoil Kitty's and Jane's chances."

"Yes, Mama," Miss Elizabeth replied with no hint of remorse in her voice.

As she issued that affirmation, Darcy and his companions drew near a large set of open doors. The butler cleared his throat as he stepped into the doorway. "Mr. Darcy, Mr. Bingley, Mr. Hurst, Mrs. Hurst, and Miss Bingley."

Miss Elizabeth rose from a stiff-backed settee, graceful and lovely in a sky-blue gown. Her hair was arranged in a style Darcy had not yet seen on her, the loose curls framing her face in a gentle, almost intimate way. Her gaze, coolly polite, met his, and he wrenched his attention away so he might issue proper greetings to the whole of the room, which he belatedly realized also held Mrs. Oakwood, Miss Bennet, Miss Mary, and Miss Kitty.

Once greetings were exchanged, Mrs. Oakwood invited them to sit and called for tea. As the settee on which Miss Elizabeth perched also held Miss Mary, Darcy found himself in a chair between that furnishing and the sofa occupied by his hostess and Miss Kitty. Bingley predictably took the chair on the other side, sitting as near to Miss Bennet as he could, and the Hursts alighted across from Mrs. Oakwood and her favorite daughter.

But Miss Bingley, rather than taking one of the remaining seats, turned to gesture to the far fireplace, visible past several more seating areas and a pianoforte. "Mrs. Oakwood, is that your late husband, the general?"

Darcy tugged his attention from Miss Elizabeth's profile. At the other end of the large drawing room, which boasted two fireplaces clad in cream marble sculpted into swirls and doves, a portrait hung above a pair of crossed swords. Even from a distance, Darcy recognized one as a service weapon and the other as ornamental, a mark of the general's office.

Mrs. Oakwood issued a beleaguered sigh. "Yes, that is my dear, dear Arthur."

The general himself, depicted outdoors, one boot resting on a rock and a cane in hand, appeared a slender, wiry sort of man. Nondescript, Darcy would call him, and remembered Miss Elizabeth's hint that her stepfather had been a spy. The only thing remarkable about the general, captured to perfection by the artist, was the intelligent, amused gleam in his eyes.

Miss Bingley wandered closer to the painting. "You must miss him terribly," she said politely but Darcy didn't doubt that if they could see her face, her visage would reveal startling intensity as she memorized General Oakwood's likeness.

"I do." Mrs. Oakwood tugged a handkerchief from her sleeve. "My dear, dear Arthur. I am lost without him."

"We all are," Miss Kitty added, producing a small square of cloth of her own.

The two of them, lavender and pink gowns alike covered in copious quantities of expensive Devon lace and imported silk ribbon, dabbed at their eyes and sniffed.

"But this is not to be a sad occasion," Mrs. Oakwood said brightly, her handkerchief disappearing.

With a startled look at her mother, Miss Kitty shoved hers away as well.

"In fact, this may be a day to be remembered and celebrated," Mrs. Oakwood continued. She leveled a warm look on Bingley. "This may be the day some of my girls meet their future husbands."

"Are more gentlemen expected, then?" Miss Elizabeth asked, exchanging a look with Miss Mary. "For we have already met these."

Miss Mary's lips quirked.

Mrs. Oakwood cast Miss Elizabeth a quelling glare.

Before the matriarch could speak again, Miss Bennet turned to the Hursts. "How did you find the roads? I have been told they are in good condition for autumn."

Darcy found the roads hereabouts rutted and pitted, a sign of a poor community. At least, until they'd reached Dovemark's lands. Whatever else she might be, Mrs. Oakwood appeared to be a capable landlady. Unless young Mr. Oakwood or a steward were to thank.

"They are tolerable within the village," Mrs. Hurst replied.

Mr. Hurst's chin had already begun its slow descent to his chest, his eyes glazed over with boredom.

"That is because we have been having such fine weather," Miss Mary stated.

"Oh yes," Miss Bennet agreed. "A lovely autumn thus far."

Miss Bingley came back across the room to join them and they continued on in this vein, Mrs. Oakwood making inopportune comments backed by Miss Kitty while Miss Bennet, Miss Elizabeth, and Miss Mary sought safer ground, until tea arrived.

It surprised Darcy not at all when Miss Kitty, though a middle daughter, sat forward. She turned to him first, batting her lashes, and asked, "How do you care for your tea, Mr. Darcy?"

Before he could answer, a clatter of footfalls filled the hallway. Darcy turned along with everyone else to see a young man with whom he wasn't familiar rush into the room, a spyglass held in one hand.

"Matthew," Mrs. Oakwood exclaimed. "Whatever are you about?"

"Lydia turned her ankle in the garden and she needs Jane," Matthew blurted, his gaze darting about the room. "Right now."

Miss Elizabeth caught his eye, hers dropping to give the spyglass a meaningful look. Matthew shoved it behind his back.

"Oh dear. Poor Lydia." Miss Bennet stood.

"I cannot imagine why she would need Jane," Mrs. Oakwood snapped. "Jane, sit down."

Miss Bennet, who had already started forward, paused. She cast a panicked look at Miss Elizabeth.

"Mama, if Lydia needs Jane, she needs Jane," Miss Elizabeth said.

"You go," Mrs. Oakwood replied with a negligent wave of her hand. "You have no hope of securing a fine gentleman and will be no loss to our tea."

"Lydia said it must be Jane," Matthew reiterated, his gaze likewise seeking Miss Elizabeth's, pleading. "And that Jane must hurry."

Miss Elizabeth's brow pinched with thought for a fraction of a moment, then cleared. "If Lydia has turned her ankle, she will need someone strong to help, not only Jane." She looked past Darcy, her mother, and Miss Kitty, to Bingley. "Perhaps you could assist her, Mr. Bingley?"

Bingley sprang to his feet. "I would be happy to."

The joy on his face was matched by the relief on Miss Bennet's, but fresh worry surged through Darcy. The majority of the Bennet sisters seemed quite eager to see Bingley go off with Miss Bennet. Such trickery smacked of scores of husband-hunting misses sadly of Darcy's acquaintance.

"Jane cannot go off with Mr. Bingley alone," Miss Kitty said quickly.

Young Matthew, perhaps all of eleven, stood tall, spyglass still hidden behind his back. "I'll be with her."

"You are a child," Miss Kitty sniffed.

"I may be a child but at least I don't look as if a milliner's wastebin toppled over on me," Matthew snapped back.

Miss Bingley coughed, trying to stifle laughter.

"Is this truly the impression of us that you wish to give to our guests?" Miss Mary asked in a mild, quiet voice.

Mrs. Oakwood gave no indication that she heard, but she gestured to Miss Elizabeth. "Elizabeth, go with your sister and Mr. Bingley, and tell Lydia that she will answer for this later."

Appearing surprised, and grateful, Miss Elizabeth stood.

"Lydia is a tall, strapping girl," Miss Mary stated. "It may take two gentlemen to assist her if her ankle is truly bad. Mr. Darcy had better join them."

Darcy came to his feet before Miss Mary finished speaking.

"Truly, I do not believe all the gentlemen need attend to Lydia," Mrs. Oakwood exclaimed. "A footman can assist Mr. Bingley if required. We do not need to impose upon Mr. Darcy."

"It is no imposition," Darcy said. "I am pleased to be of service to your daughter."

"Mr. Hurst will bear us company, Mama," Miss Mary added.

Darcy crossed the room. No part of him would prefer to remain in this drawing room rather than accompany Bingley and the elder two Miss Bennets, if for no other reason than to ensure that his friend wasn't trapped in an untenable situation.

Miss Elizabeth joined him, Bingley, and Miss Bennet by the door, saying, "I am certain Lydia will not require us for long."

"I'll show you where she is," Matthew offered, whirling.

Darcy bowed. "If you will excuse us, Mrs. Oakwood, Miss Mary, Miss Kitty."

Matthew hurried away. Darcy did not need extra urging to follow.

From the room they'd left, Miss Kitty's voice wailed, "Why does Lydia ruin everything? You will see her punished, won't you, Mama?"

Mrs. Oakwood's reassurances faded behind them as young Master Matthew led the way down the hall at a rapid pace, collapsing his spyglass as he went. When they reached the first turn, he said, "Not that way," as Miss

Bennet made to retrace the route Darcy recalled as leading back to the front of the house. "He's likely on his way in."

Bingley frowned, casting Darcy a confused look. Darcy could only shrug as they followed Matthew and the eldest two Bennet sisters into another wing of the house, but his worry grew.

"That was good work, Matthew," Miss Elizabeth told her brother as they walked. "I thought for certain the spyglass would give you away, though."

The lad shook his head. "Mama and Kitty aren't observant. Leastwise, not about spyglasses. If I was missing my neckcloth, that they would note."

Miss Elizabeth chuckled, a rich, beguiling sound.

"You were watching the roadway from the attic?"

Matthew answered Miss Bennet's question with a nod as they continued to hurry down the corridor.

Their pace surprised Darcy, but their strong strides did not seem to affect the two ladies at all. Nor was he winded, though Bingley appeared a touch so as they finally reached a door that let out into the garden. Matthew passed through, followed by Miss Bennet. Darcy lightly touched Miss Elizabeth's sleeve. She turned to him as Bingley went out.

"Yes, Mr. Darcy?"

"Before I continue with this ruse, I would like to know from whom we are fleeing, and why your younger brother was spying on the roadway."

Miss Elizabeth's eyebrows winged upward, her visage spritely, almost fey, in the rays of sunlight slanting through the open door. About her, glimmering motes of dust swirled as she contemplated Darcy through unreadable eyes.

He set his jaw. He did not care if his question offended her. He would not be a party to pretense. Or worse, to entrapping Bingley, for this collusion between the siblings smacked of an ambush into marriage.

CHAPTER TEN

The Walled Garden

Elizabeth contemplated the man before her, his dark eyes far more serious than the situation warranted. Her hand twitched, the sudden renewed desire to smooth the lines of worry from his brow startling her. He need not look as if the fate of England rested upon his broad shoulders, nor employ such dramatic language. Ruse? Spying? Fleeing? Mr. Darcy made their escape from the drawing room sound terribly dramatic, as if their little deception wrenched apart the very fabric of civilized society. Perhaps for someone as stiff as he was, it did.

She couldn't help but smile, and was rewarded by a confused easing of the worry on his face. "Be at peace, Mr. Darcy. Our ruse is of the simplest nature." Although she kept her tone light to convey a lack of gravity, Elizabeth also spoke softly, hoping Jane wouldn't hear. Her sister did not care to hear the name Collins. "Matthew was set to watch for Mr. Collins' carriage. We simply continue the game of last night. Sparing Jane his company."

"Then your youngest sister has suffered no sprain?"

"I will be shocked if she has." Elizabeth stepped through the doorway into the autumnal sunlight.

Mr. Darcy did not immediately follow.

She turned back, raising her eyebrows in question.

With a frown he joined her, his gaze going to where Jane now walked beside Mr. Bingley, a hand on his arm as they followed Matthew at a more sedate pace than they'd taken through the house. His reluctance palpable, Mr. Darcy came to Elizabeth's side, but did not offer his arm.

Which didn't sting. Why should it? She had no designs on the man.

"Do you often mislead your mother?" Mr. Darcy asked as they fell in step to follow the others up the garden path.

Elizabeth contained a wince. "Only when necessary."

"And how often do you consider such subterfuge necessary?"

Elizabeth assessed Mr. Darcy's stern demeanor. "What precisely is troubling you, Mr. Darcy?" she asked, suddenly certain that he hadn't meant his words about walks and the view from the hills as an assignation. The man lacked the subtlety. Undoubtedly, if Mr. Fitzwilliam Darcy of Pemberley wanted something, he would simply ask. Or, more likely, decree it to be so, as when he'd attempted to state that he and she would dance.

"I do not care to be a party to lies."

"But you did not lie. Only Matthew did, and I will speak with him about doing so." And congratulate him again on playing his part well, Elizabeth added to herself. "In truth, we have yet to establish that a lie has been issued."

Mr. Darcy's frown deepened. "You moments ago confirmed my suspicion that your sister has sustained no injury."

"I believe I said that I would be surprised if she has." Elizabeth couldn't contain a grin as she added, "Do you wish me to understand that you will only be pleased if Lydia has indeed come to harm?"

He answered that with a startled look.

Elizabeth held back a chuckle. "If you are truly so perturbed by what we have done, then I give you leave to return to the drawing room and confess our sins to my mother. I absolve you from any retribution or ill feelings."

"I would not betray your confidence so," he replied with considerable affront.

Elizabeth raised her open palms, expressing her lack of ability to provide him with an option to his liking. "You do not want to be a part of our ruse. You do not want to betray our trust. I am uncertain how to aid you, Mr. Darcy."

"You may aid me by not putting me in such a position as this in the future," he rumbled, his words kept so low as to make them nearly a growl.

A shiver went through her at the sound, though she felt no fear of the man. "If you did not wish to be in this position, why did you join us?" Elizabeth asked, lowering her voice again so their words would not reach Jane and Mr. Bingley, on whom they were gaining. The two appeared to be in cheerful conversation as Jane gestured to a fountain made of four flying doves, their wings spread wide and their beaks raised as if in song. One of Papa Arthur's favorites, and lovely even dry for the winter. Elizabeth slowed her pace, not wanting to overtake the two.

"Because I do not want to see Bingley trapped into a union," Mr. Darcy replied in low, clipped words.

Elizabeth raised her eyebrows at that. She thought they had established last night that Mr. Bingley did not require any help in the matter. "I believe I already explained to you that he, with his unsubtle inquiries, has done more to trap himself than anyone, especially Jane, has done to snare him."

"We could not help but overhear your mother as we approached the drawing room," Mr. Darcy stated, the quiet of his voice in no way hiding his censure. "She speaks as if a match between the two is a set thing. Bingley is certainly not responsible for that."

Annoyance flared in Elizabeth, though for Mr. Darcy's tenacity or her mother's imprudence, she didn't know. Nor did it matter, as Mr. Darcy walked beside her and Mrs. Oakwood did not. "My mother is a wealthy widow with five unmarried daughters. To be certain she will form such speculations. Why should she not?"

Mr. Darcy's features slackened with surprise and Elizabeth wondered again how often anyone refuted the man.

"Mr. Darcy, Elizabeth, you're falling behind," Matthew called.

Elizabeth looked up the path to see that the others had reached the walled garden. With a final frown for Mr. Darcy, she lengthened her stride, leaving him to follow or not, she did not care which.

She entered the long, narrow walled garden, one of Papa Arthur's greatest achievements and one of Elizabeth's favorite places, on the heels of her sister and Mr. Bingley. With rows of low braziers and tall walls to keep out the wind and hold in the heat, the garden was where they grew the more delicate flowers, herbs, vegetables, and fruit trees. Inside the walled space, it was always warmer than without, sometimes even stifling in summer when the braziers were cold and many of the plants required frequent watering.

Today, halfway up the garden, in the center where practicality gave way to simple green lawn for the purpose of enjoyment, Lydia and Thomas waited, a picnic spread out about them. More than a picnic, Elizabeth realized as she drew nearer, still following Jane, Matthew, and Mr. Bingley. Tea. Insofar as Elizabeth could ascertain, Lydia had procured a helping of everything that would, even now, be served in the drawing room.

Her youngest sister jumped to her feet, Thomas rising more slowly as he took in the extent of their party. "You see?" Lydia cried. "I told you Tommy, Matty, and I could help." She looked about at them, preening. "And how clever of you, Jane, to free Mr. Bingley and Mr. Darcy from our cousin's company as well." She dropped into a curtsy.

A glance showed that Mr. Darcy had, indeed, deigned to follow them into the garden.

Beside Lydia, Thomas bowed. "Mr. Darcy. Mr. Bingley."

Mr. Bingley returned the gesture, Mr. Darcy adding his own greeting, though Elizabeth felt he did so grudgingly.

"Have tea with us?" Lydia asked, plopping back down.

"Your ankle seems to have improved markedly since Matthew summoned us," Elizabeth observed. She couldn't help but slant a look to take in Mr. Darcy's pinched features.

Lydia stuck a leg out from beneath her skirt, smirking. "My ankle is much improved." She wiggled her foot. "Although I am certain I will be limping when next I see Mama."

"Oh, but Lydia," Jane said even as she sank down onto the blanket beside their sister. "You ought not to have lied."

"I didn't lie. Matty did."

Mr. Bingley folded to sit with Jane and Lydia, Thomas dropping back into his place and Matthew joining them. Elizabeth looked at Mr. Darcy, cocking an eyebrow in challenge. Would he sit with them, loom awkwardly, or depart the garden?

"That is true," Matthew said gravely. "I am the only one who lied."

His expression dire, Mr. Darcy lowered his tall form to the blanket.

"And I will lie too, if need be," Thomas said firmly. "I'll lie to Mama's face. I will not have my sister endure that odious lout whose father shot our papa."

Shocked stillness radiated through Mr. Darcy. Mr. Bingley cast a startled look his way. Elizabeth dropped to the blanket to sit, suppressing a sigh. She imagined it was inevitable that the two gentlemen learn of their family's tragedy.

"Mr. Collins' father shot yours?" Mr. Bingley asked, turning his head to take in the Bennets and Oakwoods around him. His gaze came to rest on Jane. "Is that how your father died, Miss Bennet?"

Elizabeth's sister studied the blanket on which she sat, an idle finger tracing the carefully stitched design. Just when Elizabeth was about to reply for her, Jane looked up, meeting Mr. Bingley's gaze. "Yes, that is how Papa Arthur died. He and Mr. Collins Sr. dueled."

A quick look assured Elizabeth that Mr. Darcy did not approve. His mouth was pressed flat, his squared jaw clenched.

"They dueled for Jane's honor," Lydia supplied into the strained silence.

"My father won," Thomas added.

Matthew looked from face to face with worried eyes. He'd known his entire life that they weren't to speak of the duel, but likely had little notion of why, other than that it made their mama wail and flap her handkerchief.

"What, precisely, happened?" Mr. Darcy asked.

Jane raised beseeching eyes to Elizabeth. "I do not care to speak of it. Perhaps Elizabeth will explain." In a swirl of elegant motion, Jane rose, turned, and strode deeper into the garden.

Mr. Bingley looked after her, then at Mr. Darcy, who shook his head in the negative. His expression mutinous, Mr. Bingley came to his feet and followed Jane. There was nowhere in the narrow garden where they could go that they couldn't be seen, so Elizabeth made no move to follow.

"Why did Papa and Mr. Collins duel?" Matthew asked quietly, looking about at his siblings.

Thomas shrugged, likely knowing little more than Matthew did, or than Lydia had until today.

"If you do not tell them, I will," Lydia stated. "Everyone should know how horrible Mr. Collins is."

Elizabeth raised a staying hand to fend that off. Better she should choose the words her brothers, and Mr. Darcy, heard. "It is a simple thing, really."

"What is?" Thomas leaned forward, eager.

"Mr. Collins wanted Jane's affection," Elizabeth said, not daring to look at Mr. Darcy, for fear he would read more in her eyes than she wanted to tell. "Jane had no affection for him. Hurt, he started a rather vicious rumor about her, which was petty of him, and wrong. Papa Arthur had no choice but to challenge him."

"But Mr. Collins is a coward and made his papa fight for him," Lydia put in.

Elizabeth cast her a quelling look. Perhaps she shouldn't have given in to Lydia's pleading earlier. Now that she knew the story, Lydia's active mind was obviously embellishing it. "Mr. Collins Sr. stood in for his son, rather than permit our cousin to face Papa Arthur. They dueled and Mr. Collins' father was shot dead, and Papa Arthur was wounded. Jane's honor was restored, and Papa Arthur died a week later." Elizabeth cleared her suddenly tight throat. A wave of pain assailed her. How much different life would be if Papa Arthur were alive.

She certainly wouldn't be hiding in the garden having tea with Mr. Darcy and her younger siblings while Mr. Collins sat in the comfort of their drawing room being doted on by her mother and Kitty.

"I'll fix the tea," Lydia said brightly. "Thomas, hand it here. Be careful. It's hot."

Elizabeth looked to see that a metal grate had been placed over one of the braziers, a teapot atop. Thomas scrambled to his feet to retrieve it.

Lydia accepted the teapot from their brother. "Mr. Darcy, how do you care for your tea?"

"Black," he said shortly, his expression dour.

Undaunted by his dire tone, Lydia fixed the tea and served him, offering him a plate of small sweet and savory treats as well. She next served Thomas, then, to Elizabeth's amusement, Matthew, before serving Elizabeth. All the while, Lydia chattered about the weather and the theater, although Elizabeth's sister had never set foot in London. Everything she knew, she gleaned from the newspapers that were still delivered, even though Papa Arthur was no longer alive to read them.

Elizabeth read them, however, often securing articles on Britain's current and former colonies, and about various wars. Mary, she knew, enjoyed reading about finance and business ventures. Jane and Kitty were indifferent to the paper, but Lydia practically devoured anything pertaining to society or fashion.

Elizabeth kept half her attention on Jane and Mr. Bingley, and was relieved when they returned to join the picnic. No one mentioned Jane's momentary disquiet, though Mr. Bingley cast many looks Mr. Darcy's way, seeming ready to burst with news.

"Now, who wants a second cup?" Lydia asked after Jane and Mr. Bingley had both finished their first.

"We truly cannot remain here all afternoon," Jane said quietly.

Mr. Bingley's hand reached out, as if it might cover hers where it rested on the blanket between them, but he drew it back and said staunchly, "We can if you like."

Jane cast him a wan smile.

"Matthew, would you mind checking if our cousin's carriage is still here?" Elizabeth asked.

Nodding, he came to his feet, then stuck a hand in his pocket to pull free his collapsed spyglass. "I don't even need to get close to the swine."

"You should not refer to Mr. Collins that way," Elizabeth said firmly.

Matthew gave her a willful look reminiscent of their mother. "He lied about Jane. When I'm old enough, I'm going to duel him."

"Oh." Jane pressed her palms to her cheeks.

"Papa Arthur already avenged Jane's honor," Elizabeth reminded her brother.

"Not well enough," Thomas muttered. "And you cannot duel him, Matthew, because I will first."

"And I will spread horrible rumors about him," Lydia added.

Elizabeth shook her head. If this was how Thomas and Matthew felt now, what would they say or do when they were old enough to learn the true extent of Mr. Collins' terrible behavior? She should never have told Lydia or their brothers the truth. "The matter is settled. Honor is satisfied."

"I am afraid I agree with your sister and brothers." Mr. Bingley's voice held a grim note.

Jane turned to him, her face suffused with worry and her cheeks pale.

"We do not have all the facts." The calm reason in Mr. Darcy's voice was a balm, even if Elizabeth resented his implication that her tale had been one-sided. "And, in truth, it is not our concern."

The determined look on Mr. Bingley's face spoke of how much he would like to make it his concern.

"Go see if he is gone," Elizabeth reiterated to Matthew. "We can speak more of Jane's honor later."

His expression still stubborn, Matthew nodded and hurried away.

They sat in awkward silence then, even Lydia making no effort to break it. Instead, Elizabeth's youngest sister nibbled on a slice of plum cake, her gaze abstracted.

Mr. Darcy stood. "Miss Elizabeth, a word."

Though his tone of command irked her, Elizabeth came to her feet. Whatever he wished to say, hearing it couldn't be more interminable than the uncomfortable quiet in which they sat. Gesturing, she followed Mr. Darcy to the entrance of the garden, where they halted in full view of the others. Behind them, Lydia began to chatter, sounding like her usual self once more.

Mr. Darcy studied the gravel beneath their feet for a moment, then met her gaze. "I know Bingley well enough to ascertain that your sister told him more than, 'Mr. Collins sought my affection and started a rumor.' I wish to know with what I will be dealing when I attempt to mitigate his anger."

Elizabeth pressed her lips together. While she appreciated that Mr. Darcy cared for his friend, Jane's story was not hers to tell. She darted a look at the picnickers. Jane must have a suspicion of what Mr. Darcy meant to ask, for she met Elizabeth's eyes and gave a slight, worried nod.

"When Jane was fifteen, he attempted certain liberties," Elizabeth said in a low voice. "Jane broke his nose, and he spread a rumor that he had done more than attempt. That is truly all there is to it."

The muscles in Mr. Darcy's jaw rippled. "When she was fifteen?"

Elizabeth's brows drew together. Why did that detail seem to distress him the most? "Yes. The same age Lydia is now."

Mr. Darcy's eyes narrowed. If anything, he appeared even more angry than Mr. Bingley had.

"You do mean to prevent Mr. Bingley from taking any actions, do you not?" Elizabeth asked. "My sister seems fond of him but they have only just met. If he were to do something so foolish as to challenge Mr. Collins over a years' old scandal, it would reinvigorate the tale and put Jane in a very awkward position. She would be obliged to accept an offer from a man who championed her thusly. She would be well and truly *trapped*." Elizabeth emphasized the word, one Mr. Darcy had earlier employed with such distaste, to ensure he fully grasped the potential level of calamity. If Mr. Bingley challenged Mr. Collins, Jane's prerogative to decide who she would marry would be taken from her.

Mr. Darcy blinked, her words seeming to reach through his fury. Much of the ire drained from his features. "Yes. I will ensure that Bingley considers his actions with care." His expression becoming rueful, Mr. Darcy shook his head. "Your family is certainly absorbing."

"Absorbing?" Elizabeth repeated. Normally quick to comprehend, she had no idea if she was being insulted.

"We are new acquaintances, and yet have already been drawn into collusions and confidences."

Elizabeth winced. "That was not my or Jane's intention."

Mr. Darcy studied her with assessing eyes, from which she did not look away. Finally, he nodded.

"Mr. Darcy, Elizabeth," Matthew's voice called.

Elizabeth looked to see him running up the path. As he appeared more pleased than alarmed, Elizabeth waited for him to reach them.

"He's gone," Matthew said, as proud as if he'd run Mr. Collins off. "And I went in to check if we're in trouble, and Mama isn't even angry because he had to have tea with her and Kitty and Kitty spent the whole time talking to him. But she didn't walk them out. Mary did."

"Them?" Elizabeth asked sharply.

"Cousin Robert called too."

Elizabeth hadn't expected that, but it mattered little. "Thank you, Matthew," she said before turning back to Mr. Darcy. "It seems you and Mr. Bingley are free to go. Undoubtedly, we have kept you too long already and Mr. and Mrs. Hurst, and Miss Bingley, are put out with us."

"Undoubtedly," Mr. Darcy agreed.

"The one lady looks like she's sucking lemons, but the fellow is asleep and the younger lady is sitting next to Mama, asking her questions about my father," Matthew supplied.

Elizabeth raised her eyebrows. Miss Bingley was oddly preoccupied with their stepfather. Like as not, she sought to discover whether her brother would gain anything through a union with Jane. Glancing back at where the two sat together conversing, Elizabeth doubted that Mr. Bingley cared about Jane's dowry or connections one way or the other.

With Mr. Darcy's assistance, Elizabeth broke up the picnic. Leaving Lydia and their brothers to find some of the staff, and with strict orders to assist them in clearing up, Elizabeth and Jane escorted the two gentlemen back to the drawing room. There, they endured their mother's mild reprimand, then bade their guests farewell.

Later, as she sat at the desk in her room composing a reply to her most recent letter from Aunt Gardiner, Elizabeth couldn't help but dwell on their afternoon. She hoped she hadn't unleashed anything terrible by letting new life enter the sorrows of Jane's, and their family's, past. Looking down at the blank page before her, she attempted to find solace in the notion that Lydia and their brothers would have heard rumors of Jane's scandal and Papa Arthur's demise sooner or later, especially as Lydia was nearly out.

Should she write to Aunt Gardiner of her worries, or would more words, even written ones sent to London, lend more strength to the shadows that lurked in years gone by? London was far away and Aunt Gardiner was often wise. Elizabeth picked up her pen.

A soft knock sounded, not on her bedroom door, which led into the hallway, but on the one that opened into the sitting room that adjoined Elizabeth's bedchamber and Jane's.

"It is me, Mary."

"Come in," Elizabeth called, looking over her shoulder.

Mary slipped in and closed the door behind her.

Elizabeth attempted a smile but her sister's serious mien quelled the expression before it could form. "What is wrong?"

Mary settled on the end of Elizabeth's bed, near her desk. "I know why Mr. Collins has renewed his pursuit of Jane, and how he arrived so promptly behind our other guests. He has set some of the lads at the inn to watch for Mr. Bingley or his carriage."

Elizabeth set down the pen she held and turned more fully in her chair. "So that he can interrupt Mr. Bingley's calls on Jane?"

Mary nodded.

"How did you learn that?" Elizabeth knew her sister was adept at getting information, having both a string of people with whom she gossiped in

Meryton and a great proficiency at reading lips, but Mary had not, to her knowledge, left the house yet today.

"Robert passed a note to me when I walked our cousins out."

Elizabeth frowned. "Why would he do that?" He was, after all, a Collins.

"His note said he is worried about the anger with which Mr. Collins seems to regard the idea of Jane and Mr. Bingley."

"Because he does not want Mr. Bingley to win her?" If Mr. Collins wanted Jane, he should have tried to make up for his horrible behavior years ago…not that Elizabeth wanted him to make the attempt or thought he could ever succeed.

Mary shook her head. "Because he does not want Mr. Bingley to purchase Netherfield Park. He believes Jane is why Mr. Bingley chose to let the place, and that as long as she remains unwed, there is a risk of Mr. Bingley deciding to stay."

Elizabeth considered that. "It amounts to much the same thing, though, does it not? We still must work to keep Jane away from our odious cousin and to help her find time to spend with Mr. Bingley." A swine, Matthew had called Mr. Collins, and he wasn't wrong.

"We do need to keep Jane from Mr. Collins," Mary said slowly. "I am not so certain about helping her spend time with Mr. Bingley. Robert's description of his brother's anger makes me fear for Mr. Bingley."

Elizabeth hadn't considered that, and suddenly knew why Mary had come through the sitting room. She'd wanted to make certain Jane was not there, to overhear her words. Jane would make all effort to never speak with Mr. Bingley again if she thought her attention put him in danger. Elizabeth had no notion if that meant that they should tell Jane of this fear or keep it from her. Taking in Mary's strained, questioning gaze, Elizabeth knew she felt the same.

All Elizabeth could do was answer Mary's worried look with one of her own.

CHAPTER ELEVEN

A Strange Request

It surprised Darcy not at all when Mrs. Oakwood and her eldest four offspring called at Netherfield Park the day following their somewhat odd visit. What did confound him, when he stood along with Bingley and Bingley's sisters to greet them, was Miss Elizabeth's attire. She'd made no special effort with her coif, and her gown was a pale yellow that complemented her delicate skin not at all.

The afternoon after the assembly she'd been especially lovely, having obviously taken extra care with her appearance. As he'd reflected on the call, Darcy had been flattered to believe that care might be on his behalf. But now, when she knew with a fair certainty that she would be in his presence, that effort was absent.

Had her preparations the previous day been for someone else? Surely not for Mr. Collins, whom she regarded with unconcealed loathing. Some other gentleman? Darcy did not care for that notion. He'd yet to meet anyone in the local populace worthy of her.

And even were there, what of the connection he felt with her? His suspicion that she was his mist-woman? That shock of recognition when they'd met on the street outside the magistrate's office?

She did not even award him particular care as greetings were exchanged, though she was perfectly cordial. Darcy was accustomed to more than cordiality from unwed misses, however. It was almost as if Miss Elizabeth didn't understand the life that would be hers if she could secure the master of Pemberley in marriage.

Perhaps, Darcy mused as seats were taken, Miss Kitty claiming the one nearest to him and Miss Elizabeth sharing a settee with her older sister, Miss Elizabeth had no knowledge of what such a life would entail? She did reside in a backwater. If she had never been to London, her only examples of living well came from her mother and the Collinses.

Not that he was seeking to marry. He was a bit young yet for that. His father hadn't taken a wife until his fortieth year. George Darcy had waited, and planned, and kept a cool head, until he could secure the daughter of a peer and further elevate the Darcy name. As the current steward of their line and holdings, it behooved Darcy to do the same.

Still, it was aggravating to be ignored by a country miss. Especially one he couldn't drive from his thoughts. The true cure, of course, would be to discover if Miss Elizabeth were his mist-woman. That mystery solved, he would be able to put her from his mind.

A goal which would likely be furthered by attending to the words being spoken around him.

"…lovely for this time of the year," Mrs. Oakwood was saying as Darcy fought to focus on the conversation.

"Indeed, it seems that way to me," Mrs. Hurst replied dutifully. "But I have never before visited this area, nor Hertfordshire in general."

"It does tend to remain warmer for longer in London," Darcy said, seizing his chance to discover if Miss Elizabeth was simply too rusticated to know the Darcy name. "But then, I am certain you will have observed as much on the occasions you have been in Town."

"Town?" Mrs. Oakwood shook her head. "My poor, dear Arthur did not hold with going to Town, even though my brother Gardiner and his wife often requested our presence."

"Then you never go to London?" Miss Bingley asked, appearing surprised. "The general did not seek society there?"

"Papa Arthur never went to Town," Miss Kitty replied, though rather than address Miss Bingley, she batted her lashes at Darcy. "He said nothing good could come of socializing there."

"Jane, Mary, and I have been," Miss Elizabeth put in. She slanted a look at Miss Bingley. "We have visited our aunt and uncle quite a few times at their home on Gracechurch Street, near Cheapside."

Miss Bingley's eyes rounded. She exchanged an alarmed look with Mrs. Hurst, which Miss Elizabeth took in with wry humor. Darcy didn't miss the twitch to Miss Mary's lips either, but Miss Bennet appeared not to notice her sisters' amusement, nor the consternation of Bingley's relations. She carried on observing the room with a pleasant, calm demeanor.

"Elizabeth," Mrs. Oakwood snapped. "You will have our new friends thinking ill of us. Do contain yourself."

"Ill of us?" Miss Elizabeth turned an overly innocent visage to her mother.

"Are we not to mention Aunt and Uncle Phillips, then, either?" Miss

Mary asked with an equal appearance of confusion.

They were rather skilled dissemblers, these Bennet sisters, Darcy decided.

And Miss Elizabeth had been to London, but not to circles where his name would be known, or where she could observe what it was to truly live well. Not that it mattered in the least, as a country miss with ties to trade would only sully the Darcy name, not add to it. Especially one who appeared quite willing to seek amusement at her mother's expense.

"Next you will tell them that Uncle Phillips is an attorney," Miss Kitty cried, bereaved.

"Mr. Phillips?" Bingley put in, a touch of strain to his smile as he took in his sisters' closed expressions. "We've already met, when Mr. Morris and I were finalizing the lease. A fine fellow."

"He is." Miss Bennet smiled warmly at Bingley, erasing all unease from his features. "When our father died, Aunt and Uncle Phillips took us in. We would have been lost without them."

"Yes, well, that was only until my dear, sweet Arthur saved us," Mrs. Oakwood said quickly. "We were with the Phillips hardly a year before my Arthur rode into the village. I am certain my girls do not even recall living in such a place as the Phillips' home. They have grown up well with my dear Arthur to guide them and provide the finer things in life."

Curiosity easing the condemnation from her face, Miss Bingley asked, "How did you chance to meet the general, Mrs. Oakwood?"

"He nearly trampled my Kitty," Mrs. Oakwood replied.

"But he did not," Miss Kitty added.

"He avoided her." Miss Mary's words were spoken with much less emotion than her mother or sister evidenced. "He was thrown, and injured, and Mama nursed him back to health."

"Just like in a novel," Miss Kitty breathed, smiling at her mother.

"And you had not met him before?" Miss Bingley pressed. "He was not from this area?"

Miss Elizabeth and Miss Mary exchanged an unreadable look.

Mrs. Oakwood shook her head. "He was passing through. He had recently returned from the Continent."

"Passing through to where?" Mrs. Hurst asked, caught up in her younger sister's enthusiasm.

Mrs. Oakwood shook her head. "He never told me."

"Never?" Miss Bingley pressed.

A glance showed Miss Elizabeth now wore a contemplative expression.

Her gaze met his and she winged an eyebrow upward in question. Darcy quickly looked away. He wouldn't want to give her the impression that he was interested.

As soon as she turned away, the movement observed from the corner of his eye, he resumed his study of her.

"Surely, you must have some notion of where General Oakwood was going when he was waylaid here," Mrs. Hurst said.

"My dear sweet Arthur was so devoted to me and my girls that he cared not at all for anything that had come before meeting us," Mrs. Oakwood replied.

"He was such a good papa," Miss Kitty added. With a sniff, she pulled out a handkerchief.

"And he enjoyed warm autumns," Miss Elizabeth said blandly.

That effectively returned the conversation to safer ground, where it remained throughout tea, which Miss Bingley served with deft competence. All about Darcy conversation flowed, talk of the roadways, the weather, what performances were likely to grace the London stage once the Season began. He took no part, preferring to mull over Miss Elizabeth's apparent lack of regard for him.

As the call drew near its natural end, Miss Mary abruptly and somewhat loudly stated, "I have heard it said that Netherfield Park is in possession of an excellent pianoforte. May I be permitted to see it?"

A heartbeat of silence met that before Miss Bingley plastered on a smile and rose. "Certainly. I am happy to show you."

The two departed the drawing room, leaving frowns in their wake. After a floundering moment, Mrs. Hurst began a monologue about an exhibit she'd viewed in London. Treasures brought back from far off lands.

"It seems so odd to me," Miss Elizabeth said as Mrs. Hurst's voice stilled.

"Odd?" Darcy asked. Was Miss Elizabeth so uncultured that she had never visited a museum?

She turned to him. "Yes. I recall the exhibit well. Household items. Clothing. Jewelry. Underthings. I remember wondering precisely how the items on display were obtained, and if the people they belonged to truly wished for us to have them, simply to gawk at."

"Is it the same exhibit we saw with Aunt Gardiner two years ago?" Miss Bennet asked.

Miss Elizabeth nodded. "Yes. You and I thought it was, well, rather sad to see peoples' lives put on display in such a manner."

Mrs. Hurst sat straighter. "I am certain the savages from which the items came have no notion what a museum is, let alone a worthwhile opinion on the value of one."

"Quite right," Mrs. Oakwood agreed.

Beside her, Miss Kitty nodded.

"Not knowing their ways, I cannot speak to that," Miss Elizabeth said. Just as her mother seemed to relax, Miss Elizabeth added, "But I can speak to how I would feel if someone came here, ransacked my home, and brought my chemise back to their country to hang on the wall for everyone to see."

What Miss Elizabeth might look like in her chemise filled Darcy's mind so fully that he hardly noted the way Mrs. Oakwood's eyes narrowed at her second eldest.

Miss Elizabeth opened her mouth to say more.

"I preferred the paintings in the other wing of the museum," Miss Bennet said in her usual dulcet tones, with no note of hurry or reprimand. She did not even glance at her sister, but Miss Elizabeth clamped her mouth closed. "Especially of vases of flowers, or fruit."

"I do enjoy those," Bingley said enthusiastically. "And the hunts. Some fine renditions of hunts. Give me a handsome hound to hang on the wall any day."

Miss Bennet awarded him a smile, effectively derailing anything more Bingley might add.

"I paint," Miss Kitty said brightly.

"My Kitty is ever so talented," Mrs. Oakwood added, though she still glared at Miss Elizabeth. "Surely you noticed her skills when you called? Her work adorns the entrance hall."

"Those were your paintings?" To her credit, Mrs. Hurst's voice betrayed only a hint of her horror.

"Oh yes." Mrs. Oakwood turned a doting look on her daughters. "They are so lovely, are they not? Kitty has been painting since she was fifteen."

Darcy's eyebrows shot up, for she looked hardly older than fifteen now.

"Truely?" Mrs. Hurst asked. "You are very prolific, Miss Catherine."

"That is a testament to her skill," Mrs. Oakwood replied before addressing her daughter with, "Tell them how many you can paint in an afternoon."

Miss Kitty looked about, preening at all the attention aimed her way. "I can do at least a dozen."

"Remarkable," Mrs. Hurst murmured.

"I wish I had your dedication," Bingley added.

"I believe you would excel at Miss Catherine's style of painting," Mrs.

Hurst said blandly. "When you compose letters, they are nearly illegible with the speed at which you write."

Bingley's cheerful demeanor didn't waver. "It is due to the speed of my thoughts, sister dear."

"Precisely." Miss Kitty leaned forward excitedly. "The ideas come to me so quickly when I paint, I hardly have time to finish one before starting the next."

Miss Elizabeth's eyes danced as she exchanged a look with her older sister but before anyone could speak, footfalls in the hallway signaled the return of Miss Bingley and Miss Mary.

That, in turn, signaled an end to the call. Farewells were made and the ladies escorted out. Servants gathered up the tea service, and silence fell.

"Miss Mary and I had an interesting conversation," Miss Bingley said once the tray-laden staff departed.

"More interesting than their revelations as to their connections to trade?" Mrs. Hurst's words sounded as sour as her face looked.

Bingley glared at his sister. "An attorney and an uncle in Cheapside do not detract from Miss Bennet's loveliness."

"Charles," Mrs. Hurst said, the word a mingled reprimand and sigh.

"You have previously stated that you wish to marry where it will further remove your name from trade," Darcy felt obliged to point out.

Bingley crossed his arms over his chest and glared at Darcy and his sisters. "Miss Bennet is the daughter and stepdaughter of a gentleman."

"I said, Miss Mary and I had an interesting conversation," Miss Bingley reiterated, louder.

Along with her siblings, Darcy turned to her.

Miss Bingley sat up straighter, folded her hands in her lap, and made no move to speak.

"Caroline," Mrs. Hurst snapped.

"Yes, Louisa?"

Mrs. Hurst glared for a moment, then said haughtily, "If you do not wish to converse, I will go wake Mr. Hurst from his afternoon respite."

"Spit it out," Bingley demanded.

Miss Bingley smiled sublimely for a moment longer, then burst forth with, "She asked that we not call on Dovemark."

Darcy sat back, startled.

"What?" Bingley demanded.

"They asked us not to call?" Mrs. Hurst radiated offense.

"Because of Mr. Collins," Miss Bingley added.

"Explain." Darcy surprised himself with the snap in his voice.

Miss Bingley's eyes went wide at his tone, her siblings turning to him, startled.

He shrugged by way of apology. He had never, no Darcy he knew of had ever, been asked not to call somewhere.

"Miss Mary said that Mr. Collins has paid some of the local lads to watch for our carriage, or for you riding, Charles. Whenever they see us visiting Dovemark, he means to follow, to press his suit on Miss Bennet. She also said that Miss Lydia can turn only so many ankles."

Bingley's face went red, his eyes murderous. "The villain."

Miss Bingley turned a curious look on him. "What did she tell you that has you so up in arms? On the carriage ride back yesterday, I thought you might throw the door open and rush the magistrate's office when we passed."

Darcy, too, wondered what details of the history between the two had filled Bingley and Miss Bennet's whispered conversation in the walled garden. Knowing the long and short of it, he agreed with Bingley's loathing for Collins, but the rage in his friend's face went beyond simple anger.

But Bingley merely shook his head. "I will not betray the confidences of a lady. Suffice it to say that his suit is wholly unwelcome and he knows as much. He seeks only to torment."

Miss Bingley watched her brother for a moment longer, then shrugged. "Be that as it may, Miss Mary asked us not to call, on behalf of Miss Bennet, and I believe we should respect her wishes."

Bingley looked about.

Mrs. Hurst nodded. "Caroline is correct."

Bingley slumped back in his seat, deflated.

"They may be watching the roadway, but they are unlikely to pay similar attention to the fields," Darcy said before he could think better of encouraging Bingley.

Who immediately brightened. "True enough. We will simply ride over."

"I am not riding over," Mrs. Hurst stated.

"Darcy and I will," Bingley replied with a shrug.

His sisters exchanged one of their looks. The ones that jointly condemned the suitability of Bennet women and the intelligence of their brother.

"The post," Netherfield Park's butler said, entering the room on nearly silent feet.

Miss Bingley waved him over. "Have I received a letter from Miss Grantley?"

"I do not believe so, miss," the butler said, crossing to proffer the salver, no expression on his face.

A solid butler, especially for such a provincial backwater. Nothing compared to the two on Darcy's staff, one in London and one at Pemberley, but competent enough.

Miss Bingley rifled through the letters, taking two but frowning. "I do wish Miss Grantley would reply."

"You have hardly given her time to do so," Mrs. Hurst said mildly as she plucked a letter from the tray.

Darcy claimed two missives, one from his sister Georgiana and one from Richard, and Bingley quite a few, as he was avid in his correspondence, laudable even if his handwriting was hardly legible. The butler retreated while they all opened their letters.

It pleased Darcy to read that his sister was well, especially after the incident the previous summer, even while it pained him that he could not help thinking on how near he'd come to losing her. Would word from his sister be forever tainted by how she had nearly eloped with their childhood companion, Mr. Wickham?

His gaze flicked up, but the others continued to read. Darcy folded Georgiana's letter to finish later. He did not care to even think of his sister's scandal in the presence of others, less they somehow sense his distress. He also did not care to think of George Wickham, his dearest friend turned greatest enemy. The man's perfidy, his duplicity, distressed Darcy nearly as much as whatever Miss Bennet had whispered to Bingley troubled his friend.

The letter from Richard, among other things, informed Darcy that the militia to be stationed in Meryton would arrive soon, headed by a Colonel Forster. With surprise, Darcy realized that in his preoccupation with the Bennets and Oakwoods, he'd nearly forgotten about the pair of bandits who'd waylaid him and Bingley. Now that he was reminded, a touch of relief washed through him, along with a hint of embarrassment. He hoped Richard didn't think him incapable of defending himself. Darcy hadn't asked the favor simply for his safety, but for that of the whole community. No matter how handsome the ladies of Meryton found Azile and Enaj, Darcy wouldn't countenance bandits rampaging about an English community.

The militia unit would deter them, and perhaps even capture them. Soon enough, Azile and Enaj would be in gaol where they belonged, and the citizens of Meryton, the Bennet sisters among them, could all rest easier.

CHAPTER TWELVE

Here to Enforce Justice

Several days after their call on Netherfield Park, Elizabeth looked up from her reading as Lydia careened into the parlor where she sat with her three other sisters and their mother. Lydia's face was alight with glee, her eyes shining. Appearing equally excited, Thomas and Matthew trailed her.

"Redcoats," Lydia exclaimed. "Meryton is awash in redcoats."

"A militia has been stationed in Meryton," Thomas added. "Real live soldiers."

A shock of worry went through Elizabeth. She struggled not to look at Jane or Mary for their reactions and tamped down her fear. No one could connect them to the Boney Bandits.

Mrs. Oakwood sniffed. "I daresay none of them have served as your papa did."

"Are they handsome?" Kitty asked, setting her needlepoint aside.

Even at an angle, Elizabeth could see that her sister was ruining another handkerchief. Kitty's stitches were erratic and uneven, even less thought out and less competently applied than her brush strokes when she painted.

"They most certainly are not handsome," Mrs. Oakwood snapped. "Not a one of them is worthy of you or your dowry."

Kitty's face fell.

Lydia bounced up on her toes. "Are they worthy of my dowry, Mama?"

Mrs. Oakwood shrugged. "How should I know? That is between my dear, sweet Arthur and Mr. Phillips. Neither consulted me on the matter. I wouldn't be surprised if you have not a penny settled on you."

Lydia sighed, but with no real distress. That was the same answer their mother always gave.

"Could you not ask Uncle Phillips, Mama?" Elizabeth asked. Normally, she gave little thought to her dowry, but it did irk her not to have any notion what, if anything, Papa Arthur had settled on her and her sisters. More importantly, Jane may care to know soon.

Not that Elizabeth had never attempted to learn about their dowries. She had asked, and been subsequently rebuffed by Uncle Phillips. That was years ago now, though. She slanted a look at Jane, who'd reached her majority and who no one could deny. If Jane asked…

"What does it matter?" Mrs. Oakwood narrowed her eyes at Elizabeth. "You, Miss Lizzy, are too contrary to marry. Mary is too plain to catch a gentleman's notice. Lydia is not out." This was accompanied by a quelling look for Lydia, who popped up onto her toes again. Their mother turned to Jane, a smug smile overtaking her features. "And Jane will marry Mr. Bingley, who is too wealthy to care about her dowry."

"But I want to know," Lydia said, undeterred.

"Then ask your uncle yourself."

"But we never see him," Lydia complained. "And you haven't invited Aunt Phillips for tea in days."

"Certainly, you never see your uncle," Mrs. Oakwood snapped. "We do not associate with attorneys. Your father was a gentleman and my dear Arthur a general, and I cannot have Mr. Bingley or his relations, or that handsome Mr. Darcy, call here and find my sister who married an attorney in my drawing room."

Elizabeth couldn't help pulling a face. The Phillips had been their salvation when Mr. Bennet died and were usually welcomed.

"Nor will we be calling on my sister. Not while Mr. Bingley and Mr. Darcy are staying at Netherfield Park." Their mother turned a hard look Elizabeth's way. "They are not to be reminded of our lowly relations."

"I meet with Uncle Phillips once a quarter," Thomas said, slipping around Lydia to take a chair at the little table where he and Matthew liked to play cards. "We go over the estate books."

Elizabeth turned to him. She knew of the meetings but it hadn't occurred to her to seek information about their finances from her little brother. "Is the estate doing well?" Were there funds to set aside for dowries?

Matthew sat at the table as well, as Thomas said, "There is usually a profit but Uncle Phillips always says to put it back into the estate, so we do. It's his decision. He's only teaching me for when I'm older."

Elizabeth nodded. Dovemark, being on a swath of land dominated by stony hills, had little in the way of farmland. Mostly, their few tenants kept sheep.

"My dear sweet Arthur put his funds into building us this lovely home." Mrs. Oakwood looked around with a soft smile, for she truly did love their home and the man who'd caused it to be built. "That, he did to ensure our comfort and that we would never be without a home again, as happened with Longbourn."

"When he turns one and twenty, Thomas could evict us," Elizabeth said blandly.

Jane looked up from her mending to purse her lips at Elizabeth. Mary merely shook her head. Neither understood her need to antagonize their mother. Elizabeth hardly understood it herself, except that Mama said such aggravating, nonsensical things much of the time and it goaded her.

"I would never," Thomas said staunchly.

"And besides, I am going to marry Mr. Collins and so we will have Longbourn back," Kitty added.

Mrs. Oakwood smiled happily at that, but Jane, whose face was angled to her work, paled.

"I am going to go back to watching the redcoats," Lydia declared. "We only came to see if any of you want to join us."

"I came back because it's nearly time for tea," Thomas contradicted.

"I'm hungry," Matthew added and reached for the deck of cards in the center of the table.

"Who can think of food with all those lovely redcoats marching into Meryton?" Lydia dropped her heels to the floor again, her eyes dreamy. "I don't care if any of you are interested, I'm going back to see them."

"Not alone, you are not," Mrs. Oakwood said. She looked about, as if someone might have joined them unnoticed. "Where is Nanny Hill? Were you out alone?"

"Nanny Hill is taking her afternoon nap," Lydia replied. "And you know I wasn't alone. Thomas and Matthew were with me."

At their table, Thomas and Matthew nodded along.

"Your brothers are too young to be proper chaperones," their mother said firmly.

Ignoring that, Lydia turned to them. "Let's go watch a bit longer."

Thomas shook his head. "They all look the same, Lydie."

"And Mama says we aren't proper chaperones," Matthew added.

Elizabeth stood, curious to see these redcoats that were invading the village...and to assess whether or not they constituted a threat. "I will accompany you, Lydia."

That earned a frown from their mother.

"I will as well." Mary came to her feet.

Jane looked up.

"You will remain here." Mrs. Oakwood aimed her words at Jane. "I will not have you falling for some useless redcoat when you could have Mr. Bingley."

Jane shrugged and returned to sewing.

Elizabeth followed Lydia out, then went up to collect her bonnet, gloves and cloak.

Soon enough, she, Mary, and Lydia walked streets dotted with men in red coats. In a way, they did all look the same, as Thomas had said. Mostly tall. Mostly well enough formed. Their faces clean shaven and their hair neat. They sauntered about, and more ladies than usual wandered the main street. Everywhere, the women of the community endeavored to act disinterested, while still watching the newcomers. For their part, the redcoats wore wide grins, as bright as their polished buttons and boots. They looked far too cocky to be any real trouble, but it would be best if Azile and Enaj were scarce while they remained.

"They seem pleased," Mary said quietly where she and Elizabeth trailed Lydia.

"The local female population or the redcoats?" Elizabeth cast back.

Mary smiled slightly. "Both."

"Enaj and Azile are going to lose half their admirers," Lydia said, looking over her shoulder.

Elizabeth, who'd thought Lydia wasn't paying them any mind, reminded herself again not to forget how observant her youngest sister was.

Halting, Lydia turned to Elizabeth and Mary again to ask, "How can we meet them?"

"Psst."

Elizabeth whirled at the sound.

Robert Collins stood to their right, tucked out of sight in the alleyway that ran along one side of the magistrate's office. He gestured, his expression eager.

"What does he want?" Elizabeth muttered.

"I will find out." Mary was moving away before Elizabeth could protest.

She looked back to see if Lydia had noticed Mary's defection, just in time to see her sister toss a handkerchief at the feet of two officers.

"Oh," Lydia exclaimed. "How clumsy I am."

One of the men, grinning, dipped down to scoop up the lace-trimmed cloth. "I believe you dropped this, Miss…?"

Elizabeth strode forward to snatch the handkerchief from his fingers before Lydia could. "I am sorry if my sister troubled you, sir. Her nanny takes afternoon naps, providing the freedom for sneaking out of the schoolroom."

Both men cast surprised, assessing looks at Lydia.

Who tossed her curls where she stood beside Elizabeth, half a head taller. "It is a good thing she will retire soon, as I am too old to require a nanny or a schoolroom." She smiled widely. "I'm Lydia Bennet and this is my sister Elizabeth."

The men exchanged a look. The one who'd picked up the handkerchief shrugged. The other raised his eyebrows, appearing uncomfortable at the inopportune meeting.

"I'm Lieutenant Denny, and this is Pratt," the shrugger said easily. "We're to be stationed here for some time, I believe."

"I hope until after my birthday," Lydia said, her smile even wider.

"And when might that be?" Lieutenant Denny asked, looking her up and down.

"We will not trouble you gentlemen any longer," Elizabeth said firmly. She caught Lydia by the elbow.

"In the spring," Lydia called over her shoulder as Elizabeth turned her away.

Elizabeth all but dragged her sister over to a shop window, away from the two men.

Lydia yanked her elbow free. "You're ruining everything."

"I am saving you from being labeled the biggest flirt in Hertfordshire."

"I only wanted to meet them."

"And you did."

Mary appeared on Lydia's other side. "What are you two whispering about?"

"I met two redcoats, Mr. Denny and Mr. Pratt, but Elizabeth wouldn't let us talk with them."

"Rightly so," Mary said firmly.

Lydia huffed a sigh.

"We had best get back."

Elizabeth agreed with Mary's assessment, but her sister's grim tone surprised her. She met Mary's gaze and received only a slight shake of her head.

"Or we could stop at Aunt Phillips," Lydia said. "She always has the best tarts, and she's certain to know all about the redcoats already."

"Elizabeth and I have work to do in the garden," Mary said in a voice about as soft as ice.

Wondering what Robert Collins could have done to upset Mary so,

Elizabeth nodded. "Yes. We have garden work."

"Can you not leave me with Aunt Phillips?" Lydia pleaded. "I'm certain she can spare a maid to walk me home."

"Mama just forbade us—" Elizabeth began.

"If you promise not to tell," Mary cut in.

Elizabeth blinked at her. It wasn't like Mary to go against their mother's rules. Even the ridiculous ones.

Lydia clapped her hands together. "I promise. Mama will never know."

"Very well." Mary set a brisk pace to their uncle's office, above which he and their aunt lived.

Elizabeth stood beside her sister, silent as they watched Lydia knock. Nor did they move until their sister went in and the door closed behind her. Still without speaking, they turned and started home.

They walked through the village, ignoring the interested looks of redcoats, and took the road north. Coming upon the westward turn that led to their home, they turned. Elizabeth eyed Mary as they walked, her worry growing with every moment of silence.

Finally, alone on the open roadway, the line of hills that ran from Longbourn, through Dovemark, and all the way to Netherfield Park visible as low lumps in the distance, Mary said, "The militia is here to find and arrest the Boney Bandits. Some colonel, Fitzwilliam by name, requested a troop be sent to apprehend them."

"What?" Elizabeth exclaimed, fresh worry shooting through her. "Why would he?"

"Apparently, it was at Mr. Darcy's request."

"Mr. Darcy?" Elizabeth repeated, the name suddenly bitter in her mouth. She should have known that he wouldn't stand for being robbed. He wasn't the sort to let an offence go unanswered.

She pursed her lips. What would being hunted mean to them and the work they did? They weren't in need of funds to distribute at the moment, thanks to Mr. Darcy and Mr. Bingley. Could they simply wait out this militia? She would not permit people to suffer because redcoats had come to Meryton. "You know for certain that Mr. Darcy is involved, and that hunting us is why they are here?"

Mary nodded. "Cousin Robert told me. He saw as much in a letter sent to Mr. Collins."

"Why should we trust him? And why would he tell you that?" That was twice of late that Cousin Robert had given Mary such pertinent, important information…which was suspicious.

"I trust him because he has never lied to me. He told me as a matter of interest." Mary's face was very blank. Very closed.

A horrible fear filled Elizabeth. "You...tell me you have not told him about us."

Mary shook her head. "Do not be absurd."

"Then why would he tell you anything about the Boney Bandits?"

"Because he and I have conversed about them before. He believes I am in league with him in his attempts to discover who they are."

Elizabeth stared at her sister, then turned her attention back to the roadway, lest she trip. She knew Mary had contacts. A network of sorts which she used to learn what took place in the village. She had not realized that network included Robert Collins so fully.

Mary slanted a look at her. "You took quite the sum off Mr. Darcy and Mr. Bingley. We should not require anything more until after the Yuletide."

Elizabeth nodded. They'd given out enough funds to ensure that everyone could have a good Christmas. Still, winters were lean and the new year would bring more of Mr. Collins' taxes, and once the snow came, she and Jane worried too much about being tracked to take to the highways seeking unsuspecting travelers.

"That is, we have enough funds for so long as Jane's resolve holds," Mary added. "I worry that if she does marry Mr. Bingley, she will insist we repay what we took."

Elizabeth pulled a face. That did sound like Jane. But rather than speculate on their sister's goodness, she worried over the villainy of their cousins. "And you are certain Robert Collins knows nothing, and is telling you the truth?"

Mary nodded. "I am certain he has no thought that we are the Boney Bandits, and I have no reason to doubt his words about the militia and Mr. Darcy."

"Except that he is a Collins," Elizabeth muttered as they stepped through an ornate gate set into the low stone wall that delineated the Dovemark lands.

Mary shook her head. "He is not a real Collins."

"His last name is Collins." And Elizabeth had no use for any Collins. Even 'not real' ones.

"Yes, but everyone knows that his mother was with child when she agreed to marry Mr. Collins' father, which is borne out by how entirely different Cousin Robert is from Mr. Collins."

"Cousin Robert was raised by the same man who raised Mr. Collins," Elizabeth countered. "He was brought up by the same man who cast us from

Longbourn and who shot Papa Arthur, and if Mr. Collins dies without issue, it is Robert who will claim Longbourn, not any of us. That is as Collins as Collins can be."

"But he is not a real Collins," Mary reiterated.

Elizabeth shrugged, her mood spoiled. She didn't want to give consideration to Robert Collins. Nor did she want to acknowledge the fear that had shot through her at Mary's revelation. A whole militia, there to capture her, Mary, and Jane. A militia that suddenly rendered their game of highwaymen far less enjoyable.

What she did want was to go to their cavern and exact a toll on a practice dummy. One she would imagine had Mr. Darcy's face.

CHAPTER THIRTEEN

Caught in the Act

Darcy conceded, as he and Bingley rode across turned under fields of rich dark earth resting in wait for spring, that the countryside in this region of Hertfordshire was not unlovely. In some respects, it could be compared to his beloved corner of Derbyshire, and certainly the line of low hills that ran from Netherfield Park northeastward to Dovemark and onward were an attractive addition to an otherwise flat countryside.

Approaching Dovemark through the fields, they sighted the stable first and, with a gesture to indicate his plan, Darcy made for the structure. They could hand their mounts off to a groom, brush off the mud of travel, and go around to the front of the house on foot.

"A pretty sort of place, isn't it?" Bingley said over the plod of hooves on earth softened by the dampness of October.

Indeed, the stacked stone stable, rather than mimic the French Mediterranean style of the manor house, gave the impression of having been built into the hillside generations ago. Narrow windows, their panes too thick to do more than permit diffused light and flanked by green painted shutters, marched along one side. The stable door, tall and set to roll open, was of the same stout wood as the shutters, painted the same time-worn green, which mimicked the moss that pillowed on the stacked stones of the stable and the craggy hillside alike. Beside the stable's entrance, a smaller green door was obviously meant for non-equine passage. The roof of the structure was densely thatched, and the far side let out into a paddock, the door not visible from where they rode but the whitewashed fence wending away like a swath of lace decorating the base of the hills.

"Charming," Darcy finally admitted, unable to think of a single structure at Pemberley that embodied a similarly ancient, slightly enchanted feel. Perhaps he would commission a folly of stacked stones and moss, to replicate the fey glory of this place. He had a lovely birch grove in the middle of which one would blend seamlessly into the already pleasant clearing.

They drew to a halt before the stable and the smaller door opened, causing Darcy to begin to revise his impression that the thick window panes didn't permit sight until Miss Elizabeth and Miss Bennet stepped out, their faces mirroring Darcy's startlement at seeing them there.

Both wore utilitarian gowns of drab brown, and both surprised visages glowed with good health and vigor. Miss Elizabeth, her coif slightly askew for all it was tightly coiled, had never looked more lovely.

Her brows drew together, no hint of warmth reaching her dark eyes as she regarded them. "Mr. Darcy. Mr. Bingley. This is a surprise."

"For us as well," Bingley said, swinging free of his mount. "But the most pleasant of surprises."

"Do you often frequent the stable?" Darcy asked, dismounting as well. Something about Miss Elizabeth's closed demeanor put him on guard.

"We were riding," Miss Elizabeth replied at the same time as Miss Bennet said, "We were stowing our gardening tools."

Bingley looked back and forth between the two, confused, but Darcy kept the bulk of his attention on Miss Elizabeth, trying to read her face.

Miss Bennet cast her sister a panicked look.

Not seeming to notice, Miss Elizabeth slipped into an easy smile. "Jane was gardening but when she brought in her tools, I persuaded her to help me brush down my mount." She gestured and Darcy took in the traces of straw and horse hair on Miss Bennet's skirt.

Looking down, Miss Bennet's face went red. She brushed at her gown. "I ought not to have removed my apron."

"You brush your own horse?" Bingley asked. "Very industrious of you, Miss Elizabeth. I daresay neither of my sisters have ever held a curry comb."

"Do you not keep a groom? A stablemaster?" Darcy asked, unable to shake the suspicion that he was being misled.

Miss Elizabeth turned her easy, pleasant expression on him. A façade that did not quite hide the flicker of some less amiable emotion deep in her eyes. "One of the tenants comes every morning to care for the horses, but we have only three, all for riding. When we need to use the carriage, he brings his team."

"Mama does not care for horses," Miss Bennet said softly, dropping her gaze to the gravel path. "Not since…" She broke off, casting Miss Elizabeth another look.

"Not since our father was thrown and died," Miss Elizabeth finished for her, the smile leaving her face. "So, you see, the less trouble our mounts are to our mother, the better, lest she decide that Jane and I do not need to ride at all."

"You are not dressed for riding," Darcy stated, wondering at her less than welcoming mood. For all her attempt at pleasantness, she seemed almost confrontational.

Miss Elizabeth raised her eyebrows. "Perhaps if you did not sneak onto our lands and come upon us so unexpectedly, I would be garbed more to your liking, Mr. Darcy."

Darcy took a half step back. His horse, whose reins he loosely held, tossed his head. "I meant only to observe, not to criticize."

"Then I accept your apology," Miss Elizabeth said primly.

Miss Bennet still studied the ground, her hands clasped before her, but Bingley looked from Darcy to Miss Elizabeth and back again. "Yes, well, we came across the fields because of Miss Mary's warning to my sister," Bingley said haltingly, obviously wishing for a return to cordiality.

Miss Bennet raised her gaze, her smile dispelling all unease from Bingley's face. "That was very considerate of you."

"We may stable our mounts and walk with you, then?" Bingley asked eagerly. "I would be pleased to see what you were working on in the garden."

Miss Bennet's smile faltered.

"Jane was trimming back the ivy when last she worked in the garden," Miss Elizabeth said. "It grows so quickly in the spring that it is best to cut it back before winter."

Miss Bennet's shoulders relaxed. "Yes. I did trim the ivy."

Darcy felt as if he were missing half the conversation.

"There is more than enough room for your mounts." With an elegant sweep of her arm, Miss Bennet turned back to the stable.

She moved to yank open the tall door, but Bingley hurried forward to do so for her. He struggled for a moment, the door apparently heavy, and Darcy wondered how a slight, though tall, creature like Miss Bennet had thought she would be able to handle it. But then, if not the two ladies before him, who did open and close the door when they rode? A footman?

Inside the stable was as picturesque as outside, the stacked stone of the four walls, even the one set against the hillside, braced with stout lintels and beams. In addition to a large tack room and a loft stuffed with hay, the stable boasted over two dozen stalls, though only three were occupied. Two by hot-blooded, capable looking bays and one by a slightly round, white mare.

Catching Darcy's gaze on the mare, Miss Elizabeth said, "Our sister Mary's horse. She is not so much of a rider as Jane and I."

"You once told me that you are not a great rider," Darcy countered, clearly recalling the exchange. "That you prefer to walk."

"I believe I told you that I am not *known* as a great rider." Mischief danced in her eyes, her mood becoming lighter as she corrected him. "And that I prefer to walk, which is true."

"Which is yours, Miss Bennet?" Bingley asked, leading his horse to one of the empty stalls.

"This one." Miss Bennet went to one of the bays, holding out a hand for him to nuzzle.

From the stall across from her, where he was stripping off his mount's bridle, Bingley said, "A lovely mount. What is his name?"

Miss Bennet smiled fondly at the bay. "Robin."

"And yours, Miss Elizabeth?" Bingley asked as Darcy took his horse deeper into the stable to an empty stall.

"Tuck," Miss Elizabeth replied.

"Tuck?" Darcy echoed, finding the name odd.

"As in, Friar Tuck?" Bingley asked.

Miss Elizabeth chuckled. "If you must know, yes." Darcy looked back to see her gesturing at the horses as, amusement in her voice, she continued, "Robin, Tuck, and Mare Marian."

A bark of laughter escaped Darcy.

Miss Elizabeth's eyebrows shot up.

Darcy shrugged and returned to stabling his mount.

"From the tales of Robin Hood." Enthusiasm colored Bingley's voice. "I used to read those as a lad."

"Papa Arthur read them to us," Miss Bennet said, stroking a hand down her horse's neck. He nuzzled her hair.

Bingley came out of the stall, closing it behind him. "I know Robin Hood is meant to be the hero, but Allen-a-Dale was always my favorite."

"Mine will always be Robin." Miss Bennet gave her horse a final pat and turned to Bingley.

"And you, Mr. Darcy?" Miss Elizabeth called. "Which of Robin and his Merry Men did you like best? Be forewarned that if you select poorly, you will be harshly judged."

He stepped free of the stall he'd selected to find her at the front of the stable, bathed in the sunlight slanting in through the open door. Her left side was gilded in a golden glow and light streamed in around her, gleaming, giving him the odd sensation that she was not quite real.

"Mr. Darcy?" she pressed.

"I agree with your sister," he said, striding up the aisle between the stalls.

"May I assume you have a preference for Friar Tuck?"

"Only for my Tuck here." She cast her horse a smile that, to Darcy's shame, stirred envy in him, and Tuck's ears swiveled forward at the sound of his name. "Insofar as the stories go, I am rather fond of Will Scarlet."

"Will Scarlet?" Darcy tried to dredge up memories of the character.

"He is dashing, skilled with a blade, and quick witted." Miss Elizabeth studied Darcy with unreadable eyes.

What was he missing? What game lurked beneath their innocent discussion? Darcy had thought on Robin Hood recently, or at least something to do with the tale, but he could not bring to mind what or why. He studied Miss Elizabeth as he drew near, searching her fair visage and his mind for answers.

She met his gaze with amused calm.

"Shall we walk in the garden?" Miss Bennet asked brightly.

Acquiescing, Bingley offered her his arm as they left the stable, prompting Darcy to do the same for Miss Elizabeth, and they set out along the neat gravel path to the walled garden. There, the air about them softened by the enclosure's warmth, they started down the length of walled in greenery, though much of what had been green now blazed red, yellow, and orange.

While Miss Bennet pointed out various plants to Bingley, Miss Elizabeth slowed her pace, obviously giving the two space for conversation. Darcy felt a prickle of concern, but Bingley had come to speak with Miss Bennet, and there was nowhere out of sight in the long, narrow garden.

Giving up worry over Bingley being trapped in any way, Darcy turned his attention to the riddle of the woman beside him. Miss Elizabeth behaved so very differently from other young ladies of his acquaintance. Foremost, she made no effort to engage him at all. Nor, lovely as she was, did she take overmuch care with her appearance. Most ladies would be mortified for him to see them in drab brown with their coif slightly askew.

Once more, the suspicion that she had a suitor welled up, unwanted. The only times he'd seen her take pains with her appearance were at the assembly, and on the day he, the Bingleys and the Hursts had called on Dovemark. For whom had Miss Elizabeth gone to such trouble? Not for him, apparently.

The sourness of that thought surprised Darcy.

Her words quiet, Miss Elizabeth ventured, "A militia has come to Meryton."

"Yes," Darcy answered, aware of an odd note lurking in her voice. Did she dislike redcoats?

She slanted a look at him. "I am afraid they will steal many a heart from you and Mr. Bingley. You have become old news."

"I cannot be disappointed in that."

"No?" Miss Elizabeth cast him another assessing look. "You do not enjoy being at the heart of every young lady's aspirations?"

He halted, turning to study her face, and found himself asking, "Every young lady?" He struggled not to hold his breath as he awaited her reply, silly of him, for he had no intentions concerning her. Even if she was his mist-woman, she was also a country miss with ties to trade. She had nothing to offer the Darcy name.

Miss Elizabeth chuckled. "You have me there. I daresay not every. Some." She pursed her lips in a parody of deep thought. "No, most."

Though Darcy had asked the question that sent them down this path of conversation, he was at a loss as to how to reply. A different sort of gentleman, a rogue, would ask Miss Elizabeth if she were among most ladies, but he did not want to encourage her hopes. More than that, mockery lurked in her gaze.

She cocked her head to the side. "If you are not pleased with the adoration of the local misses, perhaps you summoned the redcoats here to save yourself?"

Darcy frowned at the note of accusation lurking in her voice. Was her goal to discover the impetus of the militia unit's arrival? Why? And why suspect that he would know? "I did request their presence. Something needs to be done about the bandits hereabouts."

"And why is that?"

How could so much steel lurk in so light a voice? He shook his head, uncertain of the source of her ire. "Because they rob with impunity."

"They robbed you and Mr. Bingley with impunity, true, but they are not known to trouble anyone who cannot afford to be liberated from some of their wealth."

Darcy did not for a moment believe that. "They did not know us, and so could not know if we could afford to have our money taken."

Her eyebrows rose. "Do you mean to tell me that you believe them incapable of judging your wealth based on your exquisite carriage and matched team of four? Your driver whose livery is finer than the garb of most of the people in Meryton?"

"It was Mr. Bingley's carriage, team, and driver," Darcy said stiffly. So, Miss Elizabeth idolized the Boney Bandits. He should have known. In truth, all three of the elder Bennet sisters likely did, given the names of their horses. "And him employing a fine carriage does not excuse them taking our money at gunpoint."

"So you sought revenge for the affront to your dignity?"

Annoyance shot through him. "Indeed, no. They are not significant enough to offend me in such a manner."

"Then you have been imposed upon?" she pressed intently. "You suffer from a lack of funds?"

Darcy could not claim that. He shook his head. "I suffer from being threatened and robbed."

"Even though rumor has it that what they took from you was used for charity?"

"Charity should be given voluntarily, and I do so regularly."

"Then you differ greatly from gentlemen hereabouts." Anger sharpened each word she spoke.

"Am I to understand that you applaud what these bandits do?" Darcy cast back. "You believe that the gentlemen of your community are not generous enough, and that it excuses a pair of Frenchmen flouting English law?"

"I do applaud them, for they act when everyone else is either too filled with greed or fear to do so."

Darcy took in how she pressed her full lips into a thin line, her eyes narrowed, her displeasure clear. She wasn't displeased with him because she already had a suitor. Or at least that, were that true, it was not the lone reason. Somehow, she'd learned that he'd requested the militia, and that was the source of the animosity she'd evidenced since sighting them outside the stable. She respected that pair of bandits and did not want them to face justice.

Or did it go deeper than that? Did she know who they were? Was one of them the unknown caller she'd expected? Did a Boney Bandit warrant a lovely gown and extra care with her coif?

"What they do is wrong," he snapped. "Wrong and against the laws of the land. No amount of good intention justifies such moral and legal transgressions."

"And yet moments ago, you said that Robin Hood was your favorite."

"Of the characters in a tale to which I gave little credence as a lad and even less now."

"I see." Her eyes almost glowed with the anger that burned in her. "So you used your influence to call in a militia, even though what takes place in Meryton and on the surrounding holdings is none of your concern."

Darcy ground his teeth together. "The law is every man's concern."

"How weighty the world in which men live," Miss Elizabeth replied.

Darcy sought about for a reply that would dampen her fury. A glance showed that Bingley and Miss Bennet had reached the far end of the garden and not yet turned back. Seeming to have no care for what the two of them did, Miss Elizabeth stood before Darcy, chin raised and eyes flashing, in an obvious state of pique.

He'd never seen a more lovely visage.

Or an unmarried miss who looked on him with such a total lack of avarice and a considerable amount of ire. How could he make her see that he was in the right? That violating the King's law was wrong, no matter how terrible the roadways were hereabouts or how unjustly the populace felt they were treated? He required words that would explain his care for all of England and all Englishmen…including her.

As she studied his face, her visage softened. "You truly did not cause a militia to be stationed here out of spite over being robbed, did you?"

He frowned at her. "I had not considered that as a reason. I simply sought to right a wrong. To assist a populace overseen by such incompetence that a pair of bandits can go about in broad daylight robbing carriages. Bingley and I took no harm. We could, as you suggest, afford to lose the funds we lost, but what of their next victim? What if someone is shot? Or ladies harassed?"

"The Boney Bandits have never been known to do such things."

"And yet they could. They are bandits. By their very nature, they flout the law and all that is right."

She sighed. The look she aimed at him was touched with what might be pity, but the remainder of her ire drained away. "Walk with me. I will give you a tour of our garden. It will not be as illuminating as Jane's surely was, but as I have caused you to miss her words, you must make do with mine."

Darcy nodded, happy for a return to conviviality, though somewhat baffled by the sudden change in her mood, and offered his arm.

They walked down and back several times, crossing paths with Bingley and Miss Bennet at each pass. They spoke of the plants for which the elder three Bennet sisters cared, of hours spent making preserves. Of Miss Mary falling from a tree after trying to climb up after Miss Elizabeth, and of a five-year-old Miss Lydia cutting the heads off all of Miss Bennet's roses one spring.

Miss Elizabeth's anger gone, walking the garden with the two sisters turned out to be a lovely way to spend an afternoon, but as he and Bingley rode back to Netherfield Park, Darcy's mind lingered on the stable, the

Boney Bandits, and Robin Hood. He wondered what he was missing.

Once they returned and changed from their riding clothes, Bingley called for a late tea, for they had not set foot inside Mrs. Oakwood's home and had received no sustenance. Darcy supposed their visit to have been somewhat unorthodox, though nothing untoward had been done or said. Had they come upon the two sisters walking to the village, they could have strolled along a country lane with them instead. Still, if they repeated the experience, he vowed to insist that he and Bingley go around to the front of the manor house. Mrs. Oakwood had a right to know who visited her home.

He and Bingley were settled into the blue drawing room, their tea before them and Mrs. Hurst ready to serve while Mr. Hurst played cards at a table nearby, when Miss Bingley burst through the open doorway. Even Mr. Hurst paused at the exuberance of her entrance, looking up from his solitary game.

She fluttered a thick missive before her. "I have news about the Oakwoods."

Darcy frowned, uncertain he wished to be privy to gossip, but rather looking forward to tea.

"From Miss Grantley?" Mrs. Hurst asked, pausing in the act of reaching for the pot.

Miss Bingley came around the couches to alight on the other end of the one Darcy employed, across from her sister and brother. Her eyes were so bright, they could have sparked candle wicks. The heavy vellum pages in her hand rattled with excitement. "They are relations to the Earl of Pillory in Nottinghamshire."

Darcy stared at her, startled. Nottinghamshire…home to the mythical Robin Hood?

"How singular," Mrs. Hurst said mildly, but tension seemed to leave her frame and she offered Bingley a faint smile. "It seems Miss Bennet is a worthy conquest after all." Then her eyes narrowed and she turned back to Miss Bingley. "That is, depending on how closely related they are?"

"That is just it." Glee colored Miss Bingley's tone. "I think they, that is, Young Master Thomas, is the next earl. Miss Bennet is the sister of an earl." As she proclaimed that, the pitch of Miss Bingley's voice rose high enough to set Darcy's teeth on edge.

"Why, that is better even than being the cousin of an earl," Mrs. Hurst exclaimed, then colored slightly as her gaze darted to Darcy and away again.

"Indeed," he said, trying to keep his tone bland. "Far better."

Bingley cleared his throat, looking from his sisters to Darcy and back again.

"It hardly seems credible, though, does it?" Hurst drawled from his table. "Mrs. Oakwood does not strike me as a woman who would keep such a connection secret."

"And that is the best part." Miss Bingley flapped the letter at them. "I do not believe they know." She slapped the pages down on the table. "Miss Grantley writes that the old earl has been seeking his son, Matthew Rodrik Arthur Oakwood, Viscount Scathelock, for years. Apparently, Lord Matthew, a third son, enlisted without his father's permission and they became estranged. When he returned, he did not go home. He simply vanished somewhere in England."

"You mean, vanished into Hertfordshire," Bingley exclaimed. "Did not Mrs. Oakwood tell us that her late husband was passing through when he sustained his injury?"

"So he met Mrs. Oakwood and…" Mrs. Hurst frowned as she spoke. "And simply remained here, in this backwater, rather than return and claim his birthright?"

"You said he was a third son," Darcy stated, drawn into the story despite himself.

Miss Bingley nodded, shuffling the pages of the letter. "The elder son died suddenly without issue, as did the second. There was a cousin, next in line if Lord Matthew or his heir are not found, also deceased. His eldest son died as well but he has two others. The older of the two is the heir presumptive and set to inherit."

"If Lord Matthew or his issue are not found?" Mrs. Hurst repeated, her words a question.

"Precisely." Miss Bingley didn't look like the cat who got the cream. She looked like a cat who had just learned how to persuade cows to offer up their bounty at will.

Stunned looks were exchanged about the table. Finally, Mrs. Hurst murmured, "It cannot be true."

"We shall soon know." Miss Bingley set to ordering the pages of her letter. "Miss Grantly is acquainted with the twin sister of the current heir. She has written to her. An Isabella Hargreaves."

Isabella Hargreaves? Darcy frowned. "As in, sister to Lord Franklin Hargreaves, Viscount Scathelock?" A young man about Bingley's age, Hargreaves was not the sort with whom Darcy would associate. Titled, wealthy, and possessed of a streak of cruelty as wide as a country lane.

Miss Bingley turned to him. "She did not say. Are you familiar with the Hargreaves, Mr. Darcy? I imagine that they would be in your circles, you being the relation of an earl as well."

"I am familiar with Lord Franklin," Darcy said crisply in a tone he used when he did not wish to speak further on a topic. He did not care for the viscount, but he would not add to gossip.

Miss Bingley opened her mouth as if she would ask more, but Bingley cut in with, "Well, if a letter has been written, and the earl truly is seeking his lost heirs, I daresay we will know the truth soon enough. How is that tea coming, Louisa?"

"Oh, yes." Mrs. Hurst took up the teapot and proceeded to pour, then handed a cup to Darcy before assembling a small plate for him.

He accepted her offerings with his thanks, but had somehow lost his appetite. If this Isabella Hargreaves was indeed sister to Lord Franklin, he would turn up eventually. Even at only two and twenty, he did not seem the sort of man to permit an earldom to slip through his hands and into those of a mere lad. Darcy sat back and sipped his tea, Mrs. Oakwood's declaration that her husband had wished for nothing to do with his family clear in his thoughts.

With how much Miss Elizabeth resented his interference with the local bandits, would she be equally furious if Miss Bingley brought estranged relations to Dovemark? Even though Miss Bingley's theory might make Miss Elizabeth and her sisters relations to a future earl, Darcy could only picture her angry at the intrusion.

CHAPTER FOURTEEN

Rising Stakes

"Please, Elizabeth," her youngest sister's voice whined, distracting Elizabeth from the mending she'd spread atop her coverlet several days after Mr. Darcy and Mr. Bingley had appeared outside the stable to call on them. "I can't ask for Nanny Hill or a maid to walk me to Aunt Phillips because they all tattle to Mama. I only want to spend time with my aunt and it isn't fair that Mama won't let me simply because Mr. Bingley is smitten with Jane. As if he cares one whit who our relations are. All he can see are her big blue eyes." Lydia emphasized this by making her eyes round and batting her lashes, a dreamy, vacant sort of expression that Jane would never wear on her face.

Elizabeth chuckled. Her attention returned to the various stockings and other bits of mending she truly ought to do, before shifting to the window and the bright afternoon sunshine. It appeared to be an absolutely gorgeous autumn day. "Oh, very well. I will walk with you to Aunt Phillips' house."

Lydia clapped her hands together, her smile radiant. "I knew I could persuade you. You're my favorite sister."

"You said the same thing to Jane yesterday when she gave you her apple tart."

"Because when she gave me her apple tart, she was my favorite sister, but now you are," Lydia replied without a hint of remorse. "I will fetch my bonnet." She skipped from the room.

Reflecting that it was not a terrible thing that her youngest sister wasn't yet out, Elizabeth stowed her mending and donned her bonnet as well.

Soon, after a brief stop in the parlor to inform Mrs. Oakwood of their walk, which resulted in Jane and Mary joining them and Kitty remaining behind, they set out. As none of them employed mincing little steps like Kitty or their mother, it didn't take them long to reach the village.

"It is a pleasant day for a stroll," Jane said, breathing deeply of the crisp autumn air. Her gaze roamed the central street of Meryton down which they walked and Elizabeth knew her sister hoped to meet Mr. Bingley.

"You will not say that once you know our goal," Elizabeth cautioned.

Jane turned to her with mild alarm. "You said that your objective was to walk."

"We lied," Lydia chirped.

On Elizabeth's other side, Mary snorted

Jane's eyebrows crept up. "You lied?"

Elizabeth cast Lydia a quelling look. "We did not lie. Walking is one of our objectives. The other is to visit Aunt Phillips."

Worry eased from Jane's face. "Well, I can see why you did not mention as much. Mama's restriction on visiting our aunt is severe."

"Especially when Aunt Phillips is holding a card party for the officers," Lydia added.

Elizabeth turned a surprised look on her. "You said nothing about a card party. You lied to me."

Mary issued another snort, this one sounding suspiciously like a laugh.

Lydia smirked. "I did not lie. Visiting our aunt is one of my objectives."

Jane laughed. "You cannot fault her for that, Elizabeth."

Elizabeth shook her head, aware that her youngest sister was in danger of becoming something of a monster. "Very well, but we will not leave you there, nor will we linger overlong. Half an hour."

"What? Three times that is required for cards," Lydia protested. "An hour and a half."

"Half an hour," Elizabeth repeated more firmly as a gust of cold wind rustled the dry leaves piled into corners all along the street.

"An hour and a half." Lydia's voice brooked no argument.

Mary sighed.

"Three quarters of an hour," Jane said mildly.

Lydia pursed her lips for a moment, then nodded.

Jane looked to Elizabeth.

"Very well," Elizabeth agreed.

They reached their aunt's door and were let up to the home above Uncle Phillips' office to find that quite a few men in red coats, as well as other ladies and gentlemen of the community, already sat at the tables that had been set out around the Phillips' fair-sized drawing room. Aunt Phillips rushed over to greet them and any lingering ire Elizabeth felt at being tricked dissipated as she took in the joy on their aunt's face.

Aunt Phillips reached to clasp Jane's hands first, then Elizabeth's, before moving on to Mary and Lydia as she said, "Oh, you came. So many of you, too. I shan't for a moment miss Kitty and your mama with the four of you here." She beamed a smile at them.

Memory of the year they'd lived with their aunt and uncle, of the warm kitchen and sweet treats crafted with great care for the scarcity of sugar in a house suddenly burdened with five growing girls, yet crafted nonetheless, filled Elizabeth's senses. She smiled warmly at her aunt. Jane was correct. Their mother's restriction was severe, and silly as well. Their aunt and uncle were a credit to them, no matter what Uncle Phillips' profession.

"I have the precise places for the four of you," Aunt Phillips continued, still clasping one of Lydia's hands as she turned and led the way deeper into the room.

Elizabeth nodded to those she knew as they passed, noting Mr. and Mrs. Lucas but unsurprised Charlotte wasn't among those assembled. She would certainly be minding the shop.

Aunt Phillips halted before a table of four officers, one about to deal and two of them known to Elizabeth.

"Mr. Denny, Mr. Pratt," Lydia cried as the men looked up.

Lieutenant Pratt blinked in surprise but Mr. Denny smiled warmly.

"I see you already know my lovely nieces." Mrs. Phillips beamed at the officers, as if knowing Lydia were an accomplishment.

"Two of them." Pratt dipped his head in greeting. "Miss Elizabeth. Miss Lydia."

"And we know two of these gentlemen," Elizabeth added.

"Oh, but you must all become acquainted so you may play." Aunt Phillips gestured to them in turn. "These are four of my nieces, Miss Bennet, Miss Elizabeth, Miss Mary, and Miss Lydia."

Denny frowned slightly. "You have another, a Miss Kitty Bennet, do you not?" He looked about as if Kitty might appear, an avaricious glint in his eyes.

Elizabeth concluded that rumor of Kitty's five thousand pounds must have made its way through the militia's ranks.

"Kitty didn't join us," Lydia said, recapturing Denny's attention. "She thinks she's too good for cards with officers."

That earned four freshly surprised looks.

"And these are Lieutenants Denny, Pratt, and Chamberlayne, and Captain Carter," Aunt Phillips continued blithely. "And if some of you fine gentlemen will assist, I have another table we can bring in and you can become two groups of four."

Denny smirked. "Why not? I'm certain Carter and Chamberlayne are tired of me and Pratt taking their money."

Pratt looked abashed at that but Denny began scooping up a sizable pile of half-pennies.

The additional table was brought, though the space was tight, and soon enough Elizabeth and Jane sat with Chamberlayne and Carter, while Lydia and Mary joined the apparently lucky Denny and Pratt. As Chamberlayne shuffled, showing considerable skill, Elizabeth couldn't help but hear Lydia prattling on at the table beside them.

"Hopefully he will not take all of your sisters' money," Carter said dryly, apparently noticing Elizabeth's straying attention.

"Is he that good?" she asked.

Carter shrugged. "I try not to play him."

"And yet you are here this afternoon," Elizabeth observed as Chamberlayne began to deal.

"If I had known your aunt would pair us, I would not have attended," Carter replied.

"Could you not have refused?" Jane asked, sympathy in her voice.

Carter shook his head. "Your aunt is such a kind, motherly sort, I could not bear to raise a fuss."

"I had no idea he would be here," Chamberlayne muttered, setting down the remainder of the deck. "Not his usual sort of haunt."

"No?" Jane asked lightly as she looked from face to face, her expression mild.

Elizabeth wasn't fooled. Her sister was a keen observer.

"Lately his usual haunt's been the magistrate's office," Carter said with a chuckle.

Elizabeth fought down the urge to gape at him.

"Magistrate's office?" Jane repeated with a distinct lack of interest.

Elizabeth had seen her sister employ this tactic many times. Jane, who liked to volunteer little, would simply repeat back a few words and permit the other person to carry on the conversation. She maintained, and Mary always agreed with her, that people had things they wanted to tell you and you would get much more from them by letting them tell you what they wished than via Elizabeth's more direct method of asking for what she wanted to know.

Chamberlayne nodded, studying his cards while Carter leaned nearer to Jane, lowering his voice to say, "He has already been before your local fellow twice for being disorderly."

"Is his discipline not the province of your commanding officer?"

Elizabeth asked, aware that she lacked Jane's subtlety but not caring.

"Colonel Forster?" Carter's gaze went to a table across the room, where a man in a colonel's uniform played cards with Miss King, her aunt, and another officer. "It is, and he tried, but Denny has a way of finding trouble."

"You will have them thinking that officers are not true gentlemen," Chamberlayne protested. "I believe you are first, Miss Bennet." He gave Jane a winning smile.

Jane played and the game moved on from there, Elizabeth shifting the conversation first to the weather and then to where the two gentlemen had traveled during their service. All in all, it would have been an enjoyable interlude had half her attention not been on the table behind her, where Lydia laughed loudly and flirted with both Denny and Pratt.

She also, to Elizabeth's dismay, asked them why they were stationed in Meryton, to which Pratt replied that they were there to hunt down a couple of French bandits who'd got under the skin of the locals. Elizabeth could only be glad that she sat nearest their table and that Jane was focused on her cards, for she and Mary had not shared that revelation with their older, more prone to worry, sister.

After nearly an hour, Elizabeth thanked their tablemates, with whom they'd broken even, and said they were due home. Lydia, having lost her pin money one half penny at a time, didn't resist and soon they'd bid their aunt farewell and were on their way back down the staircase leading to the street.

When she reached the bottom of the stairwell, Lydia stepped out with a surprised exclamation of, "Mr. Bingley," which caused Jane, who followed her, to hurry her steps.

Elizabeth would have done likewise, but Mary caught her arm. Elizabeth turned a questioning look on her, finding Mary's face difficult to read with only light filtering in from below and down from above reaching them.

"Denny cheats," Mary said quietly.

"Are you certain?" Elizabeth asked. She had an inexplicable dislike for the man, but cheating was a rather large accusation.

Mary merely raised her eyebrows.

Elizabeth accepted that silent reprimand. "Yes, to be certain you are or you would not have told me." She pursed her lips, wondering if she should return to confront him. But then, they'd only played for half pennies, and maybe losing her pin money would teach Lydia more caution. "Perhaps Lydia needed to learn the risks of gambling?"

"But he is not her relation, so her learning is not his concern. And I gathered from talk about the table that he and Mr. Pratt are fully aware of

Lydia's youth, for all she's taller than either of us."

"Yes. I made certain on their first meeting that they know Lydia is not out." Elizabeth tipped her head. "Was he inappropriate?"

"No. My concern is simply what his behavior says about him. What gentleman would cheat two young ladies for half pennies?" Mary shook her head. "One who is very desperate, or who cheats for the sheer thrill of doing so. Both are dangerous."

Considered in that light, Elizabeth could only agree with her sister. "I will endeavor for us not to be in his company again."

Mary nodded and slipped past her down the staircase.

Elizabeth followed more slowly and came out into the waning afternoon light to the sight of her sisters speaking with Mr. Darcy and Mr. Bingley, who stood at the heads of their mounts, reins in hand.

Mr. Darcy looked past her sisters to meet Elizabeth's gaze. He dipped his head. She returned the greeting and the faintest smile graced his mouth before he turned serious eyes back to Lydia, who spoke animatedly to Mr. Bingley.

"…a ball at Netherfield Park, Mr. Bingley," Lydia was saying as Elizabeth joined them. "It would be so delightful."

"And you would not be permitted to attend." Mary's tone was as quelling as her words.

Lydia looked down, crestfallen.

"Then perhaps not a ball but a simple gathering of friends from around the community," Mr. Bingley said cheerfully. "One at which music might perhaps be played, and therefore where people may choose to dance."

Lydia looked up, smiling so brightly that Jane and Mr. Bingley answered in kind. Mary merely appeared thoughtful. Mr. Darcy, as he so often did, frowned. Catching Elizabeth watching him, he eased his glower.

"A gathering of friends would be perfection," Lydia replied. She looked over her shoulder at Elizabeth. "Would it not be, Elizabeth?"

Finding Lydia's excitement just as infectious as the others seemed to, Elizabeth nodded.

"What have we here?" a masculine voice drawled from somewhere behind Mr. Darcy and Mr. Bingley.

Elizabeth's stomach knotted. She knew that voice. Almost against her will, she looked past the two gentlemen and their mounts.

Mr. Collins strode up the street. His cane, topped with a golden lion whose emerald eyes clashed with the large ruby clutched in his upraised front paws, thudded in time to his plodding footfalls. His coat, a garish red that appeared orange compared to the ruby, was covered in gold embroidery that glinted in the late afternoon sun. Above it all, a smirk cut across his sallow face.

Paling, Jane stepped back, Mr. Bingley moving in front of her as if they'd rehearsed the maneuver. Mr. Darcy's frown deepened to a glower, and Mary's lips curled with contempt. Elizabeth moved forward to intercept their unwelcome relation, Lydia beside her.

"My fair cousins." Mr. Collins bowed, quickly bringing up a hand when his hat threatened to topple from his head. "Mr. Darcy. Mr. Bingley. I have not seen you about these past few days. I hope our community does not disappoint you?"

"Far from it," Mr. Bingley said a touch loudly. "I find I enjoy Hertfordshire quite a great deal."

Mr. Collins' gaze flicked past Mr. Bingley. "You are looking particularly lovely, Cousin Jane, but not so lovely, I hope, as to raise a gentleman's hopes when we all know your mother wishes to return to Longbourn so very, very much, and that you, the daughter who deprived her of the father of her sons, have the means to make her wish come true."

A tremble of rage went through Elizabeth. How she wished she were masked and armed for dueling, not just with the knife hidden in her boot. Mr. Collins would not dare speak to Jane thusly with Azile championing her.

Lydia brought her hands to her hips. "Why don't you go call on Mama and Kitty? They enjoy your company."

"Lydia." Elizabeth put no reprimand in her tone. "That is no way to talk to a gentleman." And were Mr. Collins one, Elizabeth would actually chide her sister.

"You are correct, certainly." Lydia tossed her curls. "I will endeavor never to speak to *a gentleman* in such a way."

Mr. Collins' smirk slid into a sneer. "Soon enough, your elder sister will be married, cousins, and her husband will have a great deal of sway over you. Therefore, I would advise you to mind your manners."

"I am to be married?" Jane said quietly, only a trace of tremble in her voice. She stepped up to Mr. Bingley's side. "It is amazing to me, sir, that you know this when I do not."

Mr. Collins' smile made Elizabeth's fingers curl into fists. "It is only a matter of time. You will come to your senses and accept an offer from me."

"I believe Jane gave you her answer years ago," Elizabeth snapped, unable to hold back her anger. "Unless you require a reminder of what it was, I suggest you continue on your way."

Looking down his slightly crooked nose at her, Mr. Collins replied, "I believe you forget, dear cousin, the laudable words of Fordyce. 'The majesty of your sex is sure to suffer by being seen too frequently, and too familiarly,'" Mr. Collins intoned. "'Discreet reserve in a woman, like the distance kept by royal personages, contributes to maintain the proper reverence.'"

Elizabeth glared at him. "Then I suggest you augment that distance by remaining away from my sister."

Mr. Darcy cleared his throat. "I believe we, all of us, would be aided by a bit of distance in this moment."

"Are you advising me on how I may speak to my cousins, Mr. Darcy?" Mr. Collins' brows drew together. "This is not Derbyshire and we are not on your estate. Here, I am the rule of law."

"You would not be if I were to purchase Netherfield Park," Mr. Bingley stated.

Anger flashed in Mr. Collins' eyes. "Netherfield Park is a rather large estate for someone so young and so sullied by the shadow of trade. Take care you do not take on more than you can hope to manage."

Mr. Bingley sputtered. A glance showed his face beet red.

Mr. Darcy put a hand on his shoulder. "Mr. Bingley will have my full support and any advice he may require, but I have the utmost confidence in him as a landholder."

Still sneering, Mr. Collins opened his mouth to speak.

"Moreover, if my knowledge is not sufficient, I can inquire of my aunt, Lady Catherine de Bourgh, or of my uncle, the Earl of Matlock," Mr. Darcy continued coldly. "I am certain their advice will be invaluable."

Mr. Collins squeezed his thin mouth closed.

"If you will excuse us." Elizabeth struggled to keep her voice even. "We are due home."

Mary and Jane curtsied immediately, causing Mr. Darcy and Mr. Bingley to bow. Lydia continued to glare at their cousin.

Elizabeth looped an arm through her tall little sister's, saying, "It was a delight to see you, Mr. Bingley. Mr. Darcy." She yanked on Lydia's arm, turning her.

With quick farewells, the four of them started up the street. For a moment, silence reigned behind them, then Elizabeth heard the dull thump of Mr. Collins' cane as he retraced his steps. A quick glance showed that Mr. Darcy and Mr. Bingley still stood with their mounts. Mr. Darcy's hand remained clamped firmly on Mr. Bingley's shoulder.

CHAPTER FIFTEEN

There will be a New Sheriff in Town

Darcy struggled to balance prudence with remaining in sight of his friend as Bingley set a reckless pace back to Netherfield Park. Fortunately, the country lane between the estate and Meryton had little by way of traffic that afternoon, though they did startle a pair of maids walking into Meryton as they galloped past.

Outside the stable, Bingley swung free of the saddle, turning to Darcy with a foreign-seeming scowl on his face. "The man is insufferable. Preening and claiming Miss Bennet as his own. After what he did. I ought to have challenged him."

Darcy swung down, casting a quick look over the grooms coming out of the stable. He caught Bingley's arm and half dragged him up the path out of earshot. "You will do no such thing. Need I remind you that dueling is illegal?"

"I don't care." Bingley pulled his arm free. "It needs to be made clear to the man that he has no right to Miss Bennet. If her breaking his nose and the duel their fathers fought didn't instill that truth, I will."

"Even though you have no right to Miss Bennet either?"

Bingley jutted his lower jaw at an obstinate angle. "Someone must protect her. Her brother is only a boy."

"If you challenge Collins on the lady's behalf, it is as good as declaring an engagement, and Miss Bennet—"

"I see no issue," Bingley cut in before Darcy could make his point.

With a glare meant to quell further interruption, Darcy continued, "Perhaps you should speak with Miss Bennet before forcing her to choose between marrying you or bearing the stain of a gentleman with no claim over her defending her honor. We have spoken of being trapped into unions often enough. Would you not apply the same care to Miss Bennet's future as you would ask young ladies to apply to yours?"

Bingley stared at him, his anger dimming into a muddle of confusion.

Finally, he grimaced. "You are correct, as always. I do not want to trap Miss Bennet into a union not of her choosing, or force her to bear the shame of a gentleman to whom she is not attached defending her honor as if it were his to defend."

"Good." Darcy drew in a breath. The crisis of Bingley's anger averted, he could now focus on his own. How no one in the community had yet dealt with the odiousness that was Mr. Collins baffled him.

Miss Elizabeth's belief that the Boney Bandits were indeed needed flashed through his mind.

"I will simply have to ask her to marry me," Bingley added. "Then, the next time Collins troubles her, I'll have every right to challenge him."

Darcy's attention snapped back to his friend. "Propose? You have not known her a month."

"It has been over a month," Bingley protested.

"I do not believe we should count our chance meeting outside the magistrate's office when we came to inspect the estate."

"Whyever not? Her kindness and consideration were on ready display."

Darcy shook his head, uncertain if there was any reasoning with Bingley at this point. With a gesture, he indicated that they should return to the house.

Obligingly, Bingley started up the path, Darcy keeping pace as his friend asked, "Besides, what is there to know? Miss Bennet is the loveliest creature I've ever had the pleasure of meeting."

"Which would say more if you possessed a greater number of years," Darcy countered, for Bingley was but two and twenty.

"Well then, as you've half a decade on me, have you met a lovelier miss?"

Miss Elizabeth, Darcy's mind whispered. "Perhaps equally so, but never more so, no."

"You see?" Bingley broke into a smile as they neared the back of the manor house. "It's settled. I will propose."

Darcy scrubbed glove encased fingers across his forehead. "A decision this momentous should not be made in the heat of any emotion, especially not anger."

Bingley waved that off as they entered through a door near the kitchen. "I am no longer angry, and I do not come to this conclusion in haste." He glanced back, his resolute visage visible by the light of sconces that burned even in this little used corridor, because Bingley could afford both the staff and candles to keep Netherfield Park as well lighted as he liked.

And could have his pick among most women, from all except the top echelons of the ton.

"You will pardon me if I believe any statement about a lack of haste on your part is not entirely true," Darcy ventured.

"I will indeed pardon you, but still maintain the stance." Anguish touched Bingley's tone as he continued, "You have no idea the torture of watching the cretin torment Miss Bennet today. I could put an end to that, and you cannot deny that she seems amenable to my attentions."

Darcy cleared his throat, disliking what he must next say, but feeling as if he would be less of a friend if he did not ask, "Has it occurred to you that her amiability may be born of hope that you will purchase this estate and replace her cousin as magistrate? That would free her nearly as well as marriage."

Ahead of Darcy, Bingley's shoulders stiffened. They reached the entrance hall in silence, but Bingley turned at the base of the staircase. "Then you believe that I should purchase Netherfield Park first, replace the man, and then test Miss Bennet's affection?"

"That is not what I said."

"It is worth thinking on, though." Bingley started up the staircase.

Feeling a touch abused by his friend's deliberate misconstruing of his words, Darcy followed. "I must emphasize, that is not what I meant."

"But it is a solid plan. Once her cousin is relegated to minding his estate and nothing more, his shadow lifted from the region, as it were, Miss Bennet will be free to prefer whomever she likes, whether they will benefit society here or not."

"And if she does not prefer you?" Darcy countered. "You will own an estate in a region where some of the only acceptable society is in the form of a woman you care deeply for, who does not return your affection. Think on the torture of that."

Bingley turned at the top of the staircase. "I am confident I will win her."

"And if you do not?" Darcy pressed, joining him in the upper hall.

A line of thought appeared on Bingley's brow. Slowly, he said, "I daresay if I do not, it will be awkward, although she is likely then to marry and move away, for if she favored a gentleman in this area, she would surely have wed by now."

"And you? How will you find a wife here? Miss Bennet is the only woman who has struck your fancy." Was he finally getting through to Bingley?

Bingley snorted. "You make it sound as if once I own an estate, I may never return to Town again."

Darcy frowned, not appreciating Bingley's levity.

"Look, I do understand your concerns." Bingley's mien became serious. "I agree that if things do not work out as I plan, I will be miserable, but I will be miserable whether I buy this place or not, and you said yourself that I cannot hope for an honest answer from her until she is freed from the temptation of wedding me simply to oust her odious cousin from power."

"Again, that is not what I said." Darcy spoke in a low voice, not comfortable having such an important conversation at the head of the stairwell. In a house such as this, there were many servants, all moving about on many tasks, and servants had sharp ears. "I merely pointed out that Miss Bennet might behave pleasantly when in your company because she does not want to discourage any chance that you might purchase Netherfield Park and depose Mr. Collins, rather than out of a regard for you as a companion and possible husband."

Bingley waved that off. "It is all one and the same. I will give your words careful consideration, but we are speaking in circles, and I am off to change for tea." With that, he pivoted and strode down the hall.

Aggravated at Bingley's adamant refusal to see wisdom, Darcy retreated to his chamber. He changed from his riding clothes as well, unsurprised to meet Bingley again in the hall a short time later. In silence, they made their way to the drawing room where the remainder of their party congregated.

"Charles, Mr. Darcy," Mrs. Hurst greeted from where she perched on a narrow settee, a book in hand. "How was your ride?"

Seated across from her sister, Miss Bingley rattled several folded pages at them, giving them no time to do more than nod to Mrs. Hurst in greeting as she said, "I have another letter from Miss Grantley. She has made an introduction for me to Miss Isabella Hargreaves, who is indeed sister to Lord Franklin. She says Miss Hargreaves awaits my letter."

"I have no notion what you hope to accomplish by meddling in all this," Mrs. Hurst said tartly.

Mr. Hurst nodded in silent agreement with his wife where he sat at a table off to the side, laying out cards. He preferred to practice for his occasional late-evening bouts in the village, played with some of the local gentlemen, over reading.

"What I hope to accomplish?" Miss Bingley's full eyebrows winged upward. "Why, to see Charles married to the sister of an earl. One sublimely grateful to us, for we will be the instrument of reuniting him with his grandfather."

"We have no means by which to know for certain if young Master Thomas is this lost heir to the Earl of Pillory," Mrs. Hurst protested as Darcy joined the two at the low table, Bingley crossing to observe Hurst's cards. "Mr. Darcy, would you care for tea? I was about to call for some."

"I would. Thank you." He settled into an armchair.

Mrs. Hurst lifted a silver bell, jangling it.

Miss Bingley clamped her mouth closed as a footman entered and took the request for tea. Once the man departed, she recommenced the conversation with, "Our lack of knowledge is precisely why I hope to convince Lord Franklin and Miss Hargreaves to join us here." A smug, satisfied smile overtook Miss Bingley's features. "Only think, me hosting a viscount."

"He won't be a viscount if your theory about Thomas Oakwood is correct," Bingley observed. "No more than Darcy is for being the cousin of an earl."

"And he will not be pleased." The dire note in Hurst's voice caused Darcy to turn to him, for the man was usually resolutely bland. "You may want to reconsider this course, Caroline. Franklin Hargreaves is not a pleasant man."

Miss Bingley turned to her brother-by-marriage with eager eyes. "You have met him?"

"We belonged to the same club. I have seen him commit numerous transgressions. He once even kicked a pup on a wager. Sent the poor thing whining and scurrying across the room." Hurst shook his head. "From the look on his face, I would say Hargreaves enjoyed it, too."

Miss Bingley's eyes went wide with horror, but she quickly schooled her features into amused condescension. "He is young, and I daresay was even younger when this so-called puppy incident took place. Young men are often ambiguous in their morality. That is why we women must take them in hand."

"Believe that all you want," Hurst replied, returning his attention to his cards. "I would wager half my fortune that none of the gentlemen in this room have ever been so cruel."

Miss Bingley's eyes narrowed.

"I daresay I have some lighter news," Bingley said before his sister could speak. He straightened where he'd been leaning over Hurst to study his cards. "I mean to purchase this estate."

Shocked silence met that, then a babble of words from Bingley's relations.

"Oh, but Charles, you have hardly lived here a month."

"Many felicitations, Bingley. Fine place."

"Should you not travel England more first?"

"You must wait until we know her brother's lineage for certain."

"Derbyshire is known to be so lovely. You could reside near Mr. Darcy."

"A house in Town might be a better use of funds."

"Are you certain you are making the right decision?"

Finally, her voice pitched loud enough to quiet her husband and sister, Mrs. Hurst asked, "Do you agree with this, Mr. Darcy?"

"What Darcy does or does not agree with doesn't signify," Bingley said stiffly. "I appreciate his experience and advice, but the decision is mine, and I will purchase Netherfield Park."

A gasp sounded in the doorway.

Darcy turned to the sight of two wide-eyed, tray-laden maids. Both dropped their gazes. They practically vibrated with interest, though neither moved to step into the room.

Darcy grimaced. Everyone in Meryton would be speaking of Bingley purchasing Netherfield Park before the sun set.

"Well, enter," Mrs. Hurst snapped. "Bring in our tea."

The girls rushed forward. They put down the trays with a clatter then straightened. Exchanging a quick look with the other, one ventured, "Will that be all, missus?"

"I daresay it will be more than enough," Hurst drawled at his card table.

"That will be all," Mrs. Hurst said curtly.

The girls gave hurried curtsies and scurried away.

"Now you will have to buy the place," Hurst said into the silence.

"That suits me, as I plan to." Bingley came around the couch as he spoke, taking a seat beside his younger sister. "I will send for Mr. Morris tomorrow to see what must be done."

Mrs. Hurst frowned at him. "Then let us hope that all this nonsense with Thomas Oakwood sorts out well."

"It will," Bingley said cheerfully.

Mrs. Hurst sniffed and began fixing the tea.

Darcy could only pray his friend was correct.

CHAPTER SIXTEEN

I Spy

Leaving the trees that gathered at the base, Elizabeth climbed the steep hillside, following Jane up at a punishing pace that made the autumnal day feel nearly hot. Obviously, something troubled Elizabeth's older sister for her to engage in such exertion, and she suspected she knew what. Jane must fear that Mr. Collins' provocations would end with Mr. Bingley challenging him. After what had happened the last time someone challenged Mr. Collins on Jane's behalf, Elizabeth understood her sister's worry.

They reached the top of the highest in the line of hills, Oakham Mount, and gazed out over groves and dales still touched with yellow and orange even though November drew near. Elizabeth's gaze roamed fields brown with turned earth, then rose to take in a leaden sky.

"It may rain," she ventured.

Jane's eyes shifted, taking in Elizabeth from the corners. "I imagine it may."

Did Jane sound...angry? "Should we go back before it does?"

Swiveling, Jane regarded Elizabeth with a frown and asked, "When were you going to tell me that the militia stationed here is hunting for us?"

"They are not," Elizabeth said quickly. Yes, Jane was definitely angry. "They are hunting for the Boney Bandits, who happen to be French and male. I cannot see how that has anything to do with us."

Jane's balled hands found their way to her hips. "Can you not?"

Elizabeth winced. "We did not want to worry you."

"We?" Jane said sharply. "Then Mary already knew as well? I could not see her face from where I sat at cards."

"You have become quite adept at hiding your feelings. I had no idea you heard Mr. Denny."

"And you require more practice masking yours. I could tell you were not surprised, merely worried, and deduced that your worry was for me."

"We should have told you," Elizabeth said. Especially as Jane had been bound to find out eventually. "I am sorry."

Jane turned back to the view, wrapping her arms about her torso under her cloak. "I am not one of Mama's porcelain figurines, Elizabeth."

"You have seemed so happy, though. Happier than I have seen you in a long time. Mary and I did not want to spoil that. We did not want anything to fracture your newfound peace."

Jane sighed. "Because I am pleasant and kind does not mean I am weak or fragile. I might argue that facing every day, every obstacle, with amiability, understanding, and hope is far more difficult, takes much greater fortitude, than turning to anger or vitriol to give me strength."

Elizabeth looked down at her boot encased toes. "I do not turn to vitriol."

"Mockery, then."

Elizabeth pressed her lips into a hard line, Jane's reprimand stinging.

"I worry for you, sometimes," Jane added softly.

A startled bark of laughter left Elizabeth. "You worry for me?"

"You are so quick to find fault. I worry you will end up alone."

"We kept a concerning piece of information from you and now I will end up alone?" Elizabeth snapped. She couldn't keep an acerbic edge from her voice as she added, "As I already said, I am sorry we kept the militia's reason for being here from you."

Jane turned to face her again. "I have already forgiven you for that. We are speaking now of your quickness to form opinions and of your tendency to mock." Jane's eyes narrowed. "Should I add to that list that you are quick to anger?"

"I am not quick to anger."

"You are angry now."

"Because you said that I will end up alone."

"No. I said I worry that you will. I worry that you spend far more time being a Boney Bandit than a young lady, and that perhaps that is in great part my fault, for going along with you." Moisture built in Jane's eyes. "And I worry that if I were to leave, you will have nothing left because you have cultivated a quick, sharp wit and deadly expertise with a blade, but no skills by which to find a husband." Jane dashed at her eyes. "I am your older sister and I am failing you."

Elizabeth's anger drained away, and in that moment, she truly grasped how much her sister had already come to care for Mr. Bingley. Loss stabbed through Elizabeth but she fought it down to say, "I cannot imagine you failing anyone, ever, let alone me. And I am certain that once I decide to apply myself to the task, I will have no trouble securing a husband." If she could find a gentleman she wanted as one. Perhaps someone like Mr. Darcy, but who did not frown quite so often, because in his rare moments of ease, he was quite engaging.

Jane offered a watery smile.

"And I truly do apologize for—" Lower on the hillside and north of them, something metal glinted among the trees.

"What?" Jane said softly, wariness instantly replacing her sorrow.

"I am not certain, but I believe someone watches us." Not turning her head, Elizabeth slanted her eyes northward.

"I see it as well," Jane murmured. "Do you think it is a threat?"

"Here? On our own lands?" Elizabeth shook her head but she wished she carried a sword.

"Especially here on our own lands, for, whoever it is, they already trespass."

"It is likely a poacher," Elizabeth said, but Jane made a fair point. Still, it was on Elizabeth's tongue to ask where Jane's vaunted hope and kindness were now, but she bit back the words as petty. It was one thing to look for the good in people, but quite another to assume someone sneaking about Dovemark, spying on them, was a friend.

"We should return home," Jane said.

Without turning her head, Elizabeth darted her gaze about again. Metal still gleamed among the trees lower down the hill. "When we reach the tree line, I will circle around to learn who is spying on us."

"That is too dangerous."

"They will not know I am there."

Jane pursed her lips, but her lack of immediate refusal told Elizabeth she'd given in. Besides which, if she wanted to stop Elizabeth from hunting for the interloper, Jane had little choice other than to cry out or chase her.

They set out down the hill, soon reaching the line of trees at the base. There, Elizabeth dipped down to draw her knife. She held it loosely, pressing the blade into the folds of her skirt to help it go unobserved. Jane watched with disapproval but made no protest when Elizabeth gestured for her to continue on.

Leaving her sister, Elizabeth slipped through the trees, wending her way closer to the denser copse in which the trespasser lurked. She moved slowly, both in a bid for quiet and so she might listen, until the rustle of something large moving through the underbrush before her reached her ears. Crouching lower, Elizabeth inched forward.

Ahead, movement caught her eye. She went still, then reached out with a gloved finger to gently press back a scraggly, thorn studded bramble.

Before her, pressing through the brush, was a man in a red coat, the color garish against the autumnal backdrop of grays and browns. Elizabeth shook her head at the hubris of attempting stealth while dressed in such a bright color.

He wore no hat, giving a clear view of limp, middling brown hair, a color that matched too many of the officers she'd seen. Darting a look about the detritus at her feet, Elizabeth found a pebble. With a flick of her wrist, she sent it sailing out in front of the man, to his right.

The stone clicked against a branch. His head jerked, seeking the source of the sound.

Lieutenant Denny.

Elizabeth was still as stone as he scanned the forest ahead and to his right. Finally, nothing meeting his gaze, he returned to pushing his way through the underbrush. With slow care, Elizabeth let the bramble she'd pulled aside slide back into place.

She waited while all sound of his passage faded, certain that if she could not hear him, it was impossible that he should hear her far stealthier steps. Once she was again alone in the woods, she made her slow way back, then sought the stable.

As Elizabeth suspected, Jane waited inside their cavern, Mary with her now, their faces pinched in the wavering lantern light. At the sight of Elizabeth, Jane's shoulders dropped to a more natural angle, worry draining from her face. Mary watched with serious eyes as Elizabeth closed the secret door by which she'd entered.

"Well?" Mary asked.

"It was Lieutenant Denny."

Mary pulled a face. "I knew I did not care for him."

"The real question is," Jane said slowly. "Why was he spying on us? He did mention Kitty at cards. Could he be seeking a chance meeting with her?"

"Then why depart once you and I left the hilltop?" Elizabeth asked. Her gaze roamed the large, open space, most of the rock smooth, evidence of the power of whatever had long ago hollowed out the hill.

"Because neither of us is Kitty?" Jane offered.

"If Lieutenant Denny's trespassing has something to do with the Boney Bandits, rather than Kitty's dowry, Cousin Robert will know."

Elizabeth dropped her gaze from studying the cavern to scrutinize Mary. "And why should he share what he knows with us? How would you even ask him without rousing suspicion?"

"Suspicion?" Mary's eyebrows rose. "I will simply mention, in conversation, that I am worried rumor of Kitty's fortune has made a target of her. If he knows otherwise, he will be quick to tell me."

Distrust welled in Elizabeth. Cousin Robert had seemed eager to speak with Mary that day in Meryton, and she, with all her skill, hadn't managed to avoid conversing with him at the assembly. Was she deliberately seeking out Robert Collins' company? "You are not forgetting that he is a Collins, are you?"

"He is a Collins in name only," Mary replied primly. "And no, I am not."

"Regardless," Jane cut in before Elizabeth could press Mary, "I do not think we dare another robbery until the militia moves on."

"But that may not be until spring," Elizabeth protested. If they didn't hold up another carriage until the militia left, would they ever again? How long would Mr. Bingley go before proposing to Jane, who Elizabeth strongly felt would accept? She hadn't known that robbing Mr. Darcy would be her final moment as Azile. She would have... She didn't know what she would have done differently, but at the least she could have savored the moment better.

"We have only given out half of that you took off Mr. Darcy and Mr. Bingley. If we stretch what is left, it will last the community well into spring," Mary said. "I agree with Jane. Another hold up at this time is simply not worth the risk."

"We did take quite a good deal from them." Jane's teeth worried at her lower lip. "Are you certain we should not—"

"The funds are already allocated," Mary cut in crisply.

"You only now said that we still have half." Jane's voice held a note of pleading. "We could at least return that, with a note of apology."

"Apology?" Elizabeth said with a laugh. "I do not feel at all apologetic." Even if she hadn't known that was their last holdup at the time, Elizabeth had thoroughly enjoyed robbing Mr. Darcy. "You have heard the rumors of their fortunes. They can spare the funds."

"I am of age," Jane stated. "I could go to Uncle Phillips and ask him about my funds. I know Papa Thomas did not live long enough to put aside the dowries he would surely have given us, but perhaps Papa Arthur left us each a sum. I could repay Mr. Bingley and Mr. Darcy from that."

"And what would happen, then, if you do marry Mr. Bingley and he ever finds out that you gave him your money?" Elizabeth shook her head. "You worry for no reason. Both gentlemen can afford to contribute to the local populace and it speaks highly of them that they did."

"They do not know that they did," Mary said dryly.

Elizabeth held up her thumb and forefinger, nearly touching. "It still makes me think a bit better of them. A tiny bit."

Jane pursed her lips. "I may inquire of Uncle Phillips nonetheless."

"Or you should not," Elizabeth countered.

"Enough." As she spoke, Mary started for the secret door. "We are talking in circles and I would like tea. Jane will do as she wishes with her funds and tomorrow morning I will walk into Meryton and see what I may overhear, and if I can glean anything useful from our cousin." She shot a look over her shoulder, at Elizabeth. "Our everyone-knows-he-is-not-truly-a-Collins cousin."

Elizabeth raised her gaze ceilingward in a dramatic bid for fortitude. "Very well. Only, take care in your dealings with him. He is not to be trusted."

"I did not, in fact, say that he is." For all the crispness of her words, Mary used care when she slid back the rectangle of wood that hid the spy hole. After a moment, she pushed the door open and slipped out.

Elizabeth made to follow but halted when Jane didn't move. She turned back, looking a question at her sister.

Taking in Elizabeth's look, Jane folded her delicate features into a wince. "Do you...do you think that Mr. Collins set Lieutenant Denny to spy on me? To ensure that I am not receiving calls from Mr. Bingley?"

Elizabeth glanced at the cracked open door. In the stable beyond, she could hear Mary talking to Mare Marian in a cheerful voice, likely spoiling her with pilfered apples while she waited for them. "Unless he has convinced Mr. Denny to physically intervene between the two of you, I cannot see what harm that would do. Let him report any visits from Mr. Bingley as he likes."

"It is only, Mr. Bingley seemed so angry when we met Mr. Collins in the village. As if he might challenge our cousin." Jane's eyes were wide with worry, shimmering nearly indigo in the flickering lantern light. "I could not bear it if another duel were fought over me. Especially with a Collins."

"It will hardly come to that," Elizabeth scoffed. "For one thing, Mr. Darcy would never permit his friend to duel. Or do you forget that the practice is outlawed?"

"That did not stop Papa Arthur."

"It will stop Mr. Darcy, and he will stop Mr. Bingley." Elizabeth gentled her tone. "You worry for nothing. Come. It is nearly time to receive calls. If we do not go in soon, Mama will send Lydia to find us." Rather, to find Jane. For years, Mrs. Oakwood hadn't cared how they spent their afternoons, only how Kitty did, but now, she wished for Jane to be present in the drawing room. That neither Mr. Darcy nor Mr. Bingley had entered their house since the day after the assembly deterred Mrs. Oakwood not one bit.

Jane nodded and left the cavern with Elizabeth, who extinguished the lanterns and made certain Mary had closed the spyhole, and then carefully shut the door. Even if Azile and Enaj might never ride again, they couldn't have anyone discover their secret. Anything else aside, if what they'd done became public knowledge, Jane would be unmarriageable. Elizabeth as well, but she cared not so greatly as Jane did.

Of course, Jane was far more likely to charm a man so thoroughly that he would accept her strange, wild past and marry her regardless. Elizabeth, in contrast, might very well end up with someone argumentative and contrary. She couldn't imagine spending her life with someone who didn't challenge her.

Mr. Darcy's frown flashed through her mind. She shook her head as she followed Jane and Mary from the stable. Elizabeth wanted a challenge, not endless condescension.

But her mind conjured his visage back, not frowning this time. She easily recalled his commitment to keeping Jane away from Mr. Collins at the assembly. The wry amusement he evidenced at times. His clear dedication to the bonds of friendship.

He could so easily be the sort of gentleman she would wish to marry. An ounce less condescension. A slight lessening of his tendency to glower…

She shook her head again. She was daft to even think it. She couldn't marry a man who, even unwittingly, condemned so large a part of her life so adamantly. Mr. Darcy was too intractable to marry, no matter how her breath caught when she witnessed the rare moments he didn't glower.

CHAPTER SEVENTEEN

The Time Grows Short

Seated in their favored drawing room at Netherfield Park with the rest of the party, Darcy concentrated on the book he held. He refused to be drawn into conversation with Bingley's younger sister as she paced the room, seeking distraction from waiting for the post. Days had passed since Miss Bingley penned her note to Miss Isabella Hargreaves, and each afternoon without a reply increased her level of agitation. Today, she did not even attempt to sit quietly, and had already rebuffed an offer of cards from Hurst and a dictate to go practice the pianoforte from Mrs. Hurst.

Footfalls sounded in the hallway and Miss Bingley hurried to the open drawing room door. A footman stepped in bearing a tray of letters, all of which Miss Bingley immediately seized. She sorted them with quick fingers.

With a crow of delight that caused Hurst to let out a low oath as he toppled the house of cards he'd been building, Miss Bingley tossed the remaining missives back onto the tray. "She wrote."

"That is wonderful," Mrs. Hurst breathed, ignoring the sour look her husband cast her sister. "I had begun to fear she would not condescend to do so."

Bingley gestured for the footman to leave the tray and depart. Setting aside his book, Darcy went to the tray to flip through the missives. Only one was addressed to him, the familiar handwriting causing him to grind his teeth together.

Wickham.

Miss Bingley paced away from the doorway, cracking open the letter, her gaze devouring the words therein. "She writes that she and her brother are quite intrigued by the Oakwoods and asks if she might visit. She and Lord Franklin, and their younger brother Nathan, a lad of seventeen." The face Miss Bingley raised glowed as one who had received benediction. "Lord Franklin, here. Oh, I am going to be hostess to a viscount."

Taking up Wickham's note, Darcy weighed the thin paper. Should he read it or burn it? It would have cost Wickham effort to track him down, for the letter was directed to Netherfield Park. Had Wickham realized that Darcy's staff knew his handwriting as well and had been ordered to burn any missive from him, rather than forward them on?

Hurst looked over from where he was gathering up his strewn cards. "I still do not believe inviting Lord Franklin to be a good idea."

Darcy could only agree. He'd seen little of Lord Franklin, but even their brief encounters had left a lasting dislike. His gaze dropped to the letter in his hand. Not as much dislike as he felt for George Wickham.

Miss Bingley huffed. "I have achieved a triumph and you are still worried that a gentleman kicked a pup in his youth."

"He was twenty if he was a day," Hurst countered, snapping the pile of cards against the table to line up the edges.

"And I cannot see how you can be so particular about him when you are members of the same club," Miss Bingley continued over Hurst.

"We *were* in the same club," Hurst emphasized, turning the cards and snapping another side down.

"You no longer are?"

Hurst shook his head as Darcy crossed to the fireplace, wrestling with the temptation to read Wickham's words.

Miss Bingley stared at her brother-by-marriage in obvious confusion. "Whyever would you leave a club with future peers in it?"

"I told you the story about the pup. That was a single, and tame, example of the conduct there. It is a rowdy, unruly, irreverent sort of establishment."

"Still, if being a member afforded you the opportunity to associate with a future earl, you should have been willing to endure a bit of good-humored rowdiness."

Hurst merely shook his head and began building a new house of cards.

"If he is truly that horrible, do we want him here?" Mrs. Hurst asked, watching her husband uneasily.

Bingley turned to Darcy. "You are familiar with the man, are you not? Would you invite him?"

Darcy looked up from the letter he held. "He is only a passing acquaintance."

"You see?" Miss Bingley interrupted before Darcy could continue. "Mr. Darcy claims him as an acquaintance."

"But even in passing," Darcy directed his words at Bingley, "I did not care for the man." He cracked open the seal.

"Well, it matters not," Miss Bingley cried. "I will not pass on this opportunity. Lord Franklin cannot be so unbearable that we cannot endure him for a week or two."

As Darcy found most people so unbearable that he would not endure them for a day, he heartily disagreed, but it was not his place to answer. He was merely a guest. He opened the missive to Wickham's erratic scrawl.

Darcy, please do not consign my words to the flames.

Darcy flinched slightly at that. How well Wickham knew him…and how adept he'd always been at using that knowledge to get what he wanted.

I need you as I have never needed you before. I have borrowed funds from a very disreputable element, and I am afraid that my inability to repay them has put my very life in danger. After Ramsgate, I would not come to you were I not desperate. You must know that. If you bear me any love, or even the memory of affection, I beg you, please, I need only this one final favor, one more—

Darcy crumpled the page and tossed it into the fire. After Ramsgate indeed. Any love, or memory of affection, as Wickham put it, that he'd borne the man had died with Georgiana's tears as she confessed how near she'd come to running off with their childhood acquaintance.

Turning back to the room, Darcy found the three siblings glaring at one another while Hurst carefully arranged cards.

"—must put to rest our speculations over who Miss Bennet's relations are," Miss Bingley was saying, a note of triumph in her voice as she cast a challenging gaze about the room.

"That is true," Mrs. Hurst said slowly, nodding. "We do need answers. They should be invited."

Bingley's brow creased in thought.

"I will be unbearable if you do not grant me this, Charles," Miss Bingley said.

With a wince, Bingley nodded. "Very well. Invite them, but it is on you to make them welcome. I will be but a reluctant participant in this."

Miss Bingley clasped her hands together, almost prayer-like. "Thank you." She rushed across the room to ring for a footman, then asked for her maid to bring her writing box.

Darcy returned to his seat and his book, trying to put Wickham's plea from his mind as Miss Bingley began a recitation of what she would put into her letter, Mrs. Hurst offering advice. He'd become nearly as adept as he suspected Hurst of being at ignoring the chatter of the two, but Miss Bingley's voice made an unpleasant backdrop to reading. Especially as his attention was already fragmented by thoughts of Wickham. Darcy hoped she would begin the actual penning of the missive soon, a quieter occupation than the planning of its contents.

Even through his disquiet, Darcy noted the butler's footfalls approaching the open drawing room doorway. He lowered his book, struggling not to give in to the intoxicating hope of seeing Miss Elizabeth. During their last encounter, on the street in Meryton, he hadn't exchanged a word with her, but she'd been stunning as she stood between her odious cousin and Miss Bennet, her shoulders back and her eyes flashing. When her anger and wit were not turned on him, they were quite beguiling.

The butler stepped into the doorway, halting Miss Bingley mid-sentence, and said, "A Mrs. Oakwood and four Miss Bennets ask if you are at home."

The pleasure that surged through Darcy startled him.

"We are," Miss Bingley replied promptly.

As the butler left, Darcy set aside his book, then circumspectly checked his cravat. Miss Bingley composed herself in a chair, as if she had not been pacing and ranting for half the day. Quiet settled on the drawing room. Mr. Hurst continued to carefully stack cards.

They all rose when the butler returned, Mrs. Oakwood and her four elder daughters in tow, and greetings commenced. So pleased was he to see Miss Elizabeth trail her mother and Miss Kitty into the room, Darcy nearly smiled. A strange giddiness swirled through his chest at the sight of her, but soon twisted tightly into something akin to fear when she did not acknowledge him. His unease grew as Miss Elizabeth surveyed the room, the Bingleys and the Hursts. Everything and everyone except Darcy until, finally, her gaze met his.

She smiled slightly, one fine brow raising in inquiry, and the worry that tightened Darcy's chest eased.

Her efforts aided by Mrs. Oakwood, Miss Bingley made certain that Bingley ended up seated on a sofa with Miss Bennet. Darcy, meanwhile, employed years of practice at ensuring that he didn't end up sitting next to husband-hunting young misses to claim a chair beside Miss Elizabeth, though Miss Mary slipped between them at one point, jeopardizing his plan. Fortunately, she passed him by, surprising him by being clumsy enough to brush against his coat. He hadn't realized she was so much less graceful than her elder sisters.

Once they were seated and tea called for, Miss Bingley sat forward eagerly. Taking in the gleam of avarice in her eyes, Darcy wondered if Miss Elizabeth would notice. If she did, would she understand what lay behind that telling sparkle?

"Mrs. Oakwood, I was hoping you and your lovely daughters would call," Miss Bingley began. "I have the best of news. We are to have additional guests."

"Oh, let them be more handsome and wealthy gentlemen," Miss Kitty cried from where she shared the settee upon which Miss Elizabeth perched.

More? Amusement washed through Darcy as he realized that meant that he was the first 'handsome and wealthy gentleman.' He slanted a look at Miss Elizabeth. Did he detect a faint blush at her sister's words? But out of mortification or in agreement?

Ignoring Miss Kitty, Miss Bingley fixed her attention on Mrs. Oakwood. "I have been corresponding with my acquaintance, Miss Isabella Hargreaves, and—"

"Miss Hargreaves?" Mrs. Oakwood cut in sharply.

"Why, yes." Miss Bingley scrutinized the matron. "Are you acquainted?"

Mrs. Oakwood gave a vigorous shake of her head, gray-streaked curls bouncing. "Most certainly not."

"Yet, you reacted so strongly," Miss Bingley pressed.

Mrs. Oakwood pressed her mouth closed, for once silent.

Miss Elizabeth exchanged confused looks with her older and next younger sisters.

"Mrs. Oakwood?" Miss Bingley made the name into a question.

"Mama is only upset because you have invited a lady." Miss Kitty accompanied her words with an uncertain, worried look at her mother. She gestured with the fan she'd brought, as if Bingley kept his home overwarm. "We have more than enough ladies about."

Regarding Mrs. Oakwood intently, Miss Bingley asked, "Is that the trouble?"

Mrs. Oakwood drew in a huffing breath, then nodded. "More ladies are not what is required."

"Then never fear." Miss Bingley smiled sweetly, still studying her prey. "Lord Franklin, Viscount Scathelock, and the younger brother, Mr. Nathan Hargreaves, will also visit. That is two more gentlemen, one titled, wealthy, and I am certain handsome, albeit the other is only seven and ten years of age."

Mrs. Oakwood offered a strained smile. "How lovely for my girls. How kind of you to invite such good prospects into our neighborhood, but I am certain you must have your eye on Lord Franklin, Miss Bingley, and will not have cause to share him." Mrs. Oakwood fluttered a hand as she spoke. "Understandable, to be certain. Unavoidable. My girls do not poach."

"But I want to meet Lord Franklin," Miss Kitty groused. "And I am certain Miss Bingley, as our dear friend, will share him. Who is his father?"

Watching Mrs. Oakwood closely as she spoke, Miss Bingley replied, "His father is no longer with us, but Lord Franklin is heir to the Earl of Pillory in Nottinghamshire."

The matron paled.

A strange reaction indeed, but Darcy was far more interested in the increasingly confused looks exchanged by Miss Elizabeth, Miss Bennet, and Miss Mary. Whatever troubled their mother, he was certain they knew nothing of it. How singularly odd, and not at all the reaction he'd expected to Miss Bingley's news.

Bingley, who had been doing his best to catch Miss Bennet's eye, said loudly, "We will hold a ball, I should think. Show these Hargreaves how grand Netherfield Park may be, and how superior the neighborhood." He smiled at Miss Bennet. "And the neighbors."

"A ball," Miss Kitty cried, clapping her hands together in glee. "Oh, how marvelous of you, Mr. Bingley."

Bingley grinned at Miss Kitty for a moment before turning to seek Miss Bennet's reaction.

She met Bingley's eyes briefly. Sorrow overtook her features. She gave the barest shake of her head and dropped her attention to her lightly clasped hands.

Bingley stared at her in surprise. A line cleaved his brow. Mrs. Hurst looked back and forth between the two in confusion.

"I believe you promised our youngest sister a friendly gathering, rather than a ball," Miss Elizabeth noted.

"Did you, Charles?" Mrs. Hurst asked.

Bingley shrugged. "Well, yes, there was talk of a gathering of some sort that Miss Lydia would be welcome to attend."

"Oh, but a ball would be much more the thing," Miss Kitty cried. "And you do not want Lydia here. She ruins everything."

"I see no reason we cannot have both a friendly gathering and a ball," Miss Bingley said, still studying Mrs. Oakwood.

"Yes, well, we must see when this ball is, to be certain." Mrs. Oakwood nodded along with her words. "We are very busy. The Yuletide approaches.

Very busy indeed."

Miss Kitty turned a surprised look on her mother. "Nonsense. November has only now begun, and we have no obligation we cannot put off to attend a ball here at Netherfield Park."

"Yes, well, we will see," Mrs. Oakwood said with surprising firmness.

Darcy took in the room, wondering what transpired before him. Everyone seemed . . . off. Mrs. Oakwood obviously did not care for the idea of their additional guests. Miss Elizabeth and Miss Mary appeared as flummoxed as he was. Miss Bennet studied her hands as if they contained the secret to eternal life, her shoulders slumped forward and her demeanor quite miserable.

Mrs. Hurst looked to her husband, who shrugged his lack of understanding, that confusion echoed in Bingley's dejected face. Her voice pitched with considerable cheer, Mrs. Hurst said, "The weather is holding so well for this time of year."

That set off a flurry of benign conversation that carried them through tea. Bingley rallied, but each attempt to engage Miss Bennet was rebuffed, sending him back into misery. Darcy contributed little, content to observe the others. Especially Miss Elizabeth, who sent him amused, assessing looks each time her mother or Miss Kitty said something particularly silly. Miss Mary spoke not at all, watching everyone with keen eyes.

Finally, with conversation about them on a normal, even keel, Darcy leaned a bit closer to Miss Elizabeth and dared to say, "Not all of your party seem their usual convivial selves." He did not trouble to glance at Miss Bennet. Miss Elizabeth, with her keen intelligence, would know who he meant.

Miss Elizabeth met his gaze with intent, gleaming eyes. "I believe, given *the* time, the reason for that will become clear to you."

Darcy frowned. "Given *the* time?"

Miss Elizabeth nodded.

Did she not mean, 'given time?'

"Why, Miss Elizabeth, whatever have you said to make Mr. Darcy glower so?" Miss Bingley asked with a laughing lightness that did little to mask the annoyance beneath. She looked about the room. "I cannot comprehend how four such fair misses have made both my brother and our dear guest so displeased."

Miss Bennet's cheeks pinked.

"I? Displeased?" Darcy shook his head. "Miss Elizabeth merely presented me with a riddle. Far from displeasing me, it leaves me intrigued."

"Do share it," Miss Bingley urged.

Miss Elizabeth's expression went blank, yet somehow Darcy could sense she didn't particularly care to have her words shared. Her gaze darted once to her mother, then back to him.

Everyone watched him now. Darcy mustered something akin to a smile. "I will ponder it a time first, lest anyone beat me to the solution."

Miss Bingley engaged in a pout. "Oh, how ungallant of you."

"Elizabeth is forever making up nonsense," Mrs. Oakwood said, waving a hand dismissively at her second child.

"There likely is no solution if it is one of her riddles," Miss Kitty added. "I daresay she invents them simply to cause consternation."

"Because you can never find a solution does not mean there is not one," Miss Mary said, speaking for the first time since greetings were exchanged.

Miss Kitty tossed her curls. "You would defend her. You think clinging to Jane's and Elizabeth's skirts makes you as pretty and sought after as they are? Because it does not."

"Kitty," Miss Elizabeth snapped.

"Girls." Mrs. Oakwood stood as she uttered that single, condemning word. "I believe we have remained quite long enough."

"Yes, Mama," the four chorused, rising as well.

Indeed, tea had been served and consumed, and it was obvious that Miss Bennet, at least, was relieved to quit their presence. Farewells were made, and promises to call issued, though Darcy was uncertain if they were meant on either side, and their guests began to file out. On her way past him, Miss Elizabeth murmured to Darcy not a farewell but a reiteration of, 'the time.'

Darcy watched them leave with the feeling that he'd missed something important. And why this emphasis on the time? His gaze went to the mantel clock but the afternoon hour read as he expected. Could the timepiece be off in some significant way? He reached for his pocket watch, to check.

His fingers encountered a folded page. Darcy pulled it free in astonishment. How had a note come to be in his watch pocket without his knowledge? That seemed impossible, yet he held the evidence.

"What an odd visit," Miss Bingley said, retaking her seat. "I am certain Mrs. Oakwood recognized Lord Franklin's name, but if so, why did she react so poorly?" She reached to pour more tea. "I am having a second cup, if anyone would care to join me."

"I don't understand." Bingley stood near the empty doorway, gazing down the hall like a forlorn pup. "She would not even speak with me."

No one needed to ask who 'she' was.

"What have you there, Darcy?" Hurst asked as he crossed back to his card table, a plate full of sweets in hand.

"A note." Darcy studied the tightly folded square.

"Is it in some way special?" Mrs. Hurst asked from where she sat near her sister, helping herself to more victuals.

"I have no notion from where it came," Darcy admitted.

Bingley turned from the doorway with a frown. "How do you mean?"

"I mean, I went to remove my watch to check the time, and there it was."

Miss Bingley's eyebrows winged upward. "Well, open it. Do not keep us in suspense."

Darcy unfolded the page with care, for the paper was very thin. To save money, or to save space, he did not know.

Mr. Darcy,

My inquiries have found that a Mr. Denny has been prevailed upon to spy on us, to report back any meetings between Mr. Bingley and my sister. Moreover, a reliable source assures me that Mr. Collins will do, in his words, 'Whatever it takes,' to ensure that Mr. Bingley does not purchase Netherfield Park. We ask that Mr. Bingley no longer show an interest in either the purchase of said property or my sister, for his own safety as well as hers.

Please pardon my impropriety in writing. I do so with the knowledge and support of both elder siblings.

M.B.

Darcy looked up to find a sea of curious eyes, and so read the missive aloud.

"So that is why she would not speak with me?" Bingley cried. He crossed to drop down into a chair, his relief palpable. "Not because she has found some sudden flaw in me."

"Spying on their land?" Miss Bingley's words were sharp with indignation. "Surely, that is a matter to take before the authorities?"

"You mean, Mr. Collins?" Mr. Hurst said dryly.

"Oh." Miss Bingley pursed her lips. "I do see your point."

Bingley surged back to his feet. "I am no coward. I will purchase this estate, and I will put someone else up for magistrate. That will fix Collins."

"She said your safety and hers," Darcy said quietly, emphasizing 'hers.'

Defiance drained from Bingley's stance. "He wouldn't harm her. He means to marry her."

"As the Miss Bennets are far better acquainted with their cousin than we are, we must bow to their superior knowledge." Darcy turned the note over as he spoke, but the back was blank.

"I will not be prevented from seeing her," Bingley said hotly.

"Nor should you be."

Darcy turned to Miss Bingley in surprise and countered, "Caution is warranted until we more fully understand the situation before us."

She shook her head. "There is no time for caution. Lord Franklin is wealthy and by all accounts attractive. If Miss Bennet truly is the sister of a future earl, she will be a coveted prize. Charles must fully secure her affections before Lord Franklin learns of her."

"If you are correct in your suppositions," Mrs. Hurst said as she studied her plate, her fingers hovering over various delectables, "Lord Franklin is no lord at all, and so will not have any more to offer above what Charles has than Darcy does, and Miss Bennet does not seem to be swayed by Darcy's wealth and connections."

Miss Bingley shook her head. "Mr. Darcy made no attempt to woo her, and he lacks Lord Franklin's keen motivation. If Master Thomas is the true heir, Miss Bennet will be Lord Franklin's best chance to recapture some small part of what Thomas Oakwood will take from him."

Darcy crossed to the fireplace and tossed Miss Mary's note inside, for no good would come of keeping such a missive. Flames engulfed the thin paper, none so bright as Miss Elizabeth's eyes. Agitation roiled through him, for the circumstances of their budding relationship with the Bennets and Oakwoods became ever more complicated. Darcy did not care for complicated. He merely wished for the opportunity to come to know Miss Elizabeth better.

But why? At first, he'd wished to learn if she was his mist-woman, but he had not thought on that mysterious figure in days. He knew he could not marry a country miss. Although, if Miss Bingley's mad notion about Master Thomas somehow being secretly the heir to an earl...at least, the notion had seemed mad. Something about Mrs. Oakwood's reaction spoke of more.

"I am due an afternoon ride," Darcy declared, tired of suspicions and machination. "Feel free to join me Bingley, Hurst." With that, he strode from the room, Miss Bingley's and Mrs. Hurst's speculations renewing to follow him down the hallway.

Surely not all women were so mercenary. He couldn't picture Georgiana speaking thusly, nor Miss Bennet and Miss Elizabeth. No, with her active mind and keen wit, Miss Elizabeth would have far more engaging topics to speak on than who must marry whom, and why. What those topics were, Darcy did not know, and after the strained nature of the call they'd just endured and Miss Mary's even stranger note, he was uncertain he would ever have the opportunity to learn.

CHAPTER EIGHTEEN

Family Secrets

Elizabeth stared into the darkness above her bed, wishing sleep would come but knowing that wish to be futile. Jane had been so miserable during their call to Netherfield Park that afternoon. Her misery, more than anything else, told Elizabeth how deeply her sister cared for Mr. Bingley. Jane should not be spurning the gentleman.

But Jane was stubborn. The moment Mary had returned from the village with confirmation that Mr. Collins was paying Mr. Denny to skulk about Dovemark spying on them, that their horrible cousin had said he would do *anything* to keep Jane and Mr. Bingley apart, Jane's mind was made up. She cared too much for Mr. Bingley to have him go the way of Papa Arthur.

How Elizabeth wished Jane wouldn't cling to that guilt. Yes, Papa Arthur had died from a wound sustained while dueling for her honor, but Jane was not at fault. She had not asked to be accosted or for their cousin to spread vile rumors about her, or challenged him. She had not agreed to permit the elder Mr. Collins to act as a proxy. She hadn't gone out that morning to duel him, and she most certainly had not shot Papa Arthur. These acts all belonged to others, to the men who had carried them out. Just because Mama blamed Jane for Papa Arthur being shot did not make his death Jane's fault.

Elizabeth ground her teeth, wishing she could make Jane believe that as strongly as she did.

A light tap sounded at her door.

Elizabeth blinked. Had she been asleep? Imagined that sound?

The tap came again.

It wasn't Jane or Mary. They had a secret sequence of knocks. Several, actually. One to summon each other in stealth. One to alert the others to danger. Others to indicate who was with them in the hall. And one, for their amusement, to signal that the moon was full and they should sneak up onto the roof to see it.

Wondering who was without, Elizabeth slipped free of her bed, her bare feet silent on the cold wood floor.

The tap sounded a third time.

Despite the lack of any of their codes, it must be Mary with more secrets to share. Mary, with her so-called informants all over the village, none of them aware that they did more than gossip with her. None of them realizing they dripped paint onto Mary's canvas of information and secrets.

Elizabeth eased the door open.

Her blonde hair in a single braid, coupling with wide blue eyes and a stark white nightgown to make her appear younger than usual, Lydia stood without. She held a single, flickering candle and had one hand raised, as if she might knock yet again.

Elizabeth stepped back in surprise, gesturing for her sister to enter. Closing the door with a soft thud, she whispered, "Whatever are you doing?"

Lydia gave the room a quick glance, although who she might find in Elizabeth's bedchamber aside from possibly one of their other sisters or a maid, Elizabeth couldn't imagine. Turning to face her, Lydia said quietly, "I need to show you something in Papa Arthur's study."

Elizabeth frowned. "What is it?"

"I have no idea," Lydia replied with a shrug.

"You do realize that makes no sense?"

Lydia smiled, adding to her youthful appearance. "Yes, I realize that, but I still have no idea what I mean to show you. Not truly. A letter, I suppose."

Her mind tired from the strain of the day, Elizabeth retreated to sit on the edge of her bed, aware that dragging sense from Lydia could often take a while. "Please explain, and then I will decide if I should go creeping off into our stepfather's study in the middle of the night."

"It is not yet the middle of the night," Lydia countered. "Only quarter past twelve. I had to wait until I was certain everyone was asleep before coming to tell you."

"Tell me what?" Elizabeth asked, annoyance flickering at Lydia's lack of forthrightness. Usually, Lydia was too frank.

"When you all returned from your call earlier, and you, Jane, and Mary went out to garden or to ride or *whatever* it is you all do all the time." Lydia stopped speaking to glare balefully at Elizabeth.

It troubled her that Lydia seemed not to believe in any of those activities, but Elizabeth met her gaze, waiting her out.

"Mama was in a mood," Lydia finally continued. "She ordered Kitty to go paint, and she sent me and Thomas and Matthew to our schoolroom, even though it was Nanny Hill's naptime."

Elizabeth nodded. She, too, had noted their mother's sour mood. A mood she couldn't quite believe rose only from the knowledge that another eligible miss, one with connections to the peerage, would soon be among them.

"Well," Lydia went on, "I snuck down to get us some tarts because, really, they only go to waste if we have no callers, and I saw Mama in Papa Arthur's study."

"She went in there?" Elizabeth asked sharply. Their mother had ordered the room closed after their stepfather died, and nothing touched. She said it would all wait for Thomas. Four times a year, maids went in and dusted, but aside from that, the door was never opened.

Lydia nodded. "I don't think the door was open when I went down, but when I came back, it wasn't all the way closed and there was light in there, so I peeked and Mama was there. She'd opened the curtains, I guess so she could see, and she stood beside a drawer reading a letter, her face all white. Then she shoved the letter and something small back into the drawer and slammed it closed, and I hurried away on account of I didn't want her to see me with so many tarts."

Elizabeth nodded, although she suspected the spying would aggravate her mother more than the tarts. "It is odd for Mama to go in there, but I cannot see why that means that we must."

"Because the drawer was on the side of the desk, where there is no drawer." Lydia regarded Elizabeth with wide eyes. "It's a secret drawer."

Elizabeth's pulse ticked up but she shook her head. "Surely not." She and Mary had, one night, sneaked into Papa Arthur's study and searched his desk and shelves for anything of use. They hadn't found any secret drawers.

But they hadn't looked on the side of his desk. They'd looked on the front, and inside the non-secret drawers, and underneath. Not on the sides.

"I am telling you, it was a secret drawer and something inside upset Mama, and we need to know what, because she looked..." Lydia balanced, lowering her voice to whisper, "She looked so scared, Elizabeth."

That clinched it. Elizabeth would get Mary and go search the desk again, but first she must put Lydia at ease and send her to bed. "Even if she was, which she likely was not, I fail to see what we can do about it."

"Whatever it is that you and Jane and Mary do about things," Lydia replied with a shrug.

Elizabeth stared at her, uncertain what to say to that. Did Lydia know something? Had she somehow figured out that they were the Boney Bandits? "What are you saying?"

Lydia tipped up her chin, defiant. "Only that you spend a lot of time gardening and yet I never find you in the garden."

Elizabeth frowned. This was getting out of hand.

"I am going down there to read that letter," Lydia said firmly. "Even if I need a hammer to get that secret drawer open."

Believing her, Elizabeth came to her feet. "We had best get Mary."

"Mary? Truly?" Lydia's eyes shone. "And I can come, too? You won't shuffle me off or lie to me?"

The hope bright in her little sister's eyes, suffusing her voice and mien, cut into Elizabeth's heart. Lydia was a very social creature. It hurt her to be denied sisterly bonds, and the affection of a mother who would never forgive her for being the babe who sent Papa Thomas to die. Or, perhaps worse, for being born a girl, when a boy would have saved them from being cast out of Longbourn.

Impulsively, Elizabeth placed a hand on Lydia's shoulder. She met her little sister's gaze, still a bit startled at how far up she needed to look to do so, these days. "We will not shuffle you off or lie to you. You are coming with us, but you must be quiet."

Donning her dressing gown, Elizabeth led the way from her room on silent feet. Outside of Mary's door, she rapped out five soft knocks, the cadence alerting Mary to who stood without. By Lydia's interested gaze, she noted the signal.

The door opened to reveal Mary, fully clothed but with her hair freed from the usual, deliberately severe chignon she usually wore. She took in Lydia standing beside Elizabeth and raised an eyebrow.

"Lydia has something to tell us," Elizabeth said softly. "May we come in?"

Mary nodded and retreated into the room. Elizabeth didn't miss how her sister casually dropped a shawl over the content of her writing desk before turning to face them. "What is so important at half past twelve in the morning?"

Lydia drew back her shoulders. "I saw Mama read a letter that she hid in a secret drawer in Papa Arthur's desk, and she looked terrified, and I mean to go down and find out what the letter says, no matter what."

Mary turned a questioning look on Elizabeth.

"Lydia thought she might employ a hammer," Elizabeth said, trying to fight a smile.

"I see." Mary studied their younger sister.

Lydia maintained her pose of defiance.

Finally, Mary shrugged. "I daresay a hammer will not be required." She turned back to her writing desk, slipped open a drawer, and extracted a small bundle of tools, which disappeared immediately into her skirt pocket. Turning back, she said, "Come along," and set out across the room.

Lydia let out the breath she'd been holding, grinned at Elizabeth, then followed.

They made their way down the wide, solid staircase, staying to the inner edge where they were least likely to encounter any creaks. Before each turn in the hallways below, Mary held up a hand, halting them while she listened. Mrs. Oakwood kept a candle burning in every corridor, and every few hours footmen patrolled the halls, but Mary knew their routine, and they encountered no one. For her part, Lydia seemed to realize not to talk, and her feet, while pattering on the floors like drumsticks on Elizabeth's nerves, did not in truth make that great of a sound. Still, Elizabeth vowed to take the time to educate her younger sister on how to move with greater stealth.

When they reached Papa Arthur's study, Mary carefully tried the door, only to find it locked. Lydia let out a huff, opening her mouth, but Elizabeth touched Lydia's sleeve to capture her attention. When her little sister looked, Elizabeth put a finger to her lips to indicate silence.

Mary slipped her tools from her skirt pocket. The door yielded to her in moments. The locks commonly used in houses offered little trouble to Mary, and she'd picked this one before.

Lydia watched Mary return her lockpicks to her pocket, their little sister's eyes round with interest and surprise. Ignoring her, Mary slipped into the room. Elizabeth gestured for Lydia to follow, then took a final look up and down the corridor before joining her sisters and closing them all in.

Mary turned to Lydia, her face ghostly by the light of their single candle. "Which side?"

"Here," Lydia whispered back. She went to the right side of the desk to stare at the inlaid wood. "The drawer was open here."

Elizabeth and Mary joined her, and Mary crouched down to study the side of the desk. After a moment, she ran her hand over the smooth inlay, frowning, then along the underside of that end of the desk. Elizabeth resisted the urge to start pushing and prodding the wood, giving Mary time.

Standing, Mary reached both arms out. She pressed a decorative carved floret on the front corner, and another on the back, hardly able to reach both sides of the large desk at once.

A drawer popped out.

Lydia gasped, then covered her mouth, her expression apologetic.

With care, Mary extracted a folded letter with a cracked open seal, a ring, and three sealed missives. She held the ring near the candle to reveal a sculpted, stylized tree in a circle of diamonds. Entwined in the branches of the tree was the letter O, a large emerald set in the center. Setting it aside, she took up the first of the three unopened letters, the wax of the seal rendered dull by age and imprinted with the signet engraved into the ring.

The missive was addressed to Robert Arthur Matthew Oakwood, Earl of Pillory, at his estate in Nottinghamshire. The second sealed missive held the same name, but was addressed to the earl's home in London. Looking up from the letters, Elizabeth met Mary's gaze. Her sister appeared as confused by them as Elizabeth felt.

Mary took up the third and final missive, this one very thick. The flickering candlelight revealed not another letter for the earl, but rather, *To My Sons, Thomas and Matthew Oakwood*, with the additional instruction penned under their brothers' names of, '*To be delivered on Thomas's twenty-first birthday.*'

Elizabeth swallowed. To have left these, Papa Arthur must have feared he would die.

But why had their mother not sent the first two, and why had their stepfather left letters for an earl...one who shared Papa Arthur's surname?

Mary held the unopened letters for a long moment, finally shook her head, and returned them and the ring to where they had rested in the drawer.

Finally, she moved her attention to the opened letter. Though the paper was heavy, the folds were worn through in places, as if the missive had been opened and read many times. The ink was faded, no longer a stark black. On the outside was written, 'Francine Oakwood,' giving Elizabeth a pang of guilt as Mary held the thick paper up for them to read. Not so much guilt, however, that Elizabeth didn't lean in along with her sisters.

My Dearest Fanny,

You cannot know the sorrow I feel in writing this, for the only way you will know of the secret drawer in my desk is if your brother Phillips informs you, and he will do so only upon my demise. For whatever reason I have done so, I apologize for leaving you.

If the reason is my upcoming confrontation with Collins, I doubly apologize. I would not have accepted the man's plea to stand in for his son had I any thought he could vanquish me on a field of honor. Even though your reading this points to that being the case, I still fail to comprehend how Collins could best me.

And poor, sweet Jane. If I should fall defending her honor, she will bear that burden to the depths of her soul, I fear. You must be gentle with her, Fanny. She is a delicate girl.

Elizabeth pressed her lips firmly together, fighting back fresh sorrow over the loss of Papa Arthur, and fresh annoyance with her mother's treatment of Jane.

But perhaps it is far later and we have had many happy years, even decades, and I have simply had no cause to rewrite this letter. I shall hope for that, and hope that you will not be too dismayed by what I must herein impart to you.

You are familiar with my reluctance to speak of my relations. You are not familiar with the origin of that reluctance. You should know, and must fully believe, that my family is horribly corrupt and evil. I, who have served King and Country in battle for years, do not employ these words lightly, so permit me to explain.

I am the third son of the Earl of Pillory and, at the time of this writing, his heir, Viscount Scathelock. Yes, my love, you are a viscountess. Lady Francine Oakwood, Viscountess Scathelock, but you must never employ that title. In fact, you must mention this to no one.

Elizabeth snapped her mouth closed, uncertain when her jaw had dropped open. She rubbed her eyes, then reread her stepfather's words in the flickering candlelight.

Their meaning did not change.

Beside her, Lydia, who did not apply herself to learning to read as well as she ought, let out a gasp. Ignoring that, Elizabeth returned to reading.

Our family has a deep history of villainy. We are unapologetic liars and murderers. The Oakwoods, along with the Hargreaves and several other branches of the family now extinguished at the hands of their relations, have long settled the ascension of each new Earl of Pillory through the most devious and vicious means possible. Both of my older brothers have already succumbed, with their murders hidden and hushed as always. I do not want myself, or you, or our sons, to follow.

"Hargreaves," Mary murmured, exchanging a worried look with Elizabeth before returning to reading.

Therefore, I have hidden my heritage. I have caused fake documents to be made, indicating that I am but a distant relation with no hope of gaining the earldom, who happens to share the name General Oakwood with the earl's third son. Mr. Phillips is in possession of these documents and has standing orders to supply them to anyone who comes to enquire after me. I will never make any attempt to claim my father's title. I am more than happy for the earldom to enter into Hargreaves hands and to let that nest of vipers murder one another and leave us be. I refuse to expose our sons to their villainy.

I tell you all this so that you can be on guard, my love. I will do my best to teach Thomas and Matthew to be good men, and how to defend themselves and to fight, as I've been teaching our three older girls and will teach Kitty and Lydia when the time comes, but the best way to keep Thomas and Matthew safe is to prevent my father from ever finding them.

For he searches still. I may be content to let the earldom pass from the Oakwood line, but my father plotted and murdered just as all his ancestors, and he longs for an Oakwood to take his place, rather than a Hargreaves. He will not give up hope of finding me alive and with issue. If he does, he will use his influence and power to wrest Thomas and Matthew away from you.

So I beg you, my love, keep this secret. Keep our children and yourself safe from my family, and if ever you hear the name Hargreaves, be on guard. Do not trust them. If possible, do not know them.

Please believe that I miss you, my love. Know that I am so sorry to leave the life we have built together. I wish you many wonderful years in our home and with our lovely sons and daughters, but I am counting the days until you join me. I will be waiting for you.

With all of my affection,

General Matthew Rodrik Arthur Oakwood, Viscount Scathelock, heir to the Earldom of Pillory

P.S. If the Hargreaves do somehow find you, and if the situation becomes too dire to bear, send the letters addressed to my father. If he doubts you, show him my ring. Do this only under great duress, for he will take Thomas and Matthew from you. – M.R.A.O.

Silence hung heavy in the study as Elizabeth finished reading. The candle's flame wavered, light and shadow dancing about the room. Slowly, Mary lowered the letter.

"I don't understand," Lydia whispered, but the fear in her voice told Elizabeth that she did.

"I cannot believe that Mama has known all this time that she is a viscountess and she has never once told anyone," Elizabeth said, as shocked by that as by the rest of the letter, all of which was far more dire than their mother's fickleness. None of which she felt able to dwell on yet.

Mary folded the letter with care, then replaced it in the secret drawer. That, she slid closed, her head cocked to the side until a faint click sounded. Dropping her hand from the side of the desk, she turned to Elizabeth with serious eyes. "This is not good. Not good at all."

All Elizabeth could reply was, "I know."

CHAPTER NINETEEN

A Point of Honor

Darcy sat before the rather plain, though imposing, desk in the study of Bingley's leased manor house, Hurst in a similar armchair beside him. They both waited for Bingley to voice his reason for asking them to join him there, away from the ladies. Across from them, Bingley drummed his fingers on the smooth wood of the desk, the dark green curtains behind him casting him in a somewhat sallow light as they filtered the weak autumnal sunlight.

"I have no notion what to do," he finally blurted.

"About?" Darcy asked. Though he suspected he knew the answer to that question, he felt it better to be certain before offering advice.

"About Miss Bennet. About Netherfield Park." Bingley shook his head. "About any of it." He slid a page across the desk. "I received a reply from Mr. Parkland. He's put an exorbitant sum forth as the price of the place. I appealed to his sense of justice, but he writes that Collins does his job well and makes everyone wealthy, and says that unless I do buy the place, what goes on locally is none of my concern."

"He is correct in that," Darcy admitted. As corrupt as he'd come to believe the local landholders and magistrate were, it truly was none of their concern.

"What is it you want to do?" Hurst asked.

"I want to court Miss Bennet without her being threatened, or me." Bingley shrugged. "That should not be so much to ask."

Darcy considered that for a moment. "Let us say that we believe Collins would harm her, or you, in some way, which I put forth for the sake of argument only, as I cannot quite credit that."

"I cannot take the risk that he'll hurt Miss Bennet in any way," Bingley interrupted.

Darcy nodded in acknowledgment of that. "Which is why we will move forward under the supposition that his threat is not hollow. Therefore, the safest thing to do is to end your suit. To, in fact, leave Hertfordshire altogether. For her sake, and your own. I will add, as well, that we have evidence in the form of the letter Miss Mary left that Miss Bennet sees that as the best solution as well."

Darcy knew his suggestion made sense, but he was uncertain he could abide by it even if Bingley accepted the idea. Leave the Bennet sisters, all of Meryton, to the machinations of Collins? This region was not Darcy's concern. None of the land or people here were his responsibility, but turning his back on them seemed wrong.

The muscles in Bingley's jaw rippled as he clenched his teeth. "Abandoning my suit of Miss Bennet is the one thing I will not do."

"You could elope with the girl," Hurst suggested. "Take her and run."

Darcy turned to him in shock.

Hurst shrugged. "It would solve a lot."

"It would sully her honor, and Bingley's," Darcy cast back. "And what of her sisters? Who would marry them then?"

"They are comely girls. Looking at Dovemark, they must have some sort of dowries." Hurst shrugged. "Someone will wed them."

Horrified by the notion, Darcy slanted a look at Bingley, worried he would see excitement for the idea.

Fortunately, Bingley was shaking his head. "We cannot leave. My sister has invited the Hargreaves here."

"And Lord Franklin is not the sort you want to make an enemy of," Hurst said. "Especially not if he remains heir to an earl. He is a vindictive, petty man who would hold a rescinded invitation against you."

"That is a consideration, to be certain," Bingley acknowledged. "Of more concern to me, now that I've had time to think on the matter, are your impressions of the man." His glance included both Darcy and Hurst. "I fear we bring another Collins into the lives of the Bennets and Oakwoods. Though I have not met Lord Franklin, I feel the need to protect them from him."

Hurst snorted. "Are you certain that is due to our impressions of the man? Not Caroline's suggestion that he will attempt to woo Miss Bennet?"

Bingley flushed.

"Rescind the invitation, return to London, and bear the brunt of Lord Franklin's ire." Darcy raised a hand when Bingley opened his mouth to protest. "I am not saying that you should remain away forever, but that you might give tempers here an opportunity to cool. We know that Mr. Collins has not pursued Miss Bennet for years. It is only your presence and the threat that you might purchase Netherfield Park that spurred him into pressing a suit now."

Bingley looked down at the hands he rested atop the desk, thoughtful.

"Sensible as your plan is, Darcy, it fails to address one issue," Hurst said. "Two, if you are feeling chivalrous."

"And those would be?" Darcy tried to keep annoyance from his voice.

Hurst held up a finger. "For one, Lord Franklin will come to Meryton regardless. He will not leave a potential usurper to his inheritance uninvestigated." Hurst held up a second finger. "For another, from what I have gleaned mingling with the locals over cards, the only way many of them survive under the harshness of the taxes here is through the generosity of the Boney Bandits." Hurst leveled a look at Darcy. "It is rumored that you are the impetus behind a militia arriving here to hunt them down. I have no notion what is to be done about that now, but we are responsible."

Darcy scowled. Hurst sounded like Miss Elizabeth.

Bingley turned to him in surprise. "Are you responsible, Darcy?"

Heat scorched the back of his neck but Darcy squared his shoulders. He'd done nothing wrong in attempting to rid a community of bandits. "I wrote to my cousin, Colonel Fitzwilliam, and asked that he use his influence to have a militia unit brought in, yes."

Worry filled Bingley's eyes. "That was not very well done of you."

"How was I to know they are local heroes?" Like Robin Hood.

An unusual sternness overtook Bingley's visage. "I believe that was made fairly clear to us on our first visit to Meryton."

Darcy looked away, annoyed to realize that Bingley was correct. The local populace had made no secret of their adulation for the two Frenchmen. Darcy had simply assumed that he knew what was best for their community. That he knew better than they did.

Realizing he clutched the arms of his chair tightly, he eased his grip.

"Regardless," Hurst said into the silence. "Done is done, and we seem no nearer to a plan."

Bingley sighed, deflating into misery. "We cannot leave without putting the Bennets and Oakwoods into possible danger. I cannot purchase this estate, even were I willing to come up with such an exorbitant sum, without putting them and possibly myself in danger."

"Then you must remain and, as Miss Mary requested, end your suit," Darcy concluded.

Bingley stared at his hands again, clearly miserable.

He raised his face, a smile breaking through. "No. I will go to Collins and swear not to purchase Netherfield Park. You said yourself that his pursuit of

Miss Bennet stems from a fear that I will take the estate. I will remove that fear. He will return to ignoring his cousins and I will be free to court Miss Bennet."

"What of chivalry and the local populace?" Hurst asked.

A wave of Bingley's hand brushed that aside. "We will come up with a solution. In the meantime, I will be free to renew my suit."

Taking in the joy on Bingley's face, Darcy hated to say what he must. "And if she has been amenable simply out of hope that you will take the estate and remove Mr. Collins as magistrate? What then?"

"She will not know of his oath to Collins," Hurst pointed out.

Bingley swallowed, his happiness dimming into determination. "She will know because I will tell her. In truth, it will solve another quandary, the impetus of her apparent affection."

"That is your chosen course?" Darcy asked.

Bingley nodded. "It is."

Something uncoiled in Darcy's chest. The desire not to depart, he realized. Not yet. He hadn't learned enough about Miss Elizabeth. Hadn't spent enough time with her.

Had not learned if she truly was the half-sister of a future earl. Because if she was, if he dared to permit thoughts on that possibility, then Miss Elizabeth Bennet was not a simple country miss with relations in trade. She was a worthy candidate for mistress of Pemberley.

And if she was not an earl's relation…would that truly make her so unsuitable?

Bingley came to his feet, startling Darcy from his thoughts and saying, "I am off to Meryton."

"Now?" Hurst asked.

Bingley gestured to the mantel clock. "It is the hour for making calls. The sooner I speak with Collins, the sooner I can renew my attentions."

Darcy rose. "I will accompany you, if I may?"

Bingley nodded and turned to Hurst.

He shook his head, though he rose as well. "Somehow, I do not find the company of the Bennet sisters as fascinating as the two of you seem to." He aimed a knowing look at Darcy.

Ignoring that, Darcy excused himself to retrieve his hat and coat, leaving Bingley to send for their mounts.

Bingley set a quick pace along the wide country lane that led from Netherfield Park into Meryton, and Darcy did not mind. Caught up in his friend's enthusiasm, he permitted his own to grow. They would soon be done with secrecy and machinations. They would be free to call on the Bennet sisters as much as they liked. He would come to know Miss Elizabeth better, to understand if she might be worthy of bearing the Darcy name.

Paying a lad at the inn to keep their mounts waiting, they crossed the street and entered the garish antechamber that Darcy had hoped never to again see. Ignoring Mr. Collins' horrendous taste in décor, they strode across the room to where Robert Collins sat behind his desk.

Regarding them with considerable worry, he blurted, "He is not here."

Bingley looked about, as if he could refute those words. "Not here? Will he be long?"

Robert looked about as well, his jerky, nervous movements sending stabs of alarm through Darcy. The younger Mr. Collins leaned across his desk. In a low voice, though they appeared to be alone, he said, "He received a letter from Mr. Parkland. It said that you were attempting to purchase Netherfield Park and that he had set a ridiculous sum, but that if you agreed to it, he would accept. My brother flew into a rage and left." Robert swallowed convulsively.

Dread pooling in his gut, Darcy asked, "Left and went where?"

The younger man winced. "T-to Dovemark. To, he said, to make Miss Bennet his."

Bingley was across the room and out the door so fast that Darcy stood for a moment, startled at the other man's speed.

"Do not worry, I am certain Miss Bennet will refu—"

Rallying, Darcy raced after his friend, Robert Collins' words breaking off behind him.

Bingley beat him to horse but, despite the fiendish pace his friend set, Darcy caught up to him on the roadway. Together, they galloped up the drive, not dismounting until they reached the front steps.

The door flew open to reveal the startled looking butler. As a footman hurried down the steps to collect their mounts, Bingley bounded up, Darcy on his heels.

"Mr. Bingley, Mr. Darcy," the butler exclaimed. "Is something amiss?"

"Where is Miss Bennet?" Bingley demanded.

"Ah, sir, that is not for me to say. If you would care for me to escort you to Mrs. Oakwood, I—"

"Is Mr. Collins here?" Darcy cut in.

"Mr. Collins?" The butler shook his head, confusion clear on his face. "The magistrate?"

"The same."

"Not that I am aware of, Mr. Darcy. If you have urgent need of him, may I suggest his office in Meryton?"

"He's around back," the footman said from where he now held the reins of both mounts. "Sarah saw him go around back a bit ago, and she told Cook, in case tea will be needed, and Cook tol—"

Bingley didn't wait to hear who the cook told, nor did Darcy. They were off running, circumnavigating a house that was, as Darcy had suspected, larger than the façade suggested. As they ran, memory of Miss Mary's mention of a spy came to him and Darcy realized that Collins knew precisely where to find Miss Bennet, and when she was most likely to be in the garden, virtually alone.

Vulnerable.

As they drew near the walled garden, Miss Elizabeth's voice reached them, saying, "…your hand off my sister, sir."

"I think not," Mr. Collins' voice sneered. "She has much too strong a right hook. I learned my lesson last time."

"Apparently you did not."

That was Miss Mary, Darcy realized, her voice distorted by anger.

"What do you plan to do with that?" Mr. Collins cried.

"Elizabeth, do not." Miss Bennet sounded strained but not alarmed.

"You see? Your sister does not want you to protect her from me."

Bingley burst into the garden, Darcy a step behind, to the sight of the backs of Mr. Collins and Miss Bennet, his hand clasped about her right arm, squeezing. Before them stood Miss Elizabeth and Miss Mary, the former brandishing a knife.

"I do not want her to harm you because you are such a petty, vindictive excuse for a man that if she so much as knicks you with that blade, I am certain you will see her hang," Miss Bennet snapped, her words dripping scorn.

"That is no way to speak of the man who will soon be your master in every way." Collins yanked Miss Bennet's arm, pulling her against him.

From nowhere Darcy could see, a knife appeared in Miss Mary's hand as well.

"Unhand her," Bingley yelled, barreling forward.

Collins whirled, releasing Miss Bennet. He sneered. "And just what do you think—"

Lowering his head, Bingley collided with Collins.

Miss Elizabeth and Miss Mary leaped out of the way, holding no knives that Darcy could see, causing him to question his earlier impression. Miss

Elizabeth caught Miss Bennet, pulling her away as Bingley and Collins crashed to the ground.

Darcy dived for Bingley, yanking him up even as he raised his fist to deliver a blow, trying to prevent his friend from going too far. If Collins challenged Bingley—

"What the devil?" Collins roared. He struggled to his feet, his face red except where yellow-stained teeth formed the slash of a snarl. His piggish eyes narrowed to gleaming slits. "How dare you? I will see you on the field of honor, sir."

Miss Bennet gasped, pulling free of her sister. "No. I forbid it."

Uncertainty overtaking anger on his face, Bingley turned to her, shrugging free of Darcy's grip.

"You will let a woman dictate to you?" Collins sneered. "I challenged you, Bingley. Meet me or be branded a coward."

"Dueling is against the law, as you well know," Darcy snapped.

"I believe I can convince the local magistrate to look the other way," Collins cast back, smug.

Miss Bennet stepped forward, nearer to Bingley. "Please do not duel him. No harm was done to me or to my honor."

Bingley shook his head. "He is a fiend and a cad."

"I am begging you not to." For all their softness, her words held intensity.

"Cowering behind a woman, Bingley?" Mr. Collins taunted. "And she is a woman. I should know. I have seen all of her. Every. Little. Inch."

Bingley surged forward, but Collins dodged back, stumbling into a flower bed. He tripped and caught himself on a tree, but the vile grin didn't leave his face.

"I accept," Bingley cried.

Miss Bennet, her face white, rushed up to him again. "He is lying. My honor has never been stained, and a duel has already been fought to prove his words untrue."

Bingley looked down at her, confused.

"Let us all take a moment to seek cooler heads," Darcy said firmly.

"Bingley already accepted." Mr. Collins sounded so smug, it was all Darcy could do not to strike him and evoke a second challenge. "He must meet me or be branded a coward, and give my fair cousin into my care."

Miss Bennet whirled to face him. Behind her, Miss Elizabeth and Miss Mary both moved forward, more menacing than Darcy would have thought two young misses could be. Miss Bennet held up a staying hand to them just as Darcy clamped one of his own on Bingley's shoulder. Attacking Collins again would only make matters worse.

Miss Bennet looked her cousin up and down, disdain pinching her features. "I will never wed you, under any circumstances. Better I die in shame, unmarried, than ever consent to your touch."

"And your sisters? How will they fare with the stain on your honor?" Collins asked, smirking.

"We will bear up perfectly well, thank you," Miss Elizabeth snapped.

Beside her, Miss Mary nodded.

"It matters not." Collins pushed away from the tree, then straightened his coat. "Mr. Bingley accepted. He will meet his fate on the field of honor." With slow, deliberate torment, he added, "Just as your father did."

Miss Bennet drew in a sharp breath, almost a sob. She whirled to face Bingley. "Do not do this."

"I must," Bingley said wretchedly. "I did accept. I am honor bound."

Desperation and fear shone in her eyes. "If you duel with him, I will not marry you either. Ever. You have nothing to win by going through with this."

Bingley stared at her, miserable.

"But he has his honor to lose," Collins called from where he still stood in the turned soil of the bed.

Miss Elizabeth turned to him. In a voice like ice, she said, "Leave."

He stared at her.

"Now." She raised an arm and pointed.

A shudder went through Collins. He tugged on his coat again in an obvious attempt to hide the involuntary motion, and plastered on an oily smile. "I have accomplished all I came here to do. My second will meet you soon, sir." Turning, grinding a heel into the dormant flower bed, he clomped off across the garden in the direction of the stable.

With a gesture to Miss Mary to remain, Miss Elizabeth set out after her cousin on silent feet.

Releasing Bingley's shoulder, Darcy followed. He didn't know how far she meant to follow Collins, but he would not trust the man alone with her.

Darcy needn't have worried, for she did not leave the garden, merely stood in the arched stone doorway and watched while Collins retrieved his horse. Darcy stood beside her, their shoulders not touching. Once Collins had hauled himself into the saddle and departed, Miss Elizabeth turned to him.

"You must dissuade Mr. Bingley from dueling."

Darcy shook his head. "I am not certain I can."

"If Mr. Bingley comes to harm on her behalf, it will destroy my sister."

They both looked down the walled garden to where Miss Bennet stood before Bingley, speaking with a passion much in evidence despite their inability to overhear her low words.

"There is little to be done now except to hope that Mr. Collins will retract his challenge," Darcy observed. If Bingley went to him with his promise never to purchase Netherfield Park, would that put an end to this? After all, Collins could not be certain he would win. He evidenced no athleticism.

"I do not believe my cousin will be dissuaded," Miss Elizabeth murmured. "His father was not, and from what I recall, they are very similar."

"Then he and Bingley will duel." Taking in the look of stubborn determination on his friend's face, recalling the insult Collins had flung at Miss Bennet, Darcy doubted anything could dissuade Bingley now. "I am afraid it is a point of honor."

Miss Elizabeth shook her head, her face full of worry.

Darcy could only second the sentiment. Miss Elizabeth took a step, as if she would return to the others, but Darcy halted her with, "You had a knife. I saw both you and Miss Mary with knives in hand."

Miss Elizabeth went completely still for a heartbeat, then turned back to him, her expression bland. "We often have knives with us in the garden."

"In the garden?" He repeated, baffled. They had not looked like tools. Nor had either miss held them as one would a gardening tool.

"Yes. I am certain if you ask your gardener, he will agree that knives can be very useful." With that, she pivoted away again, unhurried strides taking her back down the path.

Darcy stared after her. He wasn't entirely certain what he'd witnessed upon entering the garden, but he was sure that something strange had been about to happen. The question was what?

CHAPTER TWENTY

A Plot Against Justice

Elizabeth watched, Mary beside her, as Jane paced the cavern behind the stable the morning following Mr. Collins' challenge to Mr. Bingley. Pacing was usually Elizabeth's outlet, Jane being generally calm, but she bowed to her sister's greater need. For the time being, at least. With all that weighed on Elizabeth's mind, she was uncertain for how long she could remain still.

One of her worries was not Lydia, however. Mary, and Jane once they told her of their visit to Papa Arthur's study in the middle of the night, feared that Lydia would reveal the contents of the letter to others, but Elizabeth did not. She'd taken their youngest sister aside and told her that keeping the information in the letter a secret was a test. One that, if she passed, would prove she was ready to learn more secrets. Lydia longed more than anything to be included in what her older sisters did. She would keep any secret to win that right.

Halting before them, Jane wrung her hands. "We must prevent this duel."

"I fail to see how," Mary replied. "Mr. Bingley seems determined, and we can hardly reason with Mr. Collins."

Jane hugged her arms around her torso. "If they duel, something terrible will happen to Mr. Bingley. I know it will, and it will be my fault. Again."

"None of it was ever your fault," Elizabeth snapped, then winced. Her anger was at all the gentlemen who kept putting her sister into such untenable positions, not at Jane.

"We could kidnap him," Jane exclaimed.

Twin lines appeared on Mary's brow. "Mr. Bingley? When he did not arrive to duel, it would impugn his honor and suggest to everyone that you should wed our cousin."

"We will kidnap Mr. Collins, then," Jane cried, desperation in her voice.

Elizabeth cast a look over her shoulder at the secret door that led into the stable. With the rock façade that hid it, the door blocked sound well, but Jane was being excessively loud. Turning back, she asked, "And where would we put our vile cousin should we capture him? Keep in mind that an entire militia is stationed in Meryton and would be set to look for him."

"Maybe no one would tell them he was missing," Mary muttered.

Elizabeth shook her head, hating the hope that bloomed in Jane's eyes. "Someone would, and every inch of countryside would be scoured."

"Then we bring him here," Jane said.

Elizabeth exchanged a look with Mary. Jane was never this rash.

"We cannot bring him here." Mary spoke with quiet assurance. "Even Mr. Collins will be intelligent enough to realize he is in a cave, blindfolded or not, and these are the only hills in miles."

"There must be something that can be done," Jane cried. "I will not have another good man die for the sake of my virtue." She rushed over to them, reaching to take Mary's hands in hers. "Go to Cousin Robert. Beg him to put a stop to this."

Sorrow shimmered in Mary's eyes. "He has little sway over Mr. Collins."

"Please? We must do something, and while you are in Meryton, I will keep thinking. I will find a way to keep Mr. Bingley safe."

Mary looked to Elizabeth.

"If you are going to speak with a Collins, even a not-real Collins," she added hastily as Mary's eyes narrowed, "I am going with you."

Mary's face screwed with thought. After far longer than Elizabeth had expected her to take in answering, she said, "Very well. Elizabeth will accompany me to Meryton to see what we can discover. You remain here and think. Only promise us you will take no actions while we are away."

"I promise. Thank you." Jane pulled Mary into a quick hug.

"You must also promise that you will either remain in here and wait for us, or come with us to the house to remain there," Elizabeth added.

Jane turned to her, startled.

Hating to put the thought in Jane's mind, Elizabeth said, "I do not trust our cousin. He came here yesterday to find you, and it was only good fortune that Mary and I were with you." Elizabeth was uncertain what sort of fortune to label the arrival of Mr. Darcy and Mr. Bingley. She hoped not ill, but only time would tell.

Jane paled, nodding. "I will come with you into the house."

They went in and left Jane with their mother and Kitty who, despite having just finished breakfast, prattled on about her hope of afternoon callers in blissful ignorance. As they left the drawing room, Mrs. Oakwood called, "While you are in Meryton, ask if Mr. Lucas has ordered in any more bonbons."

"Yes, Mama," Elizabeth replied, hurrying down the hall before they could be called back for more requests. She and Mary secured their outerwear, the day quite cool, and were soon on the roadway to Meryton.

As they neared the village, one- and two-floor buildings rising up before them, Elizabeth ventured, "How will we orchestrate speaking with him? We can hardly enter via the door for fear of finding Mr. Collins within, and I doubt Cousin Robert is usually lurking in alleyways hoping to speak with you."

"I have a means of summoning him."

Elizabeth raised her eyebrows. "Like a djinn from a bottle? What means?"

Mary huffed, not liking her secrets delved into. "If you must know, there is a back stair leading up from the mews behind the magistrate's office. I climb up, sneak into the empty attic, and stamp on the floor above Cousin Robert's head."

"And for how long have the two of you had that worked out?" How often did her sister speak with Cousin Robert?

Mary shrugged.

Elizabeth knew that didn't mean her sister didn't know but rather that Mary would not tell her. When this trouble with Mr. Bingley was sorted, Elizabeth would have to speak with Mary about her relationship with Robert Collins.

They entered Meryton and Mary turned them from the main street to a smaller, narrower lane that ran behind the buildings at the center of the village. With an ease that spoke of great familiarity, she strode forward along a line of small, nondescript buildings. At no landmark Elizabeth could see, Mary turned into an alleyway that Mr. Darcy would have needed to navigate sideways, or else ruin the shoulders of his coat by scuffing them on the dingy walls.

Elizabeth's sister led the way forward with continued confidence, but came to a halt before the end of the alleyway, holding up a hand for silence. Elizabeth tried to peer around Mary in the narrow space, uncertain why they'd stopped.

Mary turned back, her whisper barely audible as she said, "Mr. Collins is behind the magistrate's office with Mr. Denny."

Surprise, anger, and a touch of fear sped through Elizabeth. "Can you tell why?" she whispered back.

Mary shifted slightly, presenting Elizabeth with the back of her brown curls as she studied what took place before her. "He gave Mr. Denny money."

Elizabeth waited, certain the two men were up to no good. Vibrating with the need to act.

"Collins is going back into his office," Mary breathed. She inched forward. "Mr. Denny is taking a different alleyway. He will come out on the street behind us."

Elizabeth had to know what the two plotted. Her every fiber cried foul. "You see what Cousin Robert knows. I will follow Denny. We will meet at Lucas's."

Mary looked back at her, assessing, then nodded. "Take care. He will be on the street by now." With that, she slipped out of the alleyway into the mews behind the magistrate's office.

Turning back, Elizabeth hurried back the way they'd come. It felt odd to be in Meryton alone. Not safe, as she generally felt when walking the hills around their home. As she stepped out into the street, she was uncertain if her unease came from a lack of female companions, or the nature of her mission.

She looked up the narrow roadway, then down. No red coat met her gaze and irritation filled her. Had she failed so quickly?

Then she spotted Mr. Denny's profile as he turned onto a cross street ahead. He did not wear red, but a drab green coat. Effecting as casual a manner as she could, Elizabeth started down the street.

She rounded the corner in time to see him turn onto the main street, in the direction of both the magistrate's office and the inn. Following as quickly as she dared, not wishing to draw undue attention, Elizabeth hurried after him. She came out onto Meryton's main street, her gaze seeking Mr. Denny among the people going about their day.

There, by the inn, a green coat caught her eye as the man wearing it went around the side, to the innyard. Elizabeth rushed down the street, her strides long and her face carefully pleasant, and prayed she would not encounter anyone she knew.

She reached the innyard unhindered, but walked by the opening in the wall. It would be quite strange for her to go into the yard, where carriages and horses waited. The few times she'd entered the inn, in the company of other ladies, they had employed the front steps.

She did look into the yard, however, as she passed, trying to sort the jumble of travelers, carriages, and waiting mounts. Her gaze snapped to the steps of the side door, but she didn't spot Mr. Denny there.

Reaching the shop beyond, a tanner's, she peered in the window for a moment, then turned and passed by the open gate to the innyard again, moving more slowly. A miss with no press on her time, taking in the sights of Meryton. Undoubtedly while her relations were in a shop, since she ought not to be walking the streets alone. That was who Elizabeth sought to portray.

But no sight of Mr. Denny met her gaze.

Halting on the far side of the inn, Elizabeth pretended to stare into another shop window as she weighed her options. Should she enter the inn? To what end? Were Mr. Denny within, he would likely be dining or drinking. Learning which would tell her nothing of interest, and her presence would be noted by everyone inside.

Hooves clattered and Elizabeth slanted a look to take in the London stage leaving the innyard. It rolled along the street, coming nearer to where she pretended interest in the contents of the shop before her. She was about to turn in the direction of Lucas's Sundries, to give up on discovering any hint as to what Mr. Collins and Mr. Denny were collaborating about, when the reflection of the latter appeared in the window before her.

Mr. Denny was in the London coach.

Elizabeth tensed every muscle to keep from whirling to stare at him, letting the coach go by before she turned to watch its progress out of Meryton. Mr. Collins had given Mr. Denny money, and now Denny was off to London. What could it mean? Was their cousin sending away his spy, so Denny's actions couldn't be traced back to him? How much money would it take to convince an officer to abandon his post?

Elizabeth didn't know.

Hoping Mary had learned more, Elizabeth made her way down the street to Lucas's Sundries. She opened the door to the jangle of the bell, and two startled pairs of eyes. Those eyes were accompanied by hinged open jaws as her Uncle Phillips and Mr. Lucas gaped at her.

"Good afternoon," Elizabeth said uncertainly.

Uncle Phillips cleared his throat and hurried forward. "Elizabeth, dear, how, ah, how good to see you. If you will excuse me." He rushed past her, out into the street.

Elizabeth turned from watching his progress to take in Mayor Lucas's scowl. "Yes. Well, please excuse me as well, Miss Elizabeth. Business to attend to," he said, then left through the door that led into the storeroom. Behind the counter, Charlotte took a quick look through the doorway after him, then gestured for Elizabeth to approach.

"I seem to have cleared your shop," she said as she drew near the counter. She struggled to keep her voice light, but the behavior of her uncle and Charlotte's father had been exceedingly odd.

Charlotte glanced around again, though they were alone now, and leaned across the counter to say softly, "They were arguing quite vehemently. I could not hear much, but it had to do with your stepfather and the duel, and Mr. Collins."

Elizabeth frowned. "Not with Mr. Bingley and a duel and Mr. Collins?"

Charlotte shook her head. "That is how it began, but not what set them to whispering and arguing. At one point my father said, 'You must tell Mr. Bingley,' and Mr. Phillips replied, 'I never should have told you. No one can ever know,' and hushed him." Worry filled Charlotte's wide, clear eyes. "I have never seen either so angry as they were before you came in and halted their disagreement."

Elizabeth pursed her lips. Could Uncle Phillips have told Mayor Lucas the truth of Papa Arthur's heritage? But what would that have to do with Mr. Bingley dueling their cousin? "I take it, then, that everyone knows Mr. Collins challenged Mr. Bingley?" For once, Elizabeth was relieved that her mother felt herself above most of Meryton. Perhaps they could still keep Mrs. Oakwood from finding out about the duel. She was certain to torment Jane once she knew.

Charlotte nodded. "Mr. Collins was in the public room last night, telling everyone that Mr. Bingley came upon him kissing your sister and attacked him, unprovoked and despite Miss Bennet imploring him to leave Mr. Collins alone."

Elizabeth rubbed at her forehead. There would be no preventing a duel now.

"Then it is true?" Charlotte asked.

Dropping her arm, Elizabeth snapped, "Certainly not. How can you believe that Jane—"

"I meant, that there will be a duel," Charlotte cut in quickly. "No one believes that Miss Bennet kissed Mr. Collins."

Some of the tension that had tightened every muscle at the notion of anyone believing Mr. Collins' lies drained from Elizabeth. "Yes, there is to be a duel."

Charlotte shook her head. "Poor Miss Bennet. She must be beside herself with worry. I do hope she will marry soon."

"Marry?" Elizabeth repeated sharply. "Why?"

"She is too lovely to go on unwed. Until she is, this sort of thing will simply keep happening."

"It has happened twice in seven years," Elizabeth protested. "Both times instigated by Mr. Collins."

"And yet, how many times have duels been fought over you? Or me? Or even Miss Kitty with her five thousand pounds?"

Elizabeth stared at Charlotte. She had no answer to that.

Charlotte looked around, frowning. "Are you here alone?"

"Mary is here. She simply stopped to look in a shop window. I cannot imagine what is keeping her." Or at least, Elizabeth did not like to. Had Cousin Robert turned on her? Had Mr. Collins caught her sneaking about the magistrate's building? "Perhaps I should—"

The door opened, Mary coming in. Sighting them, she asked easily, "Have you learned anything about Mother's bonbons?"

That put them back on familiar ground, and soon Elizabeth and Mary had inquired about bonbons and bid Charlotte farewell. They set out from Meryton with the assurance that more of Mrs. Oakwood's favorite confections had already been ordered.

Elizabeth waited until they were alone on the roadway to tell Mary all she had learned, both of Mr. Denny's destination and the odd argument between their uncle and Mr. Lucas. Mary took in the news without comment, which didn't surprise Elizabeth. Her sister liked to mull over information before forming an opinion.

"And you?" Elizabeth asked. "Did Cousin Robert know anything about what Collins was paying Denny to do?"

Mary shook her head. "He knows only that Mr. Collins has asked Denny to retrieve something from London. Something that costs a great deal."

"But not what?" Elizabeth pursed her lips. It must have to do with the duel, but what could it be? A very fine set of pistols? Someone to stand in for him, as his father had? But what justification could he have for that? He was not a lad of eighteen any longer, but a man grown.

"No, not what," Mary confirmed. "Mr. Collins ordered Robert to secure the funds, but would provide no explanation as to why they were needed."

Elizabeth darted a look at her sister, assessing. "Would he have told you if he did know?"

"Yes." Mary's voice rang with certainty.

Elizabeth definitely needed to speak to Mary about this affinity for Robert Collins, but not until they figured out what Uncle Phillips was hiding from them, and what to do about the upcoming duel.

CHAPTER TWENTY-ONE

A Meeting of Seconds

Darcy left his mount with one of the lads outside the inn and strode up the wide front steps. He entered to the sight of an empty desk and the sound of murmurs as people in the public room to his left caught sight of him through the open doorway. Ignoring them, he rang the bell to summon the innkeeper.

The man came out of the public room wiping his hands on his apron and hurried to take up his position. "Mr. Darcy, sir, how may I assist you this afternoon?"

"I require the use of one of your private rooms."

"Certainly, sir. For...?"

"Privacy."

"Yes. Certainly," the innkeeper repeated. "If you would care to wait, I will have the room made ready." He gestured to the public room.

"I would not care to wait. I will endure an unlit fire."

The man nodded, his expression carefully casting no judgment. "This way. I will show you back and then send someone in."

The innkeeper turned to lead the way down the hall, but not before Darcy took in the knowing glint in his eyes. That, coupled with the hushed rumble from the public room, told him that word of the duel had already spread. He shook his head, wondering how. Certainly, the Bennet sisters would not have told anyone, and he and Bingley had been careful not to speak of Mr. Collins' challenge in the presence of others.

Darcy was shown into the same room he and Bingley had breakfasted in their first morning in Meryton. The fire, while laid, was indeed unlit, casting the room into chill darkness.

"I will send someone to light the fire immediately," the innkeeper reiterated. "Would you care to have anything brought while you wait?"

"No," Darcy said flatly. Taking in the way the innkeeper deflated, he added, "For your trouble," and extracted a banknote from his wallet. "And when Mr. Robert Collins arrives, please show him back and get him anything he requires."

The sight of the note instantly reinvigorated the man. He took it, bowing. "Thank you, Mr. Darcy. I will see that Mr. Collins is shown in at once."

"Mr. Robert Collins," Darcy reiterated. For all he'd urged restraint in Bingley, for all his disapproval of dueling, Darcy didn't know if he could be trusted not to turn one duel into two, were he forced to be in the presence of the odious magistrate. The man was an appalling example of a gentleman.

"Mr. Robert Collins," the innkeeper echoed with another bow, backing from the room.

He left the door open, presumably so that light from the sconce in the hall could enter, for without it the windowless space would be dark as a moonless night. In moments, a maid bearing embers entered and soon candles were lit and a fire crackled in the grate. After she departed, curtsying on her way out, Darcy took a seat at the table. He was almost a half hour early for the meeting he and Robert Collins had settled on, and so didn't expect the young man anytime soon.

Five minutes later, Robert Collins was shown in, likewise declining anything from the innkeeper. The man didn't seem to mind, Darcy's banknote still fresh in his pocket, and bowed himself out, closing them in. Collins doffed his hat, bowing.

Darcy rose, studying the younger Collins with fresh eyes, now that he'd been in the local region for long enough to hear the rumors of the man's heritage. Indeed, he looked nothing like his older brother. While that was no confirmation of the claims that he was no true Collins, Darcy could only take the lack of resemblance as a good sign.

Robert fidgeted with the hat he held, tapping it lightly against his leg. "Mr. Darcy. Thank you for agreeing to meet with me."

"As Mr. Bingley's second, I could hardly do otherwise."

"Can I hope that Mr. Bingley's temper has cooled and he wishes to beg off?" Robert blurted. "Only, it would be for the best, I believe, if this confrontation did not take place."

The man seemed exceptionally nervous, as if Darcy might decide to pummel him simply for being there. "I can see no way to persuade Bingley into bowing out. You do know what your brother said about Miss Bennet, do you not?"

Robert winced. "I, ah, no, I do not, but I know what he is saying all about the village and that is terrible enough."

Darcy's eyes narrowed. He shouldn't ask. Knowing would only anger him, and he required a cool head. The words leapt forth despite the reasonableness of his thoughts. "What is he saying?"

"I would rather not repeat such sland—" Robert broke off, apparently realizing he shouldn't call his brother's words 'slander' as he was the man's second. "I would rather not say."

And Darcy would truly rather not know, lest he be forced to challenge the magistrate as well. "It seems to me that everyone is aware that a duel is planned," he said, deliberately changing the topic.

"That is the rumor, yes." The young man before Darcy rapped his hat against his leg. "I am afraid Mr. Collins has not been circumspect."

Because he was a fool or because he wanted to make certain Bingley wouldn't back out? He'd certainly seemed intent on drawing a reaction from Bingley in the garden. Darcy could not help but be leery of such stratagems. "Because it appears that many people now know the source of the insult, the only way out of this is for your brother to withdraw his words and publicly apologize to Miss Bennet. Mr. Bingley will not be swayed from protecting her honor."

Robert was already shaking his head. "He will neither apologize nor withdraw his quest for satisfaction. He gave me this." He produced a folded page.

Taking it, Darcy found it contained the magistrate's official challenge. "Very well." Darcy folded the page and tucked it into his coat. "I imagine we should move on to discussing the details." He gestured to the other chair at the table, retaking his, and waited until Robert sat before continuing with, "Mr. Bingley requests pistols." Bingley was not an accomplished fencer. Collins might not be either, for all Darcy knew, but it was easy to see that he had the advantage of weight and reach on Bingley.

"Very well," Robert agreed. "Mr. Collins prefers pistols as well."

"As to the time, dawn tomorrow seems appropriate. There is no reason to drag this out."

Robert was shaking his head before Darcy finished speaking. "Mr. Collins requests five days to get his affairs in order. He has sent for something from London that he must see to, and it has not yet arrived."

"Five days?" During which the man would keep going about the village laying down insults to Miss Bennet? "I think not."

"He is the local magistrate. He says that putting his affairs in order takes longer than it does most men."

From another, Darcy might believe that. "What is this thing he has sent for from London?" London was not far. Darcy could only conclude that

Collins was either plotting or afraid.

Robert shrugged. "He has not confided in me, but I do know that he paid one of the officers to employ his leave time to retrieve whatever it is. He departed yesterday."

So, Collins had sent someone to London as soon as Bingley had accepted his challenge? Darcy's suspicions grew, though he could think of nothing from London, or elsewhere, that could aid a man in a duel. "Tomorrow at dawn," he said firmly.

"Two mornings hence?" Robert suggested tentatively.

Darcy studied the earnest young man across from him. "Very well. Two mornings hence."

Robert's shoulders dropped to a more natural angle. "Thank you. He won't be happy, but at least it is something."

"As to a location, I am open to your suggestions." Darcy held up a staying hand before Robert could speak. "But know that we do not want witnesses. This is to be a private matter." It was one thing for there to be rumors of a duel, even evidence in the way of an injury, and quite another to have a bevy of witnesses able to testify that the illegal act had taken place and to give details of the event.

"My brother suggested…that is, there is a valley. It is in Netherfield. It is where our father dueled General Oakwood. You and Mr. Bingley could walk there, in truth, although I do not see why you would. It is accessible by mount only from the northwest end, and by carriage not at all, though one can reach the head of the valley. Few know it is even there."

Darcy considered that. It sounded like the ideal location, except that Collins had suggested it. But then, he and Bingley did not know the lay of the land. They would be forced to rely on suggestions, and to whom else could they turn for one? Asking any of the locals for the best location to hold a duel would only result in half the village turning up to watch.

Finally, he said, "Show me."

"We will need our mounts."

Darcy's was summoned and Robert's sent for, and they thanked the innkeeper for his hospitality. With Darcy's banknote in his pocket and only a bit of firewood expended, the man seemed quite pleased with the transaction. Soon they were mounted and riding west out of Meryton.

To Darcy's surprise, Robert Collins led him up the selfsame slope he'd ridden up on his very first morning in Meryton. At the top, no fog waited. Only a fine view of Netherfield Park. Still, Darcy felt a disjointed sense of already having done everything he now did, as if walking through a waking dream. He scanned the hilltop, but no mysterious woman, who in his mind now wore Miss Elizabeth's face, waited.

"We must leave our mounts here and go on foot, to come at the valley from this direction."

Darcy turned, almost startled to hear Robert Collins speak. "Do you not fear they will be stolen?"

Robert blinked at him. "Stolen?"

Did no one care that there were bandits lurking somewhere in the vicinity? Shaking his head, Darcy dismounted.

They left their horses tethered to some scrubby bushes and continued along the hilltop. It didn't surprise Darcy that Robert led him to the steep cleft where his mist-woman had disappeared. Were he dreaming, that was precisely where this day would take him.

They descended into a shallow valley, trees thick to each side. The dell, for that was all it truly was, was neither deep nor long, the far end opening to a field, but was wide and relatively flat along the bottom. It would serve their purpose well.

"If you go out the end of the valley or through that copse," Robert gestured left, "You will find yourself in Netherfield Park's fields. If you go up the northeast slope, the forest is far more dense. Dovemark lands. General Oakwood did not convert much of his holding into fields."

Darcy walked about the dell, finding the footing good. "You say a carriage may be kept waiting at the far end, there?"

"There is a farm track that a skilled driver can easily manage."

Darcy nodded and turned his back on the open end of the valley to study the hill down which they'd come. The sun rose in the southeast at this time of year, which would give one combatant a slight advantage, but which one would be decided by the flip of a coin, so that couldn't be part of Collin's plan. At least, not if Darcy supplied the coin.

The trees gave them shelter. The land was private and removed from the village. It was, in fact, land Bingley currently leased. Darcy could see no reason not to agree to the location, except for a vague, lingering doubt. That doubt, however, overshadowed the entirety of this affair, and Darcy knew of no other location to propose.

He came full circle. "Very well. Two mornings hence, at dawn, in this valley. Coin toss, or a count?" He offered only those options, though he suspected Collins would attempt to insist that, as challenger and supposedly the wronged party, he held the right to shoot first.

"Mr. Collins prefers a count."

Again, doubt filled Darcy. Why would Collins forgo the right to take the first shot without even an argument? He looked about again, trying to ascertain why he felt they were being led astray, then turned back to Collins to say, "We will come ahorse. Aside from the four of us, I require that the local doctor be present nearby."

"That would be Mr. Jones, the apothecary in Meryton. We can bring him in the carriage."

"Then we are agreed." Grimness edged Darcy's tone. He could not shake the feeling that, despite being warranted, this duel was a treacherous undertaking.

They climbed back up the slope in silence, but when they reached their horses, Robert Collins turned to Darcy. "Is there any way you can persuade Mr. Bingley to forgo this?" Worry lined his features, adding gravity to his youthful countenance.

"I do not see a way." Darcy wished he did. Or, at least, that he saw a way that wouldn't end up with him or Bingley challenging Collins anyhow. The man was a cad.

"I hate to…that is, he is my brother, and has had the care of me since our father died. He employs me and treats me well enough, even though we both know the rumors about my parentage, so it pains me to speak this way, but I feel, in my bones, that a plot is afoot. I fear for Mr. Bingley."

Darcy did as well, but could see no way out. No world in which Bingley would permit what Mr. Collins had said about Miss Bennet to stand. Especially now that a challenge had been issued and accepted. "All duels are dangerous."

Glumly, Robert nodded. "Yes. Well, true enough." He turned to his horse.

"But I thank you for voicing your concern. It is honorable of you."

Robert turned back. "If I learn anything, anything at all that impugns my brother's honor and expunges Cousin Jane's, I will come to you." With that, he mounted.

Darcy considered that as they rode back down the narrow track and could only conclude that Robert Collins was a good man.

Where the trail into the hills met the roadway, Darcy turned for Meryton, receiving a look of inquiry from Robert Collins that he ignored. He had a second task to carry out on Bingley's behalf. Darcy did not quite know how he would go about it, but he must call on the Bennets and Oakwoods and persuade Miss Bennet to rescind her words. More than the prospect of a duel, the weight of her declaration that she would not wed Bingley if he carried through on the act weighed on him. Bingley wallowed in a misery that could only hinder him during the bout.

When they reached the center of the village, Robert drew up before the magistrate's office. Darcy halted as well, to give his farewell, but the words were curtailed by the office door opening and Miss Bennet, accompanied by a maid, stepping into the street.

She clutched a handkerchief and tears stood out against her white cheeks. Sighting them, she gasped, rapidly dabbing at her face, and attempted a smile.

Surprised as he was to find the miss with whom he must speak before him, Darcy still dismounted with alacrity, Robert on his heels. They both hurried forward, their trailing mounts shielding them from the rest of the street as they converged on Miss Bennet.

"Cousin Jane." Though worry colored his voice, Robert Collins bowed. "Whatever is the matter?"

She looked up at them with pink-rimmed eyes. "Oh, do not tell my sisters I was here. Please."

Robert looked to Darcy, who shook his head. She was not Darcy's cousin. He had no notion what the trouble was.

Robert peered past her at the closed door. "What did he do?" The question held a surprisingly hard edge.

Miss Bennet shook her head. "Nothing. Truly. He simply refused me."

Behind her, pinch-faced, the maid dropped her gaze to study the walkway at their feet.

"Refused you?" Darcy repeated.

Miss Bennet drew in a deep breath, applied her handkerchief a final time before stuffing it away, and drew back her shoulders. "I told him that I would accept his proposal if he would call off the duel."

Darcy gaped at her.

"Never," Robert said with considerable vehemence. "You cannot bind yourself to him."

She turned her now composed face to him. "I would rather that than see Mr. Bingley end up the way P-p-papa Arthur did, but Mr. Collins said that he would be rid of Mr. Bingley soon enough and would instead take Kitty's five thousand p-pounds." She looked away, her recently claimed composure cracking.

"Your cousin is correct." Darcy gestured to Robert Collins as he spoke, to make certain Miss Bennet knew he did not refer to the magistrate. "As much as I decry this duel, any dueling, it would kill Bingley more surely to have you marry Mr. Collins than any ball from a pistol can."

She closed her eyes, her misery so acute as to awake a like emotion in Darcy's chest. "I do not know what to do," she murmured. "I will not be able to bear it if Mr. Bingley is slain, especially over my honor."

Lowering his tone to match hers, Darcy could only reply, "There is nothing to be done."

"Mr. Darcy and I have inspected the location," Robert said hurriedly, his expression nearly as wretched as Miss Bennet's. "And I will examine the pistols ten times over. Everything will be fairly done."

Her gaze snapped to him. "Why would it not be?"

Robert blinked, startled. "I-I do not know. I simply thought to reassure you."

If anything, the worry in her eyes amplified.

"It is unlikely that Bingley will come to any great harm," Darcy said firmly, then gentled his voice to add, "But he is in a state of misery in which no man should go into danger."

Miss Bennet flinched, offering no prevarication but rather, "I am sorry for my hasty words. I was desperate to prevent a duel."

"Then I may tell Bingley that you rescind your declaration?"

She nodded. "I do. Please tender my apologies to Mr. Bingley. My words were spoken in desperation and hold no truth." Pink chased away some of her pallor.

"He will be pleased to hear that."

Robert Collins looked back and forth between them in confusion. "I imagine that I ought to return to my post," he said glumly.

Darcy turned to Miss Bennet. "Do you require an escort home?" Hope bubbled in him that he might still see Miss Elizabeth.

But Miss Bennet shook her head. "As I intimated, I do not wish my sisters, or my mother for that matter, to discover the offer I made today. They do not know I am out." She stood straighter and offered a watery smile to her maid. "Lucy is with me. We will be perfectly well returning to Dovemark, but I thank you, Mr. Darcy." She looked from him to her cousin, her gaze sharpening. "Is it tomorrow, then?"

Darcy did not need to ask what. He shook his head. "No."

"May I ask when?"

He exchanged a look with Robert Collins. Would Miss Bennet spread word about?

"Please," she said softly. "So that I may know when to expect news. It would be heartless to leave me in undue suspense."

"I ask that you keep the information from becoming generally known."

Darcy infused firmness into his words.

Miss Bennet dipped her head in acknowledgment.

Darcy's gaze slid past her, to her maid.

Lucy appeared surprised at being noticed, but nodded vigorously. "I won't tell a soul, sir."

"Lucy can be trusted," Miss Bennet added. "That is why I chose her to accompany me today."

The girl flushed, appearing pleased.

Darcy studied the two a moment longer. "Two dawns hence."

Sorrow filled Miss Bennet's features and she nodded again. "Very well. Thank you for telling me."

After a round of farewells, their impromptu meeting broke up. Miss Bennet and her maid carried on up the street. Robert Collins led his horse away, and Darcy turned for Netherfield. He did not urge any speed from his mount, happy for time to ponder what he'd learned. While it pleased him that he could reassure Bingley of Miss Bennet's affections, Darcy could not tamp down his growing fear that Collins plotted in some way. Despite his lack of evidence and Robert Collins' reassurance, Darcy did not believe that Bingley would be allotted a fair duel.

CHAPTER TWENTY-TWO

Evil is Afoot

Elizabeth studied Jane from the corner of her eye as they walked down the main street in Meryton, seeking their uncle's law office. Jane was keeping something from her. Elizabeth felt certain of that. What, she'd no idea, for what secret could Jane possibly have that she would not willingly share with her dearest sister?

"What is the matter?" Jane asked, though Elizabeth knew her sister had not so much as glanced at her.

Elizabeth snapped her gaze forward. "I beg your pardon?"

"Do not for a moment believe that I cannot feel you watching me, Elizabeth."

Elizabeth drew in a deep breath. For all Jane's general sweetness, her sister held not one ounce of weakness or give at her core. If Jane wanted to keep a secret, she would keep it. "I sought you yesterday afternoon. In the garden, and our cave. You were nowhere to be found and Robin was in his stall, yet somehow you discovered when Mr. Bingley and Mr. Collins will duel." Jane had informed Elizabeth and Mary. She had not volunteered who told her. Only that she'd promised to keep the information private.

Jane answered the question implicit in Elizabeth's statements with silence.

Elizabeth pressed with, "This morning when I asked Lucy if she knew where you'd been, she went pale, shook her head, and hurried away."

"There you have it, then."

"There I have what?" Elizabeth asked in mild exasperation.

"All the proof you require to ascertain that I have no intention of you knowing where I was."

A burst of laughter escaped Elizabeth at that. "I imagine I must be content with that, so long as you can assure me that you are well."

"Perfectly."

They reached the building occupied by their Aunt and Uncle Phillips, the upper living space and small garden the source of happy memories, but did not enter either. Instead, they went into their uncle's office, where his clerk, Mr. Smith, sat as sentry before Mr. Phillips' door.

Fortunately, a sentry amenable to them. As they approached, Mr. Smith rose to bow. "Miss Bennet, Miss Elizabeth, how may I assist you?"

"We hoped to speak with our uncle," Elizabeth answered promptly.

"May I ask regarding what?"

She exchanged a look with Jane, then uttered the not-quite-a-lie they'd agreed on. "My sister and I wish to inquire about our dowries."

That earned a knowing look from Smith. "Very well. I will check that he is available."

Smith disappeared through the door, then reappeared with alacrity, followed by their uncle.

"Jane, Elizabeth, what a pleasure," he said with such genuine happiness that a pang of remorse sped through Elizabeth. Uncle Phillps gestured to his office. "Do come in. Do you require anything? Smith will fetch it."

Elizabeth shook her head saying, "No thank you," and vowed that she would make more of an effort to visit the aunt and uncle who'd sheltered them in their time of need, no matter what Mama said.

Once they were inside and seated on the couches near the front of the room, the formality of Uncle Phillips' desk waiting beyond and the door closed behind them, Jane turned immediately to Mr. Phillips. Her expression earnest, she said, "I am so sorry, Uncle. We have misled you. We have an inquiry other than about our dowries."

"Although I would not mind knowing about them," Elizabeth added.

Uncle Phillips frowned. To Elizabeth, he said, "They are in order, the funds invested just as your stepfather required and awaiting your need of them." He then turned to Jane. "What do you mean, you have misled me?"

As intriguing as Uncle Phillips' answer was, because Elizabeth had been uncertain until that moment that they even had dowries, she took in how wretched Jane looked and answered for her. "We know that you and Mayor Lucas were arguing about the duel Papa Arthur fought, and we want to know why."

Color drained from their uncle's face.

Spurred by that confirmation that a dire secret waited, Elizabeth leaned forward.

Before she could speak, Jane said with soft earnestness, "Please tell us. I believe that I am in love with Mr. Bingley, and I cannot bear the notion of him ending up like Papa Arthur."

A shock went through Elizabeth to hear her sister say aloud what they all suspected.

Uncle Phillips pushed a hand through his hair, disarraying the thinning mass, but still didn't speak.

"Please?" Elizabeth studied his face, seeking anything useful. "We have a right to know what transpired that day."

He sighed, dropping his palms to his knees. "I have always vowed to tell Thomas once he is of age."

"We do not have eight years," Elizabeth countered. "We need to know now. They duel tomorrow."

"Tomorrow?" Uncle Phillips reiterated, even as Jane cast Elizabeth a quelling look.

Elizabeth shrugged. Jane had promised to keep the time of the duel from becoming public. Elizabeth had not.

"Perhaps it can be stopped," Uncle Phillips said eagerly. "We could inform Colonel Forster. Rouse the militia."

Jane turned to Elizabeth, hope in her eyes.

Elizabeth shook her head. "They will simply select a new day. Mr. Collins is intent on issuing insults to Jane, and Mr. Bingley will not forgo defending her honor."

Uncle Phillips' clamped his jaws together so hard that Elizabeth could hear his teeth meet, then opened his mouth to mutter, "I have heard some of his slander. Collins is a cad. Were I a younger man…" He trailed off, deflating, likely uncertain of the truth behind his boast.

"Our cousin is a cad," Elizabeth agreed. "Which is why you must tell us what took place."

"I cannot ascertain what good it will do you," their uncle protested, but the fight had left his voice.

"You must permit us to decide that," Jane said in her quiet, sure way.

As many a man's had, his will crumbled in the face of Jane's sweet calm. He drew in a deep breath, slapped his palms down on his knees, and blurted, "Collins did not shoot Arthur."

Elizabeth's mouth dropped open in surprise. "He did not?"

Uncle Phillips shook his head. "He hired a man to hide in the forest and take the shot if he missed."

Elizabeth stared at her uncle, horrified. "Mr. Collins paid someone to kill our father?"

"Who?" Jane asked, that single word choked.

"It matters not." When they opened their mouths to protest, Uncle

Phillips hurried on with, "A local farmer who is dead now. He was always a bad sort, and he took the money Mr. Collins' father paid him and drank himself to death with it."

Elizabeth sat back in her chair, trying to understand what her uncle was saying.

"And you?" Jane asked softly.

Uncle Phillips bowed his head. "You must understand, honor had been served, and justice. Collins was dead. The shadow of impropriety was lifted from you, Jane. It was…honor was served," he reiterated in the desperate voice of a man trying to convince himself.

"You did nothing." Jane said it flatly.

Uncle Phillips raised haunted eyes. "No one would have cared about the testimony of that old drunk, even if I could have brought him to tell the truth. It was my word to Robinson's, and he threatened to ruin me. Maybe if Arthur had woken up, or if Robinson had not been appointed magistrate…" He trailed off, shaking his head.

Elizabeth frowned. She didn't recall Mr. Robinson ever being magistrate. Only tax collector.

"And now, Collins holds it over me," Uncle Phillips continued, wretched. "Whenever I attempt to defy him, he swears that he will tell everyone that I stood by while his father had Arthur killed. He says he will say I was in on it, and that everyone will believe him."

"But was not Mr. Jones there?" Elizabeth asked, dredging up her memories of that day. Recollections she usually sought to keep from her thoughts. "He returned in the carriage with Papa Arthur. Surely, he would have vouched for the truth of your words."

"Mr. Jones waited in the carriage at the end of the valley in which they fought. He did not witness the duel. When Robinson summoned him, he found only the four of us, Collins already dead. I did blurt out the truth. I even pointed out that Arthur had obviously been shot from the wrong angle, but Robinson cast down my words as lies immediately." Uncle Phillips passed a hand over his face. "You must understand, it was all very shocking and chaotic. I am not a man bred for battle. I—I am afraid I faltered."

Jane studied their uncle with sorrowful eyes. "I see."

"Robinson took me aside while Jones worked on Arthur," Uncle Phillips continued. "He told me he was certain to be named magistrate with Collins gone, and that he would see me ruined if I attempted to disseminate the truth."

"Mr. Robinson was magistrate?" Elizabeth asked, still unable to recall him ever holding the post. Her mind whirling, anger mounting as she fought to reorder all she knew of what had happened seven years ago. "Mr. Robinson the tax collector?"

"Old Mr. Robinson, his father," Uncle Phillips clarified. "He held the position until your cousin William came of age. The Collins, Robinsons, and Gouldings have worked hard to keep Meryton under their thumbs."

"And to raise taxes, to bleed local businessmen and tenants dry while making landholders rich," Elizabeth snapped. "And all this time, you have known a key piece of information that could have—"

"Could have what?" Uncle Phillips cut in. "Seen them all turn on me? When I am the only one left to protect your family until Thomas is of age? I cannot risk their retribution."

Elizabeth clamped her mouth closed, exchanging a look with Jane. She had a good idea from whom Uncle Phillips meant to protect them, and the list did not include only local gentlemen. Now, however, was not the time to delve into the Hargreaves and the letter they'd found in Papa Arthur's desk.

Defiance bled from their uncle. He hung his head, murmuring, "The truth would not have brought Arthur back."

A harsh silence fell between them, only the crackle of the fire in the grate sounding in the stillness of that fact.

"Thank you for telling us," Jane finally said, softly. "And thank you for doing your best, and for looking out for us. Your decisions could not have been easy ones. To make, or to live with."

Elizabeth didn't allow any words to leave her lips, for they would not be so kind nor so forgiving as Jane's. The extraordinary thing about her sister was that Jane meant what she said. She had heard Uncle Phillips, been angry and disappointed, of that Elizabeth felt certain, and then forgiven him. Perhaps she'd imagined herself in his place, and come to understand his choices. Elizabeth did not know how her sister came by her grace, only that Jane possessed enough for the both of them.

"I am sorry," Uncle Phillips said wretchedly.

"You are doing the best you can," Jane assured him. "It is a difficult predicament."

Elizabeth imagined it was, but that did not excuse her uncle for not doing what was right. "You said you told no one, but Mayor Lucas knows."

Uncle Phillips nodded, already appearing somewhat recovered, likely due to Jane's kindness. "When I heard that Mr. Collins challenged Mr. Bingley, I went to Lucas for advice."

"You fear Mr. Collins will do the same as his father," Jane said on a gasp, her serenity shattered. "You believe he will pay someone to shoot Mr. Bingley."

"The fear haunts me," Uncle Phillips admitted.

"Mr. Bingley should be told," Elizabeth said firmly. "You must go to Netherfield Park immediately."

"If you do not, I will go and I will demand to speak with him," Jane said with quiet surety. "It will be a new stain on my reputation, to arrive there without Mama and insist on a private word, but I will do so."

Elizabeth turned to her sister in surprise. Not due to her determination, but to words that amounted to coercion.

As if reading her thoughts, Jane continued, "I do not mean that as a threat. I merely seek to inform you of what will take place if you refuse to speak with Mr. Bingley."

Uncle Phillips wilted. "You are correct, certainly. Mr. Bingley must know, and I will be the one to tell him. Lucas argued the same." He drew his shoulders back. "If the two of you can hear my sins and still look upon me kindly, forgive me, even, I imagine Mr. Bingley can as well."

Elizabeth forwent pointing out that only Jane had forgiven him. Uncle Phillips was under enough strain.

"Will you go now?" Jane asked.

"I will." He rose.

They bade their uncle farewell, Jane with more grace than Elizabeth could muster, and left him as he called for his horse before going to seek his cloak and hat.

Leading the way back out into the street, Elizabeth turned to Jane to voice her anger over what they'd learned, but halted her words as she took in Mr. Denny and a tall, fair-faced gentleman walking in their direction. Struck by the stranger's air, and mindful of Uncle Phillips' revelations, Elizabeth went still, assessing the newcomer.

Mr. Denny sighted them and adopted a pleasant smile, gesturing their way to his companion. Both men lengthened their strides, long legs carrying them quickly up the street.

Reaching them, Mr. Denny bowed. "Miss Bennet. Miss Elizabeth, what a happy coincidence. I have been telling my new acquaintance how lovely the ladies are hereabouts." He gestured to the other man. "May I have leave to introduce Mr. Wickham? He has returned with me from Town and, I am happy to say, has accepted a commission in our humble troop."

Along with her sister, Elizabeth offered a curtsy. For his part, this Mr. Wickham bowed with perfect grace. Studying him, Elizabeth took in a fine countenance, a good figure, and a very pleasing address. He appeared everything a gentleman should be, and suspicion roiled through her.

"Mr. Wickham, it is our pleasure to make your acquaintance." Jane spoke with her usual conviviality and yet, somehow, Elizabeth felt that her sister was as mistrustful of Mr. Wickham as she.

"And I yours, for Denny here neither exaggerated nor lied in his description of the beauties to be found here."

His smile was too easy. Too wide, Elizabeth decided.

"Are any of your other sisters about?" Mr. Denny asked. "I would like to further my point. Perhaps Miss Kitty is in a shop nearby?"

"I am afraid our sisters are at home," Elizabeth worked to keep her manner easy, her eyes as devoid of thought as many a young miss she'd observed gazing on a handsome gentleman.

"Sisters?" Mr. Wickham repeated. "How many fine Bennet ladies grace this region?"

"There are five of us," Jane said, smiling.

"But our youngest sister is not yet out," Elizabeth couldn't help adding, though she resisted the urge to pin Mr. Denny with her gaze as she spoke. Like as not he did not even recall that he'd flirted with, and cheated half pennies from, a girl still in the schoolroom.

"I am certain four of you are enough to enliven any occasion."

Mr. Wickham obviously thought himself charming, but his sugary words made Elizabeth queasy. Had he been summoned from London to make an attempt on Mr. Bingley's life? Did he know who they were?

Mr. Denny looked back down the street. "As pleasant as it is to see you both, I am afraid we must be going. We have an appointment."

"An appointment?" Jane repeated.

"One I would beg off if I could, in order to stroll the streets with two ladies as lovely as you." Mr. Wickham added another of his smiles to those words.

Apparently, he had no thought that they wouldn't care to stroll the streets with him, and did not realize that they stood on Meryton's lone street upon which one might stroll. Elizabeth decided she would rather take the opportunity to bid Mr. Wickham farewell than correct him.

Politely taking their leave, the two gentlemen carried on down the street. While it did not surprise Elizabeth to see them enter the magistrate's office, it did cause a cold ball of fear to coalesce in her gut. As one, she and Jane turned and set a quick pace out of Meryton.

Once they were alone on the lane leading to Dovemark, striding through cold November air, Jane said softly, "Unless we get word that Uncle Phillips has succeeded in dissuading Mr. Bingley, we will rise before dawn tomorrow and go to the hilltop overlooking Netherfield park. When Mr. Bingley leaves for the duel, we will follow him."

Elizabeth nodded. They had no other choice that she could see. If Mr. Bingley proved determined to face their despicable, treacherous cousin, Azile and Enaj would be there to keep him safe.

CHAPTER TWENTY-THREE

A Dire Warning

Darcy stared blankly at the book he held, unable to muster the focus required to read when Bingley's life might end on the morrow. At a table behind him, blissfully unaware of her brother's plight, Miss Bingley muttered about the lack of sophisticated ingredients available locally as she wrote and rewrote menus for the Hargreaves' stay. She had already exhorted the housekeeper, Mrs. Nichols, to begin preparations for making up a large quantity of white soup.

Seated on the sofa across from Darcy, Bingley made no effort at normalcy, staring with blank moodiness. Behind him, Hurst had drawn his wife into a game of cards. Mrs. Hurst's pleased exclamations each time she won were the only sound in the room other than Miss Bingley's muttering.

They'd been able to keep news of the duel from Bingley's sisters, who decried interactions with the townsfolk, but Hurst's evening games put him in possession of the information. Darcy deduced from the many worried looks Hurst cast at the back of Bingley's head and the man's unusually poor performance at cards that he, too, was worried to the point of distraction.

"A Mr. Phillips to see you, Mr. Bingley."

Bingley started, letting out an exclamation, a sentiment with which Darcy sympathized. He had been too wrapped up in his thoughts to hear the butler as well.

"Really, Charles, what sort of language is that for a drawing room?" Mrs. Hurst asked.

"Mr. Phillips? Is that not the local attorney?" Miss Bingley said from behind Darcy. "What could he want?"

Coming to his feet, Bingley cleared his throat. "Ah, likely something to do with my notion of buying this place." He turned to the butler. "Put him in the study, won't you?"

The man nodded and turned to retrace his steps.

"I still cannot believe that such a lovely creature as Miss Bennet is related to an attorney," Mrs. Hurst said into the silence that followed the butler's departure.

"Soon enough we will know if she has more suitable relations to balance that out, thanks to me," Miss Bingley replied, then returned to muttering about potatoes.

Bingley came to his feet, his movements jerky. "Darcy, care to join me?"

Relieved to be asked, to be doing anything other than pretending calm, Darcy nodded and stood.

"May I?" Hurst asked.

"Really, Steven," Mrs. Hurst said tartly. "Are you so disgruntled to be beaten by me that you will pretend interest in my brother's estate matters to escape? You are going nowhere until we finish this hand. I have my eye on a new bonnet that besting you will pay for admirably."

Hurst offered them a grimace and dropped his attention to his cards without protest, to Darcy's relief. He had suspicions about why Miss Bennet's uncle would come to see Bingley, and the last thing the tension that roiled through the house needed was for Mrs. Hurst and Miss Bingley to learn about the duel.

Darcy followed Bingley out and to the room that would hold Netherfield Park's books and ledgers, were the estate currently not overseen by a steward. Mr. Phillips awaited them there, his bow nearly as shaky as Bingley's and tension radiating from him. After greetings were exchanged, Darcy dropped onto one of the sofas at the front of the room along with Bingley. Mr. Phillips perched opposite them.

"First," he began, "I need to apologize for not coming sooner. I confess that my courage left me. It took a visit from my nieces to bring me around to do what is right."

Bingley leaned forward eagerly, his worries momentarily forgotten as he asked, "Miss Bennet?"

Mr. Phillips nodded. "And Elizabeth. They came to me for answers and I am afraid that, despite vows I made years ago, I was persuaded."

Darcy imagined that both misses could be quite persuasive when they chose.

Mr. Phillips fiddled with the knot on his rather limp cravat. "You see, what you must know, Mr. Bingley, is that you cannot duel Mr. Collins tomorrow. It is not safe."

Darcy's eyebrows rose. "That it is not safe to be shot at is not a revelation."

Bingley nodded his agreement.

"Let me begin again." Seeming unable to remain still, Mr. Phillips dropped his palms to scrub them on his trouser legs. "You must understand, I cannot have what I am about to confess become public knowledge."

"On my honor," Bingley vowed.

Darcy held up a staying hand, although his friend had already offered his word. "And you must understand that we cannot promise to keep a secret without knowing the implications of doing so. I will not be a party to anything criminal." Darcy kept his voice firm, though he could feel the knowledge of tomorrow's duel undermining his words, for what was a duel if not criminal?

Mr. Phillips studied him. "That...well, yes, that is a consideration. I am not..." He pressed his mouth closed, sucked in a deep breath, and met Darcy's gaze. "I will impart what my nieces enjoined me to impart and then you may decide."

"Thank you," Darcy replied, aware of the annoyed look Bingley cast his way.

Mr. Phillips took another deep breath, then said, "When General Oakwood dueled Mr. Collins Sr., he was not wounded by his opponent. Collins hired a man to hide on the hillside and shoot the general."

Darcy stared at Miss Elizabeth's uncle, horrified. "And this was permitted to stand?"

"It was my word against that of Collins' second," Mr. Phillips began in a pleading voice.

He went on like this for some time, excusing his cowardice and attempting to justify compromising his honor for the price of ensuring he was there to care for the Bennets and Oakwoods. Darcy heard him out but made no pretense of understanding. Phillips, an attorney no less, had permitted some now-deceased local farmer to murder General Oakwood in cold blood. Perhaps worse, he had not impugned Mr. Collins' name as he should. The man would never have been appointed magistrate were the truth known.

"So, you permitted Mr. Collins' father to escape justice for his cowardly, vile behavior, and now fear his son will take like action?" Darcy stated when Mr. Phillips stopped speaking.

Mr. Phillips winced, containing his reply to a single nod.

Darcy turned to Bingley. "He is correct. You cannot duel Collins tomorrow."

Bingley, who appeared to study his hands, did not look up for a long moment. Finally, he raised his face to reveal a blank look. "Miss Bennet urged you to come to me with this story?" he said at last.

Darcy narrowed his gaze. What was Bingley thinking?

"She did," Mr. Phillips said wretchedly.

"I do not believe you."

Mr. Phillips frowned. "On my honor, she all but coerced me into coming here to tell you the truth of what took place."

Shaking his head, Bingley said, "No. I mean, I do not believe that is what took place when General Oakwood dueled Mr. Collins' father."

Mr. Phillips blinked several times, clearly confused. "But, that is what happened."

"Miss Bennet swore never to accept an offer from me if I went through with this duel," Bingley said slowly. "When I accepted regardless, she went to Mr. Collins and offered to marry him in order to prevent it." He choked somewhat on those words, red rising up his neck.

Mr. Phillips gasped. "She did what?"

Darcy cast Bingley a glare. "If you will recall, Miss Bennet specifically requested that information not be shared with her relations." He should have left that part out of his tale of meeting Miss Bennet before the magistrate's office, keeping in only her declaration that she had not meant her words about refusing Bingley.

"You told her that you would not pass that information along to her family." Bingley shrugged. "You did not."

Darcy took little solace in that.

"She is going to marry that...that..." Mr. Phillips, his face molten, fumbled for a word.

"She is not," Darcy assured the attorney. "He refused her. He is determined for the duel to take place." To Bingley, Darcy added intently, "Which is surely a sign that what Mr. Phillips told you is the truth."

"I cannot see how it is. All I see is that Miss Bennet is willing to do anything to prevent this duel, even sacrifice her every happiness, because she so greatly fears that I will end as her stepfather did, and that she is so persuasive that she convinced her uncle to come here and lie to us." Bingley's expression gentled. "It is understandable of her. Even laudable, but her honor is at stake, and mine. She is too tender a soul to understand the importance of that. I will not leave her to the treatment to which she will be subjected if the stain of Collins' words is not wiped clean."

"I swear to you that what I have told you is the truth," Mr. Phillips said desperately.

"You could offer for Miss Bennet regardless," Darcy urged, adding his will to that of the attorney. "Marrying you would do much to clear her name."

"Not enough, and you know it." Bingley held up a staying hand before Darcy could say more, adding, "And can you truly tell me that you believe a secret such as Mr. Phillips imparted could have been kept all these years? In a community such as this?"

"But it was kept," Mr. Phillips cried. "I kept it."

"You have my apology, sir, but I simply do not credit your story."

Mr. Phillips stared at Bingley helplessly.

"At least let us take a score of men with us tomorrow," Darcy urged, his mind going to the shallow dell. A location Robert Collins had suggested at his brother's urging. "They can scour the hillsides."

"Bring twenty witnesses to a duel?" Bingley cast Darcy an incredulous look. "So that Collins has twenty potential witnesses if I wound him and he decides to cry foul?"

Darcy began to feel as helpless as Mr. Phillips looked.

"Go speak with my nieces," Mr. Phillips urged, sitting forward on the couch. "Speak with Jane. You will see that I am telling the truth."

"The truth of a tale she learned only today?" Bingley asked skeptically.

"But you do wish to speak with her, do you not?" Darcy asked, seeing the brilliance of Mr. Phillips' plan. Bingley was correct about one thing. Miss Bennet was quite persuasive. Yes, she had already tried to dissuade Bingley once but he'd been in a passion. Now, his head cool and his final afternoon before the duel waning, he would be more susceptible to her entreaties.

"I do wish to see her," Bingley admitted.

Darcy came to his feet. "Then let us see her." And Miss Elizabeth.

Mr. Phillips rose too, appearing relieved.

They saw Mr. Phillips off and sent for their mounts, and in no time were riding away from Netherfield Park. They took the main roadways, seeing no reason for stealth. It made little difference if Mr. Collins' spies spotted them on their way to Dovemark now.

When they reached the house, a footman came out to secure their mounts, his expression worried and closed. As they took the steps up to the front door, Darcy noted that the man made no attempt to lead their horses away.

Even before they knocked, wailing reached them. Muted though it was by walls and door, Darcy could make out little more than the sound of it, but it filled him with worry. Bingley, not appearing to hear, knocked eagerly.

The door cracked open to Dovemark's butler. "I am afraid the family is not at home."

The wails raced down the broad staircase, moans and shrieks pierced by, 'Not a duel,' and, 'Oh, Mr. Bingley. Oh, my poor Arthur.'

Darcy exchanged a look with Bingley and said, "Even so, we would like you to convey our desire to walk with Miss Bennet and Miss Elizabeth in the garden."

The man frowned. He almost certainly knew what was to take place come morning. He must sympathize with Bingley's desire to see Miss Bennet, if he possessed any heart.

"Who is at the door, Hector?" a bright voice asked.

The butler turned his head to say, "A Mr. Darcy and Mr. Bingley, asking to walk with Miss Bennet and Miss Elizabeth, miss."

"Oh." Miss Lydia's blonde head appeared in the cracked open doorway. "Give me a moment," she said.

The door closed, cutting off another bout of, 'Not a duel. A duel with a Collins! Oh, my poor Arthur.'

Darcy exchanged a look with Bingley, who shrugged. They went back down the steps to wait. Darcy stoutly ignored the man holding their horses. He would realize they were remaining soon enough.

Bingley pulled out his watch, checked the time, and shoved it back away.

A gust of November wind whipped by, causing Darcy to put a hand to his hat.

Bingley dipped two fingers into his pocket and pulled free his watch again. He checked the time and put it away.

This went on for perhaps five minutes. Darcy was fighting the urge to remove Bingley's watch from his person when the door opened and Miss Lydia and both of her brothers spilled out.

Leading them down the steps, Miss Lydia marched up to them. "Jane, Elizabeth and Mary are in the garden. I sent a maid to warn them you're coming. We'll show you the way." She smiled brightly, whirled away, and started down a path that led along the front of the house.

Warn them we are coming? Darcy mused as he and Bingley followed the two lads. An odd turn of phrase. Why would they require warning? For Miss Bennet to compose herself? Like as not, she was in a rather tearful state.

"You are going the long way," Thomas Oakwood called to his sister's back.

"I know how to get to the garden, Thomas."

Turning to his younger brother, Thomas groused, "She's going the long way."

Matthew Oakwood nodded.

"I told Thomas and Matthew that I could take you around to see them," Miss Lydia said loudly from where she led the way around to the side of the house.

"And I told Lydia that it would not be right for her to be alone with two gentlemen," Thomas stated.

"And I said, but we'll be outside and I am not even out, and Mr. Bingley is practically family."

A glance showed crimson staining Bingley's neck.

"But he is not family yet," Matthew said. "And if he dies tomorrow, he never will be." He cast a quick look over his shoulder. "Ah, my apologies."

Ahead of them, Miss Lydia tossed her curls. "Mr. Bingley loves Jane too much to die."

"Father loved Mother very much and he died," Thomas said quietly.

Where he walked beside Darcy, Bingley rubbed at the back of his neck, grimacing.

"But they were older," Miss Lydia countered, raising her voice rather than turning her head to be better heard. "That was boring old people love."

Enduring, lasting, accepting love, Darcy thought. The sort of love his parents had. What he dreamed of for himself. A love that could only grow where there was respect on both sides.

He respected Miss Elizabeth. Her wit. Her vivacity. Her surety. Why was he waiting until he knew if her half-brother was heir to an earl to court her? Did the precise nature of her relations truly matter?

He shook his head, sure that it did not. Wondering how he'd ever thought that it did.

Miss Lydia led them around the house and onto a path leading to the familiar sight of the walled garden. Darcy longed to hurry his pace, for Miss Elizabeth waited within, but he refrained from trampling her young relations out of eagerness to see her.

A giddiness built in his heart as they drew near the garden. He was decided. No matter what else took place here, he would find a moment to take Miss Elizabeth aside and state… He broke off that thought with a wince, recalling when he'd informed her that they would dance.

He would not state his intention of courting her. He would ask her permission to do so.

Later, when Mrs. Oakwood was in a better frame of mind, Darcy would beg a meeting with her and Master Thomas, but for today, he wanted to share the joy of his resolve with Miss Elizabeth. He looked forward to coming to know her better and, in the hopefully not too distant future, to entering into a union. His reservations over her relations dismissed, there existed no reason why they could not come to a happy agreement before Christmas.

CHAPTER TWENTY-FOUR

The Promise of a Courtship

Elizabeth didn't know what possessed Lydia to send a maid to warn them of Mr. Darcy and Mr. Bingley's arrival, but she would have to thank her little sister later. Fortunately, Mary took note of the girl in the stable calling for them, for Elizabeth and Jane had been too busy fencing to notice. They'd cleaned up as quickly and best they could, checked to be certain the maid had given up looking in the stable, and made their way to the garden.

Jane had never before been so fierce an opponent as she was today. Elizabeth knew her sister's desire to sink into a bout came from her anger and worry, and a few times Jane had been nearly savage enough in her attacks to warrant ending the match. But Elizabeth was the more proficient of the two, and had withstood her sister's fury. She would have endured worse to help Jane through her tumult.

Now, her face serene, Jane sat on a bench in the center of the garden, weaving a rough basket for transporting flowers and vegetables in the spring.

Elizabeth was not fooled for a moment by her sister's composure.

Mere minutes after they were settled into their task, Lydia's prattling voice reached them, followed moments later by her appearance through the southern gate as she led both of their brothers, Mr. Darcy, and Mr. Bingley into the garden. The group, nearly twice the number Elizabeth had expected, surprised her, but what surprised her more was the warm smile on Mr. Darcy's face as he met her gaze over the heads of her siblings. Struck by how engaging the expression made him, Elizabeth's breath caught. She smiled back, unable to resist such a delightful expression. Mary, seated on one of the benches that faced north, cast Elizabeth a questioning look, in answer to which she shook her head and schooled her features, for this would not be a joyous meeting.

"Weaving baskets again?" Lydia asked brightly, reaching them. "Are those the same ones on which you've been working? You haven't got very far." She smirked at Elizabeth, Thomas and Matthew coming to stand with her in the open center of the garden about which the benches stood.

"Sometimes we get to talking and forget to weave," Elizabeth replied blandly.

"I do not," Mary announced. She held up a completed basket for all to see.

Elizabeth struggled to hide her surprise, uncertain how Mary had found the time. Had she been weaving in the cave while Elizabeth and Jane fenced?

"Miss Bennet, Miss Elizabeth, Miss Mary," Mr. Bingley spoke their names in hurried greeting as he came to stand before Jane. He bowed. "Miss Bennet, may we walk?"

"I believe that is advisable," Jane said with a certain amount of firmness in her voice, rising.

Mr. Darcy bowed as well, doing so from the head of the path so as to include them all in the gesture. Even as Elizabeth took note of that careful courtesy, he straightened to ask, "Miss Elizabeth, if it would not be an imposition, would you care to join me? I am desirous of walking as well."

Intrigued, Elizabeth stood. "Certainly." She looked to Jane, but her sister was entirely focused on Mr. Bingley as he extended his arm and they started up the path in the direction of the stable.

"I suppose I get to just sit here and watch," Lydia groused as Elizabeth crossed to Mr. Darcy. Her expression already portraying boredom, Lydia plopped down on the bench Jane had vacated.

"You can finish Jane's basket," Mary said crisply.

Elizabeth glimpsed her youngest sister pulling a face, and Thomas and Matthew taking benches opposite one another, before Mr. Darcy turned her down the path up which they'd all come. She wondered if Mary would actually succeed in getting Lydia to weave.

But she wondered more what news Mr. Darcy brought that had him smiling so appealingly earlier. "Dare I hope you have come to report that the duel has been called off?" she asked as they meandered away from the others.

His expression firmed into disapproval. "No, you may not. Bingley is determined to avenge your sister's honor."

Elizabeth let out a sigh. "I had so hoped that news was the source of your happiness as you approached." She shook her head in annoyance. "Mr. Bingley will not heed our uncle's warning?"

"He is of the firm opinion that Miss Bennet concocted the story and used her charm to persuade your uncle to bring the tale to him."

"He accused Jane and Uncle Phillips of lying?" Elizabeth demanded, indignant.

"He accused Miss Bennet of being capable of going to any length to, as she must see it, spare him the fate that befell your stepfather, and your uncle of being unable to resist her undeniable charm."

"Which is a very pretty way of saying, 'lying.'"

Mr. Darcy cast her a quick, assessing look. "It is a polite and understanding rendition of Bingley's reasoning and, if true, can be viewed as a strong testament to your sister's regard."

"You maintain that by accusing Jane of lying, Mr. Bingley is acknowledging her affection for him?"

"If it pleases you to come to that conclusion, it is near enough to Bingley's own."

Elizabeth enjoyed this, this bantering with Mr. Darcy. She'd once thought him haughty beyond bearing, but had quickly realized the impression stemmed from a correctness of character that could only be applauded. He was, upon first acquaintance, quite reserved, but was it not better to be so, and to come slowly to true friendships, than to rush into relationships that may not have the common ground and respect to last?

She would miss this. If any ill befell Mr. Bingley tomorrow, not only would that be tragic in and of itself, but Mr. Darcy would undoubtedly depart Hertfordshire, and Elizabeth would miss him.

Realizing her silence had gone overlong, she mustered a weak smile. "I believe you and I have formed a good understanding of the situation, but I do not envy Mr. Bingley if that is what he is attempting to convey to Jane." If Mr. Bingley was under the impression that Jane's kindness equated to a lack of resolve, he was likely even now being set straight.

"Perhaps she will quibble less with his choice of words and instead agree to his sentiment."

"Is that what I do?" Elizabeth's smile became slightly more real. "Quibble?"

"You insist on correct and precise understanding. That is laudable."

It came to her that she could protest the implication that if her way was laudable, Jane's agreeableness perforce was not, but she did not in truth want to quibble, as Mr. Darcy chose to define her tendency to contrariness. She wanted to know the source of the engaging, breathtaking smile he'd directed at her upon entering the garden. "If not to impart the happy news that there will be no duel, how do you explain your pleasant demeanor when you arrived?"

He slanted a look at her. Their slow steps brought them to the end of the garden, the path and house visible through the arched stone gate. Withdrawing his arm, Mr. Darcy turned to face her, rather than stroll back up the path to the center, and Elizabeth's siblings. As she met his gaze, she was aware, from the corner of her eye, of her younger siblings chatting and, beyond them, Jane and Mr. Bingley speaking with far more rigidity of stance than either usually evidenced.

"The morning after we arrived in Meryton for the first time," Mr. Darcy said, his soft words claiming her attention, "I was directed to the hill overlooking Netherfield Park's manor house." Unlike his words, his eyes gleamed with intensity, searching hers. "The fog was some of the densest I've ever seen, and the house invisible, but what I did see..." His gaze raked her face.

Elizabeth stared back, recalling that morning well. She'd walked early, because of the fog. She enjoyed how it enveloped her. How it made the world feel unreal. Magical, and full of potential, as if, if she wished hard enough, when it cleared, everything might somehow be different. Papa Arthur alive, or the gentlemen of the region proper and good landholders, or even, perhaps, her father would be there, if only for an imagined, mystical moment.

Mr. Darcy's words the night of the assembly returned to her, bringing clarity. "You were there that morning, in the fog," she realized. Once, she'd thought she heard a horse, but the sound had echoed about the hills and she'd been unable to place the source. She'd hurried back then, down the cleft she used like a stairwell, into the shallow dell, and through the trees to the entrance into their cave that hid beneath Oakham Mount.

"I glimpsed a woman," Mr. Darcy said. "Not well enough to see her face. Hardly well enough to guess her height, but there was such a presence to her. Such grace to her movements. And then she vanished." He shook his head, bemused. "At times, I have doubted the reality of her. At others, I have been certain she was you. Regardless, when we met later that day before the magistrate's office, I felt such a keen sense of recognition. As if you and I were destined to meet."

"I did walk the hilltop that morning," Elizabeth said softly, but she doubted a glimpse of her in the fog was the source of Mr. Darcy's certainty that they'd met. She recalled how he'd looked at her that morning. How she'd feared him halfway to accusing her of being Azile. Mr. Darcy felt they had a connection, and they did, but not the one he so obviously lauded.

Guilt washed through her.

"Then it was you?" he asked eagerly. "You were the woman in the mist?"

His obvious pleasure was a knife, driving her guilt deeper. "To that I cannot swear. Only that I did walk the hilltops that morning." Relenting slightly, she added, "And I doubt any other did."

He leaned forward, his eyes more alive than she'd yet seen them. "Miss Elizabeth, I know this is not an auspicious time for such a question, but I would very much like to come to know you better. Is that something that would be amenable to you?"

Dryness filled Elizabeth's mouth, her mind whirling. It would indeed be amenable to her, but how could she let him court her on the premise that they had some sort of connection, a foretold future together, when she knew the truth behind his premonition?

More than that, until such time as Jane did marry, Elizabeth was Azile. A Boney Bandit.

She looked up the garden to where Jane and Mr. Bingley still spoke with an intensity evident even from afar. If, and Elizabeth prayed it would not be so, but if anything dire happened to Mr. Bingley tomorrow, the Boney Bandits' work would not be done. They were needed, and would be for so long as Mr. Collins and his lackeys held sway.

More than that, Mr. Darcy was not the sort to marry a woman who went about disguised as a highwayman, robbing people. Elizabeth had always assumed Jane would marry, and there would be no more Boney Bandits, and that, by the time she wed, this part of her life would be long in her past. Something she could consign there, and leave there, and never need to confess to her husband. After all, men did many things before they married, and it was her impression that their wives learned little of them.

But this was different. Her illicit deeds were fresh, and Mr. Darcy was an upright, honorable man. Nor was he Mr. Bingley, or she Jane. Elizabeth could picture her sister sweetly confessing all to Mr. Bingley, and him accepting her secrets and keeping them. She was not certain she would fare as well were she to offer the truth to Mr. Darcy, the gentleman who had used his connections to summon a militia to hunt for them.

"You have not answered me."

Elizabeth returned her gaze to his face to find that the joy had departed. He stood stiffly, his eyes dark. His emotions hidden away from her. He looked like nothing so much as a fine work of art. A statue carved of the coldest marble.

"As you said, it is an inauspicious time for such a question." She swallowed against the dryness in her throat, and the hard lump forming there. "If you would ask me again tomorrow afternoon? Please?"

Twin lines appeared on his brow. "The outcome of Bingley's duel will dictate your willingness to be courted by me?" He shook his head. "In what way?"

Elizabeth floundered, the misery she felt at crushing Mr. Darcy's happiness robbing her of her usual quickness of thought. "It is complicated to explain." Reaching out, seeking to reassure him, she rested her fingertips lightly on his sleeve. "Please, give me this time. That is all I ask. If all goes as we can wish tomorrow, my answer will be yes. Enthusiastically so."

Some of the stiffness eased from him. "I cannot guess at your reasons, but if one day is what you ask, I could not call my intentions constant and not be willing to grant it."

Relief rushed through her, dizzying. "Thank you."

Movement caught her eye and she looked to see Jane and Mr. Bingley coming back down the walk, nearing the center of the garden. Jane's hand rested on his arm, but they wore matching expressions of misery. Mr. Bingley raised his gaze, seeking Mr. Darcy.

"We should rejoin them," Mr. Darcy said quietly. He offered Elizabeth his arm.

They returned to the others, not speaking, but Elizabeth made every effort not to look as agonized as Jane. After all, what was putting Mr. Darcy off for a day compared to the worry of losing Mr. Bingley forever?

Farewells were swift, Mr. Bingley's mumbled, and the meaningful look Elizabeth leveled on Lydia fortunately had her gathering Thomas and Matthew to escort the gentlemen back to the front of the house.

Once they were gone, Mary turned to Elizabeth and Jane. "Well?"

Shrugging, Elizabeth turned to Jane as well.

Her expression miserable, she said, "He will not forgo the duel. He claims that the only way to do so and preserve my honor, and his, is to force Uncle Phillips to confess what happened to Papa Arthur, but that Mr. Collins and his allies will gainsay our uncle, and we will all be sued for slander."

Mary frowned. "He is likely right."

"I do not care if he is right." Jane dashed at her eyes. "I care if he is alive. It is not as if we need to remain here, after all. If we were to marry, we would never need return here again, so it cannot matter what people here think."

Sorrow so cutting it felt like anger slashed through Elizabeth. "You would leave us forever? Never return?"

Jane turned a beseeching look on her. "What else could we do?"

"But he did not agree." Mary's words were more a statement than a question.

Her shoulders haunching, Jane seemed to shrink with misery. "Mr. Bingley said the shame would follow us, and taint all of you."

"He is right."

"I know," Jane said wretchedly.

Elizabeth gave Mary a glare for her frankness, but also applauded it. She did not want Jane to go away forever. Nor, in truth, did she want the honor of her sisters stained. What would Mary, Kitty, and Lydia do if no one would take them to wife? A small, deplorable part of Elizabeth wondered if, as well, such a blight on their family name would deter Mr. Darcy.

She did not care to believe so, yet could not quite dispel the notion.

"Well then." Mary's crisp words pulled Elizabeth from her desperate swirl of thoughts. "We need a plan. We already know when the duel will be fought. Jane, did you learn where?"

Jane drew in a deep breath, pulled her shoulders back, raised her chin, and managed a semblance of her usual calm expression. "I did. He did not want to tell me, fearing that I will come watch, but I dragged it from him." She winced. "I did not enjoy doing so."

Mary waved that aside. "Where?"

"In the valley at the base of that cleft that cuts downward from the hilltop overlooking Netherfield Park's manor house."

Elizabeth's eyebrows shot up.

"Is that not where Papa Arthur and Mr. Collins' father dueled?" Mary asked.

A shock of dread went through Elizabeth. "Mr. Collins truly must harbor the same plan as his father."

Jane's face was white as she nodded. "We must stop whomever he has paid to shoot Mr. Bingley."

"It must be that fellow who returned from London with Mr. Denny." Elizabeth knew there was something too friendly about the man. What had his name been? Wickham? He'd worked overly hard to be likable and not one bit threatening.

"Enaj and Azile must stop him, you mean." Mary's words were quiet and she darted a look about, as if someone might have sneaked into the garden to listen. "We will rise well before dawn. You will take up position on the hillside, with a view of both sides of the valley. There is that flat area, you know the one? It has enough large rocks and trees to hide you. I will guard the cleft, to ensure your retreat."

"Should we not retreat through the passage under Oakham Mount?" Jane asked.

Elizabeth, most familiar with the terrain, shook her head. "We would need to descend to the valley floor. Better to come back up and over, and disappear into the forest on this side."

"What…" Jane appeared nearly guilty as she broke off. "What if we are wrong, and the duel is fair?"

Elizabeth shook her head. "What of it?"

"Do we interfere? Do we permit Mr. Collins to shoot Mr. Bingley?"

Elizabeth exchanged a look with Mary, then said, "We cannot shoot our cousin. You do know that?"

"Not to kill him," Jane said hurriedly. "But the Boney Bandits could interrupt. Or we could, well, shoot him in the leg."

"And if he dies from the wound?" Mary asked.

Jane looked down, abashed.

"I believe that if the duel is honorable, we must permit it to proceed," Elizabeth said softly.

Jane raised stricken eyes, and Elizabeth knew she was envisioning the worst.

Mary lightly touched Jane's arm. "Elizabeth is correct."

Jane nodded, the movement jerky.

"Enaj will need his Bakers," Mary continued, referring to Jane's rifles. "Both loaded and ready, in case deterring the assassin takes more than one shot."

"We had best go fully armed," Elizabeth said. "All three of us, even though you are not meant to become involved, Mary. You will need to don your black for once."

Mary grimaced, for she never liked to put on the black lawn shirt and trousers of a Boney Bandit, but she nodded.

They carried on like this for some time, deciding precisely what to bring and when to move, and by the time they left the garden, Elizabeth felt better. This would be the Boney Bandit's final mission, and their most important, and they would not fail. They would ensure that Mr. Collins did not murder Mr. Bingley, for Jane and for all of Meryton.

CHAPTER TWENTY-FIVE

The Duel

Darcy's valet, Patrick, woke him into the chill of pre-dawn. He stoked the fire to life as Darcy rushed through his ablutions, due to the cold rather than any need to hurry. He'd instructed Patrick to wake him with ample time to prepare.

Feeling it incumbent upon him as Bingley's second, Darcy looked over from where he shaved to where Patrick was setting out coffee and dry toast to ask, "Bingley is awake?"

"He is, sir, and if I may offer the information, his man is in quite a state. He is certain that Mr. Bingley will not return from this duel and he will be out a very good gentleman." Patrick met his gaze in the mirror and added, "None of us want to see any harm befall Mr. Bingley, sir."

"Bingley will be perfectly well," Darcy replied, though to reassure himself or Patrick, he did not know. He returned to shaving, taking extra care to keep his hand steady. Perhaps he should have permitted Patrick to assist him for once, as his valet repeatedly offered to do.

Once he was properly groomed and dressed, Darcy sat down to coffee and toast by candlelight, reflecting that while they'd managed to keep news of the duel from reaching Mrs. Hurst and Miss Bingley, the entire staff obviously knew. In truth, he'd wager all of the local populace did.

He didn't encounter Bingley until he reached the stable, where a groom bearing a lantern waited to accompany them to the mouth of the valley. Beneath his hat, Bingley's face was sheet-white, and the smile he greeted Darcy with faltered, but he appeared grimly determined as he took to the saddle.

They set out, the light from the groom's lantern illuminating snaking tendrils of fog as they started along the track that led between fields and trees. To the east, the sky lightened to a more cerulean blue, prophesying the sun. Watching wisps of vapor cling to his mount's legs, Darcy realized they were fortunate the weather had been so steadily cool. If a fog such as the one in which he'd first seen Elizabeth rose this morning, they would need to reschedule this entire ghastly affair, putting Bingley through another night of waiting.

Elizabeth. He dared to think of her that way now, and he knew it for daring indeed, for she had not agreed to accept his courtship. Nor declined to, which gave him hope. A thread, at least. One to which he could cling because he did not believe she simply sought to put him off kindly. He took her at her word that she required a day.

He had no other choice.

They reached the end of the valley in good time, the darkness of night having receded to cover less than half the sky. They took the lantern but left the groom and their mounts, proceeding on foot.

"This is the place, then?" Bingley said, turning in a slow circle. "This is where I may spend my final moments."

Darcy cast him a quick, assessing look. "These will not be your final moments."

Bingley dropped his voice to a whisper to ask, "What if Miss Bennet was telling the truth about the assassin?" His gaze darted about, but nothing could be discerned in the inky darkness beneath the trees that covered both sides of the valley and dotted the far steeper end where the lower ground abutted the hill.

Nor could Darcy make out the cleft down which he and Robert Collins had come the day they'd inspected the place, but he meant to keep much of his attention there. Were there an assassin, his most likely hiding place would be among the rocks and trees at the steep end of the valley, the cleft offering the quickest retreat.

"I will be on the lookout," he said by way of reassurance. "If I advise you to run for cover or duck, do not hesitate."

Bingley nodded but the glumness pervading his features didn't ease.

Color came slowly to the valley, chasing away the blues and grays of night as the sun inched up somewhere behind the line of low hills to their east. Bingley continued to pace, fidgeting with his watch as was his wont. For once, his incessant checking of the time didn't aggravate Darcy, who could not help but consider how much he would miss the aggravating habit if Bingley were gone.

A distant creak of springs alerted them and Darcy turned to glimpse Mr. Collins' garish cream and gold carriage inching past the mouth of the valley. A moment later, a figure stood at the head, William Collins by the bulk. He started into the valley. Before he reached them, Robert Collins also appeared, burdened with the pistol case. The younger Collins raised a hand in greeting, then hurried to join them in the center of the dell.

"Good, you are here," Mr. Collins said by way of greeting. "I feared we would need to wait. Punctuality is an admirable characteristic, even if you are punctual only to the sight of your demise."

Darcy stared at him. Was that his idea of intimidation? Why would Collins bring up the laudableness of punctuality when, if anything, he was late? Darcy shook his head.

"Yes, well." Bingley cleared his throat. "Let's get on with it."

Collins smirked. "In a hurry to die, Mr. Bingley?"

Robert Collins winced.

Bingley's face went red.

"There is no need to offer additional insults," Darcy said in a tone of command. "A challenge has been issued and accepted." He turned formally to Mr. Collins. "Are you willing to make your apologies, to Mr. Bingley and to Miss Bennet, and to publicly denounce the rumors you have been spreading so that we may forget this duel?"

A sneer formed on Collins' face as Darcy spoke. "I am not."

Darcy nodded to Robert Collins.

"Ah," the younger man stammered. "Um, Mr. Bingley, will you accept my brother's words as true and admit as much in public, whilst accepting the label of coward?"

Darcy appreciated Robert Collins' phrasing, for Bingley snapped to his full height, shoulders back and eyes bright as he said, "Certainly not."

"Then let us inspect the weapons," Darcy said.

Darcy drew Robert Collins over to a large, flat-topped rock he'd long since sighted for the purpose, and the younger man opened the case to reveal two walnut-handled, brass-inlaid dueling pistols. They appeared to be fine weapons but Darcy lifted the first free with care. He checked that it wasn't loaded and then began his inspection, starting with the barrel.

As he worked, he asked, "I assume Mr. Jones waits in your carriage?"

Robert nodded. "With a warming stone, a rug, and a book." He glanced over his shoulder to where Bingley had returned to pacing and where his older brother stood scowling and, in a low voice, added, "I sent your man for Forster. With any luck, no shots will be fired before he arrives to break this up."

Darcy tried to contain the surprise that ricocheted through him, aware that William Collins watched them. "Why?" He made a show of inspecting the hammer, pan, and frizzen, which all looked to be in order.

"I do not trust my brother. He has been too…gleeful this morning."

Darcy replaced the first pistol and took up the second. He appreciated Robert's candor, and his tactic, but would honor be satisfied? Certainly, Miss Bennet would declare it so. She did not want Bingley to duel at all.

"Well?" William Collins said loudly from where he waited in the center of the valley. "Are you going to spend all morning fondling those pistols, or are we going to duel?"

"I will load both, if that is acceptable, and give your brother his choice of weapons." Darcy spoke louder than he had been, to ensure the men behind them could hear.

Robert nodded.

Once the weapons were loaded and allocated, Darcy extracted a coin from his waistcoat pocket. "The winner has his choice of sides," he began.

Before he could ask for a call, Collins' arm swept out in a dismissive gesture. "No need. I will face into the sun." He offered another sneer. "I don't need an advantage to vanquish this pup."

Worry went through Darcy. Not at Collins' boast, but his confidence. "Very well. Back to back, then twenty paces." He gestured to Robert. "Mr. Collins will count off the paces, inquire as to the readiness of each of you in turn, and then count down to the first shot."

That earned him surprised looks from all three men, but Darcy needed to be free to study the surrounding trees and slopes. Something was amiss. Collins should not be so confident. His gaze went again to the steep closed end of the valley.

Was that a glint of metal?

Whirling back, Darcy grasped Robert Collins by the arm. "Count as slowly as you can," he ordered with low intensity, then released him.

Fortunately, William Collins had already turned his back in preparation for his strides away from the sun, but Bingley cast Darcy a questioning look. He gestured to the cleft leading out of the dell, took in Bingley's gulp and Robert's air of determination, and started up the valley.

Long, hurried strides carried Darcy quickly to the far end as Robert began his slow count to twenty.

Darcy raced up the cleft, halting about halfway, where he'd seen that telltale glint beside the narrow trail. Sure enough, an even smaller path branched off, easily missed were he not seeking it. He turned, peering between a tree trunk and a large, moss draped stone. He could see a low flat area beyond, and a black-clad, masked form as someone knelt before a large rock, peering through a spyglass. Beside the man rested two rifles and a rapier.

Plunging forward, Darcy pressed between the trunk and rock, and came out into the flat area to the point of a sword at his throat.

"And what have we here?" A familiar, mocking, French accented and artificially deep voice asked.

"Azile." Darcy spat the name like a curse.

From his position behind the rock, Enaj cast them a quick glance, then returned to his spyglass. Below, Robert Collins reached fifteen. Mr. Collins' grumbled complaint about the slow count echoed through the dell.

"How dare you?" Darcy snarled, livid. "You would gun a man down? For what? How much did Collins pay you? I will double it and stand aside to permit you to depart."

"You mistake us, monsieur," Azile replied. "We come to safeguard Monsieur Bingley."

"You expect me to believe that?"

"I see him," Enaj cried. "In the trees there, on the northeast slope."

"Nineteen," Robert Collins' voice said from below.

"See who?" Darcy demanded.

"Enaj, toss Monsieur Darcy the spyglass, if you will," Azile called.

Enaj's annoyance was clear even masked as he was, his thin mustache practically vibrating with agitation. With hardly a glance, he tossed the spyglass, arcing up into the air, and reached for a rifle.

"On my count of three," Robert called below.

Darcy caught the spyglass, and threw it at Azile's head. The moment the metal cylinder left his hand, he lunged for Enaj.

"One."

With enviable speed, Azile dodged the projectile, diving between Darcy and his fellow bandit, colliding with him. Light as Azile was, the way he spun, making their meeting a glancing blow for him, flung Darcy aside. He stumbled, almost toppling, and dropped to a knee to catch his balance.

"Two," Robert cried.

Shots echoed through the valley. Too many shots, one of them Enaj's, followed hard by another from below.

Azile, sword in hand, charged Darcy. Enaj reached for his second rifle as Darcy pushed off from the ground, lunging for the selfsame gun. Men's voices cried out below.

Enaj fired again. Darcy came to his feet with the Frenchman's rapier, the only weapon he'd succeeded in grasping, as Azile reached him. They met in a clash of blades.

"He had two pistols," Enaj cried as he abandoned his spent weapons, running for the cleft.

Darcy made to intercept but Azile was there, pushing him back with several wild swings. Teeth clenched, Darcy swung at the lad's middle. He didn't have time to play at swords with a French youth. Yelling continued below. He must get to Bingley, and stop whatever Enaj planned next.

But Azile parried easily, adding a feint of his own. Darcy lunged. Azile dodged, not back but to the side. Circling, seeking an opening. Turning with him, Darcy struck again. Azile deflected his blade with ease.

Darcy attacked in earnest.

It took mere moments for him to ascertain that Azile did not merely play at swords. He had considerable skill. A few feints more brought the realization that Azile was as good as he was. Darcy would not concede that the youth might be better.

They danced about the small flat space, blades flashing. Insofar as Darcy could tell, they were evenly matched. He had the reach on the young Frenchman, and the advantage of height and a grown man's muscles, the lad before him obviously not having yet attained that. But Azile was quicker, his reflexes honed to the point of blurring speed, and agile. Nearly acrobatic in his dodges and attacks.

Their blades crossed, Azile giving a small twist of his wrist to lock Darcy's sword with his as he cried, "Monsieur Bingley may require our assistance. We fight for nothing, monsieur."

"You cannot think I will believe that?" Darcy used his greater strength to twist his blade free and attacked.

Azile flicked his blade aside, dodging to Darcy's left. "As much as this bout entertains me, monsieur, and you truly cannot know how much so, we squander time." He made a feint and leaped back as Darcy countered.

Darcy swung at him, but Azile never seemed to remain in the same place long enough for Darcy's blade to find him.

"Kill them," William Collins' voice cried below, reedy and nearly too weak to reach them. "Kill that Frenchman. Kill Bingley. I am paying you to kill them."

"I must assist Enaj. You will pardon me, monsieur." Azile lunged in close.

Darcy made to parry, but Azile didn't attempt to land the blow Darcy saw coming. Instead, the tip of his blade jabbed into the handle of Enaj's rapier. The weapon tore free of Darcy's hand, spinning through the air. Somehow, it came down in Azile's gloved grasp.

With both weapons now, Azile whirled, darting between the mossy rock and the tree. Without Darcy realizing, the youth had turned them until he fought nearest the path. Darcy cursed as Azile disappeared from view.

He spun, taking in the two spent rifles. He had no powder and no lead. His gaze fell on the spyglass. Yanking it up, Darcy rushed to the rock behind which Enaj had hidden. He brought the spyglass to his eye.

Bingley sat on the ground, Robert Collins beside him, assisting him with his arm. Mr. Collins lay propped against the large rock atop which they'd examined the pistols. Mr. Jones crouched over him, pressing bandages to his chest. Collins' mouth still moved, but he didn't seem able to bring enough breath to project his words as he had earlier.

Beyond them, at the edge of the trees, Enaj grappled with a man, presumably the one Mr. Collins had shouted to. The man had a knife and, as Darcy watched, he flung Enaj back, sending the youth flying. The man whirled, charging, his aim obviously to reach Robert Collins and Bingley.

Darcy recognized him the moment he turned. George Wickham. Darcy's jaw hinged open, shock rendering the rest of him immobile as Wickham barreled across the short distance that separated him from Bingley, knife raised.

And then Azile was there, still wielding both rapiers, a slender shadow of darkness in Wickham's way.

Darcy whirled, smashing the spyglass closed and shoving it into his pocket as he ran. He squeezed through the narrow opening that led to the cleft, the fabric of his jacket tearing. Reckless, the anger coursing through him augmented by his fear for Bingley, he plunged down the hill.

He reached the valley floor to the sight of Wickham being menaced by Azile. Robert Collins, standing now, had positioned himself between them and Bingley. Clutching his left arm and limping slightly, Enaj skirted the fight, seeking to reach Darcy's friend.

Deciding that Azile and Enaj were, for whatever reason, sincere in their efforts to assist Bingley, Darcy ignored the limping Frenchman and ran for Wickham. He skidded to a halt beside Azile to growl out, "Wickham."

Azile, rapiers weaving menacingly, asked lightly, "A friend of yours, monsieur?"

"Hardly that." He narrowed his eyes at his erstwhile companion. The man who had attempted to elope with Georgiana when she was but fifteen, in equal parts to spite Darcy and to gain his sister's dowry. "What are you doing here, George?"

Wickham crouched slightly, ready to lunge, and held his knife low. "Darcy. Is that any way to greet an old friend? Your father's godson?"

Darcy could feel the suspicion that welled in Azile but didn't dare look away from Wickham. "It is precisely how to greet a cad and an opportunist."

"And here I had hoped we could be friends." Wickham lunged at him, knife jabbing.

Azile flashed between them, knocking the blade aside with one of his own, and getting in a slash down Wickham's right forearm. Wickham roared in pain. He yanked his arm back, launching the knife.

Darcy cried out in warning.

Azile knocked the blade from the air, unperturbed, as Wickham pulled another free of his boot. "You drove me to this, Darcy. You and your vaunted pride. If you had just given me—"

A loud, shrill whistle sounded once, then again, then in three quick bursts.

"Azile," Enaj cried from behind them.

"Entertaining as this is, I cannot remain," Azile said.

"Running?" Wickham sneered. "Afraid I'll get back some of my own? I already got your friend."

For the first time, real anger sparked in Azile's eyes. Below his mask, his jaws clenched, but all he said was, "Monsieur Darcy, for you."

Enaj's rapier flipped through the air to embed, tip down, in the ground at Darcy's feet. Grasping the hilt, Darcy pulled it free.

The whistle sounded again, coming from the hilltop at the closed end of the valley. At the open end, behind Wickham, a horse appeared, a redcoat atop. The rider twisted in his saddle to wave a signal.

"You have him, monsieur?" Azile asked.

"The day Darcy can best me is the day I deserve to die," Wickham sallied with his usual misplaced confidence.

Darcy eyed Wickham, who sneered, and silently applauded Azile for giving no indication that the militia troops had found the valley. It would do no one good to chase Wickham through the forest.

"Azile," Enaj cried, his voice a bit desperate.

Azile flashed Darcy a final, quick grin, nearly as cocky as Wickham, and whirled away. Darcy didn't dare turn to watch the two bandits depart, keeping his attention on Wickham. Nor did he miss the fact that they had a third member of their gang hidden somewhere atop the hill. He wondered if the third Frenchman had been about the day Azile and Enaj had robbed them, hidden nearby in case of need. It would explain some of their confidence, although having seen first-hand Enaj's skill with a gun and Azile's with a blade, he grudgingly admitted that confidence was their due.

"Want to put down that sword and I will put down this knife, and we can make this fair?" Wickham asked. Heavy mocking in his tone, he badgered, "Or are you afraid you cannot best me without an advantage?"

Darcy straightened, lowering his blade. As Wickham's eyes went wide in surprise, Darcy replied, "No. I want to watch Colonel Forster order his men to apprehend you."

Knife raised, Wickham whirled.

Redcoats streamed into the dell. One called, pointing, and Darcy looked to see Azile and Enaj reach the cleft. Horses charged after, but their riders would need to dismount to give chase. The remainder of the troop, following Colonel Forster, converged on Darcy and Wickham, dismounting. Colonel Forster strode forward.

"Colonel Forster, thank heaven you have arrived," Wickham cried. "Those two Frenchmen hid on the hillside and shot at Mr. Bingley from afar."

Robert Collins stepped up beside Darcy. "You shot at Mr. Bingley from afar," Robert countered. "All the Bandits did was stop you." He pointed into the woods. "You will find his pistols in there. The Boney Bandits shot them from his hands."

"I was shooting at those bandits," Wickham countered. "I am certain you will find their guns up there."

"You five, search the forest for Mr. Wickham's pistols," Forster ordered several of the men massed about them. "You, go search for the Bandits' weapons."

They would find them, Darcy realized. Enaj and Azile wouldn't have time to reclaim the rifles. Would that incriminate them? He looked down at the blade in his hand, a finely wrought French rapier.

Forster studied Darcy, Robert Collins, and Wickham for a moment. "Mr. Darcy, what have you to say? Any notion why the newest member of my troop is even out here? And why did you not come to me with news of this duel, Lieutenant Wickham?"

Wickham frowned at that.

Wickham was a redcoat? The idea was laughable, but Darcy was grim as he replied, "Mr. Collins appears to have hired Mr. Wickham to hide in the forest and shoot Mr. Bingley, thus ensuring Collins would win the duel. I believe, if you ask Mr. Phillips, you will discover that this is the selfsame tactic Mr. Collins' father employed when he dueled General Oakwood, albeit with a different hired assassin."

"But, I believe, with a similar result," a voice said to Darcy's left. Mr. Jones strode forward, wiping his hands on a bloodied cloth. "At least, when it comes to Mr. Collins. I am afraid I could not save him. A ball took him in the chest, ruining a lung."

Robert Collins turned to him, all color leaving his face. "M-my brother is dead?"

"I am afraid so," Jones said with little emotion, before turning back to Colonel Forster. "I also believe, though I did not witness the actual duel, that Mr. Darcy's recounting of the previous Mr. Collins' demise is accurate. Like father, like son."

Robert stared at him, his features slack with shock.

A wave of sorrow passed through Darcy on the younger man's behalf. No matter what sort of brother Collins was, it must still hurt to lose him, and to learn that your father and brother were so very despicable as to hire men to win their duels for them.

Forster rubbed at the back of his neck. "Am I to understand that Mr. Bingley has killed Mr. Collins?"

"I did not witness this duel either," Mr. Jones said crisply. "If you will excuse me, Mr. Bingley is wounded and requires my care. A ball took him in the shoulder." Without awaiting a reply, he turned away.

"Mr. Darcy, did you witness the duel?" Colonel Forster asked. "Did you see Mr. Bingley shoot Mr. Collins, or see Mr. Wickham shoot Mr. Bingley?"

Wickham cast him a hard look.

"I did not," Darcy admitted.

Colonel Forster raised his eyebrows at that but had the good sense not to accuse Darcy of lying.

"And you, Mr. Collins?" the colonel asked Robert.

"I was looking that way," Collins said dully. He pointed into the forest, where even now Forster's men sought Wickham's weapons. "I saw Mr. Wickham stand up and shoot. He was aiming here, into the valley, not up there where the Boney Bandits were. He shot once, but his gun went flying from his hand as he did. He picked up another and aimed, and it went flying before he could shoot." Robert swallowed, a greenish tinge to his complexion. "If you will excuse me? I should…that is…" Giving up on words, he walked away.

Forster frowned. "Wickham, remain here." He cast a look at several of his men who, their expressions ranging from grim to sheepish, converged on Wickham. "Mr. Darcy, with me."

Forster led the way to where Bingley sat, Mr. Jones checking his left shoulder. The wound didn't appear as bad as Darcy feared, though Bingley was white with pain. From what Darcy could see, the ball had gouged the outside edge of Bingley's upper arm. It had likely been meant to take him in the heart.

He looked up and asked wearily, "Did I hear right? Collins is dead?"

Darcy nodded.

"Mr. Bingley, did you shoot Mr. Collins?" Colonel Forster asked in a firm, commanding voice.

Bingley cast Darcy a panicked look, but Darcy was not overly worried. The law, at least law that wasn't Mr. Collins, was generally lenient when it came to duels, and Darcy had influence. More than that, Bingley couldn't come before the local magistrate until there was one. Not that Darcy espoused corruption, but if Bingley purchased Netherfield Park, as the largest landholder in the region, he would put up the name for the next magistrate. He could even seek the position himself.

Darcy gave Bingley another nod, urging him to speak.

"Collins shot on two," Bingley said, indignation coloring his voice. "But there were more shots than that." He winced as Mr. Jones applied fresh bandages to his shoulder. "The pain hit me and I closed my eyes and squeezed the trigger. When I opened them, Mr. Collins was on the ground."

"Do you mean to tell me that no one knows who actually shot Mr. Collins?" Colonel Forster asked, sounding exasperated.

Darcy offered him a bland look.

Forster rubbed at the back of his neck again, then sighed. "I will take Mr. Wickham into custody for the time being. I will need official statements from all of you, including you, Mr. Jones."

The apothecary, busy securing Bingley's bandage, merely grunted.

"I will take a statement from Mr. Phillips as well, and get to the bottom of all this," Forster added.

"Will tomorrow be soon enough?" Bingley asked as Mr. Jones came to his feet. "I must go assure a certain lady of my lack of demise."

Bingley reached up and Darcy offered a hand, gripping Bingley's good arm to help him to his feet. He swayed once, gritted his teeth, drew back his shoulders, then winced. It wasn't until Bingley turned back that Darcy realized his ruined jacket lay on the ground beside where he'd sat.

"Allow me," Forster said, suddenly solicitous, and scooped up the bedraggled item. He held it out. "Yes, certainly tomorrow will be soon enough. You may all go now. Statements are needed, though, and we must determine if the Boney Bandits are responsible for Mr. Collins' murder."

Darcy turned then, and sighted some of Forster's men coming back down the cleft, not a bandit in sight. He felt certain Enaj had saved Bingley, not murdered Collins. In that moment, he decided not to mention that the weapon he held was the bandit's, nor his suspicion that Enaj had been injured and thus might be easier to find. Though he would not admit to as much aloud, he hoped Forster and his men had no success in apprehending the two.

CHAPTER TWENTY-SIX

A Hero's Welcome

Elizabeth reached the top of the cleft to the sight of Mary, black-clad and carrying both of Jane's Bakers.

"When I signal that you should run, you should run," Mary said tartly as Jane claimed the hilltop as well.

Elizabeth drew her rapier, which she'd sheathed while she ran. "You two go. I will hold them off."

"Do not be ridiculous." Mary walked past her and grasped a gnarled piece of wood that stuck out from under a pile of fist-sized rocks. Their linchpin freed, the rocks started to roll. Some went every which way, but the majority clattered down the cleft. "We should hurry," Mary added as curses echoed up the narrow path.

They rushed across the hilltop, seeking the forested slopes that surrounded Dovemark, and Elizabeth wondered when Mary could possibly have set up those rocks. Today, or had Elizabeth been walking past that stick and pile of stones for years without noticing? How many traps did Mary have, hidden about?

They plunged down the gentler slope on Dovemark's side of the hills and into the trees, Jane keeping up despite a noticeable limp, and another quandary sped through Elizabeth's mind. Had Papa Arthur elected to have his tenants keep sheep and hogs, rather than clear the trees for farming and pastures, to maintain the concealment of the trees? Were Elizabeth's relations even more wily than she'd realized?

Shaking her head to cast such irrelevant fancies aside, Elizabth focused on wending her way through the trees as quickly and silently as she could. Jane, trailing behind, moved with far less grace than usual and Elizabeth winced at every snapped twig and rustled bush. Ahead, ghostlike, Mary flitted through the nearly leafless maze, the forest brown for the onset of winter.

Over the excess of noise Jane was making, which Elizabeth hoped sounded overloud to her due to their desperate need not to be caught, she could hear no pursuit. She imagined that while the rocks, hopefully, hadn't harmed any of the men chasing them, they'd likely slowed them. Wary of more traps, their pursuers would have forsaken speed. Likely just as Mary planned.

By the time they reached the shelter of their hidden cave behind the stable, Jane's face was white and sweat beaded her brow, born of pain rather than exertion, Elizabeth knew. They stowed their weapons, and Jane's, putting the Bakers away in the gun cabinet hidden by their rack of padded gear, and Elizabeth realized that Mr. Darcy still had her sister's sword. Deciding there would be time to worry over that later, she discarded Azile's garb and hastily made use of a basin and water while Mary helped Jane with her lawn shirt. The left arm was torn and damp with blood. They would, as they always did with their highwaymen's clothes, have to clean and mend the garment in secret.

"Bite down on this." Mary handed Jane a leather strap, waited while she put it between her teeth, and proceeded to clean the long, fortunately narrow gash with cognac, just as Papa Arthur had taught them.

Above her gritted teeth Jane squeezed her eyes closed.

Elizabeth finished dressing as Mary bandaged Jane's arm, then said, "I'll help Jane. You get changed."

Nodding, Mary started to strip away the black highwaymen's garb she rarely wore, her expression one of relief.

Elizabeth started on the laces on the boot encasing Jane's uninjured foot first, asking, "What happened?"

"That cad Wickham stomped on my foot like a common brawler," Jane replied evenly. "I should not have shot the guns from his hand. I should have put a ball through his arm."

"What you should have done was not charge down there without a weapon."

"After I shot the second pistol out of his hand, he started for the floor of the valley. I could see that Mr. Bingley was injured, and I did not know if he could defend himself. I had to go down there."

Elizabeth shook her head but held her peace. She would have gone down as well. Of course, she would have been armed. She was always exhorting Jane to start carrying knives about her person.

Elizabeth pulled the boot free, glad they'd opted for laces. Papa Arthur had always recommended them. Laces, he'd said, allowed for better ankle movement and therefore greater agility, and were easier to remove when needed. Elizabeth wouldn't want to have to cut Jane's boot off. It had been enough trouble to get men's footwear in the first place, via an elaborate scheme that had involved inventing a widow with three sons and sending traces of their feet and measurements to London.

Elizabeth took more care with the second boot, but Jane still gritted her teeth in pain. When her stocking was removed, swelling and an already darkening bruise were revealed.

"We will need to sneak you up a cold compress for that, and ensure that no one sees it. Even Lucy," Mary said, gowned now in one of her usual drab colors.

Jane wiggled her toes. "I do not believe anything to be broken. It was a solid hit, directly to the top of my foot."

"Still, I doubt you will be wearing slippers for a week." Elizabeth glared at Jane's injured foot, but the real focus of her anger was Mr. Wickham.

Whom Mr. Darcy knew, which hardly seemed possible. What had Wickham claimed? That he was the godson of Mr. Darcy's father?

They helped Jane to clean up and dress, and Elizabeth reflected they were fortunate that the time of year dictated long sleeves. Supporting Jane between them, they made their way to the house, for, as Elizabeth had suspected, she couldn't get a slipper onto her foot. Fortunately, though their morning had been very eventful thus far, the hour was still quite early. Between the two of them, Elizabeth and Mary got their sister to her room unobserved.

They tucked Jane into bed, then Mary dropped to sit on the end. "That went well enough, I suppose."

"Jane was injured," Elizabeth countered.

"And Mr. Bingley was shot," Jane added.

"But, thanks to you, he survived," Mary said. "And it appeared as if Mr. Collins is gravely injured."

Elizabeth joined Mary on the foot of Jane's bed, a jumble of emotions washing through her at the hope that Mr. Collins might be more than gravely injured. After all, Papa Arthur had survived being shot only to die a week later, and their cousin struck her as a far weaker man. But...did she really wish a man dead? Even William Collins? She rubbed at her forehead, leery to attempt to sort through her feelings.

"I hope he will not die," Jane said softly, closing her eyes. Resting against her pillows, her bright locks spread loose about her head, for they'd taken out the tight, coiled braids they wore while highwaymen, Jane looked wan and sorrowful.

"I hope he does," Mary said, her voice devoid of warmth.

Jane's eyes flew open. "How can you say that? He is our cousin."

"He is also a horrible person and a tyrant," Mary said firmly, then went on before Jane could argue, adding, "Now, what should we tell everyone is wrong with you, Jane? Do you think we will have to stage an accident to excuse your foot?"

Elizabeth grimaced at the idea, but offered, "I imagine we will need to tell them that the strain of fearing for Mr. Bingley's life has rendered Jane ill, and we can keep her ill until such time as she can walk on her foot and use her left arm without wincing."

Jane sat up straighter. "But if I am ill, I cannot see Mr. Bingley."

"You can," Mary disagreed. "Perhaps not today, but we can help you downstairs tomorrow and you can languish prettily on a sofa while he reads to you, assuming he is even up to calling."

Jane sighed glumly, but nodded. "I imagine that is the best plan."

Elizabeth thought so too, though it galled her. Regardless of their plan, Jane would not be able to tell Mr. Bingley that she had saved his life. And to go from doing so, to pretending she was so weak of spirit, so desolate at the mere prospect of his demise, that she was too ill to rise from bed…it infuriated Elizabeth.

"It would be better not to be found here, all together," Mary said, standing. She turned to Jane. "I will see that you get that compress for your foot, though you mustn't let anyone see you put it there. Pretend it is for your head."

"Which is not addled, thank you," Jane replied a touch tartly, then her eyes widened. "I beg your pardon. Pain sharpens my tongue. I know you mean only to care for me."

Mary smiled slightly. "I understand."

"We will come to you with any news we receive the moment we may," Elizabeth added. She wished she could find that Mr. Wickham and trod on his foot. Or better still, persuade Tuck to do so.

They left Jane's room to the sight of Lydia coming down the hall, yawning widely. Spotting them, she halted. "You two are up early."

"As are you," Elizabeth countered.

Lydia looked past them to Jane's door. "What were you doing in Jane's room?"

"Checking on her," Mary said as she continued across the hall and into her own chamber.

Focusing her attention on Elizabeth, Lydia asked, "Why does Jane require checking?"

"The prospect of Mr. Bingley coming to harm has resulted in Jane becoming unwell. I am afraid she will need to stay abed for some days to recover."

Lydia's eyes narrowed. "You know, when you say things like that, I know that you're telling the truth and yet somehow lying, all at once."

Elizabeth gave her an enigmatic smile. "What an interesting speculation."

"It is not a speculation, it is fact." Lydia continued to glare at her.

Elizabeth smiled back, unperturbed.

Finally, her youngest sister huffed. "Very well. Be like that. Are you coming down to breakfast? That's where I am going. I couldn't sleep anymore because I am worried about Mr. Bingley, too."

"Breakfast would be agreeable," Elizabeth allowed, the suggestion making her realize how hungry she was. Nothing stirred the appetite so much as an early morning bout followed by a run through the woods.

They made their way down the hall. Behind them, a knock sounded. Elizabeth looked back to see one of the maids, Lucy, at Mary's door, a folded note in hand. Elizabeth frowned. Lucy must have come up the back stairwell, not odd, but a note being delivered to Mary's room at all, let alone at this hour, was.

Lydia seemed not to have noticed as she prattled on, saying, "Because, do you realize, if Mr. Bingley marries Jane, he might buy Netherfield Park, and then Mr. Collins wouldn't be magistrate anymore, and that would be good for everyone, I think. Well, not for the people of Longbourn. They would still be stuck with our horrible cousin, but good for everyone else. I think that's why he's been coming around of late. He wants to make certain Mr. Bingley doesn't propose."

Lydia's monologue took them to the staircase, where Elizabeth gave the back of her sister's head a scrutinizing look as she followed her down. For all her youth, exuberance and chatter, Lydia was obviously not unintelligent. Elizabeth simply had not realized until lately that her sister took any interest in the world beyond ribbons and redcoats.

"I imagine that is true," Elizabeth said blandly and turned the topic to the latter. Lydia could speak on the members of the local militia at length. That topic was safer than Mr. Bingley and the duel, except for Lydia's obvious preference for Mr. Denny.

"And you should have seen the newest officer," Lydia prattled as they walked. "Thomas, Matthew and I noted him in Meryton just yesterday. A

Mr. Wickham. He is so handsome, Elizabeth. He is everything an officer should be. I only managed to say hello, but he was ever so charming. I hope to see a great deal more of him."

Elizabeth contained a flinch. So much for redcoats being a safe enough topic.

They sat for breakfast and their brothers, Kitty, and Mrs. Oakwood soon filed in. Their mother did not eat, however, merely toyed with the food on her plate, her gaze constantly going to the door. Finally, she huffed a sigh and said, "How is there yet no news of the duel?"

Lydia looked up from her plate. "Jane is too ill to come down to breakfast. She made herself sick worrying over Mr. Bingley."

"Yes, poor Mr. Bingley," Mrs. Oakwood moaned. "That good, sweet man, defending my Jane's honor. Whatever was Mr. Collins thinking, saying such things about my Jane? Has anyone ever had a sweeter, lovelier, more obedient daughter? The man has obviously taken leave of his senses."

"I am as sweet and lovely as Jane," Kitty said testily. She stabbed at a slice of cold roast on her plate.

"Yes, to be certain you are." Mrs. Oakwood said hurriedly before looking about the table. "But where is our news? I am languishing for news of how Mr. Bingley fared."

Lydia turned to Elizabeth and asked sweetly, "Elizabeth, is there news?"

Elizabeth shrugged. "How could I possibly know when you do not?"

Whatever Lydia might have cast back was drowned by Mrs. Oakwood's wail of, "And Jane cannot be abed. Mr. Bingley will surely come to report on the duel. Jane must be in the parlor. He must propose to her. That he means to is the only reason he would defend her honor so."

Elizabeth dubbed it a sad referendum on their society that her mother was correct on that. A man wouldn't duel for a woman's honor simply because she was in the right. He would do so only were he family or intent on becoming so.

Mr. Darcy's handsome, serious visage formed in her thoughts. He was the one gentleman she'd met who she could see being the exception to that. Mr. Darcy would always do what was right.

And he had Jane's sword, thanks to Elizabeth. Could the weapon be traced to Jane? The rapier had been a gift from Papa Arthur. Surely, he would have been circumspect.

"...will have to be ill on the sofa," Mrs. Oakwood was saying. "I will not have her miss the opportunity to wed Mr. Bingley over a case of nerves."

"I do not believe Mr. Bingley's affections so fleeting that one missed chance to speak with Jane will deter him," Elizabeth felt obliged to point out.

Her expression eager, Kitty added, "Besides, Mama, if Mr. Bingley arrives and Jane cannot see him, that will give me more of a chance to speak with him. I am certain he will choose me over Jane, given the chance."

"He didn't fight a duel for you," Thomas said from the end of the table where he and Matthew sat.

Kitty looked down her nose at her little brother. "Only because he did not have the opportunity. No gentleman insulted me in front of Mr. Bingley."

"You want a man to insult you?" Lydia asked.

"I'll insult you if you like," Matthew offered.

Kitty scowled at them, the expression making her appear alarmingly similar to Mrs. Oakwood.

"A Mr. Collins to see you," their butler said from the doorway.

Shock radiated through Elizabeth. Their cousin must not have been so badly injured after all.

"Mr. Collins?" Kitty said eagerly.

"Ah, Mr. Robert Collins," the butler clarified.

"Show him in," Mary said, gliding into the room. "He can breakfast with us."

Elizabeth stared at her middle sister, stunned.

Mary's gown was simple, as always, but a lovely green color that brought out hints of auburn Elizabeth had never noticed that her sister's locks contained. The color also complemented her skin, which somehow seemed smoother and more luminous. Her eyes, normally appearing a dull brown, appeared green now as well, matching the gown, which, cut better than her usual choices, revealed a figure just as fine as any of her sisters'.

Moreover, beneath flatteringly arranged tresses, there was something about her mien. Some lack of reserve that had been there before. It was as if Mary had been awaiting something and, whatever that thing was, it had happened.

The butler cleared his throat, looking to Mrs. Oakwood, but she was staring at Mary as Elizabeth's sister took the place beside her at the table. "Ah, yes, Miss Mary," the butler finally said and hurried away.

"Mary, what have you done with your hair?" Mrs. Oakwood asked, blinking in confusion. She turned to Kitty. "You should wear your hair that way. It is very flattering. Why, that coif makes Mary look as pretty as you are."

Kitty scowled again.

Elizabeth tried to catch Mary's eye, to look a question at her, but Mary seemed engrossed in fixing a cup of tea.

Cousin Robert came in, quiet and composed, and they all rose to greet him. Elizabeth didn't miss the look that passed between him and Mary. Suspicion bloomed in her.

Mrs. Oakwood made Kitty move, giving Robert the place of honor to her right, and declared that coffee should be brought, even though he protested that tea would do. Elizabeth didn't even know if they kept coffee, as none of them drank it.

Once the footman given that order hurried away, Mrs. Oakwood turned to Robert. "Now, tell us the news. Do not fear. We can endure the worst, but you must know that Jane is above stairs too ill with worry to join us and if you admit to Mr. Bingley's demise, it will certainly kill her."

Robert took a moment to digest that, then said quietly, "I am pleased to report that Mr. Bingley, while having taken a wound to the shoulder, is predicted to make a complete recovery."

"Wounded?" Mrs. Oakwood wailed. "He has lost? Jane is ruined? Oh, Robert, you must take her. Please, do not let her burden her sisters with her fall. You are of age. Marry her. It is your duty as her male relation, for all everyone disparages your parentage. Do not think that will save you from doing right by your cousin. You know Jane's beauty and sweetness make her invaluable. If you take her, I will gift you five hundred pounds from Kitty's dowry."

"Mama," Kitty squeaked. "You cannot."

"Hush, child. If Jane is ruined, so are you. I must."

Robert stared at Mrs. Oakwood, his mouth slack. Beside Elizabeth, Mary carefully buttered a roll. Kitty pulled out a handkerchief and buried her face in it, sobbing theatrically.

Mary set down her butterknife. "Did Mr. Collins prevail, then?" she asked calmly.

"Ah, no." Robert shook his head. "My brother is dead."

Shock radiated through Elizabeth, followed hard by guilt, for a part of her had hoped for that news. She had thought it would take days, though, like with Papa Arthur.

Kitty halted mid wail, raising dry eyes from her handkerchief. "You are master of Longbourn?"

Elizabeth's eyebrows shot up. Kitty was correct. Robert would be master of Longbourn now. Their childhood home. Their father's estate, entailed to keep it in the male line. To keep the bloodline pure. What would Mr. Bennet think of a man everyone knew was not actually related to him receiving his estate?

Elizabeth suspected he would be amused.

Mrs. Oakwood drew herself up, her matronly form formidable, and glared at Robert. "You cannot be master of Longbourn. Everyone knows you are no true Collins, no matter what the parish records say. You must step aside and return Longbourn to Thomas."

Where he nibbled on a sweet bun and watched the scene before him in fascination, Thomas put in, "I am not a Bennet either, Mama."

"You are as much a Bennet as Cousin Robert," Mrs. Oakwood snapped.

"Cousin Robert is far too handsome to be a Collins or a Bennet." Kitty batted her lashes at him as she spoke.

Robert appeared horrified.

"Enough," Mary said crisply, setting down her roll. "Robert has lost his brother this morning, and is being shown an appalling lack of consideration for that. Moreover, in view of that loss, Robert is now master of Longbourn. No matter what speculations there may be about his birth, he is the legal heir."

"Oh, I agree," Kitty said, leaning forward across the table. "The very intelligent, deserving, tall and comely heir."

"And, when his three months of mourning are over, the banns will be read for us," Mary continued, ignoring her younger sister.

Elizabeth took in that declaration with a growing sense of inevitability, but everyone else except Robert stared at Mary in shock.

Kitty's shrill laugh broke the silence. "You believe that simply because you put on a different gown today, Robert will choose you?" She gave Mary a pitying look. "He has known you for years. He knows how dowdy you are, and how lovely I am. Or do you believe that speaking French and playing the pianoforte will sway him? I can fill our home with beautiful paintings. My paintings can be enjoyed at leisure, not simply when one is playing or needs to speak to a modiste."

"I believe you will find that Robert prefers my playing over your paintings." Mary calmly picked up her half-eaten roll.

Kitty opened her mouth but Mrs. Oakwood held up a staying hand. She turned to Robert. "Is this true? You intend to offer for Mary?"

"Miss Mary is correct." Robert turned to her and, like clouds clearing from the sky, a gentle smile broke over his face, though it didn't push all the sorrow from his eyes. "We came to an agreement some time ago. The reason I have come here this morning is not to impart news of the duel, but to inform you of my intentions, Mrs. Oakwood."

Their mother came to her feet. Her face crumpled into tears. She hurried around the table and grabbed Mary, pulling her, still seated, against her generous bosom in a fierce hug. "Oh, my dear, sweet, clever child. I always knew I need not worry over you. You are a smart one, to organize such a matter yourself."

Mary, one arm holding the last bit of her roll out of danger, her face smushed against their mother, slanted an alarmed look at Elizabeth. Kitty's voice rose in angry complaint, and Thomas and Matthew both rose to go around the table to offer well wishes to Robert. But what captured Elizabeth's attention was the expression on Lydia's face. The narrow-eyed, gleaming, suspicious way she studied Mary.

Elizabeth, too, saw their sister's error. A very un-Mary-like error. One obviously made in an excess of excitement, despite Mary's calm façade.

Mary's gown, her hair, it all pointed to her suspecting that Robert would attend them, and knowing what he would say. That would not be overly suspicious, since she apparently knew their cousin better than anyone had suspected, except that Mary's expectations for Robert's behavior hinged on, at their root, Mr. Collins' demise. A demise about which Mary should not yet have heard…except that Lucy had brought her a note.

Lydia caught Elizabeth watching her and raised an eyebrow. Elizabeth gave a slight shake of her head. Lydia shrugged, the suspicion on her face easing, but Elizabeth knew their conversation on the matter, if such it could be called, was not yet over.

CHAPTER TWENTY-SEVEN

All's Well that Ends Well

Darcy could tell by how Bingley kept urging his mount to greater speed that he meant to propose to Miss Bennet. They had been visiting Dovemark almost daily, at first to the sight of a wan, sofa-bound Miss Bennet and a hovering Elizabeth, but later to take increasingly longer walks with the two, often accompanied by Miss Lydia who, in her words, had to make certain nothing untoward took place. To this the younger girl would always add a wink, no matter how many times her older sisters admonished her to better comportment.

That day, however, when he and Bingley requested the company of the eldest two Bennet sisters for a stroll and Miss Lydia stood to join them, Mrs. Oakwood crisply ordered her youngest daughter to sit back down. Darcy didn't know if the matron read Bingley's intention in the way he couldn't seem to pry his gaze from Miss Bennet, or held hopes based on the Bennets' two weeks of mourning for Mr. Collins being over, but he was pleased with Mrs. Oakwood's intervention. He had no dislike of the youngest Bennet with her lively chatter and somewhat impertinent nature, but she always walked with him and Elizabeth, making private conversation impossible. With the sisters' weeks of mourning their cousin at an end, Darcy, too, had a question he wished to tender, one he'd wanted to ask since the day of the duel, and he did not need Miss Lydia as an audience.

The four set out along the walk that led around the Oakwoods' manor house, sans Miss Lydia, and Darcy and Elizabeth slowed their pace in mutual accord, giving Bingley and Miss Bennet more privacy. Once behind the house, they went not into the walled garden, but instead took to one of the woodland trails. An early snow that would fade long before December blanketed the forest floor, adding a crunch to Darcy's steps yet somehow wrapping the forest in a quiet, secluded feel. The path they followed appeared to be little more than a game trail, as were all the tracks they'd meandered in these woods. Despite the lack of curated walks, Elizabeth and

Miss Bennet always seemed to know precisely where they were.

"The militia is being recalled," Darcy offered by the way of interesting topics as they followed the game trail through the trees.

"Are they?" The path narrowed and Elizabeth slipped ahead of him, her light steps making no sound in the snow. "I had believed they were meant to remain into the spring."

"I understand it is an act of discipline," Darcy replied, using a gloved hand to keep a reaching bramble from sticking into his coat. Richard had written to inform him of the militia's imminent departure even before the order was given.

"Whatever have they done?"

"I am not certain if it is what they have done, or have not done. Colonel Forster is quite glum, however. He delivered the news to Netherfield Park personally."

Waiting for him where the path widened again, Elizabeth gave him a look of what he now could recognize as mock annoyance. "Very well. What have they *not done*, then, to see them leave in disgrace?"

Coming to a halt before her, Darcy deliberately began with, "What they *have* done, is to permit a duel to take place mere miles from their barracks, in which a man was slain." All levity left him as he added, "Moreover, one of their officers was used as a spy and to hire an assassin, and the newest member of their troop was that assassin. Both are being taken to London to face trial."

For which Darcy had been pleased to give his statements. Wickham had gone much too far this time, and would finally be punished as he deserved.

Her expression serious now as well, Elizabeth asked, "And will both be charged? Mr. Denny, I think, will not find anyone among his fellows to vouch for his character, but as to Mr. Wickham, I am less certain. I have conversed very little with him, but he gives me the impression of someone who is accustomed to charming his way out of trouble."

"Very much so, but in addition to his and Bingley's testimonies of Mr. Collins exhorting Wickham to murder, your soon-to-be-brother produced written records of Mr. Collins' transactions with Mr. Denny, as well as his agreement with Wickham. This included the order to kill Bingley under the guise of the duel and how much Collins was to pay. The man was a fool to write any of it down. In truth, doing so seems so ill advised that I would suspect Robert Collins of forging the record, if the ledger did not go back so many years in the same hand, and was not filled with all manner of similarly damning information."

"And if you did not know both Mr. Collinses?" Elizabeth suggested.

Darcy nodded. He could only agree that, knowing both men, it was easier to believe that the late Mr. Collins was a fool than the living one a liar.

"So, in the view of Colonel Forster's superiors, his troop permitted a duel in which the local magistrate died, foul play was afoot, and a wealthy gentleman was injured. One of their members was a spy, and another an assassin," Elizabeth summarized. She looked over her shoulder, up the path to where Bingley and Miss Bennet rounded the next bend, the trail skirting a large oak. "If all that is what they did, what did they fail to do?"

"Is that not obvious? They failed to capture the Boney Bandits."

Elizabeth's eyes narrowed at that. "Did you truly wish them to? Rather, now that you better understand the circumstances here, do you still want the Boney Bandits apprehended?"

Darcy frowned, thinking. He recalled his hope that they wouldn't be caught on the day of the duel. Finally, he shook his head. "No. I do not. In truth, I wonder if they will not simply disappear now that Mr. Collins will be replaced as magistrate."

"I imagine that will depend on who replaces him," Elizabeth said lightly, she started to turn, to continue up the path, where Bingley's and Miss Bennet's footprints wended away before them.

"You must hope that Bingley will purchase Netherfield Park?" Darcy asked, to stay her. In truth, he knew Bingley intended to do so, but it was not his news to give.

Halting, Elizabeth turned back to face him. "I do hope that, certainly, but what interests me more is that you apparently believe that if he does, the Boney Bandits will not be seen again. By what logic?"

Darcy stared down at her, taking in her dark, intelligent eyes. The gentle bow of her mouth. Normally, he might feel obliged to point out that they could no longer see Bingley and Miss Bennet, but not today, and not simply because he suspected that Bingley walked more quickly than usual, seeking privacy in which to propose. Today, Darcy sought seclusion as well.

Elizabeth smiled slightly, her expression questioning as she studied his face. "Mr. Darcy?"

"Miss Elizabeth." He loved the sound of her name from his mouth.

"I asked why you believe the Bandits will disappear if Mr. Bingley purchases Netherfield Park."

So she had. He'd been so busy taking in how lovely she was, he'd all but forgotten. "Because I concede that you were correct. The Boney Bandits merely sought to counter Collins' evil."

She smiled, as he'd hoped she would. Elizabeth, he'd come to realize, enjoyed a spirited debate. In defeat, she was gracious, but she very much preferred to win.

"Also, I have Enaj's sword and he has made no effort to reclaim it," Darcy added. "At first, my valet and I took turns guarding the blade in the hope the Boney Bandits would come for it, but it has been weeks. I cannot imagine they do not know where to find me."

"Well, then, maybe they are done." Mischief danced in Elizabeth's eyes. "Or perhaps they seek to lull you."

"If they do, they have."

"Then it may be we will soon learn which."

As much as the topic seemed to delight Elizabeth, Darcy did not wish to speak of the Boney Bandits' fates. He'd much rather speak about his, and Elizabeth's. "Before the duel, I asked you a question."

Her breath caught, her gaze locked with his.

"And you asked to have until after the duel to answer," he added when she did not speak.

"Will Mr. Bingley propose to Jane today?" Elizabeth asked softly.

Darcy frowned. "Your answer to my request of a formal courtship hinges upon that?"

She dropped her gaze, her lips turning up in a small smile.

Confusion filled him, and dread. Had she, then, been seeking a means by which to gently deter him? Was this another attempt? But they spoke nearly every day. They'd shared views on literature, punctuated by Miss Lydia's irreverent quips. They had traded tales of their childhoods. He'd told her of Pemberley and the people there, and Elizabeth had seemed genuinely interested.

She sighed and raised her gaze to meet his. "I apologize. I am clinging to something which no one can hope to keep."

He shook his head, bewildered.

Elizabeth smiled up at him and the tightness in his chest eased at the warmth he read in her eyes. "I mean my childhood," she clarified. "Not that I am a child, to be certain, but I still linger in the familiarity of that world. The unchanging landscape of youth, that seems as if it will never end, until, with one question from Mr. Bingley, it is shattered and forever gone."

He considered her words, his mind going back to when his childhood had been taken from him. The day his father had died, leaving Darcy in charge of an estate and a sister enough younger than he was to seem almost like a daughter. "I understand."

"Then understand this as well." She continued to study his face with those affection-filled, intelligent eyes. "I know that life cannot remain as it is and while I am leery, I am also hopeful, and the source of that hope is you. Before, when I would imagine Jane leaving, for certainly I have always known she would, I could think of nothing that would come after. Nothing good, at least. Simply years here alone, without her. Although, I did believe that I would at least have Mary." Elizabeth shook her head, bemusement flittering across her features before she once again focused on him. "But none of that is important. What is, is that because of you, since I met you, I can see a different future. A happy one. One that will be every bit as joyous and full of new adventures, and affection, as what I am leaving behind. You, Mr. Darcy, are the only person who has ever made my future seem wonderful."

He stared down at her, a strange tightness in his throat. Until she spoke those words, he had not realized how empty his own future had been. He'd focused on his duties, his obligations, and never looked beyond the next in an endless, lengthy line of tasks. "You make my future seem wonderful as well," he murmured, reaching up to cup her face.

She looked up at him, her eyes shining, her breath quickening, and Darcy knew that if he lowered his head, she would kiss him.

He had never wanted anything more than he wanted Elizabeth's kiss.

She pulled away, turning to face up the path, and brought her hands to her cheeks, obviously seeking composure. Darcy stared at her in shock, uncertain what he'd done to break such a perfect, precious moment.

Bingley and Miss Bennet appeared farther up the trail, hand in hand, their faces wreathed in matching smiles as they rushed down the path. "We are engaged," Bingley cried joyously.

Darcy worked to offer a happy smile to his friend as he and Elizabeth issued their felicitations, the two sisters hugging. Elizabeth must have heard them. She had pulled away because she'd heard them. Not because she would not welcome his kiss. She had not rejected him, but had rather been appropriately circumspect. They had, after all, not agreed to marriage, which being caught kissing would necessitate. They'd simply agreed to court.

Hadn't they?

Bingley and Miss Bennet leading the way, their steps quick as they hurried to share their happy news, they all retreated back down the forest trail. Darcy tried to be happy for his friend. Was, in fact, happy for him, but his mind swirled, unsteady and uncertain, wondering where he stood with Elizabeth.

When they reached the narrow section of trail, Bingley and Miss Bennet moving rapidly ahead, Darcy gestured for Elizabeth to precede him. She offered a smile before moving past him, somewhat easing his worry. He followed, then paused as a bramble caught the back of his coat.

"Mr. Darcy?" Elizabeth asked, turning back, somehow immediately aware that he no longer followed.

He gestured over his shoulder. "My coat. Patrick will never forgive me if I ruin another."

She came back, slipping around him. "Another?" she asked, gently tugging at the thorny branch that snagged him.

"I tore my favorite on the morning of the duel."

"Can it not simply be mended?"

Suddenly hearing how what he was about to say would sound to her, Darcy grimaced and admitted, "He will have mended it, and then donated it somewhere it's needed. I, ah, do not wear repaired garments."

"You do not wear repaired garments?" Laughter filled her tone. The final thorn slid free. "You may move, and do not fear, the thorns merely stuck in, not tearing. You may yet be able to keep what I must assume is your second favorite coat."

He stepped free of the narrow section of path and turned back, abashed. "It is a bit silly, I suppose. Especially as it was my favorite coat."

"Perhaps a bit," she agreed with a chuckle.

Reassured and warmed by the sound, Darcy offered his arm.

They reached Mrs. Oakwood's favorite drawing room to find her, her sons and other daughters, the Phillips, and even Robert Collins waiting, presumably all summoned. Mrs. Oakwood took one look at Jane and cried, "Pour the wine," then rushed forward to meet them in the doorway, embracing her eldest.

"Mama, how did you know?" Miss Bennet asked as Mrs. Oakwood squeezed her.

Releasing her, the matron said, "I am your mama. A mama always knows," before turning and holding her arms open for Bingley.

Without reservation, he accepted his future mother-in-law's embrace.

"Oh, you dear, dear man. Thank you for taking my Jane. I despaired for her, I truly did, and now you have saved her."

"It is not as if Jane was on the shelf, Mama," Elizabeth laughingly countered while Miss Bennet went pink.

Behind them, where everyone gathered in the drawing room, footmen were filling glasses, but rather than rejoin the others, Mrs. Oakwood kept her focus on Bingley. "Now, you will want to marry as quickly as possible, which I daresay means you will not be able to have any guests. Such a shame, but your new bride must take precedence. You will want plenty of time alone to begin begetting your family, to be certain."

Darcy raised his eyebrows at that. Bingley stared at her in bewilderment.

"Mama," Miss Bennet murmured, going pinker still.

"Are you trying to be rid of Mr. Darcy?" Elizabeth asked with a laugh.

Mrs. Oakwood turned to him, her expression surprised. "Mr. Darcy? Certainly not. Mr. Darcy must remain. I am sure you will hardly notice him."

Elizabeth shook her head. "Come, let us join the others. We will toast to Jane and Mr. Bingley, and permit them to decide on house guests."

Mrs. Oakwood pursed her lips, defiance in her eyes, but permitted Elizabeth to take her arm and return her to the gathering deeper in the room, Bingley and Miss Bennet following.

Darcy followed, but his mind went to the impending arrival of the Hargreaves, something he would have forgotten if not for Miss Bingley's ongoing and slightly frantic preparations. Did Mrs. Oakwood not wish them to come to Hertfordshire? But how could that be when she claimed not to know them? He would have to ask Elizabeth when next he had the opportunity.

A celebratory mood prevailed, even though Robert Collins still wore deep mourning, and it was with actual regret that, after half an hour, Darcy made his farewells alongside Bingley. The Phillips and Robert Collins departed as well, the three not-yet-wed men quickly leaving the Phillips carriage behind as they'd all ridden. In Meryton, Robert offered a wave, and Darcy and Bingley carried on to Netherfield Park to share Bingley's news with his sisters and Hurst.

There, Bingley's announcement was met with, "Oh, but Charles, we are mere days away from learning if she is worth marrying," from Miss Bingley, which devolved into an argument between the three siblings. Hurst excused himself to see to his correspondence, and Darcy said he would change for dinner.

In his room, he indeed found Patrick laying out his evening wear. Remembering Elizabeth's amusement of earlier, Darcy asked, "Have you already found a new home for that coat of mine? The one I tore the morning of the duel?"

Patrick looked over from where he brushed Darcy's dinner jacket. "I did, sir, but do not fear. I went through the pockets first. Your spyglass is in the desk." He gestured to the sitting room.

Darcy frowned. "Spyglass?" Leaving the bedroom, he entered the adjoining room, calling over his shoulder, "What spyglass?" as he went.

Patrick appeared in the open doorway, brush in hand. "The collapsible one you had in your coat pocket. I assumed you purchased it for the purpose of better searching the forest for would-be assassins. It is in the top right drawer. Several letters also arrived."

Reaching the desk, Darcy took in a letter from Richard, one from his steward, another from his man in Town, and two from Georgiana. He truly needed to find her more companions, such as the elder three Bennet sisters. She should have people to write to aside from her older brother and other relations.

Ignoring the missives, he pulled open the top right drawer to the sight of a spyglass. Enaj's, he realized, removing the item. He opened it, inspecting what was a well-crafted scope. Weighty, too. He'd forgotten he'd taken it, doing so overshadowed by his duel with Azile, the injury to Bingley, the appearance of Wickham, and Mr. Collins' death.

Did the Boney Bandits know Darcy had it? Did the spyglass lend weight to his theory that they were done? Their cause completed?

Darcy closed the spyglass, then noted an engraving on the rim. He moved to the window to better take in a stylized oak tree, the letter O stamped in the middle. Below were the initials, M.R.A.O. He had no idea what the M or the R could stand for, but A and O could be for…

He had seen this spyglass before, in the hands of Matthew Oakwood.

A tremble going through him, Darcy returned to the desk. Pushing the chair out of his way, he clunked the spyglass down on the desktop, then he pulled free a clean sheet of paper. He seized a pen. Not bothering to trim the tip, he opened the ink and scratched out, *Azile* and *Enaj*.

Bile rose in his throat. Azile and Enaj. It had been staring him in the face this whole time. So blatant as to make a mockery of them all. Azile…Eliza. Not foreign names at all. Not French. The stepdaughters of a man who spoke French like a native. Who had taught them all he knew. One merely need read their names backwards.

That inexplicable sense of knowing the woman in the mist that morning, that repeated shock of recognition when he'd met Elizabeth on the street in Meryton, those sensations were not a sign that she was meant for him. They had merely been some deep, obviously more intelligent, part of his mind recognizing the bandit who had robbed him. Recognizing Azile.

Darcy fumbled for the chair he'd thrust away from the desk, sinking into it. Jane Bennet had shot his hat. Elizabeth had bested him in a duel. They were the Boney Bandits.

Bingley was about to marry a madwoman, and Darcy had asked to court one.

~ THE END ~

ABOUT SUMMER

Summer Hanford writes gripping Epic Fantasy, swashbuckling Historical Romance, and best-selling *Pride and Prejudice* retellings. She lives in the lovely Finger Lakes Region of New York with her husband and compulsory, deliberately spoiled, cat. The newest addition to their household, an energetic setter-shepherd mix, has been trying, and failing, for seven years to gain acceptance from the cat, but is adored by the humans.

Since the moment she read her first novel, Summer's passion has always been writing, and epic adventures. As a child growing up on a dairy farm, she built castles made of hay and wielded swords made of fence posts. She is also passionate about animals, travel, and organizing her closet. Nothing pleases her more than a row of tops broken down by sleeve length and ordered by color…except working on her latest novel with her cat in her lap, her dog lounging on the rug dreaming of squirrels, and a cup of tea at hand.

Get Your Thank You Gifts! Sign Up for My Mailing List Today!

Visit: **www.summerhanford.com/pride-and-prejudice-variations**

Made in the USA
Monee, IL
05 May 2025

16795839R00156